BURN COLLECTOR

Collected Stories from One through Nine,
2nd Edition

Al Burian

Burn Collector: Collected Stories from One through Nine, 2nd Edition
© Al Burian
This Edition © PM Press 2010

Originally published by Buddy System/Stickfigure

ISBN: 978-1-60486-220-1
LCCN: 2010927766

PM Press
P.O. Box 23912
Oakland, CA 94623
PMPress.org

Printed in the USA on recycled paper.

Be careful

what you wish for! Every artistic expression, no matter how slight, how off-the-cuff, how seemingly innocuous, has as its base motivation megalomania—which, though it can be fun, is nonetheless a dangerous member of the mania family, and should be approached cautiously. Manias, like many other poisons, produce an initially euphoric effect, and can be used recreationally in small doses. The Beatles referred to the strange behavior of their fans in the mid sixties—screaming, weeping, tearing their hair, attempting to rip off pieces of their heroes' clothing—as "the mania." All that enthusiasm caused the band, eventually, to stop playing concerts, then to break up altogether; John Lennon was killed by an obsessed fan and George Harrison had to sign autographs for his radiologists' son on his death-bed. You might like the *White Album*, but would you, personally, want people to treat you like that? Our culture loves to iconize, and then when some stratospherically successful superstar in their chosen field has a breakdown, collapses, checks into rehab or jumps off a bridge, overwhelmed by the adulation and expectation they have brought upon themselves, we shake our heads in uncomprehending sadness, bewilderment, and perhaps a little bit of disdain; meanwhile we're in the copy room at work, sneaking off copies of our screed, which we hope, in our heart of hearts, is going to change irrevocably the life of everyone who reads it. How would we react if our own subliminal desires were realized, if our dreams came true?

It happened to me. There I was, copying in the back room, after hours in offices, on the sly in a university building, or utilizing a vast arsenal of illicit tricks in national chain conglomerates— from re-setting counters to manipulating magnetic strips, I knew them all—with the proletarian anger of punk inspiring me, plus some pretty good academic rationalizations ("we have to rethink our conceptions of literary forms or genres, in view of the technical factors affecting our present situation, if we are to identify the forms of expression that channel the literary energies of the present" —Walter Benjamin, and etc). I wrote these nine zines originally between 1994-1998; I got the idea in the summer of 1994 during a visit to Brooklyn. One afternoon as I was getting off of the subway and ran into an old friend of mine, who was, unfortunately, boarding the same train I was disembarking. We recognized each other, but only had time for a quick smile and wave before disappearing from each other's sight. I wished, at that moment, that I had something like a small brochure I could have handed over, encapsulating the basic narrative of my life at that moment, an instant version of the ten or fifteen minutes of catching up we might have ideally had.

I set to work constructing this imagined object over the next week or so. *Burn Collector* was not my first attempt; I had made similar objects before, under varying titles, with different themes and contents. But somehow this one stuck, got a particularly good reaction, and so when the next one wrote itself, a few months later on a Greyhound bus, I called it #2.

I liked the idea of a personal fanzine, and still do, fundamentally: the idea of having a small, relatively recent accounting of yourself, on hand and in pamphlet form, ready to distribute to others. It's a direct and immediate form of communication, plus I liked not having deadlines, and never getting a rejection letter. And more so, I liked the letters that I did get, which were encouraging and thoughtful reactions from real-seeming people. That was the goal, and the apex of expectable results for the format I was working in. #3 wrote itself over my second winter in Providence. Then I moved to Portland, OR, where I spent a miserable and fruitless year and managed only to produce one slim booklet of comics, which was #4. #5, 7 and 9 wrote themselves in North Carolina, while #6 and 8 were a little different. They were my first attempts at constructing a narrative from events of the past: my teen years in North Carolina in #6 and that strange, lost year in Portland in #8. I was writing to salvage some humor or certainty from those experiences, which had seemed grim and ambiguous at the time. This, I came to realize, was the theme of the zine: a celebration of failure. The best response to the downhill slide of life seemed to be to laugh it off, to find transcendent moments or situational comedy in your defeat.

Did I have literary aspirations? Of course I did, just as everyone who plays the guitar might harbor some arena rock dreams. But, like 99% of guitar players, my follow-through on the career plan was lackluster. My ambitions were low. I do not say this in a spirit of modesty or self-effacement: as usual with me, it's a matter of upholding serious moral principles. Ambition, after all, is a terrible thing. It is the root source of almost all conflict.

Compared to deep-rooted ambition, a little mild megalo is nothing, a walk in the park. Ambition destroys friendships, makes your colleagues into your competitors, whittles away your ability to feel enjoyment in your small successes. It plays you like a puppet on an eternal Sisyphusian treadmill. A healthier, saner strategy for success is to play it cool, and hope that things will fall into your lap.

I was very surprised by how well the zine was received. In retrospect, I think a lot of its success had to do with Lisa Oglesby's invariably over-the-top reviews in *heartattack* magazine, which put it on the required reading list for its demographic target audience. (Lisa was also the first to note that, while the individual stories in the zine might be entertaining, when taken as a whole, "one starts to worry about the narrator.") By 1998, I had an enthusiastic audience of like-minded individuals, a small but high quality subculture, big enough that I was struggling to keep up with demand for copies. These little pamphlets served me well, flew out of my hands, seemed to communicate a lot of things to all kinds of interesting people. What more could you want? When the Owens brothers, Mark and Matt, suggested re-printing the zines in book form via their record label, it was the icing on the cake, the dream come true, fulfillment of the secret fantasy of having my name on a square-bound, non self-stapled object, having an ISBN number, being a "real author." Why not? I thought. It would save me the trouble of keeping the old issues in print, which is a pain.

That was my moment of megalomaniacal indulgence. I knew it at the time, and in the original introduction I even expressed a little trepidation—"the idea of a book perturbs me," I wrote. A pretty mild formulation, but then I had no idea what was in store for me. Even when the first copies appeared at my doorstep, the strange effect that it would have on my life was not immediately clear. It took a little time, a bit of circulation, before I noticed that there was something odd about the cumulative effect of putting everything under one cover. It was like nutmeg: a measured dosage flavors things nicely, but eat the whole jar at once and you experience psychedelic hallucinations. People began to act strangely. "What is it like to be a *real author*?" they would ask, even though it was the same old photocopies. I hadn't changed anything, I hadn't even bothered to correct spelling mistakes. It was just a question of the binding. How could people be duped so easily, by such an obvious trick?

Maybe it goes against the original, disposable spirit of these things to be here, down at the copy store, again, preparing this for another round of circulation. These were supposed to be impermanent records, on cheap paper, quickly pawed and tattered into oblivion. Making this into a book changed it, and it took me years to understand exactly why: because the object, a book, has an *aura*, meaning it has a weight apart from its physical weight. There is a different impact. That ten minutes of catching up with a friend I'd wanted in the subway station transformed itself into a serious long-term relationship with a bunch of total strangers. I felt this when a kid from Philadelphia, crashing in my living room on his way to Chiapas, felt compelled to corner me in my kitchen and berate me for half the night about my views on gentrification. Or from a crust punk in Texas, who asked me the current whereabouts of the members of the band Manpower, and, when I told him that Bill Tsistos was teaching sociology, shook his head and scowled, as if that were the most tragically disappointing outcome he could have imagined. A major label rock band named an album after a story in the book, getting my name mentioned in both *Rolling Stone **and** Guitar Player* magazine! Without even having to touch a guitar!

The zines had an aura, too, albeit a more subtle one: they were hand-made objects. I collated, folded and stapled each one, sometimes catching my thumb on a staple and sending out copies spattered with droplets of real authorial blood. I've never believed in divisions of creative expression, I think many people have all sorts of talents and the compartmentalizing of yourself into writer, or musician, or artist, is a social construct done mainly for resume purposes. Some of the writing in here was an intense labor of love, other pages are pure filler and my main pleasure was in doing the layout. I was always, and am still, happiest when I'm doing a little bit of everything, and not taking any of it too seriously. Still, it was one of the nicest things anyone ever did for me, that gift of the Owens brothers, to place what I had produced in a different context, and thus entreat readers, and myself, to confront the question of what it means to be "real:" I had always known that being a writer or an artist was just a matter of doing it, producing pages, making things. But it wasn't until this book existed that I actually believed it.

My suggestion to the reader now would be to think of this as a series of individual magazines, as nine points of view, rather than as one book. It seems to be easier on your constitution that way. In any case, I've never liked the term "zine," but I do like the expression "personal fanzine," because I like to think of it as making a magazine expressing my fandom for the people I've encountered. They are the ones with the wisdom in here. If you take this as a series of individual components, it helps you focus less on the author, and lets you remember that he is just your humble narrator, telling you what is out there.

And to the creative people in the audience: aim higher than failure. It worked for me, but that was a one-time thing. Set your sights as high as possible and you'll probably achieve it. Just remember, and be warned: be sure that what you are going for is what you really want, because you may get it.

If you aim to fail, you probably will, perhaps even spectacularly.

-AB
Berlin, March 2010

This is a collection of zines-

photocopied, cut-and-pasted, glue-sticked, mostly written in quick bursts of nervous energy late at night, pecked out on a borrowed word processor or my own trusty antiquated artifact of the technological dark ages, the Mac Classic, whose hard drive contains exactly two programs- Microsoft Word and MacPaint. My writing is really nothing compared to some of my truly ingenious MacPaint creations, but that is, perhaps, better saved for a postmortem retrospective of my lesser-known works (something must be left undiscovered for posterity, I figure).

They are presented as they originally appeared, inclusive of typos, layout errors and tell-tale signs of haste or fatigue which leave the occasional unexplained weird margin or crammed paragraph or something- the whole point of the form, it seems to me, is its imperfection, the guiding mantra of my creative output: quantity over quality. I've churned out thousands of these things, on copy machines in varying states of decay and disrepair, changing toner cartridges in desolate all-night copy shops all over the nation, usually being mistaken for an employee as a result. That's always vaguely humiliating in some undefinable way. Is it because in my moment of artistic/ socially subversive triumph (I'm rarely paying for the copies, so it's always that glorious sense of subverting the fundamental building block of capitalism, the cash transaction, through sheer assertion of ego in the form of lifted photocopied pamphlets), someone ignobly asks me to clear a paper jam for them, or fetch them the scissors? Or do I just have the strange, docile look of someone who's been employed underneath florescent lights for too large a chunk of his life? Indeed, sometimes I get so mistaken for an employee that I end up actually working at these houses of carcinogenic ill repute, gambling my future health on the potential of immortality of some slight sort, if I can just smuggle a few more boxes of these things out the back door.

Quantity over quality: sure, there are thousands of these in circulation, many of them nearly illegible from being copies of copies of copies, or from a machine which was copying gray that day. Quality control would imply some sense of individual worth as an artifact, an implicit admission on my part of trying to do something bigger than what I'm actually doing, of trying to produce socially significant cultural documents or summations of situations, times, lives. I'm not; I'm just making zines.

As to my motivations for doing specifically that, as opposed to anything else I could be doing with my time; well, I can't really explain it- or, if I can, I can't see how it's going to hook me up to do so. If I talk you into what a good idea it is to make your own zine, well, that's just one more person trying to scam copies, or using up paper, ruining the whole racket for me by your overcrowding of the subcultural microcosm. If you get it, you're probably already doing it. If not, that's fine. More room for me.

The prospect of a book perturbs me. It seems to imply that I'm somehow graduated from the trenches, that what I wrote and put forth was somehow any more real or legitimate than anything any other kid did. Of course this is not the case. I never really meant, at the outset, to come to the point where the glue sticks started wearing out, peeling paste-up type off of yellowing sheets of non-acid-free copy paper-- I never meant to get to the point where the copies of copies started to be illegible, and still there was someone interested in reading something that I wrote. This is just a record of my impulses, nervous energy late at night, pecked out for no reason. But thanks anyway, for paying attention.

-Al Burian, Chapel Hill, NC, late December, 1998.

Printed in Canada

BURN

COLLECTOR

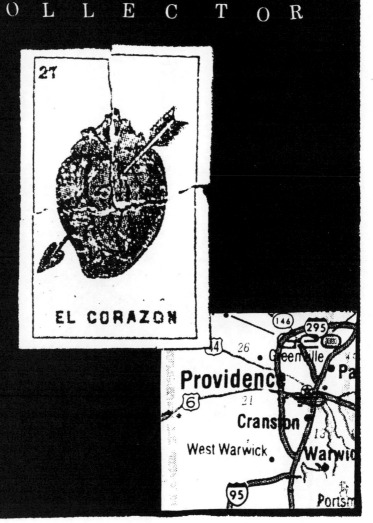

If you want a really crappy idea for something to do,

try conceptualizing your life in terms of cinematography, thinking of the dialogue as actually scripted and the awkward silences between sentences as you try to think of something, um, clever to say as dramatic pauses shot from innovative angles with dramatic back-lighting. It's one of those things, like saying to someone, "hey, have you ever thought about your tongue? I mean, really thought about it?" - it opens up this whole can of worms; you end up unable to shut off the cinematographic impulse, and you find yourself rather quickly reduced, in the eyes of the film-viewing public, to a bumbling moron, unable to speak coherently (which, by the way, also furthers the tongue analogy). Everything is kind

of like a movie; life imitates art but only the kick-ass parts and even those, art gussies up and casts babelier people in the lead roles. You end up with this really tedious, shitty movie that meanders down all these strange, tunnel-like, badly contrived sub-plots, involves way too many arty awkward silences, and including some really mortifying masturbation sequences on your part. You come off looking, basically, not that cool; your life overall is a Siskelian (or is that Ebertian?) "thumbs down." I'm watching the clock in my room: the second-hand moves forward a second, then back two seconds, then forward, and so on, moving slowly and as inefficiently as mechanically possible in a roundabout counter-clockwise direction. How did the clock get this way? What trauma occurred? Or did it simply slip imperceptibly into senility as the days turned into months? This movie sucks; it's one shot, no cuts. How long can this last, how long can I go on like this? I used to ask myself such questions in more tormented days. But the truth is, I guess, that it's not you who "goes on, " "going on" just sort of happens to you, like an endless car wreck, and the best you can hope is that they got it all on film and that you look sufficiently like Burt Reynolds so they can use the footage of you as a stunt-double in the next Cannonball Run movie.

The "life as bad film" neurosis seems particularly acute in my personal litany of hang-ups these days. Generally, I suffer not-that-stoically from a bad case of realization-that-life-has-no-plot-and-accompanying-extended-freakout syndrome, for which there is no twelve-step program that I am aware of (You know what would be funny? If I got a postcard from someone which said "there's a one-step program, Al- Jesus." Man, that would be awesome). When people in North Carolina asked me why I was moving to New England in

February, surely the worst possible timing for
traveling North to the land of grumpy bastards
and frostbite, I would respond with a stock
moralization I had developed, some spiel about
how I would be experiencing life more acutely if
I was in the most extreme climate available
(which, on a purely surface-of-the skin level, is
undeniably true) and how it all relates back to
the guy in <u>Catch 22</u> who wants to live as long
as possible so he does the most boring things he
can think of to make time seem to go by really
slowly. I would cite "the path of least
resistance" as my mortal foe in life, leaving the
phrase hanging in the air like a right-winger
does when invoking "welfare mothers:" no
explanation even needed of why that's evil, I
mean, it's just so obvious. As most everyone
picked up on, I had absolutely no idea what I
was talking about, but was in fact merely
contriving some kind of reasoning after the fact
for decisions which were either being made on
some much higher or much lower level than the
one which my cranium navigates me half-
assedly around. The artifices I rig up give me
comfort, even if they seem pretty transparent,
and I imagine I'll continue constructing them to
the best of my ability. Lately, though, everything
just seems really particularly, astoundingly
arbitrary, and that, my friend, is a grade A
blower. I take comfort in TV: on the Simpsons,
Marge tries to wrap up the episode by revealing
the moral, throwing out a barrage of trite
phrases; Homer responds, "there's no moral. It's
just a bunch of stuff that happened." Thus, I give
you an account of some of the things I've been up
to lately: just a bunch of stuff that happened.

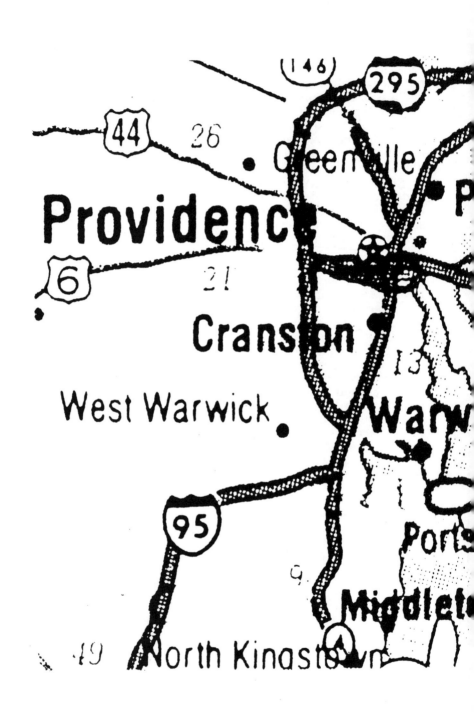

It's always been my contention that a

healthy state of psychological well-being must come from within, and that your surroundings, though a factor in determining your happiness, basically exist as a minor variable to either enhance a rich internal life or present a minor obstacle to overcome through creative use of the resources at hand. Then again, I'm probably not a good person to take advice from on the subject of inner happiness. I was fine up until the age of ten years old, when suddenly some kind of dismal, inky hormone kicked in and I just started moping and complaining to no end, a practice which I've maintained with (I think you'd have to concede) admirable consistency throughout my life thereafter. In any case, environment being or not being of whatever significance it either is or isn't to whatever it is that it is significant to (you follow me? That's the kind of

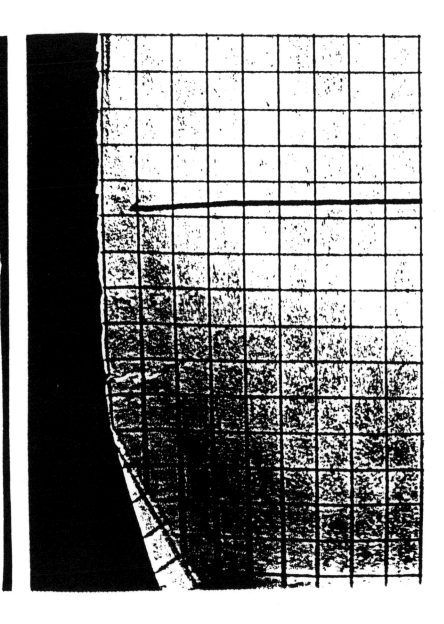

shit that gets you an A+ in college), I figured it
was time for me to expend a little quality
moping in locales heretofore only dimly familiar
to me. To this end, I packed up a few meager
belongings and set out, ending up after a short
drift at good old Harrison's little apartment in
Providence, RI. In most respects a pretty
standard student domicile, there was something
very unnerving about the apartment, and I
couldn't quite put my finger on it. Eventually I
realized: the light in the bathroom never turns
off. While this may not, on the surface, appear
to be particularly sinister, it somehow,
inexplicably, cast an aura of sketchiness about
the place which was unshakable, and, in point
of fact, kind of pleasing in an embrace-the-
apocalypse sort of way.

　　　　My first impression of Providence
upon arriving there for this somewhat extended
stay was, perhaps, not specific to the place, but
comforting in just that non-specificity: like all
locales where any number of people have to
deal with each other in any sort of interaction
which might be even remotely socially
awkward, the great social lubricant, demon
alcohol, oozes all-pervasively, like the sticky
fluid between joints. And just as the night before
I had found myself in Amherst, Massachusetts,
suspiciously eyeing the last inch of a bottle of
something with the approximate flavor of burnt
hoof, offered up by the local beatniks, so it was
with a sense of comforting familiarity that the I
watched the age-old struggle to find something
to pour down the collective gullet begin anew in
Providence on a chilly Monday night, like some
ancient ballet or those two guys in that movie
Highlander who get together every few
centuries to beat the fuck out of each other. The
chase is always better than the kill, as I believe
both Motorhead and Billy Bragg have
commented on, and the state of Rhode Island

photo- Rob.

seems to be taking these British rockers to heart
(and it figures, being how the place is so old and
Waspy- I bet you can find some old geezers
around here who still wish we were an English
colony), instituting a set of liquor laws
designed to provide a zesty challenge to the
would-be inebriate wishing to commence
activity after sundown. All venues of alcohol-
purchase locked up for the night, our
protagonists, gathered over at the house of my
friend Marie, pondered grimly the only option
available: try to score some beer from the
meatheads in the upstairs apartment. Now, my
personal position on drinking is this: anything
which facilitates you doing something kick-ass
is a good thing, (i.e., drinking a cup of coffee so
as to avoid a fruitless date with sleep) and, if
drinking seems to serve this purpose, so be it.
However, I'm not that in to drinking as an
activity in and of itself, and all too often it does
seem to be, rather than an instigator or
enhancer of kick-ass activity, a means by which
to convince yourself that sitting on your couch
is itself something pretty worthwhile. (While
I'm on the subject of myself being a weird
puritanical zealot, let me recount a little
anecdote about something that happened to me
in Chapel Hill once- it kind of tangentially
relates to drinking, but moreover it illustrates
nicely how Chapel Hill sucks. I was at this
friend of mine's birthday party, right? I walked
in and immediately was offered a beer. Being in
a room full of scary people I didn't know, I
opted to keep my wits about me and declined.
Not missing a beat, the hostess offered me a
cigarette, which I also declined. Minutes later, I
was pouring a glass of orange juice to drink,
when the same person accosted me, warning me,
in all seriousness, that I could not drink the
juice because it had preservatives and sugar in
it. The rest of the evening people kept coming up

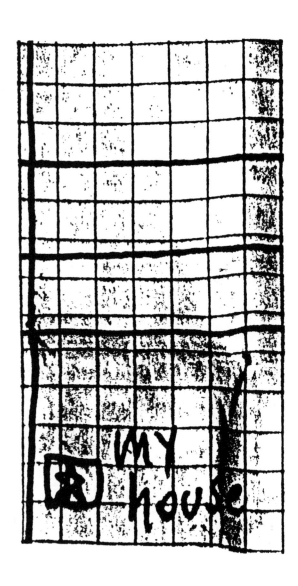

to me and telling me that they "admired my ethics.") In any event, I was far more interested in a chance to anthropologically dissect the source of the grunts, muted yelps and thundering crashing sounds emanating from the upstairs apartment than I was in procuring the bottled elixir of Beelzebub, and in my enthusiasm to lock horns with the bovine specimens upstairs, I was recruited along with this girl Debbie, whom I had developed an instant rapport with based on her rad Black Sabbath T-shirt, to be the advance shock troops in the infiltration of the retardation nation. Up the stairs we went, knocking boldly and entering under the cleverly constructed lead-in, 'hey, dudes, are you having a *party*?" This invocation of sacred scripture enthused the upstairs neighbors, who were quick to show us around their abode. I must say, I gaped in astonishment at what I witnessed there. The tenants, "entrepreneurship" majors at a local community college, were certainly putting their learning to good use, having almost completed construction in their apartment of a fully furnished and stocked sports bar! This bar came complete with pool table, wide screen TV mounted on the wall, black lights, and, of course, the *piece de resistance*, the bar itself, soon to be filled with all manner of liquor and kegs of swilly, trough-grade beer. The plan, apparently, was to run an illicit "speak-easy" of a sort, charging an exorbitant entry-fee and continuing to milk the locals by the drink. One might of course have been moved to ask how all this was going to work in these post-prohibition times, but this was a mere detail in these young goofball's grand design, besides which, the elaborate network of flaming hoops of Rhode Island liquor law (alluded to earlier) would certainly bring in, at least, under-age clientele. These

view from Harrison's house.

were men with a vision, I realized, not just a bevy of goons making a lot of trampling noises from upstairs, although their vision, the downstairs dwellers realized with furrowed brows, would certainly entail vast buffalo-stampede simulations to ensue in the future. I got so wrapped up in their world-view that I almost lost track of the mission, but Debbie snapped me out of it, casually remarking, "so, can I get a beer or something?" "Help yourself, in the fridge," the boss-man of the brigade politely offered. We sauntered into the kitchen, and proceeded to stuff our pockets with cans of beer. Unfortunately, one of the entrepreneurs walked into the kitchen in time to see Debbie stuffing a beer into her bra, at which point we saw a light bulb atop his head not exactly click on, but certainly someone was sloooowly turning up the dimmer, and it was time for us to beat a hasty retreat down the stairs, where we were welcomed as the victorious conquistadors we most assuredly were.

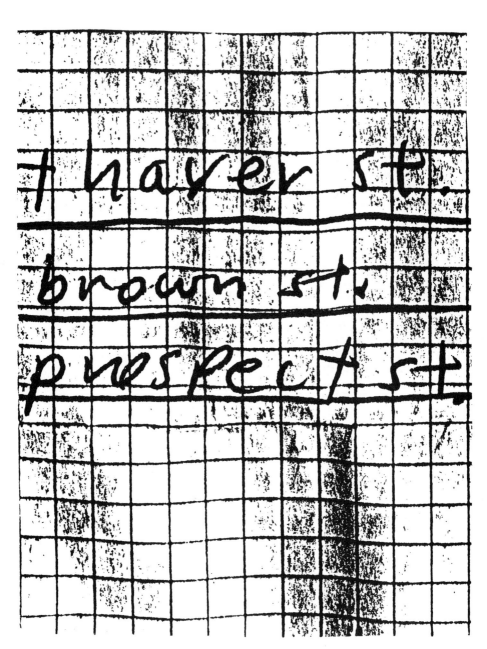
thayer st.
brown st.
prospect st

Having been "jumped in" to the ways of social life in these parts, and

finding it comforting and familiar, I woke up the next day ready to glean further comfort and familiarity from my surroundings, in the form of good deals. Harrison had drawn me a really lovely map of the town while inspired by the demon alcohol, which of course allowed the evening to fit my paradigmatic conception of productivity-rising-from-debauchery and generally made me feel pretty good about life. I set out, following this little graph-paper map, and walked around Providence, familiarizing myself with its layout as best I could. Providence is a really nice town for walking endlessly around; though rife with very steep hills, the architecture is so distractingly pleasant that you barely notice that you should be using a pick-axe and rope to get around. I like towns to be just like this: filled with interesting-looking people, and yet inexplicably boring beyond belief, so that the interesting-looking people can be found wandering up and down the street aimlessly, bleary-eyed and half-catatonic from inertia. It's like a nut with a really, really thick shell that you can't crack, and the weird conversations with understimulated kids seem enticingly to get you closer, but never quite there. The chase is always better than the kill. I got some free bread from Geoff's bakery and fifty cent day-old pastries from Silver Star bakery, and that was what I grubbed non-stop for the first few days. One thing which really sucked: New England, I was rapidly learning, is a place where the phrase "free refill" prompts coffee-vendors to perplexedly reach for there Swahili-English dictionary, in the vain hopes of deciphering this young lout who stands before them speaking in tongues. The very concept "good deal on coffee," elicited only blank stares from anyone I broached the subject with.

One day, as I was wandering about, the pangs of intense hunger overcame me, as they often tend to do, since I have (by necessity) developed a pretty fuel-oriented approach to dining (which is not to say that I can't appreciate some good food as much or indeed quite likely a great deal more than the next person- you'll often find me singing the praises of some particularly enticing meal to no end, but rest assured that I probably procured said dining experience through some sketchy invite or illicit means, which is, of course, precisely the factor which makes my palate so sensitive, because it is just an irrefutable truth that the

day → (coffee)
old
bread   deal)   ☆

tangy flavor of freedom is the best garnish), and, just as I approach fueling a car by the time-tested strategy of driving until the needle is way past empty, then panicking and frantically searching out the nearest gas station, I tend to ignore signs of oncoming hunger until the point at which some internal switch is thrown, my eyes glaze over, and my vast, towering intellect focuses like a laser on one goal, expressed by me with a finger pointed rigidly at my gaping mouth and the command, "put something to grub in here. Right now!" barked at anyone unfortunate enough to be in my vicinity. So it was on this day, and as I found myself on the campus of Brown University, I quickly put the nearest Brown... uh, what do they call them? Brownie? Browner? Anyway, the nearest student-looking type in a headlock and demanded directions to the school dining facilities. Unfortunately, the equivalent of the plans to the Death Star which R2D2 carries with him in *Star Wars* and which detail the one Achilles heel of entry to that insidious construct did not exist for me in relation to the maximum-security Brown dining hall. Despairing, I retreated to the bathroom to ponder a plan of action, unconsciously mimicking in this activity the Fonz, with his bathroom "office." My debt to Seventies culture overshadowed in enormity only by my raging hunger, I was pleased to see an employee of the dining hall, dressed in traditional college kitchen garb, in my office, and struck up conversation with him. Cutting quickly to the chase, I asked whether he could sneak me in, but he only confirmed the totalitarian methods of social control exercised in this supposed institution of free and democratic ideals. "the boss is always watching," he whispered, casting a nervous glance under the stalls. Dejected, I trudged away, pausing outside the

Rhode Island pin- found on the street.

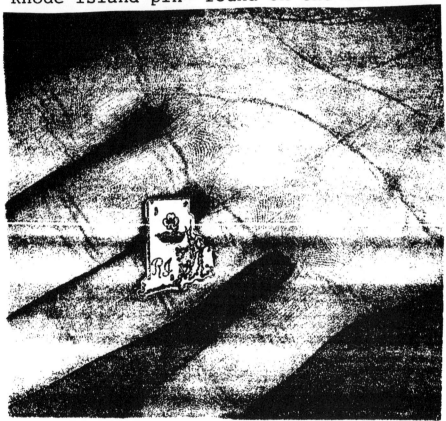

cafeteria to peruse some flyers, which I hoped might detail the activities of some renegade free food organizations in the vicinity. The kitchen worker, I was surprised to see, emerged from a side door, glanced about nervously, and proceeded towards me, clutching a small, plastic-wrapped package of approximate entrée dimensions, I was more than pleased to behold. "Here, man," he said, "I didn't want you to go away hungry." What a saint! I beamed at him, my smile only wavering slightly when I realized that he was holding out a steak. He beamed back at me. "Go ahead, man, eat it," he grinned. Hesitantly, I unwrapped it, examining the dry, brittle thing in my hand. I took a cautious bite; it had been several years since I had consumed meat in any significant sense (not counting things like chicken flavoring in oodles of noodles and the like), and this seemed like a reckless leap back into the world of the carnivorous. Satisfied with my bite and my lavish praise of his willingness to fight the oppressive system, the patron saint of non-PC culinary experience scuttled back into the kitchen. I was left with my steak and my thoughts, which were mainly along the lines of "time to eat this quite reasonably priced dinner." I ate it in a corner, feeling like a stray dog chewing awkwardly on bones and gristle. It was kind of gross, but so deep fried and dry that it was essentially gross in the way dining on a greasy piece of cardboard would be. I didn't get sick and throw up or anything, but I did have some moments of concern for my morality and ethics. What are my morality and ethics, anyway? They seem so malleable and subject to the dictates of the situation. The only real consistents seem to be appreciation for a good bargain and a vague hatred of anyone who seems to be keeping me from getting one,

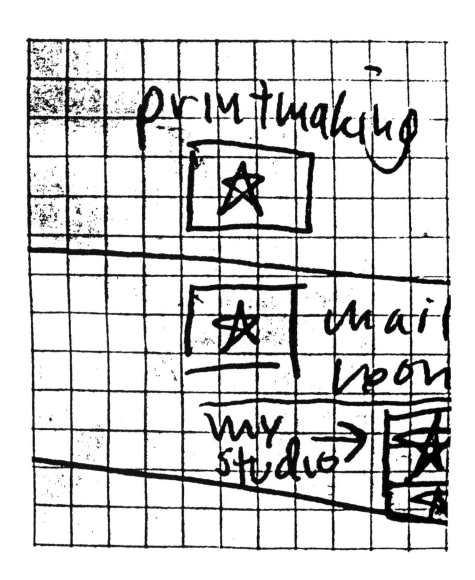

these infidels being collectively referred to in my cosmology as "the Man." I related the story and its accompanying ideological dilemma component to Marie, who explained me to myself. "Oh, that's easy," she said, "you're a *freegan*."

My main favorite place to hang out in Providence would

have to be the train station, and here's why: in terms of pure, undiluted human drama, the place is a veritable well of emotion, what people in the oil business call a "gusher;" and if emotion is indeed reducible to liquid format, it must certainly be quite oily and probably relatively salty as well, so the analogy is pretty apt. This liquid emotion, which I

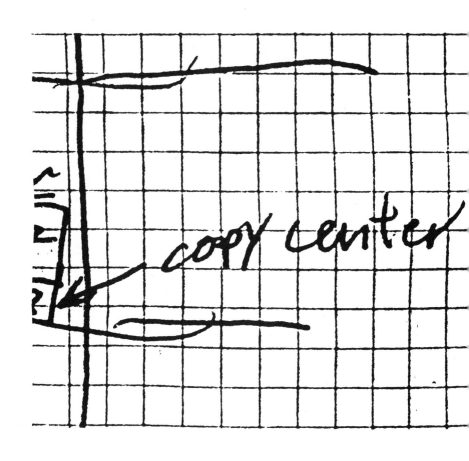

envision as tasting like soy sauce, but completely clear, mind you, accumulates on the temples and other pressure points, evaporating into the air in billowing clouds (so the theory goes), and filling the room with a static-electric charge that accomplishes totally naturally and without harmful side-effects what Bruce Lee was trying to achieve with high-voltage electrodes when he accidentally overdosed and died, which is stimulate big muscles to form (if you don't believe me, check out that movie *Dragon*- irrefutable documentation!), except in this case it's not actual, physically present big muscles, but instead big muscles of the soul, or what some more fruity people might call "building character," or what I call, "some good shit to tell people about later." In just the space of a few hours, the following phone conversations were overheard:

- An obese guy calling for a call girl, to meet him at whatever location he was taking the train to. Literally glistening like a glazed pig, he demanded: "Is she real pretty? Really good-looking? I don't want her to be too fat."

- Another guy, thirty-ish, stranded in Providence because he had missed the last train to Boston, where he needed to be within hours, apparently, to punch in to his night-shift job. His estranged girlfriend asks, "do you want me to call my dad to give you a ride?" He stares at the ground in humiliation; she screams at him, "ANSWER ME!" He nods. "Yes," he mumbles meekly. (That's actually not a phone conversation, is it? It's a conversation which occurred by a phone. Oh well, close enough.)

- The worst one: A guy who calls a number every five minutes, leaving a message each time along the lines of, "Hi, I'm calling for the birthday girl, I just wanted to wish you a

Rob.

happy birthday." On the millionth try he finally intercepts her: "Hello? Is this the birthday girl? (starts singing) HAPPY BIRTHDAY TO YOU, HAPPY BIRTHDAY TO YOU, HAPPY......... uh, hello?.....Hello...? (pause) Oh, It's you. What? What do mean I can't talk to her? Put her back on the phone! God damn it! I'm her father!" An extended argument ensues, obviously a small constellation in some vast galaxy of an ongoing custody battle. Dad finally brow-beats his ex into putting the birthday girl back on the line, and continues his song, ending with the populist twist, "you look like a monkey and act like one, too," (trying to put across zany, fun-lovin' dad, the kind of dad who will definitely let you eat Cap'n Crunch and stay up late watching Melrose Place, not like mom who makes you go to bed at eight-thirty so can you please just mention your preferences to the judge?) but the wind is obviously taken out of his sails, and he delivers the punch line grudgingly, spitting it out in a humorless monotone.

Providence, Rhode Island: A hot-bed of misery and despair. I like it.

MARIE LORENZ

interview

M arie goes to the Rhode Island School of Design, studies printmaking, but mainly seems to build boats. When I first met her she was making a pair of shoes with tire tread soles, which I thought was pretty rad. She has always impressed me as a real good artist, and also she seems to have enough of that afore-cited existential angst hormone (an overabundance of which has been my personal key to being such a scintillating conversationalist over the years) that I could probably rely on her for a transfusion if I ever run dry. On the evening in question, she made a bunch of red velvet marching band costumes, rigged a bunch of drums to people, and the makeshift parade proceeded to clatter its way chaotically and noisily over to the RISD cafeteria, for the purpose of disrupting a hippie drum circle. Things didn't go exactly as planned; the drum circle leader, it turned out, was a veteran of MCing drum jams between inner city gangs, warring religious sects, and the like, so that our motley collection of annoying art student types posed no threat to his grand design. Having defused our plan by cleverly tricking us into incorporating ourselves into one of his insidious hippie beats (God, I hate those hippies!), he continued to spread good vibes whilst Marie retreated to her house beneath the entrepreneur meatheads, where we had the following very serious debate on contemporary issues in the field of art.

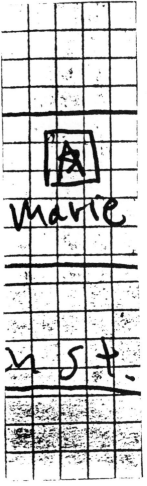

Al: A lot of the art you make is really collaborative, which I think is interesting, because one of the things about a lot of art, a good and bad thing is that it's isolating. Which is good, because it's a pain to have to depend on other people in a way.

Marie: Every time I do something collaborative I always promise myself, I'm like "fuck that! Next time- all me." With the kind of events that I do, like the thing that we just did, if I could do everything in the whole world I would do it all myself, but there's just not enough time in the world, so I have to be like, "OK, you do this part. Do whatever you want. I may not like it, but it's got to be all you for this."

Al: You have to learn to, instead of having an idea and wanting everyone to fit into it, you have to learn to fit everything into your idea.

Marie: Yeah, right. Exactly. Like that guy tonight. He was the perfect example of that. We went in there and he just made his idea get bigger. How insane was that? Specifically posted: "no snare drums. No drum sticks."

Al: Yeah, like the people who came specifically to fuck with him, and he was like, "I was hoping people like you would show up."

Marie: I've come into contact with people like that before. Working with retarded people and in schools, where they're just into being good, not being good on a selfish level, but being in to people trying. I was so set up to hate him and ruin his life.... When I first looked at the flyer I was like, "OK, there's this corporate fucker who goes around and IBM pays him;" but thinking about it now, it's a guy like us who gave a proposal to a company and said "give me all this money. I want to go everywhere and do this thing," so he's just this insane guy who had this idea and the company was "wild and crazy" enough to pick it up.

Al: It's weird to say, "yeah, he's just a corporate whore for IBM" because one thing that I've realized is that there's no such thing as selling out except in the really limited world of like, you know, our specific world-view. Like when the Eightball comic guy did the OK Cola can, you're like "what a sell-out!" but there's no anti-corporate ethic in comic books. And in the art world that's completely standard.

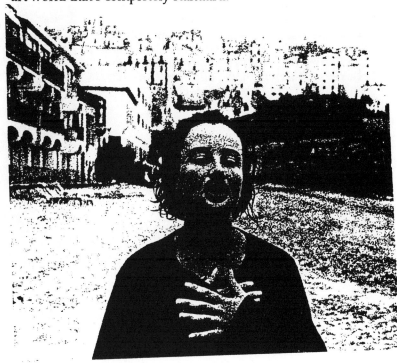

Marie: Yeah, in the seventies there was a push with performance art and stuff like that to make art that was totally un-buyable. Performance, rotten fruit, anything that can't be bought. But the thing is, then that kind of thing needs grants, so you get tied in to banks and the government.

Al: So is the lesson of that that there's no way to avoid selling out?

Marie: I guess I've always felt kind of weird about that, saying "sell-out" because I kind of look forward to the opportunity to use artwork to get money but then, I guess hearing about the band my brother is on tour with, and the ways they've had to compromise (on a major label)- they're on tour right now and getting booked in horrible places and they can't say where they want to go, they get booked with shitty metal bands.......

Al: So what's the future of art?

Marie: The art system is going down. The NEA is going to be gone in, like, 1996......

Al: Art is a sketchy thing to be pinning your hopes for the future on.

Marie: We were reading all this stuff the other day about taxes and tax deductions for making art. It's all about trading art with other people so that you can get a tax deduction, let's say we were both going to donate a piece of art to the RISD museum, I could sell my piece to you and you could sell your piece to me for $10,000 and then we could donate that to the RISD museum and get the tax deduction.

Al: The art of tax loopholes?

Marie: Yes.

Marie Lorenz fan club c/o Al Burian: 307 Blueridge Rd. Carrboro, NC 27510.

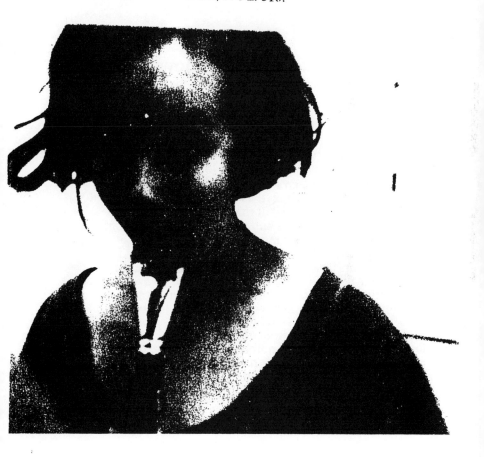

I ate a lot of good food in Providence, RI. Jeff showed me the ropes for getting into the RISD cafeteria, for which I was extremely grateful.

There were art openings with their accompanying cheese and crackers, bottles of juice and wine. Harrison and Marie made me lots of food and marveled at my stomach capacity. I told them that I was just filling up for the days when they didn't feed me. I met a lot of nice people there as well. It made me happy but also really sad; I was happy to know that you can go to some random place and meet a bunch of people that you get along with and feel entertained and possibly even inspired by, but at the same time it feels really bad to go to a random place, make a bunch of connections, and then leave. And it sort of alludes to all the millions of other random places with other random people where you didn't happen to show up, where you missed out on something great, someone amazing. This train of thought drives me crazy. I've got a backpack full of notebooks with phone numbers and addresses scrawled down, so many that it immobilizes me, I just sit there and twitch and feel stupefied by the weight of a world that is really, really big.

After I left Providence, I went to Brooklyn to stay with Elizabeth for a while. One day, I met her after work, whereupon we got a cup of coffee and I proceeded to detail my day for her. New York is brimming with strange looking individuals, and all the more so because this plethora of personas facilitates a sort of one-upmanship to occur where the only way to stand out from the masses is to look that much crazier, and so on and so on, building up like the arms race, until finally the net total of berserk looking outfits in Manhattan alone is enough to destroy the world eight times over. You see all these people all day, but you never get to talk to them, you never have an entry into their conversation, and it makes you feel that much more anonymous and hopeless in regards to your relation to that gigantic horde of humanity, an infinitesimally tiny fraction of whose numbers and addresses I carry on my back with me, pack-rat style, brainless. It made the sense of loss I felt in Providence that much more acute. This is the essential burn of New York City, I ventured, sitting there explaining the variety and shades and textures of the many burns I had been feeling in the past few weeks. "You really like to just kind of go around checking out the burns of various places, don't you?" Elizabeth said. "You're kind of a burn collector." I thought that was pretty funny.

al   burian

307 Blueridge Rd.
Carrboro, NC 27510

307 Blueridge Rd. Carrboro, NC 27510.

Provi

SPRING FEVER!!

Spring exhales its way nauseatingly into summer; things get too humid and hot. Over almost as soon as it's begun, spring stretches from some weekend in late April until the first two consecutive sunny days in May, just long enough for meaty fraternity guys to have a wild spring break weekend, these festivals of volleyball and guttural mono-syllabic conversation being the only reason, culturally, that the season even still exists in late-capitalist industrial society, the society of instant gratification and responsibility-avoidance. People don't realize how skewed their seasonal priorities are, because they can't internalize the concept that often anticipation is far better than the actual pay-off; it would, in fact, be tantamount to treason to admit this. And so, we lurch through spring, barreling headlong into sticky, languid summers, ending up face down on boiling pavement, eyeballs frying like eggs, wondering at what a tremendous let-down this all is.

In Providence, RI, the first signs of warmth do elicit an intense sense of jubilation. School is ending for the students, the bitter cold of New England is giving way to the temperate climates of summer job hunting, late nights spent walking around in shorts, beach trips. I dumpster dive a bag of donuts one night, drag them home to Harrison's house at four in the morning, and lay them out on the kitchen table. No one is awake to share in my triumph, and I begin devouring donuts with exactly the lack of restraint that tends to characterize too much of a good thing. Four donuts into my binge, I am suddenly intensely aware of how stale and sickeningly sweet these pastries are, and I am perturbed to note the vague rubbery aftertaste of garbage bag has imbued itself into these delicacies. I am mildly nauseous and overcome with inexplicable guilt. I drag the bag out of the house to the nearest dumpster, knowing that if I wake up tomorrow and see my sugary one-night stand splayed out on the kitchen table I'll really regret the past twenty-three years of life which brought me to that sordid moment. It's a warm, beautiful night, so I go sit on a park bench and listen to birds as I watch it slowly get light out. It's amazing that there is a sunrise every morning, unnoticed. The sun rises behind me and I stare out over the Providence downtown skyline, into the darkness that spans out westward for three-thousand miles. I figure out which way is northwest, staring, thinking about how it's three hours earlier in Portland, Oregon, and the people I know there just going to bed, anticipating summer. Last spring I was there, graduating college, and I remember being sucked into the vortex of emotions that comes when the weather turns nice, how everyone goes kind of crazy and you think for a fleeting moment that you will connect with everyone, because it's all about anticipation, the promise of a friendship that might be, a let-down that might not come this time. It's funny to be here in Providence, because I feel the same way here, perhaps even more intensely, and I don't actually know anyone here particularly well, suggesting that it's all reaction to climate or some kind of bizarre pheremonal contact-high from the viscous, needy sweat people produce in spring. You never want to believe the weather effects your mood to the extent that it does; it seems too arbitrary, too disempowering and simple. I like to think that my relation to the people going to bed now in Portland, Oregon are real things, based in some assessment of their and my innate understanding of each other. I like to think that the people who will be getting up in a few hours here in Providence, to find me giddy and bleary-eyed on this bench, might also mean something to me. But maybe it's all just weather, maybe it's all just lighting and the right outfits and the mis-firing synapse in the brain which spills tiny droplets of that forbidden fluid into your spine which gives things a plot, which seems like it makes life linear and well-thought out, if only for a minute.

NOTES

UNDER H

The Greyhound bus is not thirty seconds out of the gate, creeping like some hideous, blind undersea worm from its mud and fish-carcass encrusted lair, and the threat of physical violence is already palpable in the air. The passengers seated within immediate proximity of the emerging altercation, either New Yorkers or at least people really concerned about seeming urban so they won't get mugged as they transfer busses, stare fixedly ahead, wishing this was one of those fancy bus lines where they show a movie, wishing the movie had started, wishing the guy with the bulging, bloodshot eyes, puffed out like twin blowfish in attack formation, didn't reek so strongly of booze, sweat and the weight of whatever it is in his life that is crushing him, causing him in turn to seek out others to crush.

from the

OUND

"Hey, motherfucker! You just put your ass in my face!" he admonishes a stocky European man who is standing in the aisle, adjusting his luggage in the overhead rack, his rump admittedly directly at blowfish level. I can tell the man is European because he is wearing a ridiculous sweater, the kind no person responsible for dressing himself would ever wind up in, not in this country, a sweater evocative of Tintin comics and getting beaten up in junior high for wearing precisely this style of hand-me-downs from my German relatives. "Very sorry," mumbles the dishevelled, Euro-sweatered man, a bit taken aback. "You weren't going to say anything , were you?" the mean guy launches into shrill interrogation, his voice rising in pitch and volume. "If I didn't say nothing you would have let it slide, huh?" The Euro-guy starts to laugh nervously, trying to defuse the situation. "Oh, you think that's goddamn funny, huh? Huh?" The eyes strain, the eyes yearn to break free of their veiny sockets, to tear into the pink flabby throat of the flustered tourist. This stare is the universal challenge of the schoolyard, the declaration of war, the eye that sends buzzing whispers around the playground: "gonna be a beat-down." I wonder for a moment if this guy seriously intends to fight, right here, in the aisle.

These are my first thirty seconds aboard the Greyhound, and I will be on the bus for three and a half days. Behind me Port Authority Bus Station recedes into the murky haze of sin that shimmers like low-hanging fog around the porn theaters and strip joints of 42nd Ave. "Abandon hope, all ye who enter here;" Dante writes, and the sentiment is echoed in the crudely scrawled warning that I find in the bathroom of the bus: "fuck the hound." But you get what you pay for, and I am, in paying the eighty dollar special fare to get from New York City to Portland, Oregon, also receiving, as a fringe benefit, a three-day safari into the realm of the damned, a suck at the teat of the dankest, most sordid American cultural underbelly you might ever willingly end up subjecting yourself to. Welcome aboard the hound. I'm the guy at the back of the bus, smirking and uncomfortable; I know that, like all bus rides, this one is subject to the same dynamics of stratification that first manifested themselves in elementary school, as the bad kids slithered to the back, there to set up a scowling spit-ball-fortified encampment.

First half a minute notwithstanding, people on the Greyhound seem for the most part to be quite friendly, even eager to meet their fellow riders. I make two acquaintances at the first rest stop, in Pennsylvania: the first is Buddy, a mustachioed young man with that curious haircut known as the *shlong*, derived from short-long, the style of grooming where the wearer gets what appears from head-on to be a standard crew-cut, but on further inspection includes a surprising mane-like area of often permed long hair in the back. A great thing about this haircut is that fickle humanity seems evenly divided at the most basic, DNA-programmed level, into the camps of those who find this haircut intrinsically hilarious and those who consider it totally fashionable. Buddy challenges me to a game of pool and soundly trounces me. The second person I meet is Phil, who looks vaguely familiar and who, it turns out, I have actually met before, at a punk rock show in Connecticut. This coincidence, and the knowledge that someone from my particular cultural ghetto of choice is on the bus with me, is a comforting turn of events, and back on board we spend a while contentedly discussing obscure and meaningless trivia, until our surroundings encroach, this time utilizing the medium of olfactory offense. "Did someone vomit?" I ask Phil, noting the strangely perturbing smell. "No, I think that's..... feet." Phil's keen nose has accurately diagnosed the situation; indeed, a bearded, burly, red-faced man behind us has just taken off his weathered cowboy boots and is, to our horror, massaging his swollen, pustulous feet, which smell like gangrene and death itself. His body smells of fermented grain and tangy urine. Phil and I laugh bitterly: it's so greyhound.

B

99
98
97
96
95
4

DeWitt
Clinton
Park

W. 65th St.
W. 64th St.
W. 63rd St.
W. 62nd St.
W. 61st St.
W. 60th St.
W. 59th St.
W. 58th St.

W. 57th St.

W. 67th
W. 66th

Metro Opera
Hse.

Fordham
Univ.

John Jay Coll.
(CUNY)

Amst.
Broadway

Co
Bu

W. 56th St.
W. 55th St.
W. 54th St.
W. 53rd St.
W. 52nd St.
W. 51st St.
W. 50th St.
W. 49th St.
W. 48th St.
W. 47th St.
W. 46th St.
W. 45th St.
W. 44th St.
W. 43rd St.
W. 42nd St.

Twelfth Av.
Eleventh Av.

Tenth Av.

Ninth Av.

Eighth A.

Carnegie Ha

Seventh Av.

Rockel
Center

Port Auth.
Bus Term.

Times
Square

W. 41st St.
W. 40th St.
W. 39th St.
W. 38th St.
W. 37th St.
W.

Avenue of the Americas

In Cleveland a guy gets on and sits down next to the the offending smeller. His face immediately registers the realization of the miscalculation he has just made, but the bus lurches forward and he is stuck. I meet him at the next stop. His name is James, and he is a soft-spoken, square jawed guy from Washington, DC; who, like me, is going to Portland. I suggest that he sit with me and escape the guy with the pustulous feet, an invitation that he accepts with enthusiasm.

You don't really sleep on the bus; mainly you just contort exhaustedly, trying vainly to unlock the secret yoga-position that will facilitate comfort in the cramped seats. We stop every two hours and the driver wakes the passengers, whose scrambles to the counters of the mind-numbingly interchangeable convenience stores become increasingly lethargic and herd-like, the one constant routine which maintains a sense of civilization cranking along as usual, out here in the tarmac tundra where towns trickle into an oblivion of fast-food no man's lands, where the polite, toothless vestiges of regionalism are boiled away and the bleached bones of America-with-a-capital-A gaze at you matter-of-factly, and offer you beef Jerky and Mountain Dew Big Slams. This ritual will continue unabated for three days; it will not come to seem like deliberate, methodical torture until midway through the second day.

I am ensnared in conversation with a citizen of the netherworld, a thirtyish, gaunt rocker-type in tight leather pants who bludgeons away at the topics near and dear to his heart: his passion for renovating Camaros, his many romances, his childhood growing up in Germany. "Yeah, I've spreckened de douitch in my time," he allows. The talker warms up to Phil, James and myself, through no fault of our own, since we're not getting a word in edgewise, and begins really opening up, passing around pictures of his ex-girlfriends, telling us their nicknames- little Kelly, Big Kelly, Boo Boo- and then, leaning in -"You guys seem pretty alright so I'll show you this one"- he breaks out a naked picture of one of his exes. "What's wrong with this picture?" he chuckles. "That you're showing it to us?" Phil volunteers. But no, apparently the main allure of this photo is some deformity in the woman's genitals. This man is, clearly, the verbal manifestation of the Smeller's odor. He begins cracking jokes: "What did the guy with seventeen girlfriends say? One more and I've got a golf course! Two fags walk into a bar...." Phil takes offense at the fag references, I accuse the Talker of trying to

seduce us young boys with titillating photos and talk of fast cars."Hey, I'm no fag! What the hell! You guys are probably fags, huh!" he yells. This whole tangent shuts him up for a while, and there is an uncomfortable silence, broken by Buddy's address to the Smeller, "hey, man, your feet really smell!" The man's feet are actually in quite lamentable shape, and he has been fiddling with them and popping the sheet of blisters which cover them like protective bubble wrap. "Yeah, and what the fuck is up with that tattoo, man?" the Talker jumps in belligerently, making a grand re-entrance after his minute and a half of self-imposed exile. The fucked-up foot guy has, I notice, a prominently tattoo swastika on his ankle, but it's not up for discussion. "That's none of your business," he hisses, adding, "It's my heritage." "OK, OK," the talker backs off, having failed twice to go over well with the public.

In Chicago there is an extended layover, which allows us to stretch our legs, and Buddy and the Talker, two unlikely allies bonded by the universal language of vice, to go off in search of a bar, where they hope to self-medicate themselves against the next few hours of the trip. For the Talker, the medicine works a little too well: he never makes it back. In the interim, Phil, James and I strategize on how to position ourselves so as to avoid sitting with him, the barefoot Nazi, or anyone else who is really sketchy. We spot a girl with a punk haircut buying a ticket, and I am not surprised to see her sitting in the back when we reboard the bus. The Euro-guys get off in Chicago, replaced by a couple of really young-looking kids in Lalapalooza T-shirts who confer

excitedly about their plans for starting a new life in San Francisco, a lady with a tiny infant who cries for most of the rest of the trip, and a guy in a white hat who looks like a typical college fraternity type.

Food is passed around freely. Mountain Dew Big Slams seem to be the official beverage of the trip, and the high dose of caffeine imparted by the sugary, urine- flavored beverage seems to be doing everyone's mood wonders. The two Lalapalooza kids are teenage runaways, and it's very romantic. Fourteen and fifteen, respectively, they can't cite any particular repressive aspects to the families they've left behind, and their home lives are described offhandedly as, "pretty cool," but they have decided to elope to the west coast nonetheless, and sit huddled together, shivering and clutching each other in the thrall of fear and anticipation and first love.

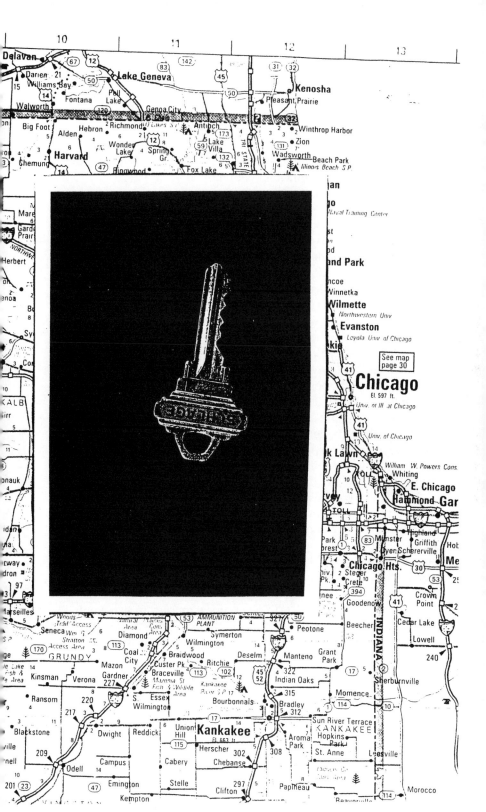

10   11   12   13

Delavan • 67 • 12 • 142 • 45 • 31 • 32
Darien • 21 • 83 • Lake Geneva • Kenosha
Williams Bay • 50 • Pleasant Prairie
15 • 14 • Fontana • Poll Lake • 50 • Winthrop Harbor
Walworth • 120 • Genoa City • 32
Big Foot • Richmond • Antioch • Zion • 131 • Wadsworth • Beach Park
Alden • Hebron • Wonder Lake • 173 • Lake Villa • 132 • Illinois Beach S.P.
Harvard • 47 • Spring Gr. • 59 • Fox Lake
Chemung • 14 • Ringwood

Naval Training Center

Mare • Gard'n Prair'e • Winnetka
Herbert • Wilmette • Northwestern Univ
Evanston • Loyola Univ. of Chicago

See map page 30
41 • Chicago El. 597 ft.
Univ. of Ill. at Chicago
41 • Univ. of Chicago

Oak Lawn • William W. Powers Cons.
Whiting • E. Chicago • Hammond • Gar
TOLL • Highland • Griffith • Hot
Park • 83 • Munster • Schererville • Me
Chicago Hts. • 30 • 53
Steger • Crete • 394 • Goodenow • Crown Point • 41

Marseilles • Woods Trail Access • 53 • AMMUNITION PLANT • 50 • Cedar Lake
Seneca • Stratton Access Area • Diamond • Symerton • Peotone • Beecher • Lowell
170 • GRUNDY • 113 • Coal City • Wilmington • Deselm • Manteno • Grant Park • 240
Mazon • Braidwood • Ritchie • 45 • 322 • 17 • Sherburnville
Kinsman • Verona • Gardner • Braceville • 113 • 102 • 52 • Indian Oaks • 2
227 • Custer Pk. • Mazonia St Fish & Wildlife Area • Kankakee River S.P. • 315 • Momence
Ransom • 220 • S. Essex • Wilmington • Bourbonnais • Bradley • 312 • 114 • 10
217 • Blackstone • Dwight • Reddick • Union Hill • Kankakee El. 663 ft. • Aroma Park • Sun River Terrace • KANKAKEE • Hopkins Park • St. Anne • Leesville
209 • 115 • Herscher • 302 • 308
Odell • Campus • Cabery • Chebanse
201 • 23 • Emington • Stelle • 297 • Clifton • Papineau • Morocco
Kempton • 114

Phil, James, and I sit in the back seats, talking to the punker girl. Her name is Diesel, and she is worse than the last guy, out-talking the Talker, promptly assuming the role of driving everyone insane. She tells crazy stories about herself, her four bouts with institutionalization, being beaten up by her dad. She talks about how she used to live with her boyfriend in San Francisco; one day she told him that she was going to the bathroom, walked out of the room, to the bus station and took the bus home to Chicago. Now, months later, she is returning to find him, not having communicated with him once since her disappearance. She hopes he won't have a new girl, but, as she philosophizes, "you have to burn your bridges so you won't be tempted to cross back over them." An ethic by which she lives: she gives James the key to her parents' house in suburban Chicago, tells him their address, and invites him to go steal their stereo and VCR. "I hate those bastards," she says,"I'm never going back there." James and I make tentative plans to meet back in Chicago and rob this house, but of course they will never reach fruition. Key-swapping is a strangely prominent activity among the Greyhound riders, people giving away or trading keys to apartments they don't inhabit anymore, storage lockers, relics of lives that don't mean anything anymore in the face of the sun coming up and the nose of the hound pointed west. The keys are exchanged to prove the lack of nostalgia for old existences. Most people are not going anywhere in particular, it seems; for the most part they are getting away. Diesel points out that pretty much anyone travelling on Greyhound during the week without a specific reason for going where they're going is probably a criminal.

This hypothesis is verified with a dramatic field test in Iowa City, where a cop is waiting when the bus pulls up. Fully two thirds of the riders seem to go into a low-level panic at the news, nervously eyeing potential escape routes. The teenage runaways get up and lock themselves in the bathroom. I saunter out, stretch my legs, and am questioned as to whether I have seen two young teens on the bus matching the description of our lovebird mascots. A curious thing occurs at this juncture: not only I, but every single person questioned on the bus denies having seen these kids. It is a pivotal, bonding moment for the passengers, not a feeling of thwarting the Man (though you'll certainly never find a group of individuals more in opposition to cops than your average Greyhound-load of societal fringe elements) so much as a feeling of protecting those on the inside from the forces on the outside; the aluminum hull has become our second skin, the metamorphosis complete.

The teenagers evade capture to great jubilation. The experience, coupled with the relief on most passengers' part that it wasn't themselves the cops were after, has brought us all closer together as partners in crime. there are sly grins all around; having recognized fellow law-breakers, the flood-gates have been opened and a microcosmic anarchy ensues, as people decide to break all the rules, sharing cigarettes in the bathroom, putting their feet up, swearing and laughing. At the next stop, a small-town cop appears to ask a few questions, but she's clearly unenthused and doesn't even bother to search the bus. The authorities have been thwarted again, and forty-ounce bottles of malt liquor and banana-flavored Mad Dog are illicitly smuggled aboard the bus. The bottles are passed around in the back seats, revelry ensues, we are elated by defiance and it goads us on to further defiance, we are vicariously in the stupor of young love. I'm sitting in the very back of the bus, the reading-light shining on my head like a heavenly ray in some velvet painting of the Last Supper, feeling like king of all losers, me and James take a few slugs off the bottles and laugh at the pure insanity of the situation. I haven't slept in a long time. Diesel is standing in the aisle reciting her poetry dramatically. I egg her on.

PEOPLE DO they MEAN
whAt they MEAN . WhAt iS
The truth? DO I CARE CARE
or DONt . CARE. where iS
Life LEADiNg? REAlAtioNships
young, olD . wHErE is the truth.
is it 'in you or mE. or
him or her'. why is the
Question. you figure it out.
NOt mE. whAt CAtAgory does
that put mE in in this
LifE Do I. cArE or DONt
i cArE! whats the rEAl QuestioN

I'm holding the banana-flavored Mad Dog in my hand at the next stop when the cops abruptly raid the bus. Elation turns to scrambling panic as the cops march down the aisles, demanding everyone's ID. "This is it, this is it," mutters the guy in the white hat. I wonder what he's got to be so worried about, as I stuff the bottle in my backpack. The runaway teens are rounded up and carted off. We watch them as they are packed into the back of a squad car to be shipped back east. They stare out the window at us, poignantly. It's like a movie; I want them to shout something compelling and wise beyond their years to us as they are loaded in the squad car, but they just climb aboard tiredly, not even casting a parting grimace in our direction.

I was in heaven one
day in search of the
neverending high. I
Blinked once, twice
an the light in the
tunnel went out!
lord have mercy on my
soul for here I was in
New york City new york
My talk was slow - as m
walk for the next light
was Bright my soul was
free as a wandering spirit
here I was the leader of the PACK
food was everywhere But still I lack
a mate. days-nights more light - then I was c
ngd for here was my mate I fought & fought - an
finally I was the light as my
People from new york to sum
Beaches - mountains & freedom
California I am Back an guess
what, every time you turn off
light an the Blub Blows just
smile b— we are all in light!

The bus switches drivers at this stop, and the new driver delivers a stern lecture to us all. "Let me remind you," he enunciates carefully over the intercom, "that drinking is illegal on this bus. I smell liquor on you people in the back. If I catch any of you drinking I will ditch you on the side of the road. I have my own bills to pay, I don't need some stupid fine or to lose my job. Keep your shoes on. I don't want to smell your feet. Keep quiet in the back." It's analogous, Phil points out, to being busted by the substitute teacher. He walks in five minutes late, says: "You and you. Out of here. To the principles office. You- I see you chewing that gum. Spit it out." The iron fist rhetoric of the cardboard dictator; the new authoritarian regime on board the hound does little to quell the berserk spirit of the populace, who are riled up by the events that have unfolded. The barefoot Nazi takes off his ratty shirt to reveal a chest-full of homemade tattoos, including his name, Red, and his destination, West Sacramento, permanently engraved in scary Gothic letters. An amazing round of dramatic poetry readings takes place, passengers crowded in the aisle in back, others scribbling frantic odes inspired by the tragic tale of our own personal Romeo and Juliet, which are then delivered in rapturous, hushed reverential whispers. I'm stunned by what is transpiring. Who are these people? What I can't fathom is that this is not some aberration, not a bus full of retarded geniuses, this is a random sampling of my fellow Americans. I pay taxes so that highways can be built so that McDonalds can be built alongside them so that greyhound can have a monopolistic contract with that franchise and my fellow Americans can in turn satiate their intense craving for salt. These people are, for the most part, on the wrong side of the law in some way, or at least on the fringes of what passes for law-abiding, and yet this whole elaborate highway system seems designed just for them, an underground railroad for the sketchy and irredeemable. I'm fucked, I have not slept in two days of total sensory overload, have not touched the books I brought to read. I write my dad a letter:

"Dear Dad: you gave me that Jack Kerouak book when I graduated college and now all I care about is distances traversed, miles an hour, the geography of despair and coffee and nonsense and beauty, of punk rock and luggage and grime and sugar and young love. You fucked up. Love , Al." I don't send it.

I collect everyone's poetry, transcribing it all in a notebook. I'll never see those teen runaways again, never know what happened to them. The bus trundles through Nebraska and I don't even make a gesture towards sleeping; it's useless. The thing that's deceptive about spending three and a half days on a bus is that these days are a lot longer than your average ones, since you are agonizingly aware of the eight hours which usually slip by unnoticed in sleep. Time crawls. I watch Red awkwardly attempt to put shoes on his swollen, cracked feet. Poor guy. I listen to Diesel's sordid sexual confessions and the white hat's explication of his adeptness at beating people up. He spends a bit of time praising the musical merits of Glen Danzig/ assessing his chances of whupping Glen Danzig's ass in a fight.

Phil has a pen-pal in Lincoln, Nebraska, who he has sent a letter to with stamps cleverly coated with glue so that the cancellation mark can be removed and the stamps re-used. He decides to call him and see if he can retrieve his stamps. Although the bus is scheduled to pull into Lincoln at quarter to four in the morning and the layover is only for five minutes, the pen-pal agrees to meet him at the station. When we pull in to Lincoln, he is there with a couple of eager friends. It's kind of funny, sweet and pointless. "Hi," he introduces the group as a unit, " we're the Lincoln, Nebraska punks." The Lincoln, Nebraska punks nod in cheerful greeting. They wave earnestly as the bus pulls out.

We stop at four a.m. at a diner and as I sit drinking coffee and listening to Diesel, Buddy and the white hat guy talk, it dawns on me that they are fleshing out a plan which involves them all getting an apartment together in San Francisco. I corner James and ask him what he thinks of this development. He thinks it's amazing, almost wanting to follow them to San Francisco just to see how it all turns out. It is also becoming obvious that the white hat guy is trying to make the moves on Diesel. She tells me later that he is starting to drive her crazy, that she plans to ditch him as soon as he gets to San Francisco, so that she can find the last guy she ditched there. I notice, though, that he's buying all her food and anything else she asks for, and in fact is exceedingly generous with his money, in fact seems to be bank-rolling about half the bus. I wonder what's going on there.

Diesel– Nothings sacred anymore, it's all tainted.

Juliet in chains.
Beefcake men
in strong starch suits
We are
Protected from
our deepest fears –
they
are given theirs,
round 'em up
send 'em back.
two open seats
to San Francisco.
— James Stockstill

Two innocent hearts
clinging to one another
like child to blanket.
— Phil Ochslippe

comic drawn by
me and Buddy.

Minutes spent watching the sun rise and turn into a bleak, burning day. Around ten the bus gets pulled over by a police car. A quiet, Hispanic man gets up without a word and locks himself in the bathroom. The white hat loses it, delirious, mumbling "OK. Just play it cool. Fuck. Just got to play it cool." He turns to Diesel. "Take this," he says, handing her an enormous wad of money. "I don't want to get involved," she replies, straring straight ahead. He presses it on her, hissing. "Just take it." "Are you wanted for something?" I asked rhetorically. "I don't want to lie to you, man," he tells me, adding, "so I'm not going to say anything."

It turns out that the bus driver is getting a speeding ticket. The significant criminal element breathes a sigh of relief. When the bus resumes motion, I make everyone play exquisite corpse and other drawing games. My muscles ache, so I try to institute a bus-wide rule that at every stop the passengers have to run laps around the bus. No one is into it except for Diesel and myself, and so we end up sprinting around the bus, panting and out of breath, while the other passengers peer out the windows and judge us to be retards. A couple lays sprawled out in their seats; we dub them the power nappers because people tripping over their flailing limbs does not rouse them. In fact, when the bus is cleared out at one stop so that the aisles can be cleared of refuse, they cannot be moved from their precarious perch, and so must be swept around. I admire them in their fetal bliss.

The last few hours to Salt Lake City, where James and I will transfer to another bus and go on to Portland, leaving Phil and the improbable would-be housemates to go on to California. The white hat and Buddy have coalesced into a vicious bludgeon of belligerent, punch-drunk annoyingness, spouting inanities at anyone in earshot. While Buddy is merely sleazy, I am coming to recognize in the white hat all the signs of the Antichrist. A game of twenty questions, meanwhile, devolves into a heated argument between Diesel and the barefoot Nazi, who ends up screaming at her. I feel sorry for Phil, having to spend another fifteen hours with these miscreants, but not as sorry as Phil feels for himself.

We stop for lunch in Arlington, Wyoming. I see a group of kids huddled in the parking lot of the McDonalds and strike up conversation with them. They are high schoolers, performing an endlessly repeated national ritual, deciding what to do on Friday night. "What is there to do here?" I ask. "Get drunk," a girl answers glumly. Inordinately high suicide rate, another kid tells me. This highway off-ramp looks a lot like the one I grew up near in North Carolina. It looks a lot like all of them.

The final hurtle to Salt Lake City achieves totally epic surreal proportions, as the Nazi attempts to mend the fence with Diesel regarding the twenty-questions fiasco, scrawling out an apology note in his feverish, tortured chicken-scratch handwriting. When his hand cramps up, he recruits me to sit next to him (an olfactory experience which the days have made no sweeter) and take dictation. The letter is basically a synopsis of his wretched life, the trials and hardships which have made him what he is today, "a clown, but crying on the inside." It then turns to profuse apology, and I realize that he is writing a love letter to Diesel, that he has, in fact, fallen for her. "I have all the important women of my life tattooed on my arms, " he instructs me to write, "may I add yours?" "You're going to get DIESEL tattooed on your arm?" I ask. "No, no, her real name," he mumbles, though unsure what it is. He does indeed have the names of his daughters and ex-wives inscribed, grocery-list-like, on his biceps; to this he wants to add the name of a sketchy eighteen-year-old girl with a half-shaved head whom he has known for about forty-eight hours. He signs it "love, Daddy Jack."

The white hat will not tell me what he has done to warrant his dread of the police, but he alludes to it continuously, making veiled references to the checkered past he is obviously quite proud of. When we arrive in Salt Lake City, famous for its Mormons and social rigidity, he and Buddy head off to get stoned and find a "tittie bar." It's the last I will ever see of either of them in my life. Diesel tells me his dark secret: he worked at a gas station in Chicago, and one day decided to knock over his own store. He emptied the cash register, took all the cigarettes and bought a one-way ticket to California. Now he has warrants for his arrest all over the country, a half-baked plan to dissappear into San Francisco with Diesel as his mistress, and a wallet fast running out of its stolen contents, as he blazes a trail of marijuana purchase and gratuitous displays of wealth across this great nation of ours. It's pretty damn tragic: he will have run out of money by the time he gets to San Francisco, and for all his troubles and the life he has irrevocably wrecked, he will have nothing to show but a hell of a lot of hamburgers and Big Slams consumed.

I part ways with Phil, Diesel and Red. "You are a fine, upstanding young man," Red lets me know, "the kind of man I wish my daughter would meet." He presses a photo of a young woman into my hand, an address scrawled on the back. "Write me and I'll send you a current photo. She's a real knockout," he confides, winking. The phrase "Daddy Jack" floats into my head nauseatingly as he gives me the potential in-law once over. I get on the Portland-bound bus as quickly as possible.

I fall asleep for a little while, totally exhausted. When I wake up I'm in Boise, Idaho, and it's six in the morning. James and I walk around downtown Boise, our eyes bleary, hard marbles in their achy sockets, smiling vague, brainless smiles to ourselves. Birds are chirping. It is a new day. The sky brightens to a pencil-lead grey as we stumble into a donut store and I blow my last buck on a really great cinnamon roll. The woman at the counter looks battered; she looks in a lot worse shape than us, and I guess objectively she is, working and stuck here, while we are just tourists in this purgatory and will momentarily climb aboard for the last leg of our ride.

I'm thinking of the people I met aboard that bus, and their perfectly tragic lives; trying to find common ground so that I can grasp the fact that I inhabit this country with these people, that we share a common culture, the common understanding that America is endless gas stations, desolate off-ramps with the fringe of ugly suburbs creeping in to view at the periphery, at the edge of where you could walk to in the ten minutes of allotted time, before the yo-yo string snaps you back into bus. In a way, of course, its so much more than that, but in a way less: I grew up in one of those neighborhoods, walked to the convenience stores on Guess road, under the highway overpass, to mix soda fountain drinks in cups with stickers on the bottom we'd peel off until we found an instant winner, keeping us endlessly supplied with free drinks. We live and die by the highway, and in between we sit in cramped seats waiting to get somewhere, forgetting where we're going.

al burian

307 Blueridge Rd.
Carrboro, NC 27510

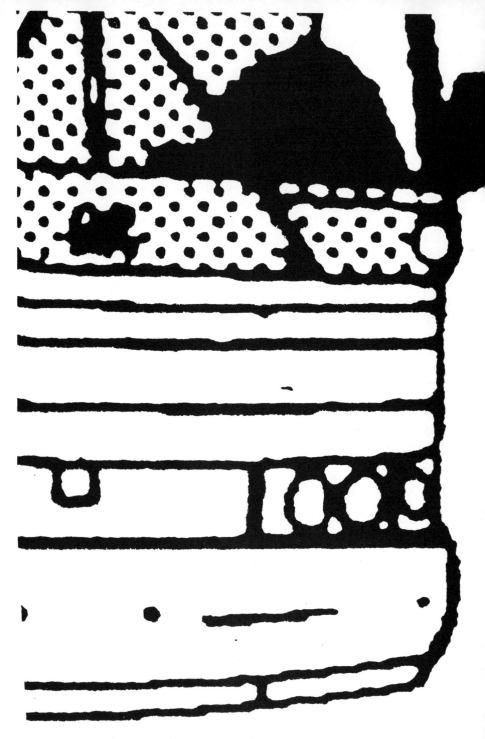

burn collector number two • summer 1995
307 Blueridge Road Carrboro, NC 27510

BURN
COLLECTOR

Greetings from PROVIDENCE R.I.

"The most merciful thing in the world, I think, is the

inability of the human mind to correlate all its contents. We live on a placid island of ignorance in the midst of black seas of infinity, and it was not meant that we should voyage far. The sciences, each straining in its own direction, have hitherto harmed us little; but some day the piecing together of disassociated knowledge will open up such terrifying vistas of reality, and of our frightful position therein, that we shall either go mad from the revelation or flee from the deadly light into the peace and safety of a new dark age."

Pretty god damn profound, huh? The above quote is, surprisingly, *not* about the Internet, but rather is the introductory paragraph of an H.P. Lovecraft story entitled "the Call of Cthulhu." It's pretty amazing just how much of all that is deeply, profoundly nerdy in our culture has it's derivation in the prose of Mr. Lovecraft; a list of his short story titles alone also forms a fairly cohesive list of Black Sabbath song titles *and* Dungeons and Dragons adventure manuals (he's kind of the "we play both kinds of music-- country AND western," of the dorky things realm). What's even more startling to me is how accurately the above summarizes my existential outlook these days.

It's always the really inane stuff which really resonates in the secret inner room of my soul. At the age of fourteen I heard that Dead Kennedys song where they go, "why don't you take your social regulations and shove 'em up your ass?" and it was a revelation; the scales fell from my eyes with an audible clunk. "Yeah, why not, indeed," I chortled, "It's got an irrefutable logic that can't be denied." So I adapted this lyrical snippet as my code of arms, consequently running my life into the ground as methodically as a guy driving a stick shift with a deep-rooted ideological opposition to using the clutch. In the glaring reverse-lights of hindsight I guess I can decipher that that song is kind of a cringer, but even now I feel that the whole "social regulation up the rear" platform has an undeniable *je ne sais quoi.*

Lovecraft's quote is a somewhat more complex, profound statement, well suited for a somewhat more complex, confused individual. It makes sense that I'd be on his wavelength because he is, after all, the local-kid-made-good of Providence, Rhode Island (and I do mean *the*: as far as I can tell, in fact, he is the *only* Providence resident to have ever made good. Pretty much the entire remaining population is on the Brown University maintenance crew and bitching about the weather in a thick New England drawl.) and as I am the new-kid-in-town-infatuated-with-the crazy-architecture-and-urban-lore it makes sense that we'd see eye to eye on issues of profundity. I love to think of H.P. hanging out downtown at the Weybossett St. Dunkin Donuts, chatting it up with the local crazies, and then walking up to Turk's Head Plaza to check out the bizarre, looming sculpted head, bottom-lit for maximum scariness, sneering down at him from three stories up, like a villain from some 1930's radio serial, and H.P. muttering to himself, as I always do in the presence of this thing, "Oh maaaaan...... that is just totally the shit." H.P. is buried in a vast,

sprawling graveyard in Providence, and his grave-site is a mecca for various fringe factions of lunatics and supporters of the black garment industry. This one guy in Providence who claims to be a six thousand year old wizard of some sort is always recruiting people to head out there and participate in some sketchy ritual of one kind or another. I gave Six Thousand Year Old Satan (as he's affectionately known behind his back)

a ride home one night, and he talked non-stop, making up past lives as he went along- "Wait, did I know Hendrix in a former life? Hold on, let me think....um.....Oh, yeah, yeah. It's all coming back to me. Yep! I was *definitely* down with Hendrix."- and scheming incessantly to take out his arch-nemesis, Michael, who, apparently, was cutting in on his chick action, and whom he referred to bitterly as "Michael.... Pan.... Odysseus.... Lucifer..... whatever it is that he's calling himself, this time around."

It seemed nutty at the time, but now that I think back on it, the thought occurs that maybe it's me who's missing the boat in this interaction. Sure, Six Thousand Year Old Satan is certifiable, but is he, as Lovecraft said, "mad from the revelation (of).... the deadly light?" Maybe Six Thou just has the ability to correlate the entire contents of his brain and I don't, and maybe it's that which makes him seem like such a weirdo to *me*, the flag-waving, picture-ID carrying citizen of the New Dark Age. I would say that it's irrefutable that piecing together the little disassociated bits of knowledge leads to some pretty damn terrifying vistas of reality, and I would posit that we're all, you, me and the Brown maintenance crew, engaged 24-7 in just barely keeping our shit together and managing to avoid totally bugging out in the face of how big the world is and how teeny we are. Given this, is my mode of dealing with things any more plausible than any random insane person stumbling down the street wearing diapers and screaming gibberish into a walkie-talkie? We raise our voices in conversation, crank up our stereos to drown it out, but underneath the distracting din we all hear the call of Cthulhu, beckoning us towards the abyss. At least I'd like to think that's what Lovecraft would have to say, if he were here today and wasn't too busy signing some D&D guys' monster manuals.

BUDDY CIANCI

Vincent A. "Buddy" Cianci (center), then in his first term as mayor of Providence. The controversial Cianci, after more than nine eventful, memorable, and productive years in office, was forced to resign in 1984 following an assault charge arising out of a family dispute.

This Fall finds me renting a dilapidated attic apartment in Providence, Rhode Island. I like Fall, tending to prefer the transitional seasons, because they don't have weather, just foreshadowing. It's not cold yet, but it's getting colder. You look hippest in this weather, dressed in your faux-proletariat thrift store jacket and long pants to hide your dorky knees. Fall seems pregnant with the possibility of simpler things, a straight-forward future. Rob asks me whether I drank from the fountain on Benefit street when I tell him I'm glad to be back in Providence. Legend has it (so he tells me) that if you drink from this fountain you will be miserable when you leave and stay that way until you return, at which time the curse is alleviated. It figures; Providence would have some kind of rig like that hooked up, a typically mafioso offer you can't refuse. Even the fountains and faucets here trickle blackmail and twists of the arm. A mafia town through and through, where the Italian neighborhoods even have streets with red, white and green stripes painted down the center of the road, where current mayor Vincent "Buddy" Cianci is reputed to have bitten the testicles off a man who slept with his wife, an old Sicilian revenge scheme, like sending a man a fish. My downstairs neighbor contests these rumors: "Everyone knows he just burned the guy with a cigar while his henchmen held him down. Who'd want to bite off someones testicles? That's gross." It does sound gross, I concur. Other variants in the Cianci myth machine include putting out his cigar on a guy at the opera who advised him that the auditorium was non-smoking (henchmen holding the guy down, of course). The fact that he seems to be so clearly mafia-affiliated doesn't seem to bother anyone. "Yeah, he's really corrupt, supposedly," my housemate Harrison says, "but I saw him speak once and he was so funny.... really charming and charismatic. He just seemed really benevolent." It's hard to believe that this Married-to-the-Mob aura could be plausible, but it is somehow.

I'm pretty fascinated with the persona of the mayor. Here are some of the weird facts and anecdotes I've collected about him:

• Exact details of the testicle-ing incident notwithstanding, it is, [ap]parently, a fact that Cianci served [so]me time for assaulting the [ge]ntleman reputedly mixed up with his [wi]fe. Cianci ran for re-election from the [pe]n, and won.

• I think I first had my heart [wa]rmed to the guy when I read about [hi]s reaction to a teacher's strike going [on] here last September. Asked to [re]spond to a statement by the head of [th]e teacher's union, Cianci retorted [sim]ply, "she's full of sh**." I mean, [tho]ught off record is one thing, but this [wa]s his official statement to the press; it [wa]s reported without ironic [co]mmentary by an apparently weary [(o]r wary) local media.

• The man has his own [sp]aghetti sauce, "The Mayor's Own [M]arinara," which is modelled blatantly [on] Paul Newman's spaghetti sauce, [do]wn to the grinning head on the front [la]bel and the cute little post-script [w]ritten on the jar's side. "A great gravy [is] like a great city," philosophizes [Ci]anci, confusing anyone who is not [fr]om New England and might fail to [re]alize that "gravy" and "sauce" are [sy]nonymous in these parts.

• A true man of the people, [Bu]ddy is often seen mingling with the [co]mmon folks, and most people have a [sto]ry about running across him. Most [im]pressive is my friend Sean's, who [cl]aims to have seen Buddy cruising the [to]wn on a moped, cigar clenched I his [st]eel-trap jaws. "Buddy! Hey Buddy!" [Se]an and the other bystanders yelled, [el]iciting a mayoral wave, which in turn [el]icited a round of riotous laughter. [Bu]ddy, sensing that his status as cult [ic]on was premised in this case on a less [th]an regal standing, flipped the voting [pu]blic a healthy bird and sped off. "The [m]ayor *flipped me off*," Sean recounts, [du]mbstruck with awe to this day.

• If any doubt remained as to [th]e guy having what my dad would call [a "]mean streak a mile wide," consider [th]e name of his daughter: Nancy Ann Cianci. Say that fast. That's right, it's "Nancy Antsy Antsy." What this means, in a nutshell, is that it's my mission in life is to befriend Nancy Ann, get invited to some fancy social engagement, and then when she comes to pick me up dawdle and putter around until she gets exasperated and tells me to get the lead out. At this point I say in the most condescending tone I can muster, "Nancy Ann Cianci's antsy!" Her bodyguards beat me to a pulp but I die a happy man.

• Befriending Nancy Ann is actually not such a far-fetched dream: my down-the-street neighbor claims to have been invited to a barbecue at the Mayoral mansion through "a friend of a friend" and to have- gasp- *smoked pot* with the mayor's daughter! After which they checked out Dad's room which was entirely mirrored on all four walls. "Dad likes to look at himself," Nancy Ann explained. This, perhaps, goes a ways towards explaining the plethora of gigantic, Ferdinand Marcos-style depictions of the mayor to be found all over town (the billboards for "Phantom of the Opera," for instance, have a huge photograph of Buddy and equally gigantic letters: MAYOR VINCENT CIANCI and then in tiny letters: welcomes phantom of the opera to providence.) But, hey, what the hell would YOU do if you were mayor of a town like Providence? Probably the same kind of shit, right? Wrong. You'd spend a lot of time gimping out over the budget and meeting with hemorrhoid-inducing legislators; you'd get really stressed out and wouldn't have a good time at all. The cool thing about Buddy Cianci is that he actually lives the dream; he really does all the excessive and ridiculous things you think you'd do in his position. Sort of an Ian MacKaye for the corrupt career politician set.

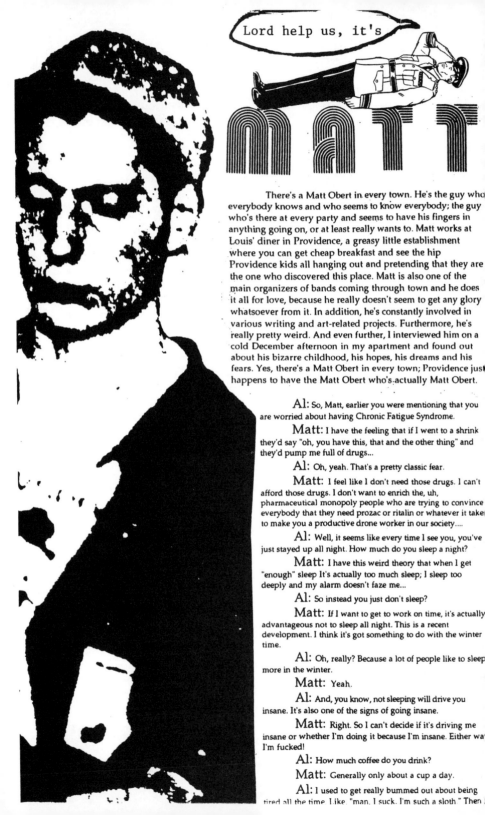

Lord help us, it's

MATT

There's a Matt Obert in every town. He's the guy who everybody knows and who seems to know everybody; the guy who's there at every party and seems to have his fingers in anything going on, or at least really wants to. Matt works at Louis' diner in Providence, a greasy little establishment where you can get cheap breakfast and see the hip Providence kids all hanging out and pretending that they are the one who discovered this place. Matt is also one of the main organizers of bands coming through town and he does it all for love, because he really doesn't seem to get any glory whatsoever from it. In addition, he's constantly involved in various writing and art-related projects. Furthermore, he's really pretty weird. And even further, I interviewed him on a cold December afternoon in my apartment and found out about his bizarre childhood, his hopes, his dreams and his fears. Yes, there's a Matt Obert in every town; Providence just happens to have the Matt Obert who's actually Matt Obert.

Al: So, Matt, earlier you were mentioning that you are worried about having Chronic Fatigue Syndrome.

Matt: I have the feeling that if I went to a shrink they'd say "oh, you have this, that and the other thing" and they'd pump me full of drugs...

Al: Oh, yeah. That's a pretty classic fear.

Matt: I feel like I don't need those drugs. I can't afford those drugs. I don't want to enrich the, uh, pharmaceutical monopoly people who are trying to convince everybody that they need prozac or ritalin or whatever it takes to make you a productive drone worker in our society....

Al: Well, it seems like every time I see you, you've just stayed up all night. How much do you sleep a night?

Matt: I have this weird theory that when I get "enough" sleep It's actually too much sleep; I sleep too deeply and my alarm doesn't faze me...

Al: So instead you just don't sleep?

Matt: If I want to get to work on time, it's actually advantageous not to sleep all night. This is a recent development. I think it's got something to do with the winter time.

Al: Oh, really? Because a lot of people like to sleep more in the winter.

Matt: Yeah.

Al: And, you know, not sleeping will drive you insane. It's also one of the signs of going insane.

Matt: Right. So I can't decide if it's driving me insane or whether I'm doing it because I'm insane. Either way I'm fucked!

Al: How much coffee do you drink?

Matt: Generally only about a cup a day.

Al: I used to get really bummed out about being tired all the time. Like, "man, I suck. I'm such a sloth." Then alized it's because I never sleep. So I think it's funny that you're worried about chronic fatigue syndrome.

Matt: It all harkens back to a theory that I had when I was eighteen years old, a homeless degenerate dude working at the Nice Paper (local free paper, now defunct), the scary vagrant guy of Providence, always looking for abandoned houses to sleep in, crashing on people's couches or the lounges of Brown..... and my whole theory then was "burn hot and heavy for five hours, then rest for two."

Al: How old are you now?

Matt: Twenty-three.

Al: So when did you get in to promoting shows and that sort of thing?

Matt: Well, I worked for the Nice Paper and I guess I was promoting shows already in my column, not actually organizing them, just announcing all the shows that would be of any passing interest at all, and then I was going to all these shows. I was just formulating my taste in music then, and listening to everything, just everything for the first time. When I was in high school I lived in this bad Christian Rock ghetto, it was... eeeughghh, I can't even say.

Al: You listened to Christian Rock?!?

Matt: Yeah, well, not so much in high school, I had already burned out on it and was listening to AOR, like Led Zeppelin.

Al: Where did you grow up? The outskirts of Providence, basically?

Matt: Yeah, my parents live in Cranston. I graduated from high school there.

Al: So you went to Cranston High School?

Matt: Yes, Cranston High School East.

Al: What was that like? What was your upbringing like?

Matt: My father is a very Christian guy. I remember, my parents both were hippies....

Al: Hippies??

Matt: Yeah, they were hippies for a while, until I was a certain age and then they decided, you know, family values and let's get involved in the church and all that. I was five when my parents actually got married.

Al: No way, so when you were born they were just free lovin' it? Did they live on a commune?

Matt: Nah, they were just living in an apartment. The church they were going to at the time, when the preacher found out he was just like (in scary preacher voice:) "FORNICATION! SIN!" That was when they were first looking for the church. To this day they celebrate two anniversaries, the one where they met and the one where they actually exchanged vows. So, by the time we moved to Rhode Island, we got involved with a really psycho Christian church. Very fundamentalist, Bible-oriented, very strict, border-line cult kind of following. Just this unswerving devotion, an unthinking, blind herd mentality towards doctrine and the leaders of the church, who were just these schlepps like you or me, except that they were the ones you were giving all your money to and confessing all your sins to. I could start quoting Bible verses at you at this point, I memorized so much of the

Al: Really? So you were pretty heavily into this.

Matt: Oh yeah, definitely. I used to go out on the street and try to convert people to Jesus Christ. Instead of handing out flyers for rock shows I was handing out John 3:16 That was me getting my feet wet in the direct sales market.

Al: It was your first D.I.Y. experience.

Matt: Except that it wasn't D.I.Y. at all, it was all part of this total corporate network infrastructure of the church. It was very much like working for Amway, like selling encyclopedias.

Al: But it had a personal meaning for you.

Matt: No. It was more like, if you didn't make a quota of inviting people to Bible-study, suspicion would fall on you, and they'd be like "brother, you're not bearing fruit! Is there hidden sin? If you were a good Christian you would have brought many into the fold.... clearly something is lacking in your zeal and devotion!" And you'd be like, "Well, uh, I masturbated again."

Al: Did you feel oppressed at the time?

Matt: I had no other frame of reference. All people in high school remember of me was, I'd approach everybody in the high school once and invite them to Bible study and they'd say no, and I'd say "OK," and never approach them again. I was a total outsider; I had three friends who were all borderline juvenile delinquents. We'd all listen to Metallica and play Dungeons and Dragons....

Al: Wait, were these kids Christian too....?

Matt: No, no. They were satanic.

Al: Oh man! You were living a Chick comic book!

Matt: And I was like, "how come no one wants to come to church with me?" And they'd say, "you just don't get it, do you? Nobody wants to go to that church, man. It's *no fun*." And I was just like, "Yeah, you're right. Every time I go to church I'm not having a lot of fun and every time I go out in the woods and drink a case of Busch light and listen to Metallica I'm like, yeah, this is where it's at." I couldn't exactly be completely up front with the people at the church about this, so it led to a lot of hypocrisy. So I got out of high school and went to community college for a little while, and then I dropped out and that's when I started to work for the Nice Paper.

Al: So then you started getting more involved in the local music scene.

Matt: In high school I had seen a couple of shows at the Living Room, like Dread Zeppelin and the Dead Milkmen. I did see one cool show, which was Sonic Youth, but I had the worst time ever at that show. I went there with my friend Doug from the church under the pretext of, "Doug, let's go to this sleazy night club and hand out tracts, try to convert people." And of course that was a total failure. Then in college I couldn't lie about things anymore. Suddenly everything was falling apart with the church- and it kind of ended up with me getting kicked out of the church. It was a real bad scene with all my friends from the church. No one would talk to me anymore unless I would talk about the Bible.

the scintillating conversation continues on page 11....!!!

I saw a guy wearing a Metallica

T-shirt the other day, standing in line to receive

his 79-cents value menu gruel at some gruel hut in a really intensely lame
suburb of Providence. You don't see these guys around too much these days.
It's like the dinosaurs; maybe a comet wiped them out, maybe it was a gradual
shift in the climate caused by fluctuations in the orbit of the earth, maybe it
was some more subtle evolutionary incompetence. The Mormons, actually,
believe that a smaller, dinosaur-habitated world collided with our own at
some indeterminate point in the hazy past, lodging the bones of these great
reptiles in the crust of our own planet, to be dug up later, in the era of

Moroni[1]. In any case, as Michael Chrichton, in his sequel to <u>Jurassic Park</u>
(which I read the first chapter of at my job the other day) astutely points out,
who the fuck really cares? They are all gone now, as are 99% of all species
that have ever existed on this planet, leaving the current populace
representing a measly 1% of life as we know or have ever known it, which is,
really, not that much at all. If we are to believe the Big Bang theory of
universal creation, our universe is essentially just composed of fading embers,
so it's all basically aftermath, and it's not implausible, from this perspective,
to view life as a sub-set of that entropy, basically all just moving in a
millennial historical trend towards extinction. And then, of course, metal is
just a sub-category of that.

Seeing as how all culture and
civilization is just a pathetic attempt
at creating structure and meaning on
the part of some free-floating crap on
it's way to fizzling out within one of
those little embers, also pretty much
cashed at this point, the recent dearth
of Metallica T-shirts being worn, and
the possible negative repercussions on
Lars Ulrich's ability to pay off his
yacht, seem so inconsequential that
even the word inconsequential seems
to lend it too much credence. But fuck
it, the flesh is weak, and here I am, my
micro-cosmic sputter of an existence
seeming to stretch on interminably
from my vantage point, a vast and
barren tundra of a life which needs to
be filled with some sort of experience
and stimuli, so what are you going to
do? I don't have the attention span to
be a movie buff. So I end up listening to
ungodly amounts of rock music. It's a
pretty good deal for me: aside from
consuming countless of those long
hours just sitting around completely
devoid of thought whatsoever, just
bobbing my head and grinning, going,
"allllllllright. Kick ass, man," I
actually spend a good deal of my
thinking time contemplating that crap,
which conveniently distracts me from
all kinds of unpleasant realities and
facts which, while floating in that
cranium of mine somewhere, would
probably bum me out a great deal if

[1] By the way, isn't it sort of odd that the Mormons are called Mormons even
though their main angel is called Moroni, not Mormoni, making them more
accurately called, uh..........
and, having finished my completely unprovoked and probably factually
inaccurate diatribe against the Mormon faith, I apologize profusely to my
friend Mike Clark and to anyone else I know who may be of Mormon descent.
I'm really sorry.

they were constantly at the forefront of my consciousness, like how one does one's taxes or what those taxes pay for 24-7 while I preen over my seven inches. There's also a lot of shit I flat out don't know at all. Take the Periodic Table, for instance. It's not like I have an excuse- educators of one ilk or another have attempted to impress the Periodic Table's significance on me on several occasions, but I have completely failed to retain that knowledge, and you know why? Because I happen to be busy retaining information such as that the drummer of Metallica's name is Lars Ulrich. With shit like that in there on file who has the data-storage capacity for the Periodic Table? Useless trivia is one thing; most information is useless most of the time, and if you are well-rounded in your informational scraps you just buy yourself a Trivial Pursuits board game, invite some people over, and Bingo, you're king of the world. But this is the sort of information which has a way, way, way higher gradient of pointlessness than most. Sometimes it drives me crazy, and I'll even pretend not to know things that are clearly right on the forefront of my conscious mind because I'm embarrassed at how retarded I'll look if I admit that I actually know the drummer of Metallica's name right off hand. I would certainly take myself in for some reprogramming if I didn't recognize, on some level, the value of this mental clutter as a buffer against thinking too much about my other main topic, the world being pretty sucky and depressing. Who wants to think about that crap all the time? Fuck that, put on some rock music. Metal's main genius lies in the way the guitars are engineered, a sonic allegory for disaffiliated youth which I'm convinced encapsulates their experience and indirectly summates their emotional landscape. Basically, a really raw chugga-chugga metal band is all treble and bass, no mid-range, which is pretty much what a teenager is, emotionally. You always catch these pimply faced kids on Geraldo going, "our music tells *the truth*, man, it peaks to us about our lives and reality;" in one Megadeth video an archetypical dad tells his archetypical pimply whelp to, "change the channel, I want to watch the news." "This *is* the news," the whelp retorts, gesturing at Megadeth on the screen. This assertion is, of course, complete bullshit. Most

metal is about some sorcerer slaying a dragon or just self-referential vapid dogma, such as Ronnie James Dio's "we rock," which asserts that, indeed, they are in the act of rocking right then. The closest the form comes to documenting "reality," is in the incessant tales of sexual conquest; however, although this may be the actual band members "reality," it probably is the furthest possible thing from a description of the lives of the pimply-faced dudes who champion it. So basically, what you have striking a chord in the hearts of the young is a set of knobs cranked up all the way on a studio control booth somewhere (usually in Sweden, engineered invariably by a guy named Snørden Rassmüssen), a metal-overkill-destructor distortion pedal with the "dist." knob turned to "max." The kids' internal "dist." knob is also cranked all the way to "max", and thus the tinny chugga-chugga means the world to them, and, in fact, expresses everything worth expressing and knowing. Pretty weird, huh?

Much like the great and grizzly dinosaurs who once existed on Earth as the main thing you didn't really want to fuck with, Metal bands used to proliferate, and, insofar as the market economy can be made analogous to the process of slow fizzling out that is life on this planet, were the main Darwinistic champs. But now, I see some kid in Taco Bell with his cheezy Pushead-skull-wearing-a-bandana shirt, and I just feel sorry for him, kind of like how the thought of the Loch Ness Monster being some dishevelled Brontosaurus who never got his shit together to go extinct is somehow really sad to me. I don't think it's a scornful or condescending pity, although I *do* often find myself grumbling "fucking teenagers," when faced with specimens of that kind of human these days, a development which I find alarming. Ultimately, despite some level of awareness as to the collapsing universe and the futility of viewing evolution as anything other than a big dead end, despite how easy it is to write off people's attempts at lives as misguided and pitiful, the human condition is all about trying to make things make sense and survival is a pretty basic instinct, whether personally or culturally, whether you're talking Western Civilization or the goofy

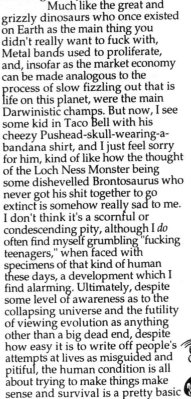

sub-culture of a bunch of lame fourteen-year olds. While metal was enjoying it's heyday of cultural relevance in the 1980's, I was getting involved in another seemingly pointless and doomed sub-culture, punk rock, which offered me some of the same treble-bass gratification, and which, in its critiques of "the mainstream" and what I interpreted as its value system seemed to me to "tell the *truth*, man," to speak to me about my existence. Back then the metal kids in their Def Leppard and Mötley Crüe shirts were the

Camaro-driving Tyrannosaurus Rexes, confident and happy in the light of their moment of cultural dominance, smugly laughing at the weird, stupid punker kids. Of course, both sub-cultures are rooted in a grassroots of genuine youth-alienation; metal was just a little further along on the evolutionary totem pole. And, just as metal was the whup-ass thing to be into if you were a jock and it was 1985, the following decade has ushered in the co-option of the next culture with it's neck on the block, punk rock, making that into the acceptable soundtrack of the guys in Camaros, much to the chagrin of the die-hard metal-heads, who are now reduced to being ridiculed as atavistic by lacrosse-playing shitheads with Rancid CD's.

What's weird about the whole thing is that you basically have this continuum of acceptability- although the Camaros never actually go out of style among the alpha males- and the smug Übermenchen go along with whatever the gears of the cultural production factory crank out for

them. I have more in common with the metal-head guy than I am really comfortable with, I think- now that it's my turn to have "my" sub-culture, or some skewed approximation of it, churned out for mass consumption, I find myself taking a defensive position as the one who "really" understands, who"gets it," and will still have the essential values (as defined by me, of course) intact when the fad passes; I imagine the kid in the Metallica T-shirt getting hazed at his school by hip kids who snicker at his dorky so-late-80's ensemble. I mean, the guy's wearing a denim jacket and tight jeans. Tight jeans, in this day and age. For Christ's sake. "Fuck them, man," he tells himself bitterly, "I'm a true believer, a die-hard metal guy, this is *my* music. They'll never understand," he thinks. His big fuck up is that music has taken on a meaning for him beyond commodity, and this, I think, more than genre or hairdo or content, is the essential schism: between people who consume the products of culture and people who feel it, to whom these artifacts speak and transmit meaning. Being a metal-head in 1995 is the societal equivalent of being a punk rocker in 1985, in terms of integrity, individualism and pure social retardation, because the mainstream acceptance of punk has made any person affiliated with that sub-culture, whether tacitly or overtly linked to the commodifd version of punk, tied into norms of acceptability, mainstream coolness and conformity which one cannot disentangle oneself willingly from. To be a true rebel you have to stick

our guns even when the culture
[la]rge has pretty much discarded
[it] and declared your raison d'etre
[to b]e totally lame, which it
[obj]ectively really is in this case,
[unf]ortunately. Shed a tear for the
[poo]r metal-head; he's fallen on tough
[tim]es. Maybe when heavy metal
[com]es back into style he'll remember
[you]r sympathy kindly and not run
[you]r pitiful punk ass down with his
[Cam]aro.

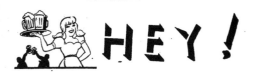

HEY !

If you find this 'zine (oh, how that word irks me) mildly
amusing, you will find these to be mildly amusing as well:

Burn Collector #1: small and scrappy, i.e, "pain-in-the-
ass-to-staple" size. Features Marie Lorenz interview, the
philosophy of freeganism, some Crassly Cromagnon
Capitalist Cretins, and some maps.

Burn Collector #2: A sordid, tedious tale of taking the bus
cross-country. Long and scary. Features teenage runaways
and ludicrously bad poetry by some very marginal
members of society.

couple stamps to: AL BURIAN•307 Blueridge Rd•
Carrboro, NC•27510

ABERT con't

Al: Are you getting more jaded about the rock
[sce]ne now then you were initially, when you first started being
[inv]olved with it through the Nice Paper?

Matt: Somewhat.

Al: You still don't seem very jaded.

Matt: Initially, I didn't really have any pre-set
[su]re ideas in my head. I liked everything. Certain local
[ban]ds, I cut them a lot of slack even though they were terrible
[bec]ause I thought, "Oh, they're trying really hard and they're
[loc]al and besides, I see them at Fellini's (coffee shop) and I
[wa]ve to them and say hi, so how can I give them a bad
[revi]ew?"

Al: So now you work at Louis', people come in there
[all] the time, you wave to them and say hi. Do you have
[obj]ectivity towards them now?

Matt: I don't have a lot of objectivity, I guess. I'm
[dev]eloping it more but I still have a lot of trouble slagging
[peo]ple out of hand. There are bands locally now that fail to
[inte]rest me whom previously I probably would have ranted
[and] slobbered over.

Al: You spend a lot of time working on flyers. Do
[you] put on shows mainly so you can make flyers?

Matt: No, I love rock. I love making posters,
[tho]ugh, it's may favorite thing to do. And I'm going to get
[real]ly into this 'zine that I'm working on now just because I
[like] putting things together that way and making text
[app]ealing, and making it so that people will see it. I'm really
[infl]uenced, actually, by working at this ad agency for a while,
[whe]re I actually designing billboards but doing the shitwork. I'm
[real]ly influenced by that. When I sit down to make a poster
[I'm] thinking, "people don't want to look at it. They'll walk by it
[on] the street and glance at it and think, oh shit, I accidentally
[read] a poster." I'm also getting really into the co-ops at Brown
[bein]g shut down, that's something that's sort of a personal
[cru]sade of mine, I think the co-ops are such a great thing and
[I do]n't want to see that happen. So I'm trying to get people to
[fight] that.

Al: So how do you think people perceive you, Matt?

Matt: Uh..... I'm a waiter. I guess I try not to think
too much about that.

Al: Do you think you're different from other
people?

Matt: I think there are a lot of people who would
rather be very sedentary and sit on their ass and watch TV,
and they don't understand that they should be making art,
they should have opinions about things that are going on in
the world; there are a lot of people who are just so lulled to
sleep by the TV-consume-excrete mentality, they don't have
a concept that there are things that you can do which don't
involve spending or making money, that are totally separate
from money, that are probably the things that would give you
more of a reason to live.

Al: Well, I asked you earlier how people perceive
you and you said "I'm a waiter." That's kind of a classic
dilemma. In some sense you are a waiter, no matter what you
do that "gives you a reason to live." So I'm wondering.... how
do you see your future?

Matt: Um.... I don't know. I like Louis', but I
would like to get some kind of graphics job, not because I
think it would be more fulfilling to be a cog in the graphics
machine than a cog in the dishwashing machine, but because
I would like to have access to the tools, just, you know, so I can
have access and do my own thing. Ideally I'd like to make
posters and flyers for other people. But there's not a lot of
money to be made in that area. Right now I'm making
enough money washing dishes that I can pay the rent and
live from day to day and still have enough money left to
waste it all on trying to make some kind of "scene" happen
here in Providence.

the end.

"Love That Burn!"

COMMON MISCONCEPTIONS

BURNIAN

BURPIAN

BOREDIAN

BIRCHIAN

BURLIAN

BURINE

BIRDIAN

burn collector
c/o Al Burian
307 Blueridge Rd. Carrboro, NC 27510 USA

B U R N

O L L E C T O R

4

North

Carolina

jobs

I HAD THREE JOBS IN 1995, MADE A TOTAL OF $2,546.83, AND WORKED APPROXIMATELY FOUR MONTHS ALTOGETHER.

MY FIRST JOB WAS DOING TEMP WORK --- EXCUSE ME, "CASUAL LABOR" --- FOR THE DUKE UNIVERSITY GRADUATE SCHOOL. I HAD MY OWN LITTLE CUBICLE AND MY JOB WAS TO PROCESS THE INCOMING APPLICATIONS.

CRACKLE
SIZZLE

MY FINGER TIPS ARE ALMOST LITERALLY BEING SINGED BY THE DESPERATION IN THESE DOCUMENTS.

MAN, "CASUAL LABOR" IS RIGHT.... MAINLY WHAT I DID WAS HANG OUT IN THE BREAK ROOM DRINKING COFFEE OR SNEAK INTO THE FORBIDDEN FAX ROOM TO SEND ILLICIT FAXES...

AL? IS EVERYTHING OK IN THERE?

HE HE HE

I HAD SOME PRETTY AWESOME CO-WORKERS:

WHY DON'T YOU PUT DOWN THOSE FILES AND LISTEN TO THIS ANECDOTE ABOUT MY KIDS.

PEGGY TRUTT WAS THE WOMAN OF A MILLION FACIAL EXPRESSIONS. MORE CHARACTER IN ONE LOOK THAN MOST MOTHERFUCKERS DISPLAY IN THEIR ENTIRE LIVES.

NANCY WAS THE MOST UN-CASUAL OF THE CASUAL LABORERS. SHE SEEMED DESTINED TO MARINATE IN A STEW OF HER OWN JUICES OF ENVY AND PRETENSION. EVERYONE HATED HER, AS FAR AS I COULD TELL.

OF COURSE, WHEN I WAS IN GRADUATE SCHOOL --- I MEAN, BETWEEN YOU AND MYSELF, I SHOULD BE A DEAN HERE, AND NOT A LACKEY SUCH AS YOURSELF ... NOT TO IMPLY YOUR INFER-IORITY, BUT ---

NOW, OF COURSE, I TOTALLY MISS HER!

LEE WAS THE OFFICE JOKER. HE KIND OF GAVE ME THE BURN --- I REALIZED THAT IF I WORKED THERE FOR A FEW YEARS, SUPPOSEDLY ICONOCLASTIC, SYSTEM-SUBVERT-ING ME HAD AN OFFICE NICHE WAITING FOR HIM --- THE ARCHETYPICAL WATER-COOLER CLOWN!

WORKING HARD OR HARDLY WORKING, MR. BURIAN?

AND THEN THERE WAS PAUL.

YOU KNOW WHAT I LOVE ABOUT THIS JOB? IT'S SO EASY TO DO IT STONED!

UH-HUH.

PAUL WAS NINETEEN AND HE SHOWED UP THREE HOURS LATE EVERY DAY. HE ACTUALLY GOT THE BOSS TO ACCEPT THIS AS "CHRONIC TARDINESS SYNDROME."

I HAD CRAZY BLUE HAIR THEN...
DURING MY JOB INTERVIEW THEY
SAID IT WOULD "GIVE THE OFFICE
SOME COLOR"... AND I WAS
CONSTANTLY THE VICTIM OF
THE SAME DUMB JOKE.

PROFESSOR, I'D LIKE YOU
TO MEET OUR NEWEST
GRADUATE STUDENT...

UH...

OH, MY...

HA HA!! JUST KIDDING, OF COURSE!

THE MAIN PROBLEM WAS
THAT IT WAS FORTY HOURS
A WEEK AND I <u>REFUSED</u>
TO LET THE FACT THAT
I WAS WORKING 8:30
TO 5 STOP ME FROM
STAYING UP UNTIL 5 AM
EVERY NIGHT.

THE SUN'S COMING
UP ALREADY? BUT
I HAVEN'T EVEN
HAD MY REFILL
YET...

WAFFL HOUSE

THAT'S THE AWESOME THING
ABOUT OFFICES.... YOU DON'T
EVER HAVE TO PRETEND TO
BE ANYTHING OTHER THAN
TIRED AND GRUMPY! IN FACT,
"TIRED AND GRUMPY" ARE
THE BUZZWORDS OF
OFFICE CULTURE....!

YOU'VE OBVIOUSLY MISTAKEN ME FOR SOMEONE WHO GIVES A DAMN

NO COFFEE NO WORKEE

TGIF!D

YOU WANT IT WHEN?!?

I WAS PRETTY OUT OF
HAND, THOUGH. I'D BRING
MY ALARM CLOCK TO WORK
AND DURING MY LUNCH
BREAK I'D TAKE THESE
CRUSHINGLY POWERFUL
NAPS IN THE STUDENT
CENTER.

MY OTHER BIG THING WAS OFFICE PARTIES, WHICH THEY'D HAVE AT THE DROP OF A HAT. BIRTHDAYS, MINOR HOLIDAYS, ANYTHING. MY JOB WAS TO TRY TO MAKE THEM LAST AS LONG AS POSSIBLE.

WELL, BACK TO WORK, EVERYONE!

SOUNDS GREAT... AS SOON AS I FINISH EXPLAINING MY THEORY ON THE HOFFA/ LEE HARVEY CONNECTION!

COLA

DON

OTHER THAN THAT, I'D JUST GENARALLY TRY TO FOMENT REVOLUTION.. LIKE THE TIME WE HAD THAT ERGONOMICS SEMINAR.....

THIS HAND-STRETCHING EXCERCISE PREVENTS TENDONITIS AND LOWERS WORKER DISCOMFORT...

WHAT ARE YOU SAYING? PROLETARIAT ALIENATION STEMS FROM BAD POSTURE? FUCK THAT! LET'S TALK ABOUT THE REAL CAUSES OF WORKER DISSATISFACTION!

MY DAD WAS AWARE OF MY BAD DISPOSITION AND PLAYED A PRACTICAL JOKE ON ME ONE DAY.....

HELLO, AL? THIS IS YOUR DAD... LISTEN, I WAS JUST LISTENING TO NPR AND APPARENTLY THE NATIONAL TEMPORARY LABORERS ASSOCIATION JUST CALLED FOR A WALK-OUT.....!

OH...MY...GOD. SO WHAT SHOULD I.... WAIT A MINUTE. "NATIONAL TEMPORARY LABORERS ASSOCIATION"? IS THAT REAL?

HA HA!

IT WASN'T TOO BAD OF A JOB, REALLY. ON MY LAST DAY PEGGY TRUTT TOOK ME OUT FOR A MILK SHAKE ON THE CLOCK.

I HOPE I NEVER WORK FORTY HOURS A WEEK AGAIN IN MY LIFE. IT BLOWS.

YEP. WELCOME TO THE WORLD.

I DIDN'T LAST TOO LONG AT MY NEXT JOB — I WORKED THE NIGHT SHIFT AT KINKO'S COPIES...

SO THIS IS MY DREAM JOB.

KILL ME.

ACTUALLY, IT WOULD HAVE BEEN FINE, EXCEPT I WORKED EVERY NIGHT WITH A STRANGE ROBOT MY FRIEND BRIAN CALLS "THE PENGUIN...."

BY DAY, I AM A REAL ESTATE CLAIMS ADJUSTER. BY NIGHT I RUN A TIGHT SHIP HERE.

I DO NOT NEED SLEEP OR HUMAN COMPANIONSHIP.

SO... WHAT'S YOUR STORY?

I WAS LIVID WITH ANGER THAT I WAS EXPECTED TO DO ANYTHING BUT MAKE COPIES FOR MYSELF ON THE NIGHT SHIFT! BUT THE PENGUIN ACTUALLY WANTED ME TO BUST ASS !!.... I THINK HE WAS JUST KIND OF LONELY, WAY DEEP DOWN.

WHAT ARE YOU DOING OVER THERE? WHAT ARE YOU COPYING? ARE YOU PLANNING TO WIPE THE COUNTERS?

HEY.... DON'T YOU WANT TO TALK TO ME?

FINALLY, ONE DAY THE PENGUIN TOOK A NIGHT OFF.

HEY....YEAH.... IT'S JUST ME WORKING TONIGHT... BRING YOUR ZINES... TONIGHT I SMITE MY CORPORATE OPRESSORS...

ALREADY SMITING ↓

KA-CHUNG

KA-CHUNG

SOON...

WHAT DO YOU WANT? FIVE HUNDRED? A THOUSAND?

I DON'T KNOW... CAN YOU GET AWAY WITH THAT?

DON'T WORRY ABOUT IT.

I COPIED LIKE A FURIOUS FIEND. IT FELT GOOD. I WAS ON A ROLL. AROUND FOUR A.M. I REALIZED:

WAIT A MINUTE.... I'VE GOT A HUGE STACK OF COPIES... I LEAVE AT EIGHT AND MY BOSS COMES IN AT SEVEN... HOW AM I GOING TO SMUGGLE THEM OUT!?

I ENDED UP JUST LEAVING MY JOB AND SPRINTING HOME ON FOOT WITH A THIRTY POUND BOX OF ILLICIT ZINES.... I DIDN'T EVEN TAKE OFF MY SPECIAL DORK SMOCK!

HUFF HUFF

THAT MORNING, I FELT SWELL... I THOUGHT I HAD COMMITED THE PERFECT CRIME. I WAS IN THE CLEAR UNTIL...

OK...WE'LL JUST CHECK YOUR CASH DRAWER AGAINST THE PRODUCTION COUNTERS ON THE COPIERS..

WHA--?

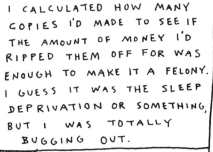

MY LAST JOB WAS THE BEST ONE — I WORKED IN THE BASEMENT OF A BOOK STORE, RECIEVING BOOKS. MY SUPERVISOR WAS USUALLY PREOCCUPIED WITH HOME-SCHOOLING HIS 5-YEAR OLD GENIUS SON, SO IT WAS PRETTY LOW-KEY.

THIS HOMEWORK IS VERY SOPORIPHIC.

HA HA! YES! GOOD, GOOD!

THE GOOD THING ABOUT IT WAS THAT I COULD BE AS GRUMPY AS I WANTED! THE WORST THING A JOB CAN POSSIBLY STRIP YOU OF IS JUST ACTING HOW YOU NORMALLY ACT. AS LONG AS YOU'VE GOT YOUR PERSONA INTACT, IT'S USUALLY OK.

MORNING, AL! HOW'S IT GOING?

CRAPPY!

HA HA

DAN

BOOKS ON THE ...

PUSH

THE BEST PART OF THAT JOB WAS WHEN MY FRIEND SEAN WORKED THERE --- WE COULD WHILE AWAY THE TIME DISSECT-ING OUR WEIRD CO-WORKERS, TAK-ING IMMENSE JOY IN HASHING THE DETAILS OF THESE PEOPLE INTO A FINE, POTATOE-EY PASTE, PUREED BY OUR RAZOR-SHARP CHARACTER ANALYSIS.

FICTION

MY BOSS WILL NOT CONCEDE THAT THE PRODIGY IS SMARTER THAN HIM!

I KNOW!

YES, SEAN'S BOSS WAS A SORRY CASE ... BUT SO IS MOST ANYONE STUCK IN A CRAPPY JOB. THAT'S WHY I LOVE TO QUIT... I'M LIKE VIRGIL MOVING THROUGH THE CIRCLES OF HELL... SO LONG, SUCKERS!

YOU'RE DOING THAT WRONG.

I THINK I KNOW HOW TO DO...!

OH, WAIT.

mugged

STORY BY SEAN LEWIS.

PICTURES BY AL.

MY BAND WAS SET TO PLAY AT MATT'S LOFT ON WEY-BOSSETT ST. SO WE SHOW UP AT 8:00, AND IT'S A GHOST TOWN.

I DECIDE TO GET SOME LIQUOR AND TAKE A STROLL DOWNTOWN.

NOW, LAST NIGHT WAS ONE OF TWO OCCASIONS I'VE LEFT MY HUMBLE DWELLINGS WITHOUT MY WALLET. THE FIRST BEING A FIT OF SPONTANEOUS SPRINGTIME EUPHORIA, RUNNING AROUND A PARKING LOT IN BOXER SHORTS, WHICH, OF COURSE, IS ANOTHER STORY.

THE OTHER WAS LAST NIGHT, IN AN ATTEMPT TO GAIN ROCK EQUILIBRIUM? HMMM.... IT MADE FOR A SAD SPECTACLE AS I TRIED TO MAKE A PURCHASE AT THE PACKAGE STORE. I THEN, EMPTY HANDED, RETURNED TO THE LOFT.

BY THIS TIME THE "REGULARS" ARE FILTERING IN AND I'M FEELING AWKWARD! LOUSY, IN FACT. SOOOO, I DO THE LOGICAL THING AND TAKE OFF FOR A BAR.

NOW, I'M KNOWN TO BE A POLAR MAGNET FOR ALL THINGS WRONG. THIS GENTLEMAN IN SFILA STARTERS AND PURPLE JEANS STROLLS UP TO ME NEAR CHESNUT ST....

HEY, WAIT UP!

GOT THE TIME? I'M LATE FOR A BUS.

9:30 OR SO...

OH... GOOD... HEY— GOT A CIGARETTE?

NO... I DON'T SMOKE. TOO EXPENSIVE.

HAH--RIGHT! GOT A QUARTER? NOT TO BUY DRUGS -- I'M STUCK FOR BUS FARE AND I NEED A SANDWICH...

UH...

SORRY... ALL I HAVE CHANGE-WISE IS PENNIES... YOU CAN HAVE THEM IF IT'LL HELP...

C'MON MAN.... HOW ABOUT A DOLLAR?

NO... LOOK, I'M LATE... I'VE GOTTA RUN...

OH... UH... OK... COOL..

SEAN TURNS AND CONTINUES DOWN THE BLOCK. ABOUT 30 SECONDS LATER, THE CHANGE IN AIR PRESSURE IS NOTED AS A STEEL (OR WOODEN) EINFORCED FORE-ARM CONNECTS WITH OUR HERO'S HEAD.

OUR ANTAGONIST GRIPS SEAN'S THROAT IN A VICE-LOCK AND SIM-ULTANEOUSLY DRIVES A BONY KNEE INTO HIS 10TH VERTEBRAE, FORCING HIM INTO A PRONE POSITION.

BE COOL, MAN. BE COOL.

HIS JACKET POCKETS ARE RAPIDLY RIFLED THROUGH AND $7 AND A GUITAR PICK ARE PURLOINED.

REMEMBER — IF I GET BUSTED.... I KNOW YOUR NAME, LARRY....!

"HA," SAYS OUR HERO TO HIMSELF. HE KNOWS THAT THIS IS NOT HIS HANDLE, BUT THAT OF THE BROWN PHYSICAL PLANT WORKER WHOSE JACKET HE AQUIRED.

BROWN
Larry
MAINTENANCE

coll

ecting

EEEUGH.

OH, MAN. THAT GUY ?!?

EW, SHE CRINGES ME OUT.

YEAH, I BET SHE DOES ...HA HA!

EEUUGHH... I CAN'T LOOK AT THESE ANYMORE. FUCKING CHAPEL HILL.... JEEZ.

YEAH.

...YEAH, NICOLE WOULD ALWAYS TELL ME ABOUT HOW SQUARE YOU ARE... SHE SAID YOU WERE REALLY BORING TO HANG OUT WITH... YOU DON'T SMOKE, YOU DON'T DRINK...

PIZZA

SO.... THINGS ARE GOING GOOD.

THINGS ARE GOING GOOD.

We went out for some Pizza, talking aimiably about nothing in particular. It was kind of weird and unsatisfying, like peering at someone through a keyhole instead of looking at them face-to-face-- you do get to check them out and maybe shout a few obligatory remarks about how you're doing fine through the crack underneath the door, but somehow it all feels lonely and makes you all the more aware of the fact that you're in a room by yourself when all is said and done. It was that way that afternoon....

....and it tends to be that way these days, which in my moments of most extreme lucicity I conjecture may be contributing to that debilatating sense of dread that's burrowed itself into the back of my head- you know the one I'm talking about? It's like that feeling you get when you've had a car wreck or a relative die on some really horrible night, and after all the trauma you finally get to sleep, only to wake up after a dreamless night to the sunlight pouring in to your window and the sound of sparrows twirbling in the arrival of a new day. "Ah, what a nice morning, so peaceful and full of promise," you think contentedly. "wait, though. Wasn't there something really crappy I had to contend with....? There's something in the back of my mind, just sort of sub-conciously making me uneasy. Hmmm..." and then the next moment it all floods back, and you realize just how much this day and all days hereafter will blow. It's that moment of vague uneasyness I'm talking about, that second or two of conciousness before all the trauma of your life punches in for it's day-shift, when the office is still uncluttered. I live within that second or two, it stretches out indefinitely, I've taken up permanent residence, I've applied for citizenship and I'm learning the national anthem by heart so I can lead the crowd at baseball games.

SURE, YOU STAY UP ALL NIGHT ALL THE TIME. NO BIG DEAL, RIGHT? BUT HOW OFTEN DO YOU ACTUALLY WATCH THE SUN RISE, WATCH THE HORIZON AT THE MOMENT IT PEEKS OUT? IT'S AN UNUSUAL OCCURRENCE IN MY LIFE.

THE NIGHT WELLS BROKE HIS SHOULDER AND HAD TO HAVE SURGERY I STAYED UP ALL NIGHT WAITING TO SEE IF HE'D BE OKAY. IT WAS SCARY, AS HOSPITALS ALMOST ALWAYS ARE.

WHEN HE GOT OUT OF SURGERY HE WAS SO FUCKED UP ON MEDICATION THAT IT SEEMED LIKE HE HAD BEEN LOBOTOMIZED. I WAS TRYING TO BE LIKE, "IT'S OK, IT'S NO BIG DEAL," BUT THE WHOLE SITUATION HAD A WAY OF INVITING PANIC... SLEEP DEPRIVATION AND ALL THAT.

HARRISON AND I DROVE TO THE LOCAL WAFFLE HOUSE AND WATCHED THE SUN COME UP. AFTER THAT WE HAD WHAT WAS, FOR ME, ONE OF THE GREATEST BREAKFAST EXPERIENCES OF MY LIFE. THINGS SEEMED MORE UNDER CONTROL AFTER THAT.

al burian

307 Blueridge Rd.
Carrboro, NC 27510

UNITED STATES OF AMERICA

PASSPORT
PASSPORT
PASSEPORT

Type/Caté-gorie P	Code of issuing / code du pays State USA	PASSPORT NO./NO. DU PASSEPORT émetteur 07348099**6**

Surname / Nom
BURIAN

Given names / Prénoms
ALEXANDER

Nationality / Nationalité
UNITED STATES OF AMERICA

Date of birth / Date de naissance
07 AUG/AOU 71

Sex / Sexe
M

Place of birth / Lieu de naissance
NEW HAMPSHIRE, U.S.A.

Date of issue / Date de délivrance
08 FEB/FEV 94

Date of expiration / Date d'expiration
07 FEB/FEV 04

Authority / Autorité
PASSPORT AGENCY
SEATTLE

Amendments/
Modifications
SEE PAGE
24

P<USABURIAN<<ALEXANDER<<<<<<<<<<<<<<<<<<<<<<<<
073480996USA7108075M0402072<<<<<<<<<<<<<<<0

plane

On a plane bound for Paris, France: a TV monitor overhead plays

continuously, drizzling the passengers with strange foreign imagery: french perfume ads, weird little animated shorts, french news (people with berets holding picket signs and yelling things). The coffee served on Air France is insanely good, so thick it borders on being a solid; I don't usually drink coffee or soda on planes because I'm abnormally freaked out about dehydration, but here in neutral airspace rules are made to be broken, a phrase which no doubt sounds even more killer in french. I feel garish and crass already, and I'm not even near Europe yet, but already the relative normalcy of life among Americans has husked off of me and I am exposed as a buffoon, as the stewardess asks in her mousy french accent, "café?" and I drawl back, "Yup. Suuure. Caw-fee. Awwwl Right." She looks at me funny and continues her rounds. I've never liked the french.

I'm only stopping in Paris long enough to switch planes, fortunately. My final destination is Munich, Germany. Don't ask me why. I've been meticulously avoiding Europe on principle for years, although not on any complex or especially well thought out principle. It pretty much just boils down to my parents deciding to get a divorce one week into a year-long stay in Rome , Italy. This happened when I was thirteen and I've been very angry with the Europeans ever since. However, there has been a conceptual shift in the old cranium lately, primarily involving a fixation which I've developed that revolves around the parallels between the social constructs of humans and chickens: it's all about strutting around and pecking at the ground and trying to ruffle up your feathers so that it looks like you own the yard. Alternatively, sometimes I like to imagine human beings as these really finely die-cut puzzle pieces, and fate as some impulsive three-year old trying to force all the random pieces to join smoothly. You can force any puzzle pieces together you want, but it never ends up looking good. It ends up a horrible mess. Well, in any case, I wouldn't recommend thinking about this sort of thing too much. I did, and look where it got me: on a plane to Germany, totally freaked out and convinced beyond a shadow of a doubt that all things are meaningless and it's all pointless, tasteless chunks of mundanity in a briny soup of despair and pain. "I need some kind of distraction from this, " I realized. " some kind of fucked up conversation or experience, and failing that, some heavy sedative medication, to offset my current trend towards paying attention to how things actually are." Fortunately for me, with the advent of the all-life-is-meaningless-crap phase of young adulthood comes absolution from all constraining moral and ethical principles constructed in youth, including arbitrary resolutions to never visit accursed Europe again. So off I flew, in hopes of there finding some stuff which would confuse me enough that my shell of jaded defeat would be cracked.

The stewardess comes back around, this time passing out a customs form which I have to fill out. "All passengers not carrying passports from European nations must fill out this form," the captain intones over the PA, and this bums me out, because I have a perfectly good German passport, which I foolishly left in North Carolina, and I'm already paying the consequences in the form of some document I have to deal with which I probably won't understand but which will no doubt result in my accidentally conscripting myself to military service for the duration of my two-hour lay-over. Although, actually, its the German passport which would probably be more likely to get me involved in some mandatory military misadventure, much like my friend Bill, dual citizen of Greece and the U.S. A, who discovered that he couldn't stay in Greece for more than three months without doing his patriotic part to safeguard the world olive oil supply. I myself feel no national attachment or nationalistic feeling towards anything, save perhaps the sight of flaming towers spewing oily, carcinogenic black belches into the stratosphere along the New Jersey turnpike, and, while I do find the resulting pollution-enhanced sunsets attractive, I wouldn't be willing to fight, die, or even do something mildly uncomfortable, like give up wearing socks for a couple of days, to preserve this "way of life." One of my German cousins, if I've got the story right, broke both legs parachuting out of a plane while doing his mandatory military service. Oh yeah, sign me up.

munich

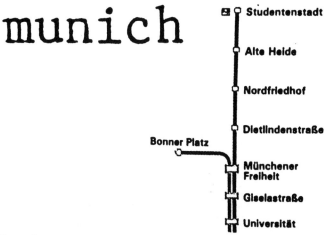

🚻 O Studentenstadt

Alte Heide

Nordfriedhof

Dietlindenstraße

Bonner Platz
O—

Münchener
Freiheit

Giselastraße

Universität

Having managed to navigate the Paris airport without creating an international incident, I board the Munich-bound plane and find myself deposited there within a couple of hours.

I promptly collapse in a heap at my mom's apartment, and then head out into town. Munich is an extremely well-scrubbed and meticulously maintained city, and I immediately realize I'm underdressed. I wander the streets in my standard winter gear, which by American mid-sized city standards would be admittedly considered less than formal wear, but I am surprised by the level of scoffing being directed at me. And that's just the street people. The actual tax-paying citizenry pretends I don't exist, treating me like I'm beyond the realm of processable sights, like someone walking down the street with a gaping head wound gushing brains and mumbling, "I want a hug." I get totally lost in the fancy downtown shopping area, but I'm too intimidated to stop someone and ask for directions. Besides, no one will even make eye-contact with me.

In any case, I find myself fairly entertained as I wander around to museums, gawk at old churches and beer-halls where people were getting loaded centuries before they piled drunkenly on to boats to go find out about America. Ludicrously talented street musicians play on street corners everywhere, standing in the kind of temperatures which lead to toe amputations and plying their trade for coins. I marvel at how seamlessly it all coexists with the conspicuous wealth of the German commercial sector. The streets are lined with upscale shops and glutted with well-dressed people in the grip of frenzied orgies of holiday buying. At times I squint my eyes to blur my vision and it looks like it could be a mall in New Jersey. But then I unsquint my eyes and check out the crazy styles people tend to rock here, and it takes every iota of concentration I can muster to not burst out laughing and point at them, shouting mirthfully, "man, check out the things you *crazy fucking foreign people wear!*"

Kids hang out in front of record stores where gigantic TV monitors play videos of Teutonic *Stone Temple Pilots* knock-offs. They smoke cigarettes and scowl at each other in sullen, universal teenage fashion. It's fun to listen to their conversation, but I'm disappointed as always in my search for German slang phrases. Their main word is "*Geil,*" which is an all-purpose blanket word whose tenuous meaning encompasses everything from 'cool" to "horny." Other than that it seems to be mostly appropriated Americanisms, and, like their dubbed TV shows, mostly ones from the seventies or early eighties. I can't believe they haven't updated their ability to swear with great nuance and say things in ways that confound their parents since I was here last, at the age of twelve. Lacking an indigenous Snoop Doggy Dogg to generate funny stuff to say, the youth culture seems stale and lifeless. I can actually support the older generation in scoffing at the apparent vapidity of the young, who seem to cling to inane talentless goons at the expense of the historically much-revered great figures of Germany's literary past, the guys who could throw around those thirty-six syllable long explosions of guttural gurgling *Sturm und Drang* to express good old-fashioned values like self-pity, existential horror, and the bone-marrow pulverizing weight of the world. Back in those days, "angst" was the most powerful monosyllabic word known in any language, before "fuck" took over. The Germans actually used to own the whole youth culture game, back when their main MC's were young bucks looking to peel some caps. Around the turn of the century you couldn't really find rawer shit than Rilke, Kafka, or Goethe; I know a guy who recently got dumped by a girl who sent him a three page Rilke quote about the futility of love, and he listed it as one of the more crushing experiences of his life. But somewhere along the way the Germans lost it. I guess that part of the problem is that the whole youth culture racket tends to be very individualistically oriented, since it caters to such a heavily narcissistic, self-centered demographic, and the Germans lost some of their claim to being the worldwide representatives of radical individuality because of, uh, Fascism.

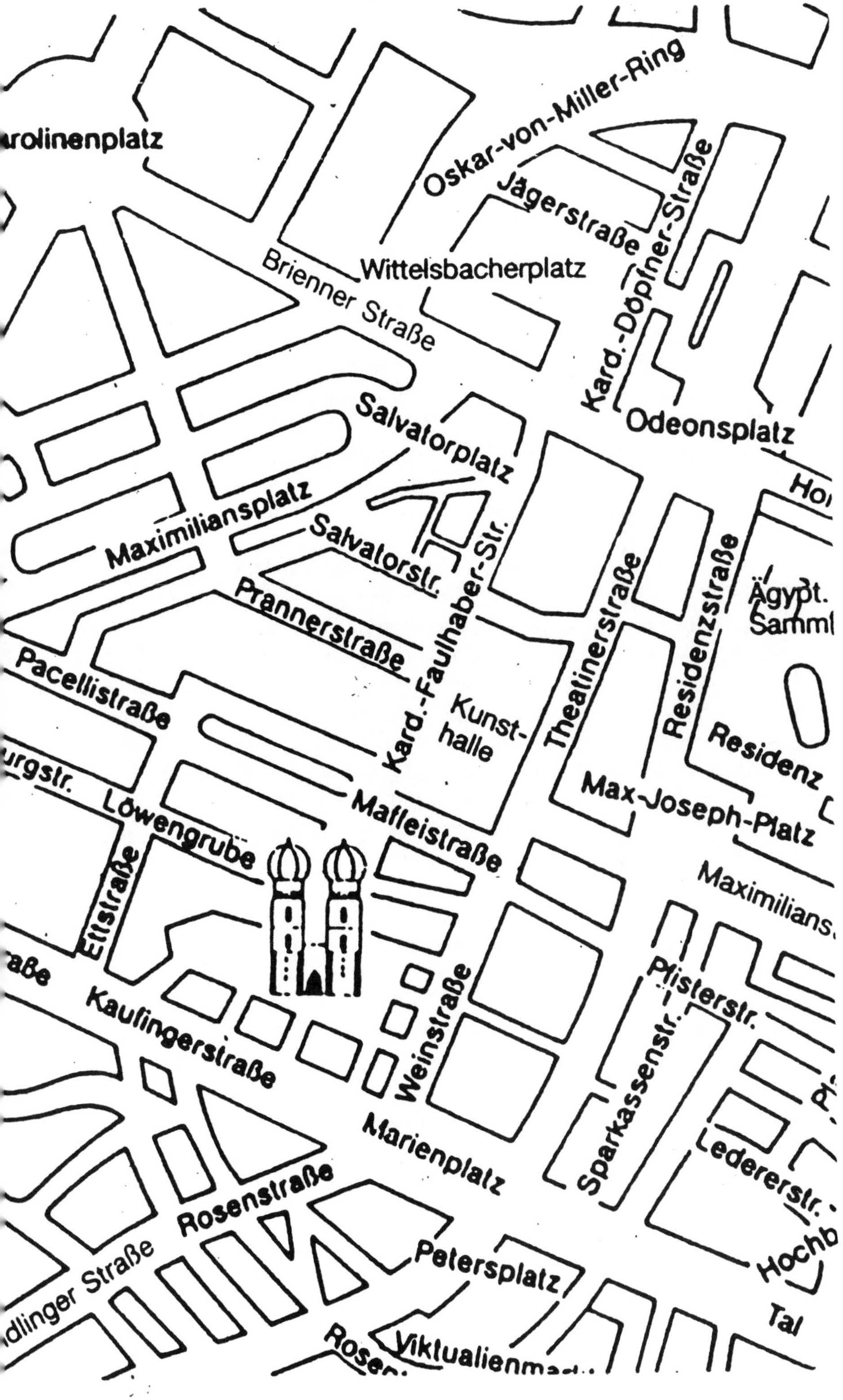

Karolinenplatz

Oskar-von-Miller-Ring

Jägerstraße

Kard.-Döpfner-Straße

Brienner Straße

Wittelsbacherplatz

Odeonsplatz

Salvatorplatz

Maximiliansplatz

Salvatorstr.

Hof

Prannerstraße

Kard.-Faulhaber-Str.

Theatinerstraße

Residenzstraße

Ägypt. Samml

Pacellistraße

Kunst-halle

Residenz

...urgstr.

Löwengrube

Mafleistraße

Max-Joseph-Platz

Ettstraße

Maximilians.

...aße

Kaufingerstraße

Weinstraße

Pfisterstr.

Sparkassenstr.

Marienplatz

Ledererstr.

Rosenstraße

...dlinger Straße

Petersplatz

Hochb

Tal

Rosen...

Viktualienmar...

After a few days in Munich, my
initial intimidation segues into my standard
counter-attack strategy of making eye contact with
everyone I see, smiling and nodding in the traditional southern-
American "howdy, y'all," manner. I assume that a day spent
giving the treatment to everyone I run into, young or old, pierced
septum or suit and tie, will result in a few conversations by the
end of the day. When it gets too cold to hang out outside
gawking at pedestrians I head home to my mom's, perplexed by
my total failure. "People just aren't really like that in
Munich," she tells me. "I'm surprised someone didn't mistake
you for a Turkish foreign laborer and tell you to get out of the
country."

"Really?" I say, "people are that hostile to
foreigners?"

"Some people," my mom tell me, "and to some
foreigners."

That night, we go out to see a play, but are delayed
because the subway line is shut down. Someone has committed
suicide on the tracks again. "This happens all the time," my
mom says, "at least once every couple of weeks." Seasonal
affective disorder? Holiday-related depression? It creeps me
out to think of people living lonely, isolated lives in Munich,
surrounded by people who won't give you the time of day
(literally!), and ending it all in an act of insane passion whose
net result is that a bunch of grumpy commuters are put out
because the trains aren't running on time. It's a bizarrely
German-seeming tragedy. A few days later, on Christmas eve, a
woman ends up going into a church with explosives strapped to
her body and detonating herself during the second hymn.
Several old ladies sitting in her proximity are "torn to shreds,"
as the paper puts it, and her own body is so thoroughly
obliterated that no fingerprints or other identifying marks
remain. miraculously, however, her head is completely
unharmed. Christmas morning in Germany, thus, involves the
bizarre spectacle of waking up to televised photos of the
disembodied head on the news, "for identification purposes."
The skin is gray and limp, and the eyes are wide open and look
to be blue through the hardened yellow of the eyeballs.
Eyewitnesses who are interviewed express outrage at the social
impropriety of the act. "if she wants to kill herself, fine," says
a women, "but couldn't she find a more appropriate location?
That's just so tasteless."

florence

My brother Martin shows up

right after Christmas. "How's Munich?" he says. "Eh,"
I say. So we decide to go to Italy. That's just the kind of thing
you do when you're in Europe.

To tell the truth, I'm almost pathologically obsessed
with Italian food. I knew it seemed kind of crazy to travel all
that way just to eat some pizza. It's kind of like deciding to
drive to Florida because you heard about a good restaurant
there. But, man, what if that restaurant was the greatest single
eating establishment on the planet? That's what Italy is- the
best restaurant in the world.

Besides, I worked out all the math. If I could just eat
thirty pizzas while there it would average out the price of the
train ticket to a mere two dollars extra per pizza, making them
still a bargain at six to eight thousand lire a piece (which in
US currency is, uh, I don't know, it's like ten trillion lire to the
dollar or something).

Martin and I hop aboard the overnight train to
Florence, Italy. We arrive at nine in the morning, semi-
delirious from lack of sleep, exchange money, and start waiting
to get hungry.

Being a tourist, and specifically the kind of tourist you tend to be when you're a well-educated, poorly-dressed American, is an odd thing. Walking through the various winding networks of tunnel-like streets and stumbling out into the expanse of one art-historically significant piazza after another, I couldn't help but notice them, packs and droves of over-sized back-pack, five-o'clock shadow, acoustic guitar-strumming, looking-to-score-some-hash-and-trip-out-on-Botticelli's-Venus motherfuckers. Well, lunch awaits. We seat ourselves in the nearest appropriate establishment, ordering in garbled Italian. "ehhhh....volere beve...uh.."

"Yes? Would you like a coca-cola to drink?" the waitress answers in chipper, fluent English. We have those awkward few moments where she's talking to me in English but I'm still trying to hold on to the illusion that I might not be one of the over-size back pack people, and continue stuttering my way through in Italian. Finally, I give up. Why bother? When in Rome, do as the Romans: speak English. It's really true that you can get by in most any situation in western Europe without even a word of non-English vocabulary. It's marginally more difficult and challenging to be a tourist here than it is to travel in the United States, but only in the sense that tying your shoelaces with gloves on is marginally more challenging than without. And gloves are less expensive than a Eur-rail pass.

The appeal of bumming around Europe for the goateed and self-consciously bohemian masses of American youngsters lies in the small challenge of complexifying the everyday, in the same way that such goateed individuals sometimes like to smoke a lot of pot and spend all afternoon wrapping their minds around the task of preparing a bag of microwave popcorn. The subtle differences, like the sink which works on a foot pedal instead of a faucet, take a couple minutes to figure out, and there's all that trying to convert Celsius to Fahrenheit or figure out what time 22.30 is. Such hurdles make the routine of the tourist heroic, and a successful trip to a restaurant becomes a Homeric Odyssey; an Arnold Schwarzenegger movie you've already seen reveals new layers of humor and strangeness when dubbed into french. It's funny how conversations with people about their trips to Europe almost never revolve around their insights into the culture and history of the places they've visited, but instead involve anecdotes about being mugged by Gipsies, getting drunk and having a run-in with the law over some quaint local custom, or making out with a stranger in a youth hostel.

"Wow, you really are a jaded, spoiled fucker," my brother astutely points out as I lay out my new American-college-kids-just-like-bumming-around-Europe-because-it's-kind-of-like-being-on-drugs hypothesis over lunch. It's so true: here I am in Florence, Italy, wracking my brain for reasons why it sucks, why the people here suck, why I suck for being here. I'm supposed to be distracting myself from the existential horror of noting the similarity between people and chickens, and here I am feeling that humanity is more poultry-like than ever. We have a map of the town but nowhere we need to be so we wander the streets aimlessly, turning down streets at random or following people who look like they might be going somewhere interesting. My normal everyday routine is already pretty arbitrary and I rely on a complex constructed sense of what is and isn't meaningful in order to not freak out about the pointlessness of it all- strolling through a gigantic amusement park of funny foreign people only super-heightens this sense of alienation.

I remember when I was a kid seeing ads on TV for this place in Virginia called Busch Gardens. It was an amusement park which marketed itself to people who couldn't afford trips abroad as an almost exact replica of Europe, which was not only cheaper to travel to but which featured many amusing roller coasters and rides which the actual Europe did not. I imagine myself, here in Florence, wearing a giant Styrofoam Busch Gardens hat, astounded to hear my own voice uttering phrases like, "dude, that is one *big* church!" and "woah, this statue's *famous*!" Now if we could just find a youth hostel.

München Hbf
→ **Berlin Zoolg.**

Fahrplanauszug – Angaben ohr
Gültig: 29.9.96 bis 31.5.97

674 km

ab	Zug			Umsteigen	an	ab
4.50	ICE	886	✕	Göttingen	8.56	9.04
5.48	ICE	884	✕	Göttingen	9.56	10.04
6.51	IC	806	✕			
7.14	ICE	682	✕	Göttingen	10.56	11.04
7.51	ICE	882	✕	Göttingen	11.56	12.04
8.49	IC	804	✕			
9.14	ICE	680	✕	Göttingen	12.56	13.04
9.51	ICE	788	✕	Göttingen	13.56	14.04
10.51	IC	812	✕			
11.17	ICE	588	✕	Göttingen	14.56	15.04
12.51	IC	802	✕			
13.17	ICE	586	✕	Göttingen	16.56	17.04
13.51	ICE	784	✕	Göttingen	17.56	18.04

berlin

A few days later, I'm standing in the Banhof Zoo in Berlin, having a revelation. The scales are falling from

my eyes: the *Scorpions* are from Berlin, and they have a song called "the zoo," which is all about *hanging out at this very train station!* It's all so clear to me now. I always wondered about their fixation with going to the zoo- it didn't seem, you know, very tough (*not* that I put a lot of thought into it or anything- no, really, I swear). Man, if I was the *Scorpions* I'd hang out here, too. It's totally seedy and the shady characters abound.

Martin and I have arrived here at nine p.m. on new years eve. It's all part of my plan to be somewhere really distracting at the moment when I traditionally have my annual mid-life crisis. However, we are now at a loss for where to go. Martin chats up the local contingent of scabby-looking punk rockers, who offer the insight that we would probably have the most fun if we scored a lot of drugs, and they happen to have some they could sell us. We are touched by the sincerity of their offer but decline. I wonder if the *Scorpions* get their drugs from those punk rockers.

We make our way towards the Brandenberger Tor, which is for all extents and purposes the Times square equivalent for Berlin. Already the streets are chaotic and exciting, with explosions going off everywhere and people running around with champagne bottles. People are a lot more friendly here than in Munich, although mass drunken debauchery can tend to have that effect. We get on the subway towards our destination. The subway cars themselves are just mobile parties, with people passing around champagne bottles and whooping and yelling. "All trains should have one car like this at all times," Martin says, "you know, a party wagon." towards the front of the car a group of Italian men are singing a kind of barber-shop quartet type folk song, while towards the back a guy beat-boxes while another incredibly stoned gentleman busts out an awe-inspiringly good rap, freestyling in German. This will prove to be my only positive encounter with the barbaric practice known as German rap.

We manage to get delayed and sidetracked enough to arrive at our destination right at midnight, emerging to surface level amidst a throng of revelers, who exit the subway station only to emerge into the midst of what is essentially a massive riot. Fifty thousand people are losing their shit, firecrackers and rockets exploding underfoot and careening inches away from our discombobulated persons. It is quite a bit below freezing, so the mass of people cluster together into a gargantuan ball of body heat generated by drunken, gyrating bodies, limbs flailing to the rhythm of some of the worst music I've ever heard in my entire life. A DJ calls out invocations to the throng in between songs, bellowing, "let's hear it for all the ladies here tonight!" Everyone whoops it up. The crowd becomes particularly ferocious in it's enthusiasm when the DJ plays one of the few songs I recognize, which is, bizarrely enough "Born in The USA," proving irrefutably once again the superiority of American popular culture. People are practically doing summersaults of ecstatic rapture all around me, grabbing my shoulders and screaming "happy New Year!" into my ear. I'm struck by the amount of dancing going on and the.... well, the kind of dance moves the Germans seem to get into. There is, someone pointed out to me, no German word for nerd. This is because the term would be so non-specific and all-encompassing when applied to an event such as this as to be rendered meaningless. "No one is going to believe this," Martin frets, looking around, 'no one is going to believe me when I say that I've just been to a nation composed entirely of nerds! They'll think I'm exaggerating or being a snob, but look around! IT'S JUST OBJECTIVELY TRUE!" Martin looks around astounded, like a person who has been picked up by aliens and taken aboard their flying saucer, knowing even as it happens that no one will believe his story when he gets home.

East Berlin has the strangest architectural mishmash of ornate pre-war facades, decaying Stalin-era communist apartment complexes (many of which are strikingly reminiscent of college dorms) and even uglier hulking orange constructs from the seventies, when even communism bowed to the prevailing trends towards tacky color schemes which swept the world like a pestilence-bearing wind. This part of the city is gray and dilapidated, with hundreds of buildings unoccupied or uninhabitable, standing black and decrepit against the night sky. Since most houses here still rely on coal heat the air all over east Berlin is thick with soot and smells toxic, giving one the eerie sense that right beyond the periphery of your vision, the next neighborhood over is on fire, succumbing to the collapse of law and civilization which seems on the brink of happening all around. In reality it's the exact opposite: law and civilization as it existed since world war II have already collapsed here, six years ago, and what's happening now is the slow uphill climb back to some kind of normalcy. Berlin looks crazy and schizophrenic- majestic old churches lean up against creepy old communist bunkers which sit alongside ultra-modern glass and plastic promises of a brighter future.

The surroundings can seem pretty oppressive here, and one wonders how in such a grim environment the people can be so intensely compelled to get down. Around every corner is some kind of makeshift sketchy little disco or club or bar, sometimes rigged up in people's living rooms or no more than a disco ball and some crappy speakers in a shelled out cement basement. These places are packed all night with people, and are for the most part illegal or only semi-legal. Many establishments are open only very sporadically or operate on complex schedules involving even-numbered Wednesdays or some such trick to confound the local authority figures, who appear to be content to be confounded and let things run their course. Most of these places seem to be run by very young people who haven't quite figured out the whole concept of the profit motive- they serve food and drinks so cheaply that you know they're just in it to

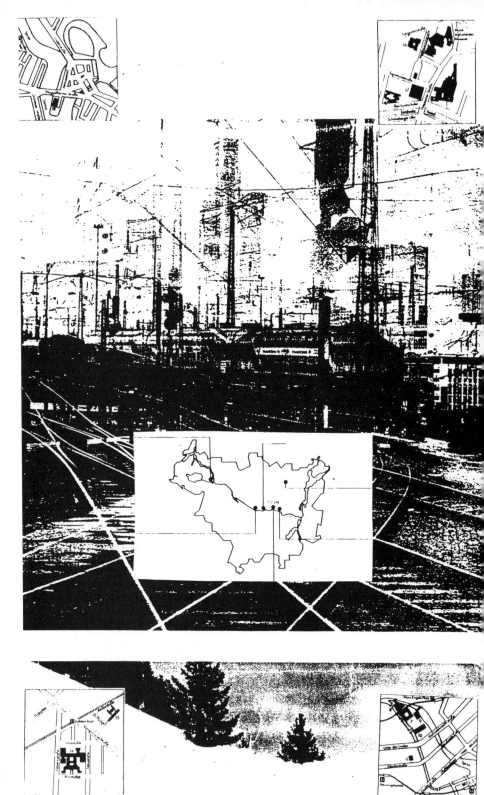

hook up the populace with the fruits of the newest youth craze-capitalism! Hey, why not? There are parts of Berlin where you can look out at the horizon and it's just rubble and destruction, and you can actually believe that the world has ended, the apocalypse has come. What response is there to this really, other than cranking up the dance music as loud as possible and doing the freak?

You can dance twenty-four hours a day in Berlin if you feel compelled to do so, and probably without spending a cent if you look around hard enough. The places where people meet to do this sort of thing are so sketchy that one person I met said he would occasionally just walk around trying random doors on abandoned buildings until he found some new places. At another spot I see a bath tub leaning against a wall in front of an abandoned storefront. "Crawl under that bath tub on certain days," my guide tells me, "and you find a basement club under a trap door in the sidewalk." People plan where to dance as meticulously as where to eat, and it's a nice way to live, getting all that dancing in, treating it like an essential bodily function, an appetite which needs to be sated as much as any other. People look really serious when they dance, almost always dancing alone and seemingly oblivious to those around them, eyes closed and face locked in a look of stern concentration. You act totally self-absorbed even as you are acutely aware of all these other people all around you writhing around. It's pretty funny, this basic human urge, like sex or peeing, the need to act really stupid in front of a large group of people.

Whenever I dance there's always that barely submerged subconscious fear that the moment I begin, the proverbial needle will screech off the record and all eyes will be frozen on my ineptly gesticulating and breakdancing body, for a horrible second before some voice blurts out from the throng, "man, that is the most ridiculous thing I've ever seen!" But it never happens, and in the tacit social acceptance you find the transcendence that makes the ritual work out for you.

I must say this, though: they do listen to some very fucked up things while they dance over there. The Germans claim to have invented Techno, a claim which I believe that they share with the British, although the Germans posit that the Brits merely invented the inferior house music, which is essentially the *C+C Music Factory* to Techno's *Ice Cube*. Techno itself is an ever-evolving and splintering umbrella term which many claim has no meaning anymore. "Jungle" seems to be just past its popularity apex, ceding the way to the up-and-coming craze of "German bass." Meanwhile, the ominous cloud of something called "Gör," which is pronounced kind of like *Gwar* and which is only spoken of in hushed, reverential whispers, looms on the horizon. Fuck, man. I believe the Germans. I can't imagine any other nation being sprockety enough to create such a completely crazy musical form.

The Germans never could really rock, but boy, can they tech. I don't know if I'm stretching it here, but my whole experience with this subculture makes me feel a lot better about my previous concerns for Germany's apparent falling off in the youth culture department. Here's my concept: even in the most anti-social and far-out products of a culture you can trace the blueprint of that cultures aesthetics' and value system. Rock music, for instance, has, as its basic guiding feature for differentiating good from bad, the same criterion as most traditionally American musical forms, i.e, if you are banging on an instrument and wailing really, really soulfully, that's "good." Techno people aren't worried about banging, and they aren't worried about soul. Their whole thing is making these meandering, extended compositions with certain themes being continuously repeated, varied and elaborated on, and you have a gradual building and ebbing of emotional peaks and valleys (if something entirely produced with drum machines, synthesizers and samples can be termed "emotional"). At this point I can invoke my status as uncultured heathen and go, hmmm, themes being repeated, peaks and valleys, hey, sounds kind of like classical music. Yes, that's right! The great classical masters +Kraftwerk= techno! Sure, to you and me it sounds like a crystal-meth-laden monkey with a casio, but you have to make room for cultural differences. They like it. It makes them freak out and shake their rumps like there's no tomorrow.

Unfortunately, there is a tomorrow in east Berlin, and it looms conspicuously in the sky in the form of the giant steel cranes which are everywhere, a portent of things to come. Berlin is currently under intensely heavy renovation and reconstruction, struggling to homogenize and give the people what the corporate powers-that-be insist that the fall of the Berlin Wall indicates they want: western capitalism. It's already amazing how many McDonalds and Pizza Huts are thriving in the recently de-commiefied Eastern zone. Still, the area retains a romantic third world charm- like the restaurant where for five marks you get a plate of whatever one menu item they made that night on their single burner stove. In cafés people hang out and sell their own sketchy wares, be they flowers or jewelry or pot brownies, without any complaints of competition or stealing customers from the proprietors of the establishments. It's a strange bizarro world, the post-revolutionary revolution of the free market, where no one would ever think of denying anyone the new-found thrill of being your own boss, turning your living room into a coffee shop or boutique or disco, never mind licenses or sanitation grades or bureaucracy of any sort.

It's strange to think of myself and the kids who run these places, who are mostly around my age, growing up in parallel opposite universes: in the U.S, being counter-cultural usually connotes some disdain for business and the commerce and commodity fetishism of the mainstream. Growing up in communist Germany, though, the most crazy, outlandish thing you could be into would be the free market. These kids probably dreamed of a time when they could just open up a shop in the same far-out science fiction way I dream about having health care one day. The student and youth culture in east Berlin is enamored of the same DIY spirit you hear American punk rockers talking about, and they don't have to carry around the weird contradiction of being entrepreneurs with anti-entrepreneur ideologies: the free market is the phoenix rising from the ashes of a war-torn and burnt-out city, and they are unabashedly psyched about it.

I'm pretty blown away by the whole thing. Everyone I talk to is sincere and enthusiastic, and it's really hard to imagine any of them as profiteering business majors out to make a buck. The main motivation for this flourishing culture seems to be the dance-urge, the urge to control your life and be stupid and crazy in public and be having a good time all the time. It's really the only way of living that makes sense in the post-ideological, politically circular and confusing times we inhabit. Unfortunately, while dancing in the ruins of civilization is a really good time, it's only going to get more civilized and less apocalyptic, like a reverse Road Warrior, as the cranes move in to these neighborhoods. Eventually the Starbucks and Burger Kings will move their franchises here and insist on sanitation grades, fire codes, police crackdowns, and then the whole subculture will be weeded out by the forces of gentrification. There's probably another three or four years of dance party left before this becomes just another historical footnote of a time when, for a brief and hopeful historical second, people didn't act like assholes to each other.

homeward

270201   0082460   ARD

CEIPT   SITI   X XXXXXXXXXXS

AGENT CODE
A33720956
ACE OF ISSUE SO CODE DATE OF ISSUE
NY USO6DEC96
ATOR   FCI SERV CARR. ID
1 0011/
STATUS   NOT VALID BEFORE NOT VALID AFTER
PT   18MAR
        ISSUING AGENT ID
X/ CW20*RG

LEAGE CREDIT
PAR AF NYC B
5XA3.OOXFEWR3

NAME OF PASSENGER
BURIAN/ALEXANDER MR
EWR
FROM
CDG AF3   T 18DEC1T
MUC AF1554 T 19DEC1T
TO
CDG AF1509 T 07JAN1T
JFK AF8   T 07JAN1T
CARRIER
CARRIER   FLIGHT CLASS   DATE   TIME

GATE   SEAT   SMOKE

PCS   WT   UNCKD   BAGGAGE ID NUMBER
NOT VALID FOR TRAVEL
0 057 1343244115 0
AA33720956

ALLOW PCS WT UNCKD
UMENT NUMBER   CK

244115 0

It is very weird to be German. It's weird in the same way that looking at my passport is weird, noticing how it says, "Alexander Burian, birthplace New Hampshire, USA." New Hampshire, because it was August of 1971 and too hot in sweltering sticky North Carolina for my pregnant German mom. As a result my point of entry into the world is a totally random place which I feel no connection to. All these various factors align to make up your identity, it seems, and so often they don't resonate with you at all when you recite them to yourself. They don't mean anything. *I'm German. I originate in the place Wienerschnitzel and Lederhosen originate.* Hmmm.

Places grow to have meaning in your life from experience, from the process of connecting. The inevitable contemplation of commemorative tattoos follows. Whenever I think of getting a tattoo, it invariably revolves around a geographical representation of some sort- for a while I thought I should get an outline of the state of North Carolina, with major highways noted (to provide fashion *and* function). I'll never not be from there, right? I mean, it's too late to be from somewhere else at this point. Then I got fixated on the state flag of Rhode Island, with its anchor and the scroll with the simple message: "hope." But I decided that I didn't want to back myself into any corners in case at some point in life I want to become an embittered cynic (in which case, I suppose, I could simply add another scroll over the anchor which read, "no.")

Germany has conflicted and tangled meanings in my life, because I haven't really had a lot of experience or connection with it since I was a small child. "German people are the worst people in the world to wait on," a friend of mine who works at a fancy restaurant recently told me, "I can say that," she added, "because *I'm* German." (Being a waiter in Germany must, it follows, be the worst job available in the industrialized world). I'm not really sure how psyched I am about the whole culture, symbols, history or the general German package, but, as destiny would concoct it, this is the package I happen to be packed into, so my options are to ignore this or remove the styrofoam peanuts and start digging around.

One thing I must say that Germans really know a lot about, as well as having a rich heritage of literary and cultural appreciation of, is the Burn. Goethe's <u>Sorrows of Young Werther</u> is one of the archetypical blueprints of the Burn, for instance. You don't even have to tell German people about the correlations to be found in the behavior of chickens and people, or about your sleepless nights tearing out your hair because you were gripped with intense fear that human interaction really is just a series of non-interlocking tabs and slots (and suddenly, Al realizes just how subconsciously sexual his whole earlier puzzle-pieces-being-jammed-into-one-another analogy was, which of course, evokes another German, the man who clinically defined and labelled the Burn as a medical condition, Sigmund Freud); they just look at you and go, "Ach, Ja- *Das Burn.*" In that way, it kind of makes sense. My mom was explaining the bitter emptiness of life to me once, and I told her that she should lighten up. "You don't understand depression," she said. "You didn't grow up in east Germany. You're an amateur. " It's true. But I'm a quick learner.

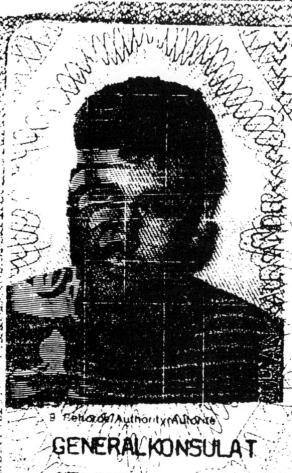

P

1. Name/Surname/Nom

BURIAN

2. Vornamen/Given names/P

ALEXANDER

3. Staatsangehörigkeit/Natio

DEUTSCH

5. Geschlecht/Sex/Sexe   6.

M

7. Ausstellungsdatum/Date o

15.09.199

9. Behörde/Authority/Autorité

10. Unterschrift des Paßinhat

GENERALKONSULAT ATLANTA

P<D<< Burn Collector #

3236057671D<<7108075M

al burian

307 Blueridge Rd.
Carrboro, NC 27510

burn collector   number six

I

I've been drunk before, on cheap beer bought by pedophiles and consumed in the graveyards and parking lots of my teenage years, or from a couple glasses of white wine too many at an art opening, where, having eaten nothing all day, I reel around and pretend to be "a good friend of the artist," lecturing people on his use of yellow and offering up fist fights to anyone who disagrees with my art-historical analysis. I've smoked reefer as well, notably once with a homeless ex-Hollywood mogul (so he claimed) under a freeway overpass in Venice beach, California. I was a naive sixteen years old, unversed in the complex social etiquette of Hollywood moguls, even homeless ones who live in the pornography-strewn hollow center of a hedge adorning a highway off-ramp, and consequently was totally unprepared for the urgency of the sexual propositions which followed the "smoking out." In retrospect, my escaping unsodomized is a real miracle. I've experimented with LSD, which on occasion has resulted in a few really horrendous situations but overall was pretty funny. I've taken mild muscle relaxants, had bizarre dreams while feverish and guzzling cough syrup; I've sucked out the nitreous oxide from a can of aerosol whipped cream and been giddy and dizzy for twenty lurid, retarded seconds. I had my wisdom teeth taken out and, while under the gas, experienced prophetic and haunting visions of things to come.

But I will tell you, nothing beats sleep deprivation when it comes to really astounding experiences of altered consciousness. I swear by it. Sleep deprivation! The sun coming up on another day and you, glassy-eyed like a fish, gritting your teeth and rubbing your eyes- your state of mind slowly shifted in such a way that you feel you've slipped out of the bonds of an illusory and narcotized waking life into an altered state which is hyper-awake, where, for the fleeting moments you can maintain this vantage point before the cruel, weak body shuts you down and you collapse into an exhausted heap, you get a glimpse of what the world really looks like, startlingly beautiful and hysterically ugly.

Sometimes this viewpoint produces euphoria, and sometimes it results in near-suicidal despair. This is fine with me. Experience can be approached in two ways: you can put things on a moral/qualitative scale, where, say, on a scale of one to ten, one represents "a really bad time" and ten represents "a totally kick-ass time," and then go about the business of trying to have all your experiences be, if not tens, at least in the four to five range. Alternatively, you can put experience on the same scale they try to allude to with those little drawings of thermometers on the side of jars of salsa, where low-thermometer equals mild and bland, and high-thermometer equals spicy and delicious. According to this rating system, traditional dichotomies of "bad" and "good" experience merely fall under the umbrella category of "spicy." The main thing to be avoided are not the "one" experiences but that low-thermometer "mild" salsa, because, really, if you like mild salsa, just face it, you don't like salsa. You like tomatoes. That's fine for you, but I myself am a spicy condiment individual and under my thermometer rating scheme your acceptable four and five scale experiences become my unacceptable mild salsa experiences.

Thus, sleep deprivation. Why not? Laughing your ass off is a great experience, but bawling uncontrollably is pretty interesting as well. It's in these moments that you realize what's really going on in the world around you, and that once you get crying you really *should* cry forever, because there's no end of stuff to weep about, and that at the same time there is so much hilarity whirling around you that to be truly in tune with it, to live a life without the filters and blinders of sticky, opium-like sleep, would mean you'd just keep laughing and laughing until you died from lack of oxygen to the brain. Moments like that are the peaks of emotional experience, and even as you have them you sometimes become dimly aware that this is one of those things that is going to stick with you, that it is going to become an archetype, a pivotal memory. Time tends to boil your life away until it's just these moments; you think back and in the camera lens of your recollection everything is stark and well-choreographed. Things seem simple and better then than in the murky, complex now. Sometimes, though, I think, if you get freaked out enough your actual life begins to resemble what the memory will be. And that's a beautiful thing.

II

I grew up in Durham, North Carolina. Sometimes, when I'm in the area, I like to stop by and spend a little time at the old alma Mater, Duke University. Not that I ever attended college there or anything, but I feel a deep connection and affinity for ye olde ivy covered walls on account of all the afternoons I spent in my youth scowling at people and roaming the campus distributing "the bird" to the assembled masses. Time was, I was on a first-name basis with the various sergeant and commanding officers of the illustrious campus security force, and we'd engage in witty banter of Oscar Wildesque proportions. I'd saucily suggest that they were "pigs" who were too lame to make it as real cops and they'd chuckle mirthfully and throw me in the Duke equivalent of the pokey. Many an afternoon was spent in the "holding cell," of the Duke security, also known (and widely discussed, in the reverential hushed whispers with which the juvenile delinquent population of Durham passed its mythology down from generation to generation) as the "trophy room." Even years later, I'd meet other kids who had done time in this auspicious chamber, and we could recall fondly (and in crystal-clear detail) the assortment of bongs, switchblades, brass knuckles, and other essential accouterments of the aspiring hoodlum. I wonder if that garish glass display case is still there, items meticulously labelled: "marijuana smoking implement-retrieved from bushes, Duke gardens," and similar references to heroisms and the death defying feats which form the core of life as a campus security officer.

Life was good back then, in the crappy, oppressive way life is good for fourteen year olds, which is to say, it completely sucked but seems pretty good in the obscuring glare of nostalgia. It's weird that I am older than most everyone who bustles about the campus at Duke now, because I still feel like a little kid when I get around them, and I still feel like giving them all the finger would be a pretty funny thing to do, as well as being a valid social commentary. However, I am more mature now, and I restrain myself. Let's face it, it's not the eighties anymore, and even if I were fourteen again, it just doesn't seem like it would be the same. The young conservative fuckers who used to roam the earth were like dinosaurs in the Jurrasic era, smug and self-confident in their sense of Reaganomic manifest destiny and God-given right to spend the rest of their life talking on car-phones and playing tennis. It was easy to despise them. Now they just seem like odd anomalies, one more cliche in a sea of tie-dyed neo-hippies, alternative-rockers, confused exchange students, and the various other archetypes that make up a college campus.

Around the age of fourteen I was living in a strange little yellow aluminum-sided hutch on Iredell street. It was hard to really put your finger on what was so wrong with the place, but there was something so palpably horrible about those days that even now when I pass by the vicinity of the little aluminum box I get a feeling of nauseous vertigo, the feeling that the past ten years have been some lulling dream of escape and that at any moment, as happens with dreams, you'll become self-conscious of the dream state and emerge from that sticky cocoon, blinking in the hazy glaring morning light. It's like going to sleep filled with anxiety about a math test you have to take in the morning; in your dreams you undergo the entire ordeal of getting up, going to school, taking the god damn test and then sigh with perspiration-soaked relief as the weight is removed from your chest. In that moment of triumph you awake to the realization that you have to do it all again, like some low grade Sisyphus, pushing the boulder of your mundane life up god- damn El-Camino-and-lawn-ornament infested Iredell street. Except this isn't a test we're talking about: this is me, fourteen years old, with my greasy, stringy seventies hair (and, yes, this is the mid-eighties I'm referring to; an indication of not only my own innate lack of fashion sense but also of my fruity European family's inability to grasp what kind of social indoctrination havoc occurs when you allow a fourteen year old boy to go around looking like Mary Tyler Moore); an ill-fitting hand-me down sweater from obscure eastern European second cousins, usually far too tight as if attempting to highlight my concave, hairless chest; flared no-name brand (or worse, lame brand) jeans, and those curious bo-bo shoes (possibly with velcro straps, if memory serves) which seemed to serve as a call-to-arms for all the local rednecks in the neighborhood to swarm into battle formation and beat me up for crimes against redneck fashion etiquette (these bo-bo shoes being, they'd gruffly inform me in between blows, ideological heavy artillery in the fashion assault of the "faggot" aesthetic- the sales staff at Pay Less shoes had not informed me of this).

The house had a peculiar time-warped quality to it as well, which was noticeable even at the time- the weathered, dull yellow exterior melding gracelessly into the brownish grass which infested the front lawn all seemed to lend it the air of a corroding snapshot, color seeping out so that the aluminum siding and the haggard, jaundiced faces of the inhabitants all flattened out into the same washed out, sickly tint. Standing in front of the residence, the edges of vision seem almost take on the rounded edges of an old photo. The sight of my father stumbling blearily out of the house to sit on the sad little porch and stare out across the little lawn would, I'm afraid, do absolutely nothing to dispel this ambiance. Recently divorced after a fifteen year marriage, my father, professor of classical studies at Duke University, graduate of Princeton, world traveler and fluent in several languages, had regressed whole heartedly into the womb of white trash bachelorhood, and spent most of his time hanging out in boxer shorts and a wifebeater undershirt. I would not be shocked to learn that he actually went to work and even taught graduate comparative literature classes in this outfit. These were hard times. I ate enough tater tots in this era to bolster the economy of several midwestern potato-producing states well into the early twenty-first century. My father clearly felt a great weight of guilt and remorse over the failure of his marriage, but being a man of the mind, a man who had rejected whatever religious upbringing he had received as a child, he was unable to assuage his guilt through penance or the clutching of rosary beads, and something compelled him to replace the religious sacrament of the rosary with fish stick consumption.

It is not hard to imagine the despair that a man in my father's position must have felt, looking up from his plate of fried and breaded grease-nuggets of one type or another, and out across the vast tundra of the stained kitchen table where, on the other end, sat his two sons, myself a seething hive of anti-social scowling spite and his other son, my brother Martin, sullen and withdrawn underneath a standard issue eight-is-enough bowl cut. Beyond the confines of the depressing kitchen, out in the dank heat of a humid North Carolina night, the neighbors blasted their novelty car horn, which played "Dixie," again and again, the neighbors apparently endlessly amused and enraptured by this diversion. I'd get up from the table abruptly, without excusing myself, and stumble out into this wilderness, to return hours later, smelling of illicitly purchased cigarettes, slugs of Mad Dog or cheap liquor bummed off of the neighborhood winos, and the acrid smoky smell which betrayed my small, though enthusiastic, attempts at developing arson as a hobby. The bachelor life wasn't all it was cracked up to be, realized my dad.

Fate, or at least some sympathetic administrative authorities concerned by reports that my dad was showing up for lectures wearing only his underclothes, intervened. The trio of maladjusted males was offered a spot in a small apartment-size dwelling on the Duke campus, in the first floor of a dormitory. My dad was given the auspicious title of "faculty in residence," and alloted a budget for catering the occasional bagel brunch for the students.   Things started to look up at this point. It was during this period that I was introduced to a number of new concepts which would have long-lasting impacts on my behavior and world-view: The discovery of punk rock changed me profoundly- it was, most of all, instrumental in my getting a haircut, and updating my overall aesthetic to one which was, at least, only behind the times in terms of years, not a full decade. Meanwhile, the relative freedom and various social opportunities of the college environment began to transform me from an introverted loner into the arguably even more annoying, but less socially deviant, extroverted smart-ass. Then there were those bagel brunches. The sheer magnitude of it all, the unearthly beauty of a table filled to capacity with bagels, free bagels, all you can eat bagels, the most perfect and ancient of man's culinary creations, the veritable shark of foods, such a streamlined, perfect killing machine of a breakfast food that thousands of years of evolution had left it pure and unchanged (until this recent blight of sun-dried tomato yuppie bagels which some demented genetic engineer of bourgeois eating has recently foisted on us, but let's not talk about that, it's a downer)- well, suffice to say that I was forever scarred, scarred in two specific ways: trained like one of Pavlov's hounds to seek out and line up at any kind of event, opening, lecture or other fascist gathering which might afford me some glimpse of a well-stocked buffet table ripe for the raiding, and with a fanatical devotion to the concept of free food, to the notion that by being at the right place at the right time, you can turn on the tap and let gush forth the waters of that eternally flowing river, the river of capitalism's bountiful excess.

But, my friends, by far the most amazing discovery I made that fateful and magical summer of my fifteenth year, was that I discovered sleep deprivation. As you might well imagine, the first step in this process was figuring out about drinking coffee. All my flirtations with substance abuse were out the window, cast into the dustbin of juvenile delinquent history when the black broth of the benevolent bean entered my life. What causes a person to do exactly the thing they are supposed to do at the time that they do it? How did you know to turn on the radio the day when you heard your favorite song, the one which changed your life? I wonder about things like that- how did anyone ever figure out about making bread? It's not a logically self-evident process, and yet in a myriad of cultures somebody comes up with some kind of bread product, as if in a trance, as if it's in their genetic makeup and they are just following orders. Who smoked the first cigarette and how did they possibly get the idea to do it? Who first refined heroin? And for God's sake, who came across the inedible, repulsive oily bean of the coffee plant and thought, "hmmm, can't really make a burrito with these beans...... say, why not grind it into powder, filter boiling water through the grounds, and then drink the bitter, stomach-cramp-inducing result?" Some genius had the prophetic vision to go through with that lunacy, setting the stage for vast empires and fortunes, for a world of bleached and unbleached coffee filters, lives of misery and toil for generations of people in vast acres of coffee bean fields the world over. On top of the pyramid of this history sits a lone Mr. Coffee, located on the counter in the apartment where I dwell. Nature versus nurture: you can't really say people are genetically programmed to do most of the things they do because most things people do are just too socially constructed. A wolf can be a great hunter, but is it plausible to ascribe the same natural, DNA-encoded primacy to the world yo-yo champion? Who knows. Somebody got the idea to invent a use for the evil bean, accouterments were concocted in that great late-industrial highly accesorized-lifestyle way that accouterments get concocted, and before you know it I'm standing in front of the aforementioned Mr. Coffee going, "Gee, I wonder how this thing works," for no apparent reason at all. I made my first briny batch much too strong, and it poured like molasses and tasted like a mouth full of charred hair. "This is horrible," I thought, "I'm intrigued."

Cup after cup of the cruel crap. My scrawny, fifteen year old frame began to twitch and palpitate even more than when under the strain of the usual dosage of brain-twisting youthful pus and spite, which even under the best of circumstances probably composed a good thirty percent of the Molotov cocktail coursing through my veins. But I felt good, oh Lord, I felt good! I stared into the oil sheen floating atop this secret, poisonous beverage, and saw my eyes reflected and shooting sparks from dilated pupils, felt the high octane fuel coursing through the engine of my brain and snaky intestines, cleaning it out, giving it the low, self-confident rumble of a car that's perfectly tuned up, a car you're treating right. "Let's give the old jalopy a tank of the good stuff," you mutter at the pump, hitting the super-super-unleaded. I was finally running correctly. Polishing off the pot, I ventured out into the sunny afternoon heat on twitchy, skittish ankles, wiggling knees, pelvis clenched into place and every spinal disc in sync, like an audience at a rock concert or football game, gripped with the unified giddiness of mass hysteria, doing the Wave up and down my back in tingly synchronicity. It was a whole new world out there. Everything seemed infinitely complex and worth exploring and expounding on. I looked down at my shaking hands; the right claw was still clutching the coffee cup, empty now of all elixir, save a small residue of gritty ink collected at the bottom. Contemplating the cup, I began to croon a Black Sabbath song which seemed particularly apropos, modifying the words to suit my particular set of circumstances:

Alright NOW!! Won't you listen?
When I first met you didn't realize
I can't forget you or your surprise
You introduced me to my mind
And left me wanting you and your kind.
Oh, I love you!
Yeah, you know it!
My life was empty, forever on a down
Until you took me, showed me around

It was early summer; my first year of high school, characterized as it was by an internal landscape of bleak horror and the waking nightmare of hormonal anarchy, had just mercifully ended. Running around, jacked up out of my skull on coffee was the first unadulterated good thing I'd felt since the onset of adolescence- a pure and untainted feeling. I was ready to go. This was my new thing.

III.

Why am I telling you this? I don't know. But listen- there
is something wrong with me, that's for sure. It seems like I could
trace the steps, backwards, and somehow I could come to the spot
where I diverged from the beaten path and became deviant,
because there must be such a spot, there must be a moment when
I threw off the cloak of civility and embraced the void: when I
became a crazed cannibal, a maniacal, misanthropic monkey.

I know this guy who decided to cultivate an extremely
irritating laugh just be, well, you know, irritating. He would
throw back his head and emit this piercing, hyena-like series of
squeals; "eee-eee-eeee-eeee," he would croak, driving everyone
around him into fits of epilepsy and muted swearing. Eventually
of course, like the weird face your mother warns you will stick,
his laugh stuck and then he was stuck with it. Life began to grow
difficult for him; he was kicked out of restaurants and seeing a
movie that was at all funny was just out of the question. But he
couldn't un-cultivate it; it was too late to go back. The laugh he
thought he was choosing had chosen him.

IV.

My dad would drive me to Chapel Hill, the next town
over, where opportunities for youthful transgression were far
more plentiful. I'd get dropped off at some friends' house in the
suburbs, where we'd outfit ourselves in the bizarre gear of the
aspiring eighties punk rocker, and then wander down to the mall
to be resoundingly beat up. The main guy I knew who I'd do this
with was this kid named Edward. The guy had a magnet in his
head or something; it attracted all manner of fists, rocks, and blunt
objects. He couldn't seem to escape pummelings. One afternoon I
was dropped off at his house, only to find him in the ditch in front
of his lawn, face down, being repeatedly whacked over the skull
with his own skateboard by Max Earl, the neighborhood bully. I
was powerless to thwart the inevitable course of nature, so I
merely stood on the sidelines, patiently, while Max whacked
away, until, growing weary of subduing his now motionless
opponent, the Earl righted himself to his full homo-erectus stature,
grunted in my direction with a subtle nuance of scowling belch
which both indicated a greeting and a threat of continued beatings
in the later afternoon, and shambled off to harvest car stereos or
some other activity for which the boy scouts offer no merit badge.
I peeled Edward out of the ditch and dragged his whimpering
form into the air-conditioned house.
    Once the minor contusions had been bandaged and ice-
packs applied where appropriate, Edward was back on track,
scheming revenge against Max as he prepared to go out on the
town.
    "We could hide on the sides of the road with a trip-wire,"
he suggested, "and when he bikes by-- BAM, we pull the wire and
he goes flying, cracks open his fucking head!"
    "Hmmm," I nodded.
    "If I just had some kind of gun," Edward continued to
rant, "Man, I'd just.... You know what? I'm gonna mace him."
    "You're what?" I said.
    "Next time I'm gonna mace him," Edward confirmed.
Thus satisfied that retribution was within grasp, we set out for
another disastrous venture to the mall.
    It was Edward who really solidified my self-identification,
in terms of aesthetic, with the punk rockers. Fourteen years old,
he was a round little kid with a bright smile and a hairspray-
intensive mohawk which the friendly barber at Glen Lennox
shopping center would meticulously trim the sides of every week.
He strutted around awkwardly in oversized combat boots and a
black leather jacket which he wore even in the hundred degree
summer heat, scowling or giving the finger as the situation
demanded it, and it often did. This was not cool or acceptable
teenage behavior in a historical era which celebrated as one of its
great cultural icons Michael J. Fox.

Down at the mall, a small group of boys gathered to taunt and brutalize us. We wandered the brightly lit corridors, passing the sanitation grade B Chick-fil-ay, the radio shack with its somber tight-lipped stooges watching us mutely from behind beeping, blinking display cases, stumbling through department stores, all the while trailed by a squadron of heckling roughnecks, serenading us with an endless symphony of jeers, like our own personal theme music in this very banal suburban sit-com.

We ducked down into an alcove which led to the public rest-room, locking ourselves in to strategize.

"We can take them," Edward pronounced, his eyes blazing with the gusto of a crazed John Wayne general from some late-night TV world war two epic. Within his pockets was an arsenal of small-time hoodlum accessories, which we divvied up, preparing for battle- a butterfly knife, a couple of skull-rings which would presumably serve the function of brass knuckles, and the small canister of mace Edward had recently procured from the army surplus store. I was, of course, terrified; although I was older I still played the role of Patrokolus, timid sidekick to Edward's dogged and spiritually uncrushable Achilles. If Edward was scared he showed not a flicker as we sauntered into battle.

The aggressor tough guys had disappeared in the meantime, and as we stood outside the men's room scanning the food court I imagined the warbling, ominous drone of the soundtrack to some Western, echoing through the bustling halls of commerce.

"They're gone," I mumbled meekly.

"All right!" Edward said brightly, strutting out of the corridor. We had won victory by default.

"Let's go," I suggested, and we headed for the rear entrance of the mall. As we shuffled along, two of our aggressors appeared before us, arms folded, stone-faced, immobile as we approached and Edward brushed shoulders with one of them roughly.

"Faggots," the tough guy stated flatly, as if he was a horticulturist identifying flora. He nodded sagely.

Edward hissed back raggedly, "you want to take this outside?" and the two sentries turned to march solemnly out the door with us. Edward shot me a glance, grinning, giving me a reassuring ass-kicker nod.

I grew up in the American South but I am, in many essential ways, not southern. There are many facets and nuances of social propriety and familial organization which I cannot comprehend or harness to benefit myself; for instance, I could never, within a ten minute span of time, muster a medium-size lynch-mob composed entirely of cousins, instructing them to wait outside the side entrance of a shopping mall in order to dismember two teenagers of questionable sexual orientation. Whatever powerful forces had been set in motion to accomplish this task, however, the end result was that Edward and I exited the mall fully intending to come to blows with these two ruffians, only to find ourselves completely encircled by a seething mob of bloodthirsty killers, any one of whom was two to four times our girth.

"Oh," I said, the situation becoming clear to me, "I get it. This sucks."

"You want to talk shit now? Huh?" The leader stepped forward to taunt.

"No, thank you," I said sadly. This was the typical situation. There was nothing to do but concede defeat. We turned and limped away, heads hung low, as the raging throng mobilized behind us, picking up rocks from the conveniently placed rock garden encircling the mall's outer perimeter, no doubt placed for easy access in the case of just such a situation. They hurled the rocks, laughing and cheering when a good-sized boulder would careen of one or the other of our skulls or shoulders with a dull ponging sound.

"Wow," I was stunned and incredulous," we're actually being stoned right now. This is like the Bible come to life." I looked over at my fellow sufferer, who did not respond, but simply stared ahead, flinching ever so slightly when a rock would get him in just the right spot.

"Ouch," he'd snarl quietly. There were scalding, angry tears welling up in his eyes. We walked through the parking lot, silently, headed home, past car loads of young girls on their way to buy gaudy plastic bracelets, past sullen grown-ups in pick up trucks whose faces brightened mirthfully at the sight of our debasement. The entire community, the town and by tacit approval the world as a whole, seemed in on the joke against us; the sky loomed big overhead, Carolina blue, as the bumper stickers like to point out, proving that God is a Tarheel. I felt small underneath the sky. The throng followed us until their rock supply ran out as we approached the edge of the lot, at which point they turned, slapping each other five and shouting "faggots!" into the early evening heavens, almost as if in celebration of the subspecies which provided so much amusement for their kind.

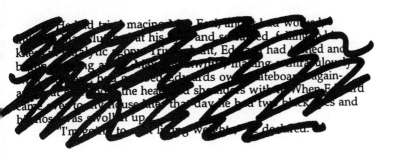

al   burian

307 Blueridge Road
Carrboro, NC 27510

sleep deprivation
and stories
of my bullshit youth

CAL LOCATION

FRONT

O Right, O Left
O Right, O Left

: O Right, O Left
O Right, O Left
O Right, O Left
O Right, O Left

cify): _____
O Right, O Left
O Right, O Left

O Right, O Left
O Right, O Left

O Right, O Left

O Right, O Left

ATE LOCATION BY
RAM

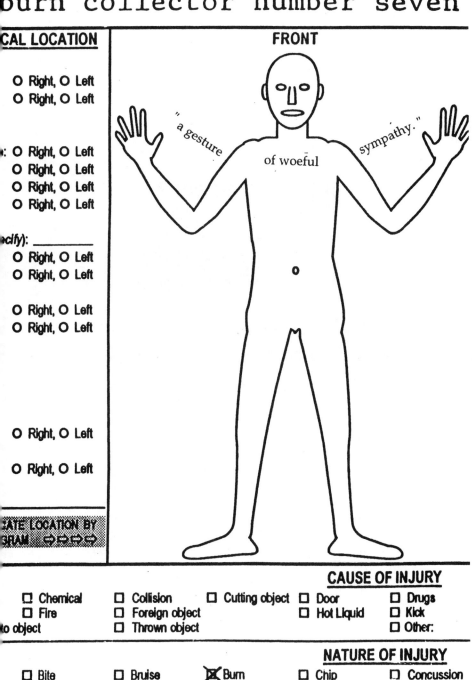

"a gesture

of woeful

sympathy."

CAUSE OF INJURY

☐ Chemical	☐ Collision	☐ Cutting object	☐ Door	☐ Drugs
☐ Fire	☐ Foreign object		☐ Hot Liquid	☐ Kick
to object	☐ Thrown object			☐ Other:

NATURE OF INJURY

| ☐ Bite | ☐ Bruise | ☒ Burn | ☐ Chip | ☐ Concussion |
| ☐ Poisoning | ☐ Pulled | ☐ Puncture | ☐ Scald | ☐ Scratch |

As I was attempting to go to sleep one horrid and dreadful

morning, lulling myself into the warm embrace of slumber with the aid of the rain's relentless and soothing pitter-pat against the window, as well as several bottles of rapidly chugged Niquil (the velvet hammer of temporary retardation- the insomniacs' ambrosia), I was roused from the old faithful sleeping bag by the sound of fists banging urgently on my door. Now, usually, this all-too familiar sound is met with muted whispers of "landlord!" from the assembled inhabitants of the less-than fully legal firetrap I rent as "office space" and occasionally lay my weary head down to rest in, and then immediately following one hears either the scurrying shuffle of housemates clamoring towards the back room to hide and cackle amongst themselves, or a stony, teeth-gritting silence as we play what is known in landlord-tenant legalese as "the waiting game." Today, however, seized by the inexplicable giddiness of the overtired, I sprung out of bed and answered the door promptly. Waiting for me beyond the threshold were two glum-looking rednecks, shifting their considerable respective bulks from foot to foot and glaring at me sullenly. "Duct repair," the motley pair muttered in unison. I shook my head in a gesture of woeful sympathy. "Are you here to fix the heat?" I ventured. They nodded. "Well, I'm sorry to inform you that the crawl space is over on the right side of the house, but the ducts that need repairing are, uh, on the other side. So... well, I guess you'll be having to crawl all the way under the house to the other side." I had already thoroughly investigated the situation, thinking that, like Robert DeNiro in the film Brazil, I could be a renegade duct repairman, smiting the massive bureaucracies pitted against me by my act of subversive home maintenance. One look in the crawlspace opening, however, was enough to convince all my housemates that the post-traumatic stress disorder incurred by any poor soul who chose to slither into the rat-and-spider-infested intestinal underbelly of our decaying shed would not be worth its weight in status quo subversion. And, speaking of Status Quo, and some dudes who were probably conceived while a song by the band Status Quo was playing, I looked deep into the faces of the befuddled duct dwellers standing before me and I could clearly see that my darkest nightmares are their day job. "Well," the leader of the two shrugged, "God damn."

I left them to bicker over tools and went back inside to lay down and pick up where I had left off in my quest for a coma. Laying on the floor in my sleeping bag, my head was directly next to a heating vent, which blows sometimes soothingly onto my furrowed brow and reminds me of wise and all-knowing Athena, wiping the sweat from my anxious forehead. It also permits me to rock some of my award-winning hairstyles. In any case, moments after laying down for my second attempt at getting some rest, I heard the voice of the duct repair men directly underneath my face. I realized, with a start, that the crawlspace entrance was situated exactly below me, and that, as I lay face-down, the cardboard thin floor was all that was separating me from french-kissing the squirming ductman, whom I could hear loud and clear, grunting and moaning obscenely as he maneuvered his frame into the claustrosphere underneath my house.

"Oh God......." I heard him snarl, "this is full of broken glass. Why is it always me who has to crawl into these hell holes?" A good question. It began to dawn on me that only inches away from my squirmed the man with the worst job in the world. "AAAGH!" he screamed. "I got glass in my back." He snaked his way further, alternately swearing, screaming in pain, and bellowing Stone Temple Pilots lyrics. "I am, I am, I Wanna get with you babe," he crooned. Arriving at some juncture in the venting system at which it was necessary for him to begin hammering maniacally, he proceeded to pound away, and I drifted eventually into a deep, death-like sleep. As I was nodding out though, I heard him scream again, and the excited exclamation to his partner: "Chris! Do you see this? Does this look like a human bone to you?"

The house in which I currently reside is indeed appropriately referred to as a "hell hole." Architecturally, it is a sterling example of the southern "eyeballin' it" school of masonry, a liquor-fortified brand of gutsy carpentry wherein the goal is to avoid all ninety degree angles. The overall result evokes a small child with a crayon, drawing up elaborate blueprints in the shaky hand of Cap'n Crunch-induced sugar spasms, and then some sadistic realty company owning dad building a house to the child's specifications, all to teach him a lesson about using rulers. The wind howls in through the jagged gaps between wall and window frames, and sketchy plywood doors hang awkwardly from rusty hinges, ill-fit for door frames they've been randomly assigned to. There are advantages to living in such a death-trap, to be sure. Sometimes it's hard to keep them in mind, though.

I myself reside within the sketchiest quarters. My "room" is essentially the crawlspace between the outer wall and a homemade, constructed wall, erected from the debris of a fence which was torn down at our old house and left to rot. It continues to rot, but now in a much more functional, semi-privacy-facilitating fashion. My housemates, Dave, Roby and Seth, don't really have it that much more palatial in the rooming department, and I feel especially sorry for Dave, whose room not only doubles as the band practice room, but also provides the stoic virtue of being unheated.

To the extent that the house can even maintain a United States zip code and thus consider itself part of the first world, various plumbing and heating improvements were performed by Roby, who has also installed shutters on her windows so that they completely shut out all light. This is helpful for shooting films or, alternatively, just modifying her light intake to the six months of no sunlight her Scandinavian heritage demands. Patrick, ideological ally and freelance superhuman, helped a lot with plumbing and wall building, as well as rendering an eerily accurate life-size likeness of Ozzy Osbourne on this wall.

The other really unfathomable thing about my housing situation is the fact that the landlord is located in a realty office right across the street. This is the element that really makes my whole life transcend a life right now, and start to take on the grainy, overly real antic timing of a *Fawlty Towers* episode, an Inspector Cleusseau movie. Not only do we live in our "office" illegally but we refuse to pay rent on it, on the grounds that he hasn't fixed the stuff we're fixing ourselves. But it's not like this is some absentee landlord- this guy literally comes by, pounding on the door, and we cower in the back room and shush each other until he goes away. It's a tough way to live, although it's pretty easy to slip into the immature frame of mind which relates the experience to *Ferris Beuler's Day Off* or some other iconic scenario of youthful triumph over vaguely defined authority, and thus be having a really good time. Mostly, it's just interesting to trace your path from the womb, the various choices, so arbitrary at the time and so crucial in retrospect, which led to this moment, and the specific set of bizarre circumstances which we wave in to our frame of reference so emphatically, inviting in the sketchfactors as if holding black and white checkered racing flags. This is a snapshot of me right now, the life I live, suspended in the moment, waiting to be kicked out or have the floor cave in, suspenseful motions in my suspended animation.

I haven't been sleeping very well. It might be

sleeping on the floor, although I've done it on and off for years, or it might be these weird dreams I've been having. They are not especially profound or terrifying, and they are pretty obvious in a Freudian analysis kind of way, but the essential theme is that I'm in a nudist colony and it's me and all people in their seventies and eighties. Yeah, I know, it sounds like I'm on comedy Central and there's about to be some really dumb punchline to that. But there is no punchline. That's the whole crazy thing, I'm actually having these lame dreams.

Worse than that, as I sat in a coffee shop feverishly writing down the sordid details of my latest nudist colony dream in a local café the other night, an obviously horrendously drunk young woman entered and made a B-line to me. "What's your name?" she drawled drunkenly.

"Um, Al," I said.

"What's this?" she croaked, snatching my journal out of my hands. She began to read, as I sat transfixed and paralyzed, a feeble no-I'm-not-embarrassed smirk on my face, muttering the words to herself at first, voice rising in a crescendo of disbelief as her incredulous eyes scanned the page. She read a poem I had written aloud, much to the amusement of the assembled clientele. (Man, I *wish* I was making this up.) She then hit her stride and, in shocked gasps, read aloud the description of my latest nudist colony dream, which included many naughty words and images, I'm sad to say. I tried to give her an apologetic look, shrugging in a gesture meant to suggest, "you shouldn't have 'gone there'" (that being the hip lingo of the kids these days). She looked at me with a scowl of wide-eyed contempt and left the building, mind expanded in unpleasant directions. All I could think was that earlier that day I'd been having a conversation about how John Hughes used to make these poignant encapsulations of the deepest, most resonant humiliations, and how no one ever really captured that feeling anymore. I don't know, geriatric nudist colonies- is that really such a fucked up a thing to have a dream about?

Any number of factors might be contributing to my weird sleep-

it could be the claustrophobic closet, the discomfort of the floor, the social awkwardness of living with a girl I'm only occasionally on speaking terms with (another bizarre and calculated attempt to make life alien and unrecognizable, and thus "interesting"- don't ask me why I act this way. I do not know.) or it could be just the general uncertainty of the whole leaseless, slum-lord situation. Whatever the case, I haven't really been "myself" lately, whatever that is. It's strange how environmental factors affect you- as much as you put into a situation, it also puts something into you. I admire Roby a lot for working hard to involve people in projects and make the most of a sketchy situation by taking advantage of the sketchiness: we draw on the walls, we can play music and have bands play shows in our living room at all hours, we can organize and carry out any event we can think of. There is a certain level of psychological freedom to this, the thrill of realizing that your limitations are self-imposed, and this seems like the most valuable thing in the world to me. Roby told me that the other night she was at a party and a number of people commented that they would like to get their shit together to work on projects in the way that she does, and, as much as I think she's a good influence on the people around her in that way, you can't help but worry about their inertia and its eventual influence on her. I think of it like magnets which people carry in their heads, radiating force fields which draw other people in, align their polarity and send them spinning on the same trajectory y ou are in. You like to think that your force field is the strongest, and that kinetic energy displayed will activate other people, but the converse is true and the more you fall in the sway

of others the more they can pull you into being like them, slow and hopeless. And then, of course, there's this house, which leaks an immense field of gravitation from the floorboards, making us all more like it despite ourselves and our ideas of conquering its essence, of making the house more like us. The house always wins, I've found. We end up satellites, going out into the world on kamikaze missions, spreading the word. Entropy, collapse, decline, sketchiness, the breakdown of civilization. Ruins and rubble, and the possibilities for post-apocalyptic dance parties. Which is, really, not a bad message.

Theology, or lack thereof

1. Life is hard

Life is hard! It is so damn hard. Back in the olden days, of course, it was really, really hard. When white people settled in North America they fucked up and settled in places like New England, a place with a climate so inhospitable and crappy that it was only acceptable to the New Englanders because they had come over from Olde England, which is not exactly a Miami beach resort type of area itself. But man, life was so hard back then! Most people froze to death in the winter. The other New Englanders gathered up the dead and ate them, or made pelts from their skins, which were not very warm because humans have little or no fur, and so a lot of those pelt-wearers froze to death themselves. Crazy. But so anyway, the way these people made it through these hard times was, they decided to be puritans, which meant, they developed a whole value system based on not having a very good time at all. This was a kick-ass strategy for New England. The simple conceptual shift of valuing a bad time made the area a veritable amusement park of hellish torture. The possibilities were seemingly endless, there was so much terrible stuff to do- kill Indians, churn butter, kill witches, chop down trees, get eaten by bears. The puritans believed strongly in God and thus all this suffering made a lot of sense to them.

2. God sucks

But no one really believes in God anymore, except for some old folks and the occasional socially retarded youngster, biking about in his little white shirt and tie, babbling some gibberish which any rational person smirks at smugly. The average, well-adjusted atheistic citizen would rather hear something at least marginally plausible, like information about extraterrestrial bodies kept on dry ice at hanger 18, in Las Vegas, Nevada, than hear the archaic prattling of some freak who thinks some big guy with a long white beard is up in the sky listening to your prayers and taking it all down on a little note-pad, like some absurd celestial maitre d'.

3. The existential void

However, this leaves some people with a little problem called the Existential Void. This is one of the many problems I do not suffer from (amongst a myriad of others, including crooked teeth, venereal disease, night blindness and brittle, dry hair, to name but a few); however I know a good number of people who have got it, bad. You might know some as well. These are the kind of people who always ask those weird questions, like, "well, so how do explain the trees?" or mope about how there should be "something more" to this life. My answers to these fundamental questions about the nature of existence are as follows: 1) acorns and 2) there's already way too much. Because of my great attitude I am able to get on with my life and do the important things, like draw or make up new dance moves to confound my enemies. Some people are not so lucky. These people are brooders. There are a good many of them.

4. Existential void in the animal kingdom

Who can blame them, I suppose. As shown in paragraph one, life is very, very hard and unrewarding. That does seem like a good reason to be depressed, although I don't know who ever said it wasn't going to be. Some say that it is a bad idea to traumatize newborns by shining bright lights in their eyes immediately after birth, turning them over and whacking them on the back, possibly snipping off a bit of the genitals. I say, that sort of thing is only right and natural. Why lull the kids with a false sense of security? The infant giraffe is expulsed from a pouch in the underside of the mother giraffe, falling seven to ten feet through the air, depending on the height of the mother, and then landing with a resounding whack on the hard and unforgiving African soil. It is the newborn giraffes responsibility to begin flailing its legs in a running-type of motion while in free-fall, so that immediately on impact he or she can commence fleeing from the predators waiting below. Now that's a tough life! And if it's good enough for giraffes, why should humans be so hoity-toity about it all? Sure, it is technologically feasible to birth our offspring in lukewarm pools of water in dimly lit rooms while the soothing music of Kenny G. plays to welcome our progeny into the world- but the fact remains: our society is so constructed that this child will not be sufficiently hardened to deal with a life time of teachers, authority figures, bureaucrats and bosses, all shining bright lights in their eyes, punching them in the back, and snipping off their genitals, bit by bit.

5. The age-old question

So yes, life is tough, and though this appears to be the animal kingdoms' natural way, some still insist on asking, "Why? Why? WHY?!?" The lack of a good answer to this question creates the black hole of uncertainty and despair alluded to earlier, the so-called existential void. Back in the old God days this issue was all worked out by a combination of theological rhetoric and selected stake-burnings. Now, the whole thing is considerably more complicated. People flounder around for a suitable replacement for the big theological cheat-sheet.

6. Side-note: Friedrich Nietzsche

Before I took it to work one day and lost it, I was the owner of a biography of Friedrich Nietzsche, a book which I got in a free box in Portland, Oregon. It is certainly arguable that the character portrayed by Kevin Kline in the film "A Fish called Wanda," who insists that he is above the monkeys because "monkeys don't read philosophy," only to be rebutted by the always saucy (and, rumor has it, born hermaphroditic) Jamie Lee Curtis: "monkeys read philosophy; they just don't understand it," is, in fact, a direct character assassination of myself (and to this assassination attempt I can only respond with a heavy-hearted "touché,"); however, one fact which I did glean from this book was that, apparently, that guy wrote some books which are considered to be quite smart and, in fact, just kept getting smarter and smarter and smarter, until eventually he went over the Niagara Falls of smartness and was just a raving lunatic. It makes a lot of sense to me that this would be the course of a smart person's intellectual development. Child math prodigies, apparently, tend to make their great contributions to the field in their early twenties and are usually insane by twenty-five. Thinking about things tends to lead to pretty grim conclusions- if not, you're probably not thinking hard enough. And while it is certainly logically sound that, life being hard and pointless and grim, we should all be really bummed out about it and lose our minds, most of us find some way to cope (at least most of the time) with the white-noise background loop of despair which replays itself over and over again in the back of our minds, like a video on constant replay, like the day the space shuttle challenger blew up. On that day, on every television channel, they just showed it, blowing up again and again, in slow motion, all afternoon. Do you remember that day? There was nothing else on. Man, it sucked.

7. One answer to the big question

Some ask, "what creates these filters which allow us to deal with the irrefutable harshness of this world we live in?" Others are more practical and ask simply, "how can I get as much of that going as possible?" Now that God is dead or unemployed or whatever, some say, "it's all chemicals." Chemicals? Yes. unctuous liquids which geyser out of synapses in the lobes of the brain, lubing and facilitating the smooth turning of various gears and pulleys in there. It sort of explains everything: when the engine creaks and whines, you simply apply more motor oil, and the thing is good to go. In the olden days, when they were first working out this whole chemicals theory, if a person wasn't appearing to be producing enough of the feel-good chemicals, they'd drill a little hole in the front of that persons cranial lobe, like tapping a maple tree, hoping to hit a good vein of the sweet stuff. People are not really that analogous to maple trees, so that whole thing didn't work so great, but on the other hand people are more like trees that they are like cars, so they motor oil analogy is even worse. Now, they have the exact chemicals you need to filter out all your bummer thoughts worked out to T, and it's just like oil in a car, or toner in a copier, or adjusting the tracking on your VCR. I find the "jiffy lube" approach to human happiness and well-being very disturbing, but then again, I'm the kind of unamerican communist nutcase who gripes about them building malls and parking decks, too.

8. Digression number two: some comments on the genius of Black Sabbath

·   Black Sabbath, on their (perhaps ironically titled) album *Master of Reality*, seem to be inordinately obsessed with this whole existential void issue. While their previous albums display a confident, zesty Satanism, the later, more mature Black Sabbath finds them touching on various potential answers to the big questions. "Sweet Leaf" celebrates the drug-induced state as the path to enlightenment, while "After Forever," is an unabashed foray into born-again Christian rhetoric. "Children of the Grave," advocates a quasi-Marxist youth revolution, while "Into the Void," proposes that the answer to life's cruelty is to build a giant spaceship and just get the hell off planet earth, a planet which is cursed with "bad vibes." Clearly, there is a lot of confusion at work in this album, and the questions raised far outnumber the answers given. Like Nietzsche, Black Sabbath edges towards the abyss, growing increasingly brilliant as they hurtle inevitably towards the tragedy of that horrible disco album *technical ecstasy*, and then the musical syphilitic dementia of the later Ozzy Osbourne/Lita Ford ballads.

9. Ozzy Osbourne

Poor Ozzy Osbourne, in fact, has himself succumbed to the dominant paradigm that people are, for purposes of maintenance, indistinguishable from combustion engines and fax machines. Thus, the man who made a career as the soundtrack to teen suicide pacts everywhere now appears before us on talk shows, discussing how Prozac has really perked up his outlook on life, "So, Oz, you're on the 'Zac!" the talk show hosts rib him, and he laughs, and wonders what it was that he was so depressed about all those years.

10. Another failed attempt at coming to grips with the big question

The abyss looms, meanwhile, a hungry craw waiting to engulf the random passer-by into its vortex. "When you stare into the abyss, it stares into you," old man Nietzsche said, and apparently that is not a good thing. Some people flee from the craw and some people run blindly towards it wearing a kamikaze headband and aviation goggles. It's kind of like how people used to make plans for what they'd do when the World War three air raid sirens started going off-some people would stockpile canned goods in the hills to prepare for their new life, while others planned to drive straight to ground zero, or they'd have a map of the stars' houses ready to go, and planned to make a b-line to Kathy Lee Gifford's house, where they'd stand on the porch and bellow, "hey, five minutes 'till the end of civilization! Let's GET IT ON!"

But of course, these days the main problem is not five minutes until the end of the world, rather it seems that things just plan quite audaciously to keep on going and going. Those not fully lubed on the 'Zac must therefore rely on the people's Prozac, dope and/or alcohol, to keep them clear of the saliva speckled lips of the crushing abyss. Most people like to indulge in some form of controlled substance, at least from time to time. Used in moderation, these substances can be helpful in sidetracking the user from the great existential questions to the more pressing worldly concerns of full bladders, the need to throw up, attempting clumsy copulation, or just staring at the walls giggling about the funny colors displayed thereon.

Then again, there are those who imagine the intake of substances to be their screaming Ferrari-ride to ground zero, a straight ticket to the heart of the vortex, where some higher truth or deeper plain of understanding will be revealed to them. It's hard not to see the puritan New Englanders in these hyper-hedonists, in that strange circular way that most extremes tend to spiral themselves into. A life of frostbitten misery and starvation in service of stoic adherence to the word of some higher power, an all-knowing God who works in mysterious ways and thus answers all of life's questions is comforting, in the same way that you can imagine the strange comfort a junkie or the neighborhood crack-heads feel when you ask them to explain the trees or what the meaning of life is. "The meaning of life? That's easy," they say, "getting some more heroin." "You've obviously just chemically constructed a sense of meaning which is completely fraudulent, based on reducing your brain to a reflexive, lizard-like state of need-satiation," you counsel them. They nod understandingly, and then when you leave they steal your stereo and sell it.

11. The futility of it all

So, essentially, it's all pretty futile. God is dead, killed off by the human invention of things being "cool:" the introduction of this scale of valuation has destroyed all hope of religion ever playing a major role in the life of Western man, since religion is clearly "lame" and practiced by "dorks." Philosophical constructs for explaining reality, i.e, just thinking through things rationally, leads you to realize that it's all totally irrational and lose your brain. Narcoticizing yourself with either the prescription tranquilizers peddled by psychiatrists or the more illicit Prozacs offered up by the shady dudes on Rosemary street who approach you muttering, "you OK, man? You need anything?" (No, those guys are not interested in having a conversation about your self-esteem) makes you into a docile and malleable robot, and this is good for keeping Angst in check, but it's kind of like answering the query "what is the meaning of life?' with "Uh... what was the question again?" Although, I did see Ms. North Carolina once, on the Ms. America pageant, answer the question, "what does the concept of the 'melting pot' mean for American society and for your life?" with an indignant, "I refuse to answer the question on the grounds that it is too hard and I don't understand it. This is unfair to me, and I demand a new question." The judges conferred for a moment and then returned to give her an extra two points for candor and self-esteem. As a substitute question they asked her to explain her spiritual side and she opened her toothy, grinning mouth and babbled about Jesus for a while. So I guess, "uh, what was the question" worked pretty well for her. But that just brings us back around to the whole issue of "coolness" vs. "lameness," and though on the one hand it seems arguable that these values are subjective and one persons' worthwhile life is another persons tremendous waste of time, I do believe deep down in my heart, that the world of these conventional morons is a very "uncool" one and that, on their deathbeds, Ms. North Carolina, the judges at that beauty pageant, and all my other enemies will, for one brief and horrifying moment, see things from my point of view, be shaken to the core by how objectively lame they are, and regret that they wasted their life in the pursuit of interests which are barely noble by cockroach standards. Then they will die, expiring in the blaze of this awful truth, and, since there is no heaven or afterlife, their momentary suffering will be alleviated and it won't really matter one way or the other, much. Hallelujah.

For best results

Always maintains a clean,
organized and safe work
environment.

Does not abuse or take
advantage of sick time or
personal days; takes
corrective action to
prevent recurring absences.

Always appears well groomed
and observes
dress code.

Demonstrates a consistently
well organized approach to
all activities.

Is willing to adjust personal
schedule in order to complete
workload.

The Unabomber is on trial

as I write this, and attempting to fire his lawyers because they want to introduce evidence attesting to his mental instability. He insists on being tried as a rational adult, of having the court base its verdict on the strength of his ideas, rather than how much lube certain glands in his brain do or don't produce. More power to him! *(editor's note: later, of course, the trial ends in an anti-climactic plea-bargain. Dawg.)*

America, we should remember, has a long and noble tradition of political assassination. John Wilkes Booth, the man who shot Lincoln, yelled "sic semper Tyrannus!" to the crowded hall of theater-goers assembled underneath the presidential balcony. That translates essentially into "thus always to Tyrants!" in Latin. Latin! And he expected the populace to get it. Or at least, he expected to be widely quoted by scholars later- you can practically hear the little "[1]" dangling by the phrase, screaming out for a lengthy footnote. I like John Wilkes Booth because he knew incendiary Latin phrases and I like Lee Harvey Oswald because he had those sinister good looks and that classy Russian wife Marina (a name which ties in with some of my own unresolved teenage romance issues from the summer when I turned fifteen, but that's a whole different set of Revelations), and because he stood around with a sandwich board that said Hands Off Cuba and passed out leaflets to the people expressing his deep romantic love for Communism before taking the final plunge into less-talk-more-rock and climbing up into that book suppository to blow JFK's head off. I like lone nuts, I like organized plots, I like it all. What I like a lot less, though, is the whole trend towards pure insanity which has started creeping into the picture like a bad fad, like the Rubick's cube or shaving "Let's Make Slow Love" into the back of your head.

Take the case of John Hinckley. He gave the noble profession of political assassination a bad name. In 1980, as I watched the Carter-Reagan presidential debates, I had my first stirrings of political consciousness while listening to Reagan's emotional indictment of the liberal 1970's welfare programs documented on television programs such as "Good Times." Reagan made an analogy which moved me deeply: "Sometimes," he smiled paternalistically, "you have to cut off a kid's allowance." Being heavily entrenched in an allowance-based economy myself in 1980, I took the metaphor. literally, and exploded in an indignant outburst of rage, turning to my father and demanding that he cast his vote against this mad zealot. My politics were shaped profoundly by that experience and have really hardly evolved since. But my point in all of this is: even as early as 1980, there were a myriad of perfectly sound reasons for killing president Reagan. A case could easily have been made for the moral righteousness of this course of action. That is why, when my fourth grade class was dismissed early one afternoon when a weeping Mrs. Richter entered the classroom after lunch recess to announce in between choked sobs that the President had been shot, I was the first person in America to applaud. The statute of limitations for prosecution on the grounds of national treason having passed several years ago, I will now admit this fact: when school was let out early (this being Washington, DC, it was considered a big deal, kind of like when it snows in North Carolina) and my father came to pick me up, we drove home listening to NPR with enormous shit-eating grins of mirth plastered on our faces. "Hee hee hee," I said, as the reports of entry wounds and exit ruptures filtered into our car from strained, somber commentators. "Of course, if Reagan dies he'll be a martyr to the Right," my dad reasoned, "and plus, George Bush will become president, which is absolutely unthinkable. Ludicrous, really." In the passenger seat, however, I sat unconcerned with martyrdom and constitutional by-laws. My allowance was safe, that was all I knew.

But was Hinckley a crazed zealot, driven by Marxist fervor? Or perhaps a radical right winger trying to polarize the extreme right and left and start a race war in America? Was he even a disgruntled airline controller? Nooooooo. Much to the chagrin of assassination buffs everywhere, John Hinckley could concoct no higher motive than to impress a girl! And he didn't even come up with the idea himself, rather opting to steal his romance moves from a film in which the object of his amorous feelings, (the admittedly pretty damn babely) Jodie Foster, acted in! So clearly, even were she to be impressed by the gesture, she was going to be on to his lack of originality. Poor, dumb John Hinckley.

However, my sensibilities are deeply offended by the assassination attempt of Hinckley not because they are a testament to the damaging effects of the cinema on the central nervous system, not because Hinckley was a half-ass who didn't even get a Travis Bickle mohawk, but because at root, Hinckley was killing for mortal love instead of the more pure motivation, the morally superior romantic thrill of politically-motivated murder. That's one of my big gripes with modern man™- the emotional spectrum is so shallow, so adolescent. People today don't fall in love with politics, in the bad way, the spouse-killing, jump-off-a-bridge, desperate, sweaty, cut-your-ear-off-and-mail-it-to-your-loved-one kind of way. This is why I like the Unabomber. He's "old school." He lives in a cabin, he writes manifestos, he has no time for Jodie Foster or People magazine's *100 hottest heterosexuals* special editions.

And, oh, how they deride him for it. No one really thinks the Unabomber sucks for killing people- most people love and revere serial killers, and it's not like anyone of note was murdered, like, say, a fashion designer or football hero. The sad truth is, people despise the Unabomber because he is "square" and "out of it." The feds who raided his hutch in the mountains knew they had their man because they found perturbing evidence of a deranged mind within, notably "a manual typewriter."

In the new Gus Van Sant film, a work which I find somewhat horrifying in many ways, Robin Williams is attempting to impress chicks at a bar and asks the surly barkeep, "who is Ted Kozinski?" "Unabomber," the bartender replies. It seems funny that they would even bother to have a trial after Robin Williams has tacitly pronounced old Theodore guilty. Still, you can feel the Unabomber's pain, can't you? After all the struggle and sacrifice, essentially all just to get your arcane and somewhat wordy manifesto published in the New York Times, to sacrifice your life in a very real sense to the power and dissemination of your ideas, and then to have your own lawyers get up and try to portray you as "two fries short of a happy meal," well- that must really hurt. It would injure Theodore Kozinski's feelings quite deeply, I am sure, to be sitting in this coffee shop where I am sitting and hear a table of sorority girls discussing his trial- they are probably psychology majors- deriding him as, "another classic case of someone who'll do anything for attention," as if they recently read all about it in <u>Women who Love too Much</u>, or <u>Men who Love Women who Love too Much</u>, or <u>Men who Love too Much and the Social Institutions which Oppress them.</u> Theodore, I would love to answer on your behalf, I would love to stand up for you since you can't be here to stand up for yourself; I'd like to get out of my seat and leap on the table, point an accusing finger in the direction of these prattling wretches and scream, "The Industrial Revolution and its consequences have been a disaster for the human race!" You get those urges, the urge to say "fuck" during a tense family dinner, or whip out your private parts during a business meeting. But I don't do it, Theodore, because I am not crazy. I think about that a lot: how easy it is to imagine "insane" things that you could do at any moment, and how the only difference in the sane and the crazy, really, is whether or not you act on those impulses. I sit still. I behave myself. I am not crazy.

al burian

BACK

307 blueridge road carrboro, NC 27510

] Electrical   ☐ Explosion   ☐ Fall   ☐ Falling object
] Knife   ☐ Lifting   ☐ Pencil/Pen   ☐ Poison

I Cut   ☐ Dislocation   ☐ Drowning   ☐ Fracture
I Severed   ☐ Shock   ☐ Sprain   ☐ Wound

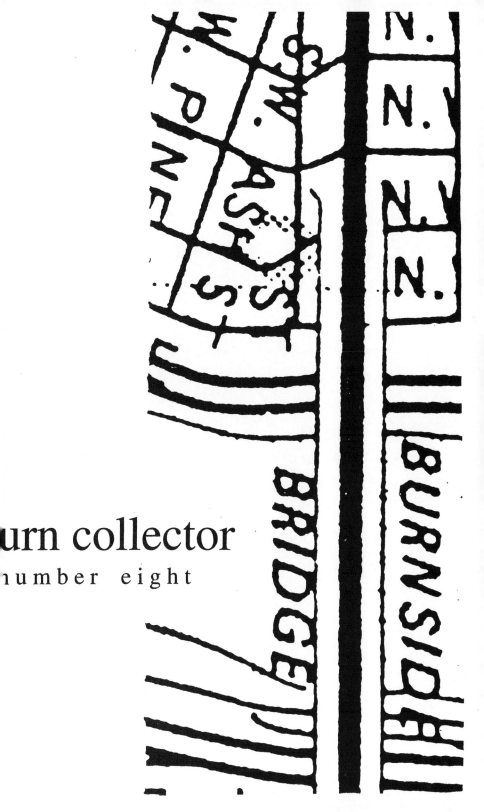

urn collector

number eight

<u>one</u>

YOUNG HEARTS BE FREE TONIGHT

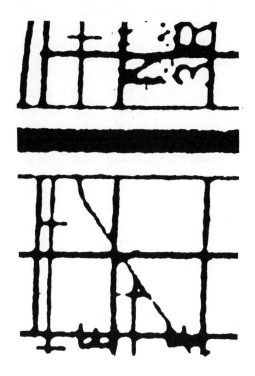

1.

I'm unemployed.
So I figure, why not stay up late?

There's nothing quite like *free time*-- out of a job and gorging yourself on that devalued commodity, ticking useless time; frittering away your existence in half-hour increments, on a sit-com or a magazine or staying out until all hours talking to no one about nothing. Hey, I got nowhere to be tomorrow. I don't have anything, actually, except an overabundance of time. Sometimes being unemployed is liberating, and sometimes it's debilitating. I've got the paralysis lately, stare blankly at the clock, make a phone call, go hang out.

Dave's dad died recently. He tries not to think about it. Dave is one of the few people I still know from college, but he doesn't like to talk about school, which is fine- I don't like to talk about it either. We have plenty of other things to talk about, to distract him, like finding a house or playing guitar. We go out to a bar in a part of town where he won't see anyone he knows; it's a blue-collar, older-crowd type of place, and settling into a booth among the Coors posters and dart boards, with the din of drunken conversation buzzing around me, I can't believe this is me and not some kind of *Saint Elmo's Fire* movie I'm acting in. We marvel at the proliferation of mustaches-Portland is so over-run with hipsters now, you see bus-loads of them, packs of them everywhere, and I wonder how the mustachioed and hair sprayed patrons of this bar perceive that phenomenon. I noticed right off that there was an inordinately dense population of crazy people walking the streets here, and I wonder if to the outside eye the green hair and ill-fitting thrift-store clothes just makes it seem like the number of free-range insane people has shot up of late. As if on cue, a pack of skater twentysomethings stumbles in the door, boards under armpits, looking around sheepishly, sizing up the camp value of the establishment. "Wow, it's like there's so many of them that they just infiltrate every crevice," I say. "like cockroaches."

"And everyone is lumping us in with them," Dave laments. It's true: thrift store sweaters and thick-rimmed retro-glasses, that's us. You get what you pay for.

We stick around for a little while longer. In the adjacent section of the bar, among the pool tables and video-poker games, a portly fifty-year old man is having a birthday party, carousing noisily with various friends and family members. Suddenly, a woman appears seemingly out of nowhere to begin stripping and lap-dancing in the birthday-boy's lap, which elicits hoots of unconditional approval from every single person in the bar. The birthday boy looks somewhat chagrinned, but then, what really is the couth way to handle a naked stranger gyrating in your lap while your loved ones hoot at you? In the time it takes me to process the scene and fully take in the weirdness of what is transpiring, Dave is out the door and sprinting down the street at a moderately brisk pace.

We take our business into another bar, this one with a dimly-lit dance-floor on which a few couples gyrate obscenely to the sound of a guy in a red tuxedo playing guitar solos over pre-recorded synthesizer versions of Top 40 hits. Dave and I have a pretty good laugh at this guy, a vapid chuckle at the same pop culture which Dave finds himself moments later once again lamenting that he can't fit in to, that he can't camouflage himself. I buy him a beer.

2.

I'm having trouble

sleeping since I got back to Portland. After I drop Dave back off at home, I go for a walk in the cool of an early spring night, the first night of clear sky after months of rain in the town I have just arrived in. Watching radio towers blink in the distance, I think about the cooling towers of the Naragassett Power Company in Providence, RI and how I would watch them out of my window, trying to decipher the pattern of three lights which blinked on the towers, waiting around for them to blink in unison. I convinced myself that this was some kind of secret sign, and I told myself when I left that if I didn't see those lights blink in unison one more time before I left I was fucked. I did. So am I not fucked? Unfortunately, I am fucked just by the knowledge of that cooling tower, the inability to live a life without constant comparison. I saw a survey in a magazine at a friend's house and one of the questions was "true or false: the thing that would make me truly happy is impossible." Too much information tends to be my downfall.

I'm not tired and so, not knowing what else to do, I walk up the street to another bar. Two fifteen in the morning-- west coast time, impossibly enough- seated in the back corner of the bar, not drinking, not socializing, just sitting, semi-catatonic. Five minutes until they kick me out. I have no idea why I'm here, in Portland. I guess there's something to be said for a place that can make you feel so intensely freaked out that you can't think or speak or sleep, that elicits such a strong chemical reaction in the synapses of my dumb-as-fuck head. Tectonic plate shifts in the crust of the earth have thrown the United States into a tilt, so that the west coast rests at the bottom of an incline, leading those with less than sturdy footing to go careening down the slope, landing haphazardly in the refuse pile of lost souls on the bottom coast. Everyone here is from somewhere else, eager to make conversation because they don't really know anyone either, yet, and no one likes to be asked the most pivotal of questions, so you learn eventually to not even ask. "So, why are you here?" "Oh, uhhh, you know....." they mumble, then turn the question back on you sharply, "why are YOU here?" "Tectonic plates," I say.

"Last call!" Jim, tending the bar tonight, good natured and boyishly cute in an off-putting way, the way you imagine child movie stars look later in life, comes around to ask me if I want anything. My head is down on the table. "Hey, are you OK?" he asks.

"Fine," I moan.

"You sure?" he pauses, hovering over me.

"Ugh. Yes. Fine."

"Really."

Jim contemplates my slack, lifeless limbs, my sprawled out, defeated form. "Look," he says, "come over to my house. Have a few beers. We'll have a good time. You'll feel better."

I look at the clock. Two twenty. I got lucky this time. Jim has unsuspectingly snatched me from the jaws of a horrible fate: I'm quite certain that, left to my own devices for the evening, the morning light would easily find me with a full beard, raving about the Nixon Watergate tapes and trying to sell balloon sculptures on Belmont street, a glazed, crazed vacant sheen over my eyeballs which nothing would ever again remove.

We walk over to Jim's house, which is strewn with debris-mostly bicycle parts, welded into grotesque and monstrous shapes, which clutter the living room menacingly. Moldy, brittle-paged Playboy magazines from the early sixties, stacks of which can be bought for a quarter from glazed-eyed vendors on Belmont, are strewn haphazardly about the coffee table. But drinking a couple of beers and having a good time is distracting, and I am grateful for this in an inexpressibly profound way, the simple kindness of picking someone up off the floor and telling them a couple of jokes or good stories. He tells me a good one about his all-time low point, a situation which occurred while hitch-hicking through Montana. "This guy picked me up," he relates, "and he was driving a hundred fifty miles an hour, smoking crack, and searching for some spot on the road where he'd dropped off a secret stash of cocaine a year and a half ago. I tell you, I'd never smoked crack before, and," he leans in, imparting the nugget of wisdom which nests at the center of his tale, "man, there is no lower feeling than coming down off of crack at a truck stop in Montana where you've just been dropped off and realizing you've just hitched a ride two hundred miles in the opposite direction from where you were heading."

"No, I imagine that's one of the great crushers," I nod.

"One of the all-time, most fantastic crushers," laughs Jim.

"See, man, that seems so terrible it almost seems good," I propose.

He shakes his head, still cackling, "No, it's just terrible."

I stumble home around five in the morning, to find the doors at Tedra's house all locked. I sit on the porch for a while, in darkness, watching the fat wedge of moon in the sky. After a while I get up and walk some more, and end up at Dunkin Donuts at six a.m. watching the sun slowly rising on yet another day. In the reflection of the window I look green and dishevelled, with sunken black holes for eye sockets and my hair sticking up absurdly in all directions. I can't help but grin foolishly at myself. Just the other morning I sat in this same Dunkin Donuts and watched a punker couple making out at the bus stop, oblivious to the bus passing by in their total rapture. I couldn't believe it. Staying up all night doesn't really mean anything, but still, when you see that old man sun start fucking up the sky with his red and gold rays you can't help but feel that you have accomplished something amazing, to arrive at this great moment, and maybe nowhere more so than Portland, which constantly seems to have the most amazing skies. This is one of Portland's main virtues- the sky drives you crazy, makes you feel small under its grandioseness, or makes you feel like the star of an opera. It's a multi-faceted sky, but always dramatic.

3.

Tedra finds me asleep on the porch as she leaves for work. "I guess if you're going to stay on the couch I should get you a key," she observes. I stumble in to wash my face and drink a cup of coffee. I have a job interview scheduled at the Kinko's copy center in Northeast. Unfortunately, I appear to be a shoo-in for the position, and this depresses me greatly.

I'm maneuvering a gargantuan blue dodge van (borrowed) through a snarl of mid-morning traffic, burning my mouth on my third cup of coffee and swearing. I've slept about two hours and the sense of sunrise serenity which had seemed to realign my world-view is eroding back into the grim desperation of a life out of control, a life which is moving of its own volition in directions I had not intended to go. All in all, it's sad to say, my work ethic is a sad and meager thing. I've often conjectured that I may well be the absolute worst worker on the face of the planet. If you think about it, why *not* me? It has to be someone. My career as a wrench in the gears of industry probably started as an academic interest- my early exposure to economic theory resonated with the daily experience around me and I found myself dividing things along Marxist class lines, which added an air of righteousness to my extended breaks and stealing of pens. But truthfully, I think, what has always lain at the heart of my work ethic is an inability to face up to the concept of having a bad time. Look, if you're going to try to purchase hourly blocks of my valuable existence, I don't blame you for trying to get the best deal you can; how can you blame me for my part in the haggle? I'm just trying to maximize my own personal profitability by giving you the least amount of work for your dollar that I can. That's nothing but fair. The same corporations who decided it was more cost-effective to deal with the occasional law-suit occurring as a result of faulty Pintos which exploded on impact than to recall the cars and fix the problem- the same corporations who jip you out of those extra few sips of cola by making the bottom of the bottle concave- these captains of industry want to come down on *me* for being cost-efficient!? It's the height of hypocrisy.

In high school I worked in a movie theater and we used to go hide out in the theaters during shows to avoid cleaning up, or even sneak back to some employees' house who was unfortunate enough to live within sneaking distance of the strip mall, there to listen to records, read comic books and generally bask in the thrill of Fucking Around On The Clock. When, eventually, I was caught and called in to the manager's office, I was completely indignant.

"Do you like your job, Al?" The manager began, rhetorically.

"Are you serious?" I yelled, "Hell NO! I've been working here a year and you only gave me that one measly raise a week before they raised the minimum wage anyway, so now I'm just back to working for the minimum! That's what you get when you pay people the minimum possible, man- you get the minimum work!"

Whether my compelling argument won the boss over or whether it was the sincerity of my convictions which reminded him of a younger, more idealistic managerial training school go-getter will remain one of those great unanswered historical questions. I did not get fired; I'd like to think.perhaps in some small way my words touched my manager. In any case, he was caught embezzling ten thousand dollars two weeks later, and so I outlasted him.

It's hot as fuck in the speeding metal box and sweat is dripping from my brow, stinging my eyes. "Good God, what am I thinking? Who are these motherfuckers? What kind of robot drones would populate such a place of employment? Jesus!" I bark in impotent rage, swerving sharply as I career into the Kinko's parking lot and slam the side of the gargantuan blue van into a Range Rover. There is a strangely pleasant tinkle of glass and the shrill whine of a car alarm.

"Whoops," I say.

That's the thing about not sleeping: one minute your head is a mass of jumbled contusions and confusions, the next moment everything is brought startlingly into focus and inflicts whiplash with its simplicity and truth. I stare into the widow of the copy store for one second, watching people mill about, cutting, pasting, collating, oblivious to the clamoring cacophony of the wounded Range Rover in the lot. *Well, that's it then,* a voice in my head calmly explains. *Park the car. Write a note. Go in there. Interview. Get the job. Start working to pay off the car you just fucked up.*

Or:

"Fuck all this," I realize, stepping on the gas and lumbering away. Back in the stream of traffic, the adrenalin surge of my daredevil escape from wage labor subsiding, and, looking in the rearview mirror to verify that no one seems to be following me waving fists or motioning me to pull over, a strange sense of apocalyptic joy overtakes me. No job, no home: equilibrium. It all adds up to zero in some sketchy arithmetic of rawness. I eat out of the bulk bins at Fred Meyer and drink what people give me when they find me near suicide, wandering the streets in the middle of the night. It's OK.....

I'm burning a bridge. It feels pretty good. If too many options is the problem, the solution seems fairly obvious. Now there's one spot on the map I will be too gimped out to ever show my face, one less sordid fate which can befall me. It's like sculpting in reverse; carving your destiny out of granite with randomly placed dynamite charges which detonate landslides, earthquakes, mass annihilation and upheaval, until the rubble clears and you look up to the face of the mountain and see that it's a bust. Either of George Washington, or the other kind of bust. Either way.

4.

Bright afternoon sun.

Van rolls down the street conspicuously. Cops seem to be circling around, like lazy predators. Did someone catch my license plate? I pull over; best to stop driving. Put a quarter in a pay phone and dial. The other end rings, tinny, sounding transcontinental, and a few blocks away a telephone is ringing off the hook.

Kevin answers. "Hello?" Syrupy southern accent in my ear.

"Kevin!" I explode. "I've had a car accident!"

"Oh God," he gasps. "Are you okay?"

"Well.... sure, yeah," I say.

"Where are you? Should I come pick you up?"

"Oh, no, It's really OK," I stammer. "I'm just kind of freaked out." I explain the circumstances.

"Is your car fucked up?" Kevin asks. I haven't even bothered to check. I let the receiver dangle, and walk around to the passenger side of the big blue bastard. There is a minor welt, a gouge in the paint and perhaps a small dent in the resale value.

I get back on the phone. "Man, where are you? Are you nearby? You should come on over here." Kevin suggests.

Right. Hide out for a while. Let the trail cool down.

"OK," I say.

Good old Kevin. Arriving at his doorstep, I find him sitting on the porch, smoking a cigarette. He waves, smiles. "Howdy."

A good-natured, quiet sketchiness under the earnest exterior, Kevin exudes calm from steel-blue eyes and his almost cartoonishly handsome sculptural protruding chin. We both grew up in the South, we both share an affinity for the early works of a number of disreputable homoerotically charged heavy metal bands, and we both feel alienated by Portland, so we have plenty in common. He makes a pot of coffee and some quesadillas. "Keh-sah-diaz," he enunciates heavily, the way commentators on NPR do when they say "ni-CA-rag-ua," rolling the r's.

"I can't hack this shit," I moan, flinging myself into a limp heap on the couch. In another universe, black and white 1950's robots pummel each other awkwardly, muted on the TV screen, performing a frenetic dance for no one. "Man, I *can't* have a job! The very thought of it makes me break out in hives."

Kevin nods, thoughtfully.

"The copy shop, too," I continue, "I mean, what a horrific institution. The whole technology hasn't even been around long enough for them to measure the health effects of it all. I swear, whenever I work around those things I can practically feel the tumors forming in my stomach."

"Well, you seem to have solved the problem, anyway," Kevin reassures me, "I mean, it's all a moot point now."

That *is* reassuring. Snapped from the jaws of death.

"Still," I realize, "I'm going to need some form of income at some point. I'm down to my last few bucks by now, and staying at Tedra's house was cool at first, but I've been in town for a while now without finding a place to live. It's a real Catch-22: as soon as I actually start earnestly trying to find a place to live I'll *really* be faced with the need to get a job, and so it's much easier to just blow the whole vicious circle off. Man, I'm incredibly poorly socialized, aren't I?"

Kevin chews, listening attentively. We grew up three hours apart and never met. My parents are artist-intellectuals who sent me to a private Quaker school so that I wouldn't get beat up in the public schools, a certain magnetic skill for attracting blows having reared it's embryonic head early on. During the Gulf War I made a sculpture to show my protest and displayed it at a community arts center. That's the kind of kid I was. Kevin tells me about sneaking out of the house when he was younger to attend a pro-choice rally. His face was broadcast on the evening news in passing, and a friend of the family, the tight-knit noose of conservative southern Christian defenders of value and virtue, called Kevin's parent's to tell them where he'd been. His parents were furious. I'm astounded.

"How did you even manage to formulate those values?" I ask. "Where did you get the idea to go to a pro-choice rally?"

"Punk rock lyrics," Kevin shrugs, turning and walking into the kitchen to get a glass of water.

The process of socialization is a strange one. Your parents map out a psychological blueprint for you, attempting to impart whatever values and survival skills they deem necessary for a functional citizen of the community, nation, or world to posses. Somewhere in there you get a Black Flag record and years of etiquette training, Bible study, therapy, and child-rearing manual reading are rendered impotent and useless; even the sacred bonds between parent and child, the bedtime stories and baseball games, become hollow and archaic. This was the case for both Kevin and myself. Neither of our parents are too thrilled about the presence of Black Flag in our formation of Gestalt. Like living in a foreign country, even when you speak the language it's nice to go to a party at the Embassy once in a while, speak the mother tongue for a minute- and in that same way it's nice to talk to someone who lets you know that you're not alone in the world, that those 80's cold-war era nihilist records, thirteen songs in twenty minutes, the ones which convinced you that everything previous generations had strived for had led to nothing but an eternity of alienation from your surroundings at worst, and instantaneous thermonuclear obliteration at best, have some resonance in the consciousness of your peers.

So now what? A strange situation now. No house, no job, not trying to find either one, really. Very precarious; what do I do all day? Nothing. I can't figure out how to get into gear.

"Why did you move back to Portland?" Kevin wants to know.

"I don't know," I shake my head, "Claustrophobia? Nostalgia? Chemical imbalance? I knew within about twenty minutes of returning here that I wasn't going to make it, honestly."

"It's definitely weird out here," Kevin nods, "After growing up in South Carolina, going to school there and everything, I was just ready for something different, a challenge. I didn't really realize how comfortable the familiarity of home and routine is-- it's sort of a humbling experience, being out here."

"Yeah, it's like you keep waiting for things to be easy. But they never are. I don't know-- Clearly some deity is testing us on something and we are failing in a fairly grandiose way."

"All the kids are headed here," Kevin laughs morosely, "I don't think anyone knows why, really."

"Man, you should get in on my whole tectonic plates theory," I suggest.

Quesadillas polished off, we decide to take advantage of the nice weather and do something outside. I'm still obsessed with my future employment uncertainty.

"Man, you should temp," suggests Kevin. We are in a park flying a kite. "I just got this job through my temp agency which is pretty good. I stand in a parking lot with a counter and click off how many people go in and out of the entrance to this building."

"What for?"

"I don't know, actually. I wasn't told that. But listen to this: my housemate Bill got a job dressing as a peanut M&M and handing out free samples of candy at a grocery store!"

"You're kidding."

"No, seriously," Kevin explains, " and they promised Andrew a job dressing as a giant bottle of Powerade. Hell, man, he's already been Mr. Peanut! They handle all the dress-as-a-chicken-and-walk-around-a-mall type jobs in the area."

"I'm qualified to dress as a chicken," I assert.

When I get back to Tedra's house, I call up my friend Wells, who has been temping for a while.

"My job is the absolute worst experience I've ever had in my life," he asserts.

"What's the name of your temp agency?"

"Manpower. You should sign up," he says. "I get twenty-five bucks if you mention my name as a reference."

5.

My ex-girlfriend Elizabeth is in town. She is interviewing at a graduate school in Seattle. There's nothing like the evocation of grad school to dampen the *joy de vivre* implicit in your story of how you almost got that job at the copy store but then hit and run a car instead.

"Yeah, so that's pretty much what I'm up to these days," I squirm over dinner, having just recited the hit and run story anyway. What else am I going to talk about?

"Hmmm," Elizabeth says, non-plussed.

It's pretty embarrassing. But then, her rationales for grad school leave me staring back at her just as blankly. All we really crave in this day and age is for someone to be self-assured, for someone to display a directional motivation and some sense of comfort in the security of knowing where they are going. It doesn't seem like a lot to ask, but you don't find many people who deliver. The muttered excuses and dismissals with which we preface our lives put all involved on edge.

Leaving the restaurant, she has to get up early to drive up to Seattle, I'm telling her that I was glad to see her and it's awkward in a way I've never really experienced before, not just over as in I-used-to-be-with-you-but-now-it's-over; this is alien and absurd, the feeling of watching a chasm grow between the tips of your toes and her toes. She's not like me at all, and I try to kiss her and get her to hang

around with me some more, but she has to get up early and besides--
she's staying at her *other* ex-boyfriends' house and where would we
hang out, anyway? On Tedra's porch? Good night, Al. Good night. See
you later. Good luck with everything.

Walking home. I never really felt stupid for not having a
car or a house or any money.... those are worries which have always
seemed universes away to me. Lower Southeast is dismal, empty, run
down with burnt-out industrial buildings and the kind of brain-
deadening nine-to-five office supply warehouses which exist only to
provide daily exercises in ritual torture for people who have done
something wrong in another life. Certainly not this one; certainly none
of us have done anything to deserve this lot right now. I won't be able
to sleep, once again. I'll walk around all night. I just keep getting
dumber, it seems.

Portland could not really be described as a twenty-four hour
town by any stretch of the imagination. There's a bowling alley,
various convenience stores, and the hot-cake house, which is where I
find myself hanging out instead of ending up back at home. Two drunks
yell at each other across the table in the booth across from mine-
"Jeff! You are lovin' those eggs, huh! What the fuck! Sit down, man!
Pass me the Catsup!!!" They crack themselves up.

One of the drunks gets up from the table and stumbles over to
the jukebox. He returns with a mischievous grin plastered over his
face underneath dried up egg-yolk. Moments later, Kenny G. begins
blaring through the dingy eatery.

"JEFF!!!!!!!!" The other drunk yells, "YOU didn't put this
on, did you? Jeff!!! Oh, man. Oh no."

"huh huh huh huh," cackles the Kennyseur.

"You know what I hate about Kenny G? He's rich. You know
why I dislike him? He can play. Motherfucker can play his horn. I'll
give that to him. I just wish......... I just wish he had some balls, man!
I just like a horn player with some nuts is all!" Then a quiet, pensive
moment, and he continues in a hushed, somber tone: "Jeff. Tell me
honestly, man..... do I have a voice? Should I do it, man? Should I
keep on playing or give it up?" Playing horn, I surmise. The thing that
would make him truly happy is impossible.

Jeff continues to play Kenny G songs on the jukebox, driving
his friend into a frenzy. "I can't eat! I cannot eat to this! Fuck!!!!"

6.

I wake up

in the morning and instantly realize I will not make it through the day. Pacing the living room in a state of agitation, biting my nails and pulling my hair neurotically; you can almost literally climb the walls at times, if you get enough pacing momentum going. I'm always reminded of Sylvester's guilt after he (mistakenly) believes he has killed the Tweety Bird: he wears a circular trench into the floor in a cartoon which horrified me as a child, almost brought me to tears.

I get a brisk power-walk going down Division street, burning off calories around the thighs and butt, swinging those arms with determination like the sorority sisters do it in my home town. It actually feels pretty good; you can imagine that the clear, oxygenated feeling of deep breaths and forcing blood through the veins on pure G-force could cure a hangover, absolve you of some low-grade sins, maybe take your tests for you and type out a resume. At the very least the physical exertion crowds out panic.

I stop at a coffee shop to read the paper. They are lying strewn about the tables, left over from the morning rush. The girl working scowls but doesn't kick me out for not buying anything. Then the realization kicks in: Tedra's making waffles. She had told me as much the previous night. There is a big waffle festival going on right now, a behemoth brunch happening a few feet away from the very couch which I currently conceptualize as home.

I don't fly into a frenzy at the thought of it; in fact I calmly peruse the paper for a while, until inevitably I realize that I am hopelessly behind on world events and can't make head or tail of a single god damn thing in there. I get up and walk out, calmly, towards home and the waffles.

The door is wide open at Tedra's house, and when I walk in there is silence and Tedra standing in the exact center of the living room, staring straight at me.

"No waffles," she says.

I look over at the chalk board, which is shaped like a brontosaurus, on which I see the chilling sentiment echoed, scrawled in chalk: *no waffles.*

"Are you having a, uh, domestic situation?" I ask.

She nods, vaguely, as if dazed, and walks right past me and out the door. So that's the way it's going to be. No waffles. The old get-in-a-fight-with-your-boyfriend and the next thing you know, it's no waffles for Burian. Fate has dealt me a bitter hand. I'm stunned, and look back at the chalk board, which leers back at me. In ghostly scrawl, jittery from frayed nerves, no waffles. Why me, Lord?

The whole waffle thing, I realize, was the only thing keeping me even temporarily together and now that that's out the window I'm back to my early morning anxiety and inability to deal with this inexplicably horrible day. I step out onto the porch and into the glaring sunlight, squinting. Around the corner, Tedra's neighbors have a pet pig in their yard- I stop to poke a stick through the fence, budging up against it's fat snout, listening to it snort indignantly as a pig is wont to do. A pig in the yard, how crazy, I'm thinking, as I walk over to the Hawthorne street 7-11 to buy a bottle of malt liquor, which I then devour somberly on the stoop in front, facing the parking lot, the motley little shanty-town of Thai restaurants and bong vendors across the street, the sluggish traffic of VW vans and roller-bladers meandering down the center, to be ensnarled by the intersection of 39th and Hawthorne, the most mundane cross roads of the world available, where you could sit on a bus stop bench and see everyone you ever knew go by eventually, and you could wave with some small modicum of enthusiasm, but you wouldn't be too psyched, really, because, fuck, it's just 39th and Hawthorne, and here you both are.

However, there is something very killer about drinking whatever battery acid and paint thinner concoction it is that they make malt liquor out of, in broad daylight, slumped down on the pavement. It's one of those acts of such total defeat that it becomes a definitional moment.

A quarter of an hour later, considerably cheered up by the way events have begun to transpire, Burian stumbles around the residential thoroughfares of southeast Portland, relatively certain that he will not get hit by a car in this winding labyrinth of picturesque rented huts. Drunk, I can sort of face up to some of the darker implications of this whole brunch fiasco and the possibility that it is, in fact, my presence on the couch which has caused the whole relational tension between Tedra and her dude that has, in turn, led to my being extraordinarily drunk on account of my empty stomach, which all leads back to the whole lack of breakfast foods being served. A vicious circle, and if there was only some way to sit the dude down, and look him earnestly in the eye and let him know that I'm really just into the waffles as far as his girlfriend goes.

But then again, that's a horrible thought. You can almost respect a man more for trying to get with your girl than you can for just wanting to get some breakfast items. All living things at some level are in pursuit of breakfast items; they wake up and immediately start foraging. Waffles, malt liquor- the whole thing makes me feel like hamster, or like the pig in Tedra's neighbors' yard, sniffing the ground for a beetle to gnaw on. Love, betrayal, jealousy- those are all the higher motives, the ones which spawn all the really quality literature and art, the useless cultural artifacts which people rig up because they've evolved to the point where they have way too much free time. Tedra and Todd are real people, having some sort of human interaction, while I'm functioning on this psuedo-pet level, running around the neighborhood like some weird, retarded mutt that got loose for a while, who will probably straggle back in time to pee on their lawn, and I'm not just extending the metaphor there.

And, sure enough, here I am, coming around the corner, and there they are, sitting on the porch, talking it out, calmly.

"Hey, motherfuckers!" I yell mirthfully, swinging the bottle around a little for effect.

They are laughing, cooing at each other, and it seems they've made up in the interim. "I guess it was a misunderstanding." Tedra says.

"Yeah? Well, fuck, man! Look at me and how much I don't have any waffles to show for this whole day," I shake a fist in the sky.

They laugh at me (lucky me- they could be throwing my stuff on the lawn) and Tedra promises me waffles some other day. But I am a completely ungracious houseguest and, still bitching, I saunter into her kitchen and start drinking out of bottles of liquor in the small stash that comprises the meager liquor cabinet.

By six o'clock I am completely wrecked and I remember that I am supposed to meet Kevin and go to a party with him. I wander down Thirty Ninth and turn at Belmont. I can't really remember where he lives exactly; the streets down there become winding labyrinths and I get lost without much effort. I keep forgetting who I'm looking for or what I'm doing.... my mind reels and I am unstuck in time, can't even remember when this is. Am I a sophomore in college? Here's the pink house I lived in then with my girlfriend-- do my keys still work and can I just walk in the door and resume that strain of alien existence? No, the keys don't work; what's more, there's someone coming to the door- I see the glimmering shadow of a movement, a face radiating anxiety through the glass pane of the window, the door opens and I am already retreating down the front steps, laughing, before an alien voice asks me what I'm doing.

Ah, yes. Kevin. Can't find house. When is this? What the hell. Here's the Seven-Eleven I used to hang out at. I stumble in, perusing the aisles with spare change in my pocket. The clerk is watching me nervously. He has a crew-cut and glasses and the scars of an acne-riddled adolescence which he's only just put behind him. This guy has worked here forever, and what's more, he's a real spaz. I can tell I'm about to get it, so I make a purchase of Lance choc-o-lunch cookies for twenty five cents. He looks at the item, then up at me, and then back at the item, scowling, "Twenty five cents," without looking back at me. I slide a quarter his way. "No sales tax," I gloat. "Not here. Not in Portland, Oregon."

He shrugs. I pop a chocolatey wafer in my mouth and head over to the magazine rack, where I begin leafing through a body building magazine. Is it the audacity of this act, a skinny drunk kid eating junk food and daring to ogle the gigantic tumors of bulk which festoon the Lee Haneys of the world, daring, perhaps to dream of a day when I might be all pumped up, which sets the clerk over the edge? I don't know. But a shrill scream erupts behind me in any case.

"Will you PLEASE hurry up! I've got a LOT of work to do tonight!"

I throw up my hands in a gesture of compliance (magazine tumbles to the floor, landing in a graceless heap, like a dead bird) and back out the door. I've heard the tales of this psychotic alpha-nerd assistant manager, who routinely refuses service to people he deems unfit clientele for his establishment, and calls the police to disband loiterers in the parking lot six or seven times a night. How quintessentially unamerican, to take a stand against the institution of teenagers hanging out in Seven-Eleven parking lots! That motherfucker!

Not that he hasn't gotten his. It has become routine sport, even in some circles revered ritual, to sally forth on slow evenings and find entertainment in torturing and hassling this self-appointed convenience mart Mussolini. All sectors of society (at least, all sectors which converge on Seven-Elevens), the street vagrant, the college student, the skater kids, all these disparate elements seem to find a common mission in the torment of this poor soul. He, for his part, interprets all this as less a personal attack than as one more sign of the world sliding into an anarchic Mad Max-style post-apocalyptic nightmare where no one, and I mean no one, has any regard for the "this is not a library" sign he has meticulously scripted in magic marker and affixed above the magazine rack. It's an emotional arms race which escalates nightly, and, as I realize all this, I turn in the parking lot and extend him a defiant bird: my contribution to the conversation.

Poor guy. Our eyes lock through the glass partition for a moment and he stares into my soul, stone faced, finding nothing of merit, no reason why I should not be swept from the earth in some great cleansing flood. He then turns away, bustling up and down the aisles, tidying up, neatening displays of candy bars which ruffians have dishevelled. "A lot of work to do." I am startled by the realization that he was being serious.

Slightly sobered by this encounter, I find my way to my destination, the aforementioned party, which is taking place in a crowded duplex further down Belmont street. The mind reels: a folk-singer is performing in the living room while bright-eyed kids in square-rimmed glasses sit cross-legged on the floor, immobile and attentive, and she sings a song entitled "we are fucking." Every song she sings is preluded by an extensive explanatory monologue, guiding us through the twists and turns of the vast epic poem she is crooning, her *Illiad* of sixteen-year old failed lesbian relationships, all songs written in the last three days.....
I'm in the kitchen telling everyone about my traumatic morning. "It was written on the dinosaur-shaped chalkboard: no waffles." I testify.

Kevin shows up eventually. I have the momentary illusion that everything is going to be OK in my life. In the bathroom, someone understands me and my existential horrors: they have written NO WAFFLES in soap on the mirror.

7.

Fucked up dreams sometimes. Sometimes no
dreams at all: less and less these days. I have the distinct feeling
that things are building to a climactic end, a magnificent unraveling
which will leave us all at a loss, naked and squinting in the bright,
bright florescent sunrise to follow this dark age. This is what they
call millennial anxiety, I guess, but I dislike those cheap shot
answers, the sociological aggregate behavior patterns which explain
our herd-like hand-wringing. I have no idea what possessed me to do
any of this. This life is a slingshot of nostalgias; every zig zag back
and forth and up and down compounds the problem, adding a new
layer to the arcane web of what vacation I'm on vacation from.

Tedra doesn't ask a lot of questions or demand a coherent
defense for living, which is a relief. Mostly, she's just into it if you eat
a lot of the pies which she is constantly baking. A fantastic use-value
friendship: if she was the kind of person who baked pies and then got

mad at people for eating them, what purpose would I serve? I'd be dead weight.

We sit around her kitchen on weekend afternoons or evenings when she gets home from her job at the abortion clinic. I've pitched my idea for a pro-choice television commercial to her a few times: Tedra in the garden, picking tomatoes. Tedra baking a pie. Tedra listening to the new *Built to Spill* album, and then critiquing it for the band members, who sit attentively on her couch, listening as they eat some pie. The hip homemaker, the friend to humanity, the good neighbor- final shot, close-up on Tedra's face, as she smiles warmly and says, "Hi, my name is Tedra. I'm an abortionist." Play that on MTV twice a day, I insist, and all the plastic fetus dolls and maniacs with bullhorns could never take away something fundamental about the right to abortion, something enmeshed far deeper in the fabric of our society than supreme court rulings or fire-bombings: abortion would be *cool*.

Use-value friendship: I pay for my pie and sleeping on the couch with an endless barrage of sit-com pilot ideas, half-baked sociological theories, embarrassing anecdotes and gossip. She smiles politely at most of it.

Tedra and and I went to the same college, briefly; she quickly realized that the whole thing was a scam for keeping directionless kids confused enough that they'd end up paying for eight or ten years of schooling before finally settling on the six-month vocational course which would actually get them a job. So Tedra dropped out of my relatively pointless college, enrolled in a nursing school, and is now on her way to being certified as a midwife. She is a person with an intense sense of direction, an unusually well-articulated notion of herself as fulfilled by what America offers its privileged class, the "pursuit of happiness"- domesticity, security, career. This is what she wants. And in that sense, I'm just as much a voyeur in her life as she is in mine, perhaps even more titillated by the petty details of her existential landscape than she by mine. "You make how much money?" I gasp in amazement. "You're actually looking into buying a house? You want to have a kid? Before the end of the twentieth century? But Tedra, WHY?!?"

She's just as incredulous about my life, of course. But it's the polar opposition of what seems to each of us like the self-evident mode for existing that makes our interactions interesting. So we sit around and talk.

"I need to get a job, I know, I know." I am saying one afternoon.

"What happened to your job interview the other day? I thought you were a shoo-in."

"I didn't end up going," I admit.

She shakes her head in mock disappointment, laughing.

"Look, I used to work at Kinko's copies of Providence, Rhode Island, and, let me tell you, it wasn't that fun," I explain. "I used to have this manager named Don there. That guy was an asshole. He was one of those people who go to managerial training school and get a degree in bossing people around. He'd never seen a copier before, his previous job was managing a drug store. What did his resumé say on it? 'CVS drug store- ordered people around in an efficient manner'?! Well- anyway, there I am one night, collating some papers alongside Don, listening to that infuriating 'greatest hits of the seventies, eighties and nineties!' radio stations which Don insisted we keep the radio tuned to at all times. All of a sudden, that Rod Stewart song, 'Young Turks' comes on. You know," I begin to sing the chorus: "*Young hearts be free tonight, time is on your side.... Don't let them ever change your point of view...*"

"And Don began singing along!" I continue, "It was obviously his favorite song. So tell me, what was I to make of that? What was he trying to communicate to me? Does Don have a young heart? Or is he singing to me? Was he subliminally invoking me to subvert his authority? And what point of view is he expressing? Is time on his side? Or has he changed his point of view? Or was his point of view always that being the manager of a copy franchise and crushing your underlings is a valid way to spend your time?"

"These are the great philosophical questions which haunt you," Tedra nods sympathetically.

"Young hearts be free tonight," I repeat solemnly, shaking my head in disbelief.

8.

Closing time at the Wonderland nickel arcade on Belmont street

is a sight to behold. On a weekend the place is packed with kids feverishly pumping nickels into ass-whupping and high-speed driving games of varying degree of virtual reality, eyes flickering and bodies rigid with tension before the screen, muttering obscenities and releasing the joystick only momentarily to wipe flecks of saliva from the corners of mouths with the backs of shaking hands. At midnight promptly, the plug is pulled. The whirring, clanging, strobing cacophony hums and sputters to a halt and the assembled throng of revelers find themselves standing silent in a dank, ill-lit den of dust and body odor. They look around sheepishly, like guys assessing each other as they leave a porn theater, and then file silently out to the exit, head ringing with adrenalin and the mild guilt of an evening ill-spent. Any connoisseur of anti-climaxes or migraines' resumé is incomplete without this experience.

I am walking past the nickel arcade one night at around midnight, just as the neon sign is extinguished and the masses begin to trickle their way out for the sorry pilgrimage home. Two young guys come sauntering out, dressed in identical black T-shirts and thick glasses; one of them sporting long, well-groomed hair with distinctly Farrah Fawcett style wings. Spindly limbs amble over and fumble in pockets for a pack of cigarettes, which he juts in my direction.

"No, thanks," I say. He nods, sticking a cigarette in between his scrawny lips, lighting up with an obviously inaccurately named child-proof lighter.

"You here to pick someone up or something?" he asks.

"No" I say, "Why do you ask?"

"You look like the type of guy who might be waiting for someone." he says. "Dad type."

"Really?" I say, laughing. "I look like a dad?"

"Well, uh.... hey, now. No offense." He tries again. "So... uh, you here to pick up your girlfriend?"

"Man, who are you guys?" I say. "you inhabit a reality I just cannot fathom."

"We have IQ's of 180," the other kid, a chubby little walrus of a boy, asserts.

"Wow," I nod, "how old are y'all?"

"Fourteen." They say in unison.

"Wow.... what kind of stuff are you into? Video games?"

"Role playing games, mostly," the thin one, who appears to be the leader, explains. "have you ever heard of a game called *Dungeons and Dragons?*" He says it like he's letting me in on one of the little known secret keys to universal understanding.

"Yeah," I say.

"I mean other than that, we're just into.... you know, teenage things."

"Teenage things? Like what?"

"You know," the walrus giggles, "Pamela Anderson Lee. Stuff like that."

"Oh." I say.

The leader smiles, "We're fourteen. You remember what it was like."

Fourteen. Born in 1981. And yet somehow the kid seems as mature and conversationally adept as me, at least. It's eerie. His face looks strangely aged, like a grown-up nerd dressed as a young hesher, unconvincing in his awkward, gangly body.

We talk a little more. I ask the kids questions and they are eager to tell me about themselves, being enamored as they are of the strange universe within which they reside. "I don't care if I end up making $5,000 or $100,000 a year," the leader says " I just never want to be alone. I always want to have friends, you know, someone I can call on a Friday night to go to the movies."

"That's your big fear for the future?" I ask, "being alone?" It seems like a strange thing for a kid to obsess about.

"Yeah."

I think about it. "You know," I realize, "I'm pretty sure at the age of fourteen I never even thought of $5,000 as a sum which might or might not be appropriate to make annually. So what do you want to do when you grow up?"

He answers without hesitation, "I want to be a marine biologist."

"Oh yeah? Why is that?"

He stares at me long and hard. " Ninety percent of the ocean floor is unexplored. Now, don't get me wrong. I'm not saying there *are* vast civilizations comparable to our own down there. I'm just saying, *it might be possible.*"

With that, the two turn and disappear into the cool autumn night, running across Belmont to the waiting station wagon of the parent who has arrived to pick them up.

two

IT'S HARD TO SURVIVE

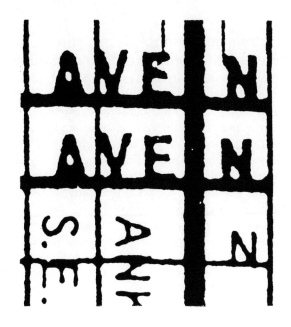

9.

Bill Tsitsos,

a man with a tremendous afro-like expanse of hair, sits in a bar, surveying the scene with feigned casualness. He is a nervous man, prone to fits of anxiety and bursts of paralyzing self-consciousness and doubt, but he is also a driven and dedicated individual, a man whose mind races constantly, examining every situation from a myriad of heretofore uncharted angles and untraversed vantage points. And, yes, he has recently found gainful employment as a giant peanut M&M. In his heart, he is well aware of the circumstances conspiring to put him in these often demeaning but invariably amusing (at the very least anecdotally, which for Bill is currency of the highest denomination) situations. The woman at the temp agency has erroneously fallen under the assumption that his surname, Tsitsos, a common Greek family name, is Tostitos. Whether the snack-food related assignments which have followed are a result of some unconscious name-association or whether, perhaps, she believes that Bill has suggestively offered up a creative *nom de temp* (and it would not be at all surprising for the office staff to be accustomed to dealing with fraudulent identities- after all, a good number of the fellow temps he has come in contact with have alluded to double lives, alimony evasion, or perhaps even displayed an understanding of the mechanics of convenience store robbery which seemed too lovingly precise to be merely an academic interest), is of little consequence to the end result. The M&M suit was fairly comfortable, in any case. A flaccid yellow sack, Bill had donned the outfit in the surplus produce room of the grocery store, initially balking at the suffocating folds of canvas which encased him, threatening a grim race to the finish between asphyxiation and heat-stroke as his cause of death. However, a battery-powered fan strapped to his back was set in motion, and soon the flaccid M&M had inflated to it's naturally jolly rotund state of being. Sweating, grimacing, stumbling at near-total blindness through the aisles of afternoon shoppers, Bill attempted his best impression of how he conjectured a yellow M&M, brought to gigantic sugary life, might behave. The huge, leering painted smile on the face of the candy offered no clue to it's operator's true emotional state, which quickly turned from quiet concentration to scowling frown to panic as the possibility of heat stroke again crossed his mind. Around his legs, young ruffians scampered, hands extended, yanking and poking in whining pleas for candy. "Ho ho," Bill gargled, wondering whether, in fact, it was appropriate for the M&M to sound like Santa Claus. An image from his childhood flashed through his mind's eye- "Kool Aid!" The merry pitcher had brought mirth to many a youngsters' face, and he looked kind of colorful and bulbous, as did Bill, right at this moment. Turning a corner to face another impending flock of miscreants, Bill decided to give this new persona a try. He mustered up a gruff voice, uttering a cry of merry greeting, albeit without actually coming up with any specific syllables to utter. "Heyoooooaghhh!" The utterance came out, sending the terrified kids scampering, and giving Bill a moment of reprieve. He leaned against the aisle, sweating buckets by now in the claustrophobic burlap contraption.

Blindly groping, his hand brushed a cool glass wall, and Bill realized that he was in the frozen foods section of the grocery store. This gave him an inspiration. He opened the door of the freezer, inserting the nozzle-like duct of the fan, which sucked air from outside into the costume, lodging it between a bag of peas and baby carrots, sucking in the frosty air and soothing Bill's parched and world-weary soul. Thus revived, he continued his rounds for the duration of his tenure at this bizarre job, and, when the time was nigh, he shed his mobile tent outfit, procured the requisite signature from the appropriate authority, verifying for the agency another satisfactory depiction of snack food on the part of Tostitos, and was on his merry way, a few dollars and several dozen trial-size packages of M&M's richer.

But now our victorious breadwinner finds himself less than pleased. After a day's hard labor, it seems the pay-off should be something more than the sight he sees before him. When he moved to Portland it was on the advice of various friends and acquaintances from his college years who assured him that it was "the place to be-" a town full of hip, vivacious, fascinating individuals brimming with energy and ideas. Perhaps this is how Bill sees himself, in his moments of greatest self-assurance, and perhaps it is even true that his friends, in selling him on the idea of moving out West, might have painted him not only a picture of a place filled with interesting people- but a place filled with people who he'd relate to and connect with, a place, it might even have been implied (or was this his imagination now, reading things into their descriptions which correlated to some popularity fantasy lingering from adolescence?) where he might find acceptance and spiritual fulfillment.

What, he asks himself, does any of this have to do with where I'm sitting now? This is where the hipsters hang out: a remodeled strip club painted all black, where currently a possé of slightly balding dudes wearing CRACKERBASH T-shirts guzzle beer, rubbing their pot-bellies and chuckling absently at Beavis and Butthead, which plays menacingly on a wide screen TV.

"Jesus, man! This totally blows," he realizes. He can feel a tingling sensation in the pit of his stomach-Ah, old man rage, boiling up, the urge to kill these fuckers. He grimaces, makes an unappetizing-food-in-my-mouth type face.

"Yeah," his housemates concur, crowded around the small corner table, slouching in towards their beers. Their glazed expressions, as if they have all just awoken from a nap, indicate that they don't seem particularly perturbed by the raw truth of Bill's statement.

"Should we go check out that party," suggests Andrew, ever the constructive one, the temperate, calm and controlled voice to balance out Bill's internal hurricanes and typhoons. Andrew and Bill seem to be inseparable, paradoxically, because their exact dichotomy of temperament makes them complementary; when they are together they become positive and negative poles of the same magnet. Or perhaps it is just that Andrew also has a monumental afro of hair atop his towering dome, and the two of them cruising around together just looks so killer.

Bill doubts very much that he will be able to deal with the people at the party. Nonetheless, he and Andrew set out in that general direction, passing the very store in which, earlier that day, Bill had paraded around in the bizarre attire. They stop in to graze on the bulk bins, which soothes Bill, and makes him realize that he is hungry. Andrew suggests they head over to the Montage for a quick bite to eat.

It is late, and the place is packed when they arrive. Ill at ease, Bill senses a strange force-field of hostility emanating from the hostess, a supercharged bubble of spite which singes the eyelashes and the fine hairs on your arms. "This way," she motions them, leading them back through the cavernous airplane hanger of a restaurant, snaking between tables at which well-dressed parties of all shapes and sizes seem to be performing elaborate pantomime routines of having a good time, eyes darting around to reference the other tables' takes on what having a good time looks like, keeping current and hip to the newest moves and inflections.

The table where they are seated is the furthest back, at the rear of the hanger. You can watch the doors to the kitchen swing as waiters burst out or bustle in, catching tantalizing glimpses of sour and grease-bespeckled dishwashers skulking about, breaking dishes and swearing. This is not, one can't help but note, the prime real estate, seating-wise.

"Well,"pronounces Bill, "we just got the big shaft."

Andrew is oblivious. Bill, however continues being livid. "I mean, we look cool enough, right? We could be cool. There's nothing which specifically points us out as not being cool. Why single us out for the dick treatment?"

"Maybe this is just the only table open," suggests Andrew.

"Oh, come on!" Bill explodes. "I think it's very obvious what's going on here!"

He looks around angrily for someone to complain to, or something to steal or break as an act of revenge. The other tables continue their pantomime, their eternal farce, oblivious. Bill wonders what they would do if he came in here and demanded to be seated in the center of the restaurant, with all eyes facing him, in full regalia, fan whirring majestically and M&M fully inflated.

10.

Seven forty-five

in the morning finds me sitting in a bagel bakery downtown, waiting to sign up at Manpower. Time marches on; the bagel, once a scarce commodity on the west coast, now proliferates like Kudzu. I'm having a serious revelation as I stare at the counter, realizing that it probably would have been a lot wiser to spend one of my precious last remaining dollars on a half dozen day old bagels instead of investing in another nail for my coffin, a cup of coffee on an empty stomach, blank canvas of intestinal lining that it is, stretched and gessoed and awaiting my masterfully executed ulcer. "I didn't think it was possible to drink coffee that fast," the kid in the coffee shop compliments me (I think it's a compliment) when I ask for my refill. "You have to be really commited to inducing a heart attack," I reply. Downtown, early morning, you get the same type swarming everywhere- guys in suits, cruising around, grinning in precise, well-groomed evil. NPR plays on the radio in the background, the eternal Greek chorus, narrating the tragedy of the modern world. There's a Black Flag song stuck in my head. "It's hard to survive," it says, "I don't know if I can do it." This song has been stuck in my head for years, ever since I first heard it, centuries ago.

People time things by the time it takes to smoke a cigarette, or drink a cup of coffee. You get a good feel for the bio-rhythms of it all. That's why people with vices don't wear watches. At eight o'clock I'm in the door for my interview at the Power, but I can't even bring myself to say the name to the doorman of the building; I mutter "uh.... I'm going up to the temp agency on the fifteenth floor." "Oh, MANPOWER?" he snickers, enunciating the words carefully enough that the hipster bike messengers milling about the the lobby will be sure to dog me later on at some party. "yeah," I mumble, shuffling over to the elevator. That guy's probably just bitter because he got *his* job from the Power, I decide.

Well, I must admit that when choosing a temp agency to sign up with, it came down to a close race between Manpower and Talent Tree- I just cracked up at those names. It's definitely important, I have decided, to pick your agency by how funny the name is.

I am greeted in the temp agency office by a bubbly lady named Kelly, who loads me down with an arsenal of forms to complete. "You brought your social security card, right?" she chirps. I have not. The social security office downtown opens at nine, so I trudge back down and over to await that office's opening and the printing of an application for a duplicate card which will verify that I am, indeed, a human; during said trip I end up having a nice chat with a seventy-six year old homeless woman who explains to me that Armageddon is beginning in the hills of Oregon even as she speaks, instigated by roving packs of Masons who are involved in a vast conspiracy to capture and eat children. When I get up to window One in the social security office, she approaches window Two and, when the lady at that window inquires what she needs, the apocalyptic old lady turns from delivering her sermon to me and picks up mid-sentence in the direction of the social security worker. The worker stares at her for a moment, trying to figure out what the hell she's talking about, then, realizing she is dealing with an insane person, takes the opportunity to take an unofficial break, staring off into space and dreaming of lunch while pretending to listen to the doomsday prattle for a good five minutes. During these same five minutes I get my humanity notarized and proceed back to the Power.

The interview lasts four hours; I cheat on one of the typing tests. I'm not sure why. Would I even ever want a job that involved typing? Why represent myself as a competent typist and then spend the duration of employment doing something I'm not that good at? I guess it's just one of those things you do on principle; I figured out how to beat the system (if they put you on a timer, just stop the timer when they leave the room!) and so I do. There are a variety of other tests. One is really pathetic: a computer proficiency exam which begins by asking you to type in your first name. The following message then appears:

"Welcome, Al! This is a test of your COMPUTER LITERACY! We want you to do the best job possible so that we can give you the BEST AVAILABLE JOB FOR YOU! So, let's begin the test. Press the F1 key!"

Pressing the F1 key elicits a low hum and the whirring of gears.

"CONGATULATIONS, AL! You're really TAKING CHARGE!" appears. What kind of simpering low-self-esteem morons apply at this place that need this sort of validation? I wonder. And further, does anyone actually buy into the premise advanced by the worker loyalty videos I am then entreated to watch? The basic plot is this: a sort of Charlton Heston looking guy and a sort of Sally Struthers looking lady appear and begin explaining some rudimentary economics to you. The economy is not so hot. Jobs are scarce. That's probably why you're here. And why is the American economy taking the pummeling that it is? The fault can be put squarely on the shoulders of you, the American worker, who for years has been taking too long lunch breaks, sassing back to the boss, fomenting anti-employer feelings by quoting certain contraband country music songs within the context of the workplace (all scenarios illustrated with great dramatizations by a team of superb improvisational actors). So now look at you. Stuck at the bottom of the chain, temping your way back up. As the video ends, an American flag unfurls into the wind behind Charlton Heston, fireworks go off, and he proclaims, "Our company's growth, as a subsection of the greater economy, will strengthen America overall, causing a return one day to the boom times of yore, and perhaps an actual permanent job for you--with benefits! But this can only happen if, as a representative of MANPOWER, you work tirelessly to make our company the best temp agency out there!" Sally Struthers wipes a tear from her eye.

Of course, my whole agenda in seeking employment through a temp agency is to take long lunch breaks, sass back at not only one boss but potentially as many as five new bosses a week, and sing all the Dolly Parton anti-work anthems I can think of, which is only one, actually.

Interview completed, Kelly shakes my hand and welcomes me aboard, and then I'm back on the bus, headed Southeast across the Burnside Bridge, feeling semi-successful--- now officially temporary, with four hours effortlessly shorn off of my life. It's a beautiful day out. I feel the sense of ease which comes with finding a job, but not the oppressing sense of having to be anywhere at any specific time. "We'll be calling you in the next week," Kelly assures me. Her words ring in my ear, to the tune of Black Flag.

11.

At first temping really seems like the ideal job situation. I wake up late a few days after signing on with the Power and call in. "Al!" the voice of Kelly greets me emphatically. She probably can't remember who I am, but her enthusiasm at hearing my voice gives me a warm feeling nonetheless. It's like I'm doing them a big favor by offering my services. "Nothing today," she offers consolingly, and, after a quick phone number verification so that she can call me on the double if anything comes up, I hang up and heave a great sigh of relief.

So, this is pretty killer, all in all. I've technically procured some form of employment, thus assuaging the guilt factor of hanging out in coffee shops all day, vainly trying to summon the necessary concentration to read the paper, or staring at the front cover of a book. However, I have not cashed in my guilt chips for that most bitter of currencies, dread. The dread of actually having to go to work is a hideous hydra indeed. I hate that desperate feeling of needing to get a job, which when alleviated, provides you with approximately two and a half seconds respite before the dread sets in. I've been in job interviews laying on my best employee smoke screen, feeling the thrill of landing the job blossom like a flower and, as I listen to the prospective boss' arcane econo-jargon spiel (the most insane thing ever said to me, in terms of indicting late-industrial capitalism, was, again, a copy store job, where a boss said to me "it's like fast food-*without the food!*"), it's like that flower is being filmed in stop-motion, hyper-accelerated, and even as it blooms it begins to blacken and whither. "Man, I think I'm actually going to land this job...this job... Oh man, this sucks, I have to fucking work here?!?" I think to myself. The flower has been reduced to compost at this point.

But now: no guilt, no dread. For a cry-baby like myself, temp agencies are kind of like those half-way house high schools they send kids to between rehab and regular school. You know, you have to kind of ease into it.

Oh, I can ease. Just as Ozzy has O-Z-Z-Y tattooed across his knuckles, I've considered having L-E-I-S-U-R-E permanently affixed to mine. (But then, I'd be one letter short. Exclamation point? But then my one hand would say "URE!") The one chink in this brilliant plan is, of course, that the reason you go out and get yourself a job is that you actually need a job. If I just needed something to call home and tell the folks about I'd make up a lie about being a partner in a law firm or something. Make up some fake stationary to write them letters on. Parents fall for these sorts of obvious ruses, because they WANT to believe.

Three days into my newfound existence on the frontlines of being "on call," I wake up around three in the afternoon to find a message chalked up on the dinosaur-shaped chalkboard. *Manpower called.* I sprint to the phone and dial the hell out of the number.

"We're just verifying your phone number again," the chipper voice on the other end chirps.

When I hang up the receiver I feel spent and restless. These are desperate times indeed for our young protagonist. I've been completely out of money for a week now. I go to restaurants and eat the left-overs off of unbussed tables when no one is looking. I approach strangers in coffee shops and ask them if I can have their refill when they are done with their cup. Strange alien thoughts are worming their way through my brain: *I need to work, damn it. I'll take anything.*

At this point my theoretical employment becomes less like eternal days off and more like a battle of wills. I set my alarm for eight o'clock and when it goes off the next morning I'm up and on the phone, being chirped at again, once again coming away from the conversation empty-handed. I go back to sleep for a few hours and call again at noon. Then I go out for a while and call again at four. This becomes my daily regimen of saturation bombing.

And then one day, the big pay off comes. It is the greatest job ever conceived, the kind of job temps dream of. It involves no boss, as many lunch breaks as I want and unlimited songs played on my own personal stereo. And it centers around coffee. Essentially, what the job entails is driving from grocery store to grocery store, meticulously cataloging the types of available coffee to be found in their bulk coffee bins. I have three days to complete the task and I can calculate my own hours. I go downtown to the office, pick up the requisite forms, and promise to show up in three days with everything satisfactorily filled out and time-card in hand.

I actually do the job the first day, so as to get a sense of how to forge filling out the forms, and what sorts of times spent laboring one could reasonably put on the time card. The grocery stores are spread out all over, many in areas I've never even been to; an Albertson's in Gresham or a Safeway in Milwaukee, all suburbs of Portland which exist to me only in mythical references to rodeos and schlong haircuts. It's pretty damn entertaining, too, to walk the aisles in these stores amongst strangers, holding a clipboard and looking serious as I make notations: "Venezuelan Antigua decaf- bin 1/3 full." No one questions my position of authority. I've got a *clipboard* after all, I'm the kind of authoritative guy who generally carries around a bunch of pens. This seems like the kind of thing I might even do in my free time; walk around with a clipboard some Friday night, intimidating people.

Navigating traffic in the more familiar downtown area, passing the Manpower office and turning to cruise past the park blocks, as I think about making my way towards the Tenth and Jefferson Safeway, trying to time it so the killer song on KNRK (the "new rock revolution!") will end right as I put the car in park, I happen to catch sight of Andrew and Bill eating lunch out in front of a Thai restaurant. I cut across traffic, a stupid move in a borrowed car, and park illegally in a loading zone, right in front of their table.

"Hey, guys, what's up!" I greet them, getting out of the car and sitting down.

It turns out that they are both at work at different temp jobs themselves, and are meeting for lunch. "Man, I'm working at the Portland State University bookstore," Andrew explains, "and they just have no idea who I am. I can pretty much show up, clock in, and leave. I feel sort of weird about it, but then again, what are you going to do? Not leave?"

"What are you doing?" Bill asks. "Are you just hanging out downtown today?"

"Hell, no, man," I gloat, "I'm at work right now! Check out my job: some kind of coffee institute is having me conduct a marketing survey of some kind," I show them the intricate, byzantine forms. "Basically, I'm sure that whatever they're going to do with this information is probably pretty crappy, so it seems pretty morally imperative to forge as much of this info as possible." I explain the whole no boss, yes stereo angle.

"Any free food?" Bill fires at me.

"Ahhhhh, well, no," I lament, "though I work around coffee, I do not actually receive any free coffee, which sucks. It's true."

"Nonetheless," Andrew congratulates me heartily, "a pretty killer score. In fact, I consider your job one of, if not even *the*, elusive most coveted temp positions. I myself had that exact same job when I worked for Manpower in D.C. and it rocked, I must say."

A pretty thrilling day of employment overall. I sit and chat with them for a while longer before resuming my chores. The real shank of the whole thing is that they don't pay for your gas. I alleviate this problem rather easily by spending the next couple of days filling out fantasy reportages of half-empty coffee bins of the mind. On day three I show up late in the afternoon to turn in my forms. I put myself down for thirty-six hours of back breaking labor.

"Oh, yes," coos Sue Ellen, matron of the Power, "these look just fine. I'll fax them out right away."

"If you have any other jobs like this, sign me up," I tell her.

As it turns out, I have a lucky streak: my next two jobs are even more bizarre, and similarly easy. In the first, I am instructed to drive to a grocery store, buy two packages of instant hot chocolate (it is IMPERATIVE that they not have the same expiration date) and deposit them at the Manpower office, where they are then shipped to some client. The following week I do the same thing with ice cream treats, which, once safely delivered to the office, are packed in dry ice and shipped off. I would like to think that it's just some executive in Texas' weird way of getting snacks, but that's probably too good to be true.

12.

Time moves in unpredictable fits and spurts. At certain moments I find

myself amazed at how days turn into weeks and months, and then at other times I realize that I've only been in Portland for a few months now, which is not that long. It's all illusory.

Tedra is happy to note that I have moved off of her porch. I now reside in a little pink house on Forty-ninth and Hawthorne, which I share with a number of odd characters.

The day I moved in, finally unloading the couple of boxes of junk which I'd hauled with me from North Carolina and kept in Tedra's basement for a month, I surveyed the scene and was, predictably, overcome with a wave of nauseous panic. The realization dawned that I do not have enough stuff to to fill a car, much less an entire room, and there is really not a great deal of silver lining to that life situation except, of course, for the convenient fact that it only takes one car trip to move out. But if transience is the goal, how can the moving in ever be less than horrifically oppressive? I stared dumbly into the gaping craw of my room, naked bulb dangling overhead, illuminating barren walls. The room is the window to the soul. My soul, apparently, is a pretty no-frills soul.

In the grip of fear and panic, and then overcome by a wave of dull Darwinian determination which had me muttering swear words emphatically, I marched over to the phone and dialed the Greyhound bus line, a number which I know by heart, as I often like to remind myself when I'm feeling geographical jitters (although the number is 1-800-GO-HOUND, so really, it's not that impressive). The Hound put me on hold. As I waited, nervously pacing the living room, I became aware of a dull, thundering cacophony emanating from the basement. I hung up the phone and went downstairs, where I found my housemate Jason playing the drums. Our basement is filled with all manner of amps and musical knick-knacks, and I watched him play for a while. He seemed oblivious to my presence. Eventually, I picked up a guitar and began to play along with him. Inertia set in instantaneously, and by the time I put the guitar down I was as pacified as a sixth-grader with a Pezz dispenser full of Ritalin. Guitars have that strangely soothing, debilitating effect: you're on hold to buy a ticket out of town to leave within the hour, but you inadvertently pick up a guitar and the next thing you know it's three months later and you're still there.

Jason is certainly an archetype: recently moved up from California after unfortunate breakups with both his band and girlfriend, he lives in the basement, where he can usually be found paralyzed with depression. Even my usual gloomy world-view is rattled by the depths of his malaise, and I shudder to find myself suggesting that he should get a hobby. "Why don't you start a band?" I ask.

"Start a band?" he smiles resignedly. "I can't get out of bed most days." This is a pretty valid argument, so I shut up.

When not sleeping, Jason is on the porch drinking. Theses are hard times for him. Still, he is always amiable and engaging, and even when he's explaining to you that life isn't worth living he does it in a charismatic, friendly way. Recently, he took a trip back down to California to try to patch things up with the girlfriend. He was gone for days, but one day as I returned home from an errand, there he was, sitting on the front steps of the house, silhouetted in the twilight, smiling mysteriously and staring into space, drunk. I sat down next to him and asked him how his trip went. He turned his head slowly and stared at me for a while, slightly cross-eyed, still smiling, before lifting his shirt to expose the shiny, scabby mark of a new tattoo, etched over his heart. It was a Cupid angel, lying on its back, dead, an arrow protruding from its chest, sticking straight up.

"Man!" I yelped. "You got that tattooed on your body! That is permanently on you!"

"She broke my heart," he said, and laughed quietly to himself, turning back towards the darkening sky. I am impressed with his romantic spirit, his dedication to the concept of heartbreak.

What I lack in material goods, the house more than makes up for. The living room is crammed full of stuff; kitchy Elvis paintings on black velvet, bookshelves with great philosophers and pulpy softcore pornography, enough furnishing for a small third world nation, all of which has been retrieved from the trash, and an endless supply of records, magazines and food to keep all senses occupied. My housemate Theresa works down the street at a health food store and the other inhabitants take turns loading up shopping carts full of food, which are paid for with food stamps that Theresa gives us before she goes to work. I load the shopping carts until I can't maneuver around corners, gritting my teeth as I approach the checkout line, wheels straining under the weight of the gourmet treats within. Theresa smiles and rings me up, usually for a dollar. I give her a food stamp and push my cart out the door.

Theresa writes down what she does every day in a notebook. It is somewhat different from a diary in that it is a purely factual account, like minutes at a meeting, the minutes of your life. I decide to do the same, writing down my activities in a daily planner for a few days. It looks like this:

TUES: Went downtown. Saw bands at Rexall Rose. Went to a party. Got drunk. Made out with someone I didn't know.

WED: Played music with Jason. Went to a show at the Power House. Then went to Fellini's with Jason and some friend of his. Talked to drunks.

THURS: Played music with Harrison. Went out for coffee with Wells. Organized my room.

This does not look good. Having it all laid out for me like that is a total crusher, and the thought that I would fill up a daily planner, day by day, until finally I was left with a document of the exact minutae of how I'd wasted my life for one solid year seems unfathomably painful. A little poetry does make the bad medicine go down, and I sure as hell can't swallow that stuff plain. Oh, it is just way to harsh to see that. I suspected as much.

13.

Powell's bookstore in downtown Portland is the largest bookstore in the free world, spanning an entire city block, and crammed full of pretty much any sort of literature you could possibly be interested in. They have no filing system or overall computer network to keep track of their inventory, as far as I can tell, which makes it a lot better place to browse for hours than to go in search of any specific book. They also have a warehouse in Northeast, where primarily text books and oversize art books seem to be stored.

I'm assigned to spend a day at the Powell's warehouse, shelving and unshelving, packing and stacking, carting on handtrucks and wrapping onto wooden pallets, books, books, books.

When I arrive in the morning I am shown around the premises, and introduced to two other temps, one a meek professorial type from Angola and another guy, Charles, who besides being one of the first fellow Men of Power I have met is also my first encounter with someone who regularly smokes crack. "You know," he is soon explaining, as he hands me books which I stack on a shelf, "you're hanging out at your house and a bunch of people come over and start smoking crack; what are you gonna do, not smoke crack?" I stare at him incredulously, but only because I'm thinking, "wow, he has the same relation to crack cocaine that I have to oodles of noodles," and he, noting my stare, responds, "damn, I know. I should probably move out." He has been up all night smoking the magic rock, and now professes an intense craving for salt, as well as expounding on his deep love of the classic rock musical genré, which we listen to out of a dented up old boom box. "That's my jam!" he intones in a deep Barry White voice when a particularly good song is played.

My first experience with actually performing labor for the temp agency is not quite as exhilarating as the string of survey/retrieval jobs I'd concocted over the past week or so, but the two other temps make it entertaining. I never catch the Angolan guy's name, but his nervous by-the-book philosophizing and Charles' contemptuous dismissals make for a running Abbott and Costello routine which can't be beat.

"Pick up the pace, pansy-ass," chides Charles.

"Big ass mustache motherfucker," the Angolan replies in a thick accent, apparently referring to Charles' big ass mustache.

"Big ass?" laughs Charles. "Whose ass you looking at? Keep your eyes on the books and off my ass, you dumb faggot!"

"You want some of this?" the Angolan waves a mocking fist around.

"Punk, come on down to my neighborhood," Charles threatens, "Northeast Fiftieth and Alberta, motherfucker, see how long you last."

"So, how long have you guys been working for the Power?" I ask.

"Man, I've been doing this shit for three years!" Charles tells me, "Temporary? Huh! Well, it works for me. I'm signed up with four agencies, man! That's how you gotta do it. That way, someone always hooks you up."

"I don't really want to work that much," I say.

"Huh! Well, man, temp work beats a job any day. Some day I don't feel like coming to work, I can just be like, 'not today.' I don't have to suck some boss' dick, you know what I'm saying?"

This cracks up the Angolan, to which Charles rejoins, "You think that's so funny? You probably wanna be sucking a dick."

By the time lunch rolls around, my eyes feel like marbles from all the dust shifted along with the books, and we stumble out into a sunny day. "Who's got some money?" Charles asks brightly. The Angolan guy and I both shrug.

"Nobody got any money?" demands Charles. "Come on. I need some motherfucking salty-ass food. Now! McDonalds got a two Big Macs for two dollars deal. Who's in?"

"Not me," I say.

"I will be in," consents the Angolan.

"You got two dollars?" snaps Charles, like he's the doorman charging admission to some exclusive club. The Angolan guy nods; he produces a couple of crumpled dollar bills which he waves at Charles, who wags his head eagerly. "Let's eat," he leers.

But the supposed two-for-one deal at McDonalds doesn't materialize.

"Damn," Charles mutters, his eyes lingering for a moment on the yellow and red awning, scientifically color-coded to induce maximum salt-craving. (Watching Charles' Pavlovian eye-rolling reminds me of an article I once read, about crack addicts who crave fast food and how the McDonalds corporation had installed florescent "crack-lights" to ward off these undesirable consumer elements—apparently the glaring, buzzing tubes really ruin the ambience for light-sensitive crack heads. I never really believed this story; in fact

I'd be more apt to believe that the McDonalds corporation created crack cocaine as an appetite enhancer and then fueled the fire by installing florescent bug-lights which attract the crack-addicted like moths. However, I did have this one really odd experience at about three in the morning in a Dunkin Donuts in Providence, where, after I'd been sitting half-slumped in a suger-addled stupor for some time, I noticed the sole night-shift employee saunter over to a certain half-concealed light-switch panel in the wall and flip on exactly the sort of glaring, buzzing overhead heat-lamp the article had described, right above my head. "Ah-ha! The notorious crack-light," I scowled, donning my homeless-vagabond-couture and dragging my carcass out the door.)

Momentarily side-tracked, the lunch-seekers straggle about without direction, Charles and the Angolan still at it, bantering and swearing at each other. Charles observes a thirty-something yuppie type jog by in tight biker shorts, his well-toned rump heaving inside the spandex, and is moved to comment, "Damn. Did you see that ass? I'd get up in an ass like that." The Angolan quickly jumps to concede the fineness of the ass in question. They both nod reverently, and then break into another round of calling each other faggots, laughing merrily. I must say, I find their behavior very bizarre.

Charles leads the way over to a nearby grocery store, where we split up. I gnaw my way through several pounds of bulk bin fodder and shoplift a roll. The two other temps are much more industrious than I am, and I catch sight of them at the costumer service desk pulling some elaborate receipt scam. Outside, I'm perusing my roll, and Charles joins me. We sit on the stoop and eat contentedly, Charles gnawing on gristley chicken legs and muttering, "Mmm-mmm. I do crave chicken after a night of smoking that crack. Did you catch that store detective following our boy around? Motherfucker..."

We exchange some shoplifting anecdotes, and I notice that while my stories tend to end in near-misses or my talking my way out of a situation, he tends to tell stories which end with him in jail. Minutes ago, walking over to the grocery store with these guys, I had imagined for a moment that I was on the level with these guys; just three workers on lunch break. But of course, it's always the privilege of those who can pass for respectable to get away with murder. I'm white, college-educated, relatively neatly dressed- this guy, on the other hand, must have security guards on him the moment he enters a room.

The Angolan guy wanders out of the store, and displays his purchase proudly: a plastic container of diced up watermelon. Charles chides him for getting a bad deal on it. "You gotta check the unit price, motherfucker," he cackles.

14.

Another day

finds me walking around the supposed "bad part of town," putting home refinancing flyers on doors and narrowly avoiding pit bulls. Northeast Portland; up the ominously named Killingsworth and back down Alberta, and somewhere in there walking by some apartment or fence-enclosed house with paint peeling off the shutters and a "forget the dog -beware of owner" sign, wherein resides mustachioed thirty-five year old Charles, just waking up from a rough nights' activity, or maybe off at work carting boxes around on a forklift somewhere in service of one of the four temp agencies which have his name on file.

It's a serene and easy job, actually: I like walking. A lot of the apartments have really low windows in this area, almost like store-front windows, and as I approach them to deposit my wares I often catch glimpses of extremely sad-looking lives. Obese, half-dead men sit in soiled undershirts gawking at televisions alone, or harried moms veg out as children run screaming in circles about them. Anyone who is not at work is watching TV, and most people do not even glance up as I stand on their doorstep, fumble awkwardly with a stack of papers, and scurry off. Occasionally, someone comes to the door, suspiciously, refusing to accept a home refinancing flyer and motioning me to be on my way, even sometimes yelling a few brief curses in my general direction.

15.

On one of my many days off, I head downtown to the social services office. While waiting in line I notice that the clerk at the desk is blind. It's very weird- he has bulbous, yellowy eyes which protrude disconcertingly as he stares vacantly straight ahead, rattling off names of forms and instructions for filling them out. Until I realize that he is blind I mistake him for some kind of intensely arrogant prick, unwilling to make eye-contact with the lowly masses, but that clearly seems to be my own hang-up talking. Then I think he's autistic, staring into space and talking a mile a minute, until I get to the front of the line and he looks past me, standing there awkwardly and not saying anything.

"Is there anyone there? Is there someone there I can help?" he asks the void.

"Oh," I stammer, finally grasping the situation, "um, yes. Is this where you apply for food stamps?"

"Oh no," he shakes his head, "there's a separate office for that." He tells me the address, adding- "they close at four-thirty, so- -" he lifts his arm, fondling a braille watch which he wears on his wrist, caressing the contours, almost like a kid boasting about a neat toy, I kick myself for thinking. "It's three twelve now; you can catch the bus over and--"

Walk up the street and catch a Southeast bound bus. The bus is slow to start because a woman in a wheelchair is disembarking with the aid of various hydraulic levers and ramps. The sight is sort of mesmerizing- the bus door itself has developed maternal, cradling limbs which gently set her down, like a mom. She controls the wheelchair, a sporty electric-motorized contraption with a video-game style joystick, which she wields deftly as soon as the tires touch cement, rocketing off, between the legs of pedestrians. It's a nice thing to see, and the combination of the woman in the wheelchair and the blind man in the unemployment office get me thinking about the life of people differently abled from myself. Handicap access is a great thing. She's off and running, no problem, rosy-cheeked and flitting between the shambling masses of the ill and impaired, the hordes of sickly or defective stragglers, wandering the streets aimlessly, an aggregate which I guess I lump into. You get attuned to it and then you can't stop looking out the window and seeing impaired individuals. I tore the ligaments in one of my knees a couple of years ago, and that knee is not really so good anymore; sometimes I'll step on it funny and the leg bends the wrong way, like a horse, and I fall down and then limp around for a few days, knee swollen up like an over-ripe grapefruit, hot and mushy with pus. But I don't think of myself as disabled because of it, I certainly subscribe to the differently abled theory. I think of it as one of my attributes, one of the interesting facts about me, along with being able to draw pretty good or drive a stick shift. The kind of thing I might put in a personal ad:

SWM, enjoys music, reading, long walks in the outdoors. Gimp knee, bad temper. Horrible work ethic, OK kisser. I can also draw pretty good.

We're all just differently abled, right? From each according to their ability. At my house the walls are plastered with full-page color photographs from an extremely disturbing recent issue of *Life* magazine, which features a story on an actual, living two-headed girl who resides in an undisclosed (for obvious reasons) town in the Midwest. It's hard not to obsess about this living, breathing six year old creature. The trains of thought are endless- she's got two heads, but only one heart, one set of lungs, one spine; is she a girl with two heads or a pair of twins sharing a body? I tend to go with the two-headed girl theory, but the parents have named each head and they seem to display distinct personalities, so what do I know. Eventually, one of the heads will go punk and the other will become a fundamentalist Christian- it will be a fashion nightmare. Outfits will be sliced down the center and sewn together in incongruous halves.

When it comes right down to it, is the body just a contraption for hauling around the brain, which is the real you, the locus of your personhood? Is your brain floating in a vat the real you without it's electric wheelchair and video game joystick to cart you around? Or is it just one of your organs, disembodied, like an appendix preserved in rubbing alcohol? These are the big questions. I think this is what Jack Kirby was getting at in those old Marvel comics- when he paraded around that one character of his, the big red disembodied head with the tiny legs and arms, who crawls into the empty face of a giant robot body and, pulling levers, levels buildings. When I fucked up my leg, did I feel like less of a person for being less a leg? No- I felt like a new person, the new, fucked-up leg me.

The lady in the wheelchair disembarks. When I was a little kid I went to Disneyland with my family, where I saw a guy in an electric wheelchair and told my dad that I wished I had one, too. He told me that that was a horrible thing to wish for. As I child, I could not grasp this. Come on, free rides all the time? Eternal bumper cars? It seemed a small price to pay for not being able to walk, an activity which I loathed at the time anyway. I've come a long way since then- I walk all over the place now, I'll walk anywhere, if I have enough time. I walk for money, even; seven bucks an hour to trudge around Northeast putting up flyers. I almost decide to save the dollar and walk across town to the food stamp office.

The poverty line is low- somewhere in the six thousand dollar a year range- but I beat it by a mile most years. Last year I made twelve hundred dollars in taxable income. I live in the wrong country for that, a country which actually looks down on me as slothful for this. The watchmaking, metronome-hearted swedes would be complimenting my thrift and handing me a check. I'm all for secession from British rule, I love to call them french fries instead of chips and all, but their whole being "on the dole" thing really holds a lot of appeal for me. The economy only functions when there's a permanent base percentage of the out of work, and I bet some of those five to seven percent really would like to have a steady job. Given that, it seems selfish and inhumane for me to fill a slot I don't even want. Is a little stipend for my selflessness, for my willingness to keep the economy roaring along, so much to ask?

In the food stamp office there is an arsenal of forms and questionnaires to fill out, a procedure which I'm mildly unnerved to notice that I'm getting fairly acclimated to. You jump a few hoops, sit in some uncomfortable plastic chairs for a few hours, and eventually you get whatever it is that you came for. Life in the safety net is a lot like high school.

I take a number and sit, waiting for an interview with whatever lucky individual is assigned to be my "case worker." It does take a while, and it's a nice day out. I look out the window at traffic snarling it's way down Powell, thinking I'd like to walk through that traffic, breathe in the exhaust and dirt. That would be nice, better than sitting in this plastic chair- but, of course, that's just what they want me to think, That's why they have this big window here, that's how they weed out the less than totally desperate. When my number is called I'm still staunchly planted in my chair, forms filled out and clenched in white-knuckle fists.

The case worker seems like a nice guy, giving me a cursory glance which tells him all he needs to know, skimming my questionnaire, asking a couple of monotone questions- "how long have you lived in Oregon?" "Have you worked in the last month?" I answer his questions and he nods, checks off boxes. I tell him that I've signed up with a temp agency and that as soon as they start calling I'll be fine, I just need some help getting on my feet that's all. He seems to like that line of argument. The case worker nods dreamily, staring over my shoulder, into space.Then the phone at his desk rings, and he whips the receiver off the hook, clamping it between shoulder and chin, continuing to check boxes, muttering into the mouthpiece. "Oh, heyyyy," he murmurs. "Yeah." pause. "Uh-huh. Yeah." I fidget, stare at the walls, watch the clock. His voice continues a monotone, monosyllabic drone. "Listen," he says, "Uh, listen. I'm with a client right now. Can I call you later." There is the pause of response on the other end. The case worker looks perturbed. "Riiight. Yeah. See you later."

He hangs up, staring blankly at the sheet he's been checking off. He's lost his concentration. A moment of silence as I wait for whatever comes next. He looks up, assesses me for a moment.

"Man," he says, shaking his head. "I just started dating this girl last week."

"Now she's calling you at the office," I venture.

"Does a week seem kind of soon to be calling me 'honey?'" he asks.

"I don't know, man," I say, "I think it kind of depends on the relationship."

"Things are moving fast," he nods, "I just got out of this pretty serious relationship and, well, I'm not sure I want to jump right back into this kind of thing. I just seem to repeat the same patterns, though."

"I have that problem." I say.

"You have a girlfriend?" he asks.

"No," I shake my head, thinking about my disastrous dinner with Elizabeth, "I just got out of a thing too. It kind of...well, I don't know. I don't really know what's up," I say.

"Yeah, no kidding," the social worker laments. "Now she wants to go on this cruise. That seems kind of heavy. She'll want to move in soon."

"Then it all goes to hell," I predict.

"That's usually how it works," he agrees.

"It's weird how you can see where it's all headed and feel totally doomed about it but you still go through with it anyway, just go through the motions."

"No kidding!" he says, "I can't believe it. *Honey*, she says. " he stares at the phone. "Ah," he mutters, shaking his head, snapping out of the self-induced trance. "So, now, what are you here for?" he looks down at my paperwork. "Hmmm, well you should be able to qualify for emergency benefits and begin picking up food stamps right away. Of course, you'll need to come in for an evaluation every three months and notify us immediately if there's any adjustment in your income."

As I get up to leave we shake hands. "It was nice to meet you," I say, "Good luck with that whole girlfriend thing."

"Thanks," he laughs.

Walking out into the lobby; anxious people clutching forms and squirming in uncomfortable plastic chairs, waiting through another couple hours of wasted life, wasted time. In the back offices, in cardboard and felt divided cubicles phones ring and dates are made, hearts are broken and mended. Lunch money is doled out. When's the prom? You learn a lot about sitting and killing time in high school; it comes in handy later.

16.

It's a crappy day, gray and drizzling.

A typical Portland day, and I'm on my lunch break from a job at the downtown Meier and Frank department store, sitting a few blocks away on a wall and killing time. I'm watching people walk by. There goes a man with one arm and a lovely burgundy sweater. Another gimp, another hip, homeless hipster. Portland drives me crazy.

I feel pretty OK, wearing an old red sweater and pants found in the trash by my mom, a nondescript dark blue prole shirt and the usual black clunkers for shoes. It helps to wear a uniform of some sort, in order to feel a bit more cartoony and less emotional and human. Most days I'll find something to get bummed out about, whether it's my weird interpersonal relations with people or just the bad weather and how spring never seems to get going. Both of these things seem to boil down to a lot of talk and not much action- I keep waiting around, but it's always one or two nice days of sun and then a lot of big mouths jinxing it by announcing that spring is here, a lot of big mouths putting a curse on my life by making plans for picnics and staying out late wearing shorts.

However, I must say that my life looks pretty rosy in comparison with this guy who I am working with today at Meier and Frank. He really has no hope. We have been spending the day doing a tedious chore known as "re-wrapping," which is pretty much exactly what it sounds like- taking returned garments and wrapping them up in plastic. The top floor of the department store is a vast warehouse-space of free-floating garments and assorted sundry crap, which our meager labors will hardly make a dent in. The other temp, who I immediately begin referring to in my mental notes as "the Robot Man," saves me the traditional minute and a half trouble of asking one or two leading questions by immediately launching into a tedious and laboriously detailed account of his life story. He begins by assuring me that, despite his current temp status, he is meant for a far grander destiny and is, in fact, currently enrolled in business school, which he attends nightly. He hopes his impending degree will land him a "real job."

"Oh, yeah?" I ask, "What kind of job are you looking for?"

"Nine to five, forty hours a week," he says, flatly.

"Um... is that your only specification? No particular, say, field of interest or anything."

"No, just nine to five, forty hours a week," he repeats slowly. "I'm not picky."

"Wow! No kidding!" I say "Well, that seems like an attainable goal."

"I had a job at a grocery store for five years," he explains "three years on the graveyard shift. I was the graveyard shift manager," he says proudly.

"How'd you like that?" I ask.

"Every month, for three years, I requested to be taken off of the graveyard shift. But they just wouldn't do it," he recounts. "Finally, it ruined my relationship with my girlfriend, who left me. I lost all my friends, who worked days. The store was all I had left."

"So why did you leave in the end?"

"One night I sold alcohol to a minor and was fired on the spot." he mutters.

It's fairly astounding. The Robot Man's life seems Tolstoyesque in tragic sweep compared to my three month visits to towns, my one day on the job temporary life, which seems as lightweight as an *Archie* comic book. Why is he telling me this, I wonder? Why do I always make it a point to ask? It's as if I think that the accrued information will all add up into a huge flow chart pie graph data spread sheet, an equation which will unravel what's OK, will unlock the secret for how to live life in the right way. Data Spread Sheet Item One: do not live your life like the Robot Man.

Later that night, as we prepare to leave, I pass my time card over to the secretary in charge. She looks at it and grins up at me from her desk: "Oh! I'm also from Manpower!"

She laughs. I restrain myself from looking her in the eye and chanting in a quiet hypnotic voice, "Ah, yes. One...of...us. One....of...us." It's weird, alright. Manpower is the largest employer in the U.S. It's like all the teachers are substitutes, like no one is in charge.

As we walk out into the cool evening air, Robot Man expresses sadness at not having a job to go to tomorrow. "I need a steady job," he pleads, "I'm willing to work any evening, every weekend," he keeps telling me. But I'm not hiring.

17.

The phone rings off the hook,

now that I'm in; a few assignments completed without
overt displays of drunkenness on the job, and no swings
taken at any of the temporary employers, has assured me a steady
stream of employment offers, mostly for various sorts of light-
industrial work, which, by and large, I turn down, because I'm too lazy
to lift. There is this sub-basement of jobs which always seem
available, and when you haven't worked in a week or two, and start
getting that tinge of desperation in your voice, the girls will
invariably deal it out from the bottom of the deck- "Well, there's
always unloading the aluminum siding trucks." At which point you
start moaning slightly and make up some story about having had a
hernia recently, unless you're Bill, in which case you actually did get
a hernia from lifting things at a temp job.

It's always nice when the ladies from the downtown office
call up. they are always exceedingly friendly, and I feel that I am
developing a good rapport with them. Is it just my imagination or do
some of them- the cool ones, the ones who always give me the jobs I
like, seem to perk up an extra notch or two above the call of duty when
I saunter in to turn in a pay stub? Just the other day one of the girls
said I was "swell." My nonchalant attitude towards doing crappy
stuff seems to please them immensely. I was even, a bit earlier,

thinking that one of the girls who works in the downtown office is pretty cute. This led me to formulate an elaborate scenario where I ask her out on a date, she accepts, we become romantically involved, and then when it starts getting really heavy and serious she is wracked with guilt at the immense conflict of interest involved. By this time she's slipped down a treacherous slope of moral ambiguity; she begins giving me all of the really good jobs (which ties into another secret job fantasy I have involving a secret "X File" where they keep all the outrageous luxury jobs stashed away for their most favored ones- I *know* it's in that office somewhere), which of course is making all the other women working at the office, as wall as my fellow temps, extremely suspicious. Our torrid affair would obviously have to be kept under wraps, and there would be a lot of sneaking around involved- but worse than that would be this whole other layer of intense deception, the dark secret which I could never tell her, but which, as time went on and our relationship blossomed, she'd begin to suspect. How long could I hide from her the fact that I am the world's worst employee? I'd be living such a tremendous lie, pretending that I really dug all the bullshit she was assigning me to do (because, really, how good is that X-file going to be?), wooing her with tales of success and customer satisfaction at some office, as she wonders darkly where all those staplers are coming from, and why my collection of rulers, scissors and reams of paper seems to grow and grow.

Hmmm. Having thought the whole thing out to it's logical conclusion, I realize it just isn't going to work, and so I've nixed the idea.

18.

While riding the bus home, I am often transfixed by an advertisement,

posted by a temp agency called "labor Ready-" the ad proclaims in bold red letters "Work Today....... Paid Today!" - a slogan as far removed from the cutting edge of subtle advertising nuance as that guy Mr. Cash, local North Carolina kitsch celebrity, who appeared nightly on TV during my youth to wave wads of dollar bills in clenched fists as he offered dubious no-strings-attached trailer home refinancing. A similar wad of dollars illustrates the phrase "....Paid Today!" and three smiling guys in hard hats grin out at the viewer alongside the "Work Today...." although their presumably worker-satisfaction-induced grimaces look to me more like they are sizing me up for an ass beating and they like those odds. I have not been temping long but I know enough to avoid places like Labor Ready, places where you get issued a hard hat at 6 a.m; get a load of bricks dumped on your head around 11, and have the dents in the hat deducted from your pay around 5. You have to read between the lines, pick up on the subtle signals- any place that advertises on the bus with a wad of crumpled dollar bills in a clenched fist is probably going to suck.

Working as a door greeter for a huge furniture warehouse sale has inspired me to concoct an elaborate plan whereby Bill and I would trade off jobs, using the old "my mom thinks I'm at his house and his mom thinks he's at my house" routine to procure us each half a day of wandering around downtown while on the clock. I spent my half-day half aimless, half tense with anxiety that something might be going wrong and that the powers that be might be uncovering my devious scheme. The only real enjoyment I got out of the whole thing was the thrill of playing hooky, which I hadn't really checked in on in a good while, and which actually is a pretty hearty little thrill.

But it's not all so heart-warming. Manpower calls to ask me if I'd like to work the swing shift at a janitorial supply warehouse one day. "You want me to work from eleven at night until eight in the morning loading trucks?" I say, cracking up. It seems so horrible that I can't even believe such a job could exist. "Sure, I'll take it," I say.

The manager of the janitorial supply place is cracking up too, when he sees me, apparently in on the whole humor-in-horror concept. "Look, man, according to your temp contract we can't ask you to lift more than fifty pounds, so if you suspect we might be making you lift too much you can just call bullshit on that, OK?" He and the other guy working the night shift convulse with laughter over that one, sobering up only long enough to throw a hand-truck in my direction and load it up with a barrel of mint-lime scent detergent clearly labeled as weighing four hundred and fifty pounds.

I spend the night hauling crates, barrels and boxes from within the snaking bowels of the warehouse and carting them into the backs of eighteen-wheelers, from there to be dispensed to various institutions and facilities in need of some minty-lime freshening-up. While my handtruck skills do improve noticeably, they do so at the price of a rather sizable chunk of my faith in the decency and humanity of the world. The two guys I am working with (I'm just filling in for a guy who has taken his paycheck and gone on a massive several day drug-binge, which apparently happens like clockwork every pay-day, after which he returns sheepishly and is rehired) have been working this shift for a good while, and it really seems to be crushing them pretty intensely. They are barely recognizable as human beings; just weird, sad drones loading and unloading, attempting to have conversations with each other during breaks but so worn out and frazzled that they can only speak in monosyllabic grunts. I never really thought about the implication of all the trucks you see on the highway: the transportation of goods is the backbone of the society, and the loading is horrible, the driving is horrible, the unloading is horrible, and the product being shipped is just the agent in someone else doing something really unpleasant. The worst thing about cleaning supplies is that they don't even address the primary function of an institution. Whatever the place being cleaned is, that crappy cleaning job is just prep work so that the institution can get around to its actual function, which, nine times out of ten, is something which involves a lot of people doing something really crappy as well. And the place I'm working is even a third tier of crappiness removed from that in that it merely distributes the cleansing agents to the unfortunate cleansers. It's a pyramid scheme, a grand and overarching conspiracy of everyone doing unbearably ugly and mundane things, in a vicious cycle whose unbearableness serves only to facilitate the production of more unbearableness.

Having stumbled upon this horrific glimpse into the hidden world of grinding gears which pulp and mash my fellow Americans into broken-willed wretches, all for the greater good of the bloated bastard beast of national overconsumption, I return home, and, around nine in the morning, call the office.

"No more jobs like that," I tell them. "From now on, it's chicken suits exclusively for me."

19.

I take girls out on dates with food stamps. The case
worker tells me to call in as soon as I start making more than three
hundred dollars a month so that they can readjust my allowance; this
prompts me to meticulously calculate my temp earnings so that I will
be certain to refuse all work the moment I make two hundred and
eighty dollars. I watch myself on food stamps and it makes me feel
right wing. Good God, I'm exactly the kind of person who needs to be
rounded up and put in a labor camp, forced to break rocks down into
smaller rocks with a pick-axe or something. I spend the majority of my
food stamps on Super Big Gulps of Mountain Dew which keep me up
all night, bouncing off the walls of my bleak box of an abode, thinking
about how pointless everything is, rationalizing all my irrational
behaviors off of that premise. What the hell is wrong with me?

20.

I call Wells at work to find out if he wants to hang out later. "I get off at five," he says firmly. "If you aren't there right when I get off work, just keep driving down the street, because the second I'm allowed to leave I start walking. I can't be in that place a moment longer than absolutely required." It's safe to say, I think, that he doesn't really like his job.

He works at an electronics wholesale company in the desolate single-digit-street area of Southeast, an area characterized by foreboding warehouses, broken glass, and lacerated right down the middle by a rusty set of train tracks, down which trains wheeze at regular intervals, carrying nothing nowhere. Sometimes, at night, when I was in school, I'd take a walk down to this part of town. The train passes within a few feet of some buildings, forming an open air tunnel-like gauntlet. I'd stand with my back against the wall of some dilapidated office space and wait there, perfectly still, as the train rumbled by, pinning me there, a wall of metal lumbering past, missing the tip of my nose by an inch or two. You could reach out your hands, grab hold, and swing yourself up- it was fun, clinging on, to catch a ride across town. I guess you can still do that if you want to.

This part of town has the same appeal that all industrial ruin holds- some promise of The End, an indication that industry has become cancerously malignant, and is rusting itself out. In the post-cold War era, with it's shattered promise of instantaneous armageddon at any moment, it's something to hold on to, at least. I was always fascinated by a college acquaintances' description of the people who lived by these train tracks, or down by the river- "people who carry no form of ID," he'd explain ominously, and somehow it evoked living on the edge for me, drew me in.

I never thought someone I knew would work in one of these ghostly sweat shops. Wells spends his break time outside, by the train track, where he amuses himself by placing pennies and other small metal objects on the tracks, and then waiting for a train to come by and flatten the objects into tiny distended art objects. He has an impressive collection- one penny features a grotesquely distorted Abe Lincoln, still recognizable with his forehead exploded and jaw distended. Abe Lincoln, hit by a train.

Wells' job involves processing forms with serial numbers on them. He has no idea what the serial numbers represent specifically, but is pretty sure that they correlate to the various circuit boards and transistors which are on display in the company catalogs, provided as the only reading material in the bathroom, perhaps as a final blow in the breaking of the employee's wills. As an additional form of self-torture, the only music in the office is the muzak which plays while a phone line is on hold, and Wells puts the phone on speaker-phone mode and cranks it to top volume, letting the lite rock fill his cubicle with the soothing sounds of adult-contemporary suicide pacts and nervous breakdowns.

He's leaving work as I arrive, hustling out the door. We walk over to the tracks to harvest the penny crop for the day. Wells holds up a mashed bolt, flattened into a paper thin sheet. "Not bad," he mutters. Sometimes I hardly recognize him, he's so angry about his job. The crushed pennies seem to help him keep a grip on things, they give him something else to focus on. Still, I wonder, why is he doing this to himself?

As we walk up the street I ask him. "Man, you're the guy who turned me on to Manpower," I say, "and it's not like I really work any great jobs, I mean, it kind of sucks to shelve books or make copies for a couple of days, but Wells, I must say, your job *really* sucks. And you work forty hours a week! I work about forty hours a month."

"My job is the worst job on earth," Wells corrects me, "and the fucked up thing is, I'll probably get asked to join on as a permanent employee in a couple of months."

"you've got to get more into the whole temporary aspect of temping," I advise him. "I never like a job to last more than two days. That way one day is your first day, and the next day is your last day- and everyone knows those are the two best days of any job."

Wells walks down the railroad track, occasionally nudging a scrap of misshapen metal with his shoe, or stopping to stare out across the bleak metal underbelly landscape there, at the foot of the various bridges which bind Portland together, right down the river, like sutures on a tremendous, wet wound. He's quiet a lot, and when he talks it's usually funny but also pretty bitter. Sometimes you appreciate the joke but feel like you want to pretend you didn't understand what he meant, just so as not implicate yourself in the world-view, the sadness of what a lot of the best jokes really mean. Wells has a great way of looking at me when I say something like "you need to get more into the temp aspect of temping," which turns what, as I said it, I really thought was a truism worthy of being printed and distributed in fortune cookies, into the most childish statement imaginable, a succinct articulation of the chasm between us.

He's got the Fear, I guess. A lot of people have it; I guess the aging process involves seeing a lot of strange poxes sweep over your people- first the Fear, then hair loss, arthritis, retirement, and eventually funerals. A sort Chernobyl-cloud of free-floating despair (it reminds me of an article I read in Newsweek about "free radicals-" not a gas, not particles, just-- actually, "cloud of free-floating despair" may have been their term) seems to roam about, occasionally seeping into people's consciousness and producing this strange, agitated state which expresses itself as bitter sarcasm, or snippy cynicism, slipping out on occasion, inadvertently, when the host's mouth was really aiming more for a bemused, sardonic sort of wit.

And there appears to be no formula for inoculating yourself. The age bracket I'm in encompasses a variety of lifestyles, economic brackets, upward or downward mobility, desk jobs, clown schools, janitorial positions. There's no excuse for people like Wells and I to be unable to match ourselves with a social position or occupation (in the most general sense) which provides the right ratio of happiness, security, contentment. And still, here we are, walking around on the train tracks, kicking rocks dejectedly. It occurs to me to wonder whether Wells' apartment has been checked for Radon. That shit may or may not be related to the aforementioned free radicals, but in any case you don't want either in the house.

Existential dread, that's all it is, an old-fashioned malady like the flu. Existence itself by nature produces existential dread, like exhaust from a car. Once you catch on to the acceleration of your life towards the final configuration, that moment when you have to look around and go- "hmmm. So, it all boiled down to sketchy roomates, a carpet I was allergic to, a pretty bitchin' car and so-so parents-" and then die, well, the acceleration realization causes one, naturally, to panic. It's a tremendous psychological pressure: that, at the crucial juncture, despite our best of intentions, we may play some card wrong and somehow end up somewhere we do not want to be.

Most people can imagine the potential, not just for future misery, but for a future which is characterized by, even more so than just some potential moments of misery- stubbed toe, etc.-, an overall general blanket vibe of hating it. I get it on occasion. You have those moments where you feel close to articulating your highest ideal, only to hear your own voice instead articulate the most banal of clichés, and that, you're startled to find, is it. Those crazy old urban legends are your high moral principles, your collective myth. In those moments you realize, the shining future is not coming, and nothing's going to work out how you planned it.

On the way to wherever we're going, the nickel Arcade on Belmont or something, we pass Wells' apartment and he seems to suddenly get an increment wearier, as if fighting off the earth's gravity were one thing, but the dual forces of that and the magnet hum of his house are just too overpowering. He excuses himself, feels tired, goes inside to rest. It leaves me feeling nervous, and I pace up Belmont briskly, hands twitchy and shaking my head a little. I feel like he just handed me all of his cagey energy and the least he could have done was spent a couple of minutes going over the instruction manual. But, ah well. I find myself tongue-tied and unnatural around Wells, weighted down by my own ability to articulate, to navigate our friendship. It happens: you get too close. I've known him since I was about twelve, and when I moved back to Portland from North Carolina he moved here as well. I guess he didn't realize how much the continental edge this is, how the end of the world it feels. It's a bad place to get the Fear.

However, when I see that look in his eyes I assess my own lot and see an even weirder phenomenon- a feeling which resonates a somewhat different, though also kind of disturbing, note in my psyche. The malady I've got is certainty, which is in some ways more comforting: while the Fear is an anxious state premised on the bleak improbability of an eventually victorious life's outcome, certainty is a more upbeat, though still quite bleakness-intensive, state of clarity as to all the bad things to come. Increasing alienation from friends and family as I grow more eccentric and irritating; no property, assets, significant other or children of my own because of my oft-espoused conviction that such things are "square" (which is code in my secret lexicon for "too expensive"). The accompanying bitterness and anti-social manifestations lead to "weird" being added to "unskilled" on a data base somewhere next to my name.

So much misery, but grim realism allows me to embrace it rather than run from it. Bad life means good art. When I think of the future, I can truly feel, deep inside me, an untapped reservoir of ill feeling, a gushing oil well, a geyser of despair and its accompanying doodles, short experimental films, Pulitzer prize winning collection of suicide notes. My livelihood is assured. Sure, free-form sufferer is not the most lucrative of career options, nor does it carry a good benefits package, but who am I going to lodge a complaint with about that? The whole premise of the venture is self-employment. I am my own boss, and as boss I feel I must make the executive decision that a good benefit package would be bad for business- it would be like giving all the workers at the beer bottling plant all the beer they can drink. Entirely self-defeating, since the workers just end up too drunk to bottle any more beer.

There is a magic Eight-ball at my house. When I get home, I shake it up, asking silently to an empty room: will Wells and I continue to be be friends much longer? The answer floats mysteriously in a soapy froth, biding it's time. "It is most definite," the Eightball finally prophesizes, cheerfully.

Fear is a different camp. It's like finding out your friends joined the Sharks and you joined the Jets. Once there, I find it difficult to infect them with my stoicism. I'd like to say, "don't worry, it'll all be OK." But I really honestly can't. All I can say with certainty is, "don't worry."

Something will happen.

<u>three</u>

INTO THE VORTEX

21.

The album "Into the Vortex"

by the North Dakotan rock group Hammerhead may
initially present itself to the listener as little more than the
retarded, painfully post-pubescent squawling of testosterone-
overloaded tough guys- what one might perhaps expect of any art
indigenous to the bleakest state in the Union, a state whose actual
license carrying residents have confided in me is "the worst place to
live in America"- however, to dismiss it as merely such is a grave
miscalculation. Bill certainly does not err in the direction. "My money
tape," he says, patting his shirt pocket; contained within that pocket
is a high-bias cassette of the Vortex as well as the far inferior
"Ethereal Killer" album ("too fast," Bill explains, "it's like the
drummer was a little bit ahead of himself, always tripping over his
fills. But then," he nods gravely, "they slowed it down. And they hit
it, man. And then when the third album came out, fuck, what a
disappointment, they were too fast again!") His tape has no case and
no song listings, and it cuts off during the last song, but still: I must
confess, there is a hypnotic, sludgy grip it exercises on the listener.
The actual arrangement of tracks is interesting in and of itself. The
album begins with a couple of pretty alright mid-tempo selections,
plods along, moving slowly, inexorably forward, each song slower and
slightly more torturous than the next. By song number four Bill is
pointing excitedly at the speaker, nodding furiously. "Do you hear

that bass?" he exclaims, "MAN, it's like a mattress!" He spreads his arms to pantomime laying his body on to a cozy bed, allowing himself to lean forward slightly into the speakers. I agree- it is kind of like an aural mattress, easy listening for the tittinus affected, soothing ocean sounds for a generation of sub-cultural mutants weaned on the screeching banshee-wails of thick necked hardcore singers.

It's the kind of record where you keep slowly edging the volume on the stereo up and up and up. I've never heard a more appropriately *titled* album: putting the best songs *in the middle*, rather than going for the easy sell of putting the best songs early on, the undiluted inspiration of that move, does indeed create a whirlpool effect which draws you in to the core, the black hole center of the album, where slack-jawed and light-headed from the bludgeoning weight, you realize you've been nodding your head back and forth without blinking or thinking a polysyllabic thought for several minutes, a state of delirious meditative mind-clearing endorsed by almost all major world religions as well as both all major cults and cult deprogrammers. It is at that point that the singer steps up to the mic and announces in a tone of raging victory[1] , "you have stepped into...the vortex!!!!" I don't know what the hell he's talking about (and, actually, I suspect that rather than being intended as metaphor, the Vortex in this case is intended to be read quite literally, and that the members of Hammerhead are, in fact, sci-fi nerds) but, man, it sounds pretty kick ass.

It helps a lot to be really stoned during all of this. "What we generally do," Andrew explains to me one afternoon, "Is, listen to *Into the Vortex* twice all the way through, smoking pot the entire time, and then, at the end of that, we go down to the basement and play music."

"That sounds pretty good," I must admit.

"Oh, it's a totally fun time," Andrew nods, arching his eyebrow and giving me a serious look.

Such shenanigans, performed regularly and over an extended duration of time, can only end in one conclusion: Bill and Andrew eventually find that they have formed a band, which, well, sounds a lot like Hammerhead. "*Manpower*," says Bill one afternoon. "We'll call it Manpower. It works on a number of levels. First, it connotes our manly style of bludgeoning testosterone music. Secondly, we both work for that temp agency, so it has personal significance, as well as connoting our rigorous work ethic. Also, implicit in the name is our particular musical genre."

---

[1] this is an example of the musical form my friend John Bowman refers to, I think quite astutely, as the "sweet victory parts."

"Which is...?" I ask.

"Light industrial," Bill states. When he tells jokes he delivers them flatly, never scanning the room for reaction or revelling in whatever social one-up they might give him. He's a workman, matter-of-fact, or, in another sense, superheroic: it's like God gave him a power he never wanted, the X-ray ears which allow him to hear the implicit punch lines of life, and he recites them, but almost grimly, as if he's an ancient oracle who can't help but tell us what's written on the cave wall, knowing we'll probably cut his head off one day for giving us what we asked for.

I like Manpower (the band), though. Their songs tend to have Appealing conceptual twists, like the song whose entire lyrics are composed of the messages which run across the bottom of Public Enemy albums ("Freedom is a road seldom travelled by the multitudes! Freedom is a road seldom travelled by the multitudes! The government's to blame!" Bill yells, as the music thunders along sounding, well, again, kind of like Hammerhead). "Seeing Stars" transcribes Bill's conversation with the singer of Jawbreaker at a New Years Eve party, and begins:

we talked about Depak Chopra
And the time that he was on Oprah

leading me to wonder whether it was Depak Chopra or Black Schwartzenbach who appeared on Oprah. I don't ask, though.

22.

I've been recently dumped

by Andrew's housemate, a girl named Ramsey, whom I've been working out a mediocre melodrama of torturous interaction with for a few weeks now. She calls me up in the middle of the afternoon, no doubt aware that I'm barely awake and so practically defenseless, and says, "Listen, I heard you went to the movies last night with a friend of mine. Is that true?"

"Yeah," I say groggily, "why, does that make you feel weird or somethi...?"

"Have all my stuff in a pile in half an hour. I'll be by to pick it up."

"Oh, man, can we...."

"No, we can't still be friends. Don't talk to me ever again after today." She doesn't sound mad, really, just authoritative and in control, the tone of voice you usually use when you're talking to a representative of the phone company.

"OK, well, see you in half an hour then, I suppose."

She hangs up the phone, and I stand in the living room, perplexed but, I must say, overcome with admiration. What an awesome dump! So clean and efficient. She should be paid to kill people. She could probably assassinate government officials in their sleep, slit their throats and you could still use the bed linens the next day.

I go in my room to find her stuff. There's not a lot, but I scrape up a few odds and ends. Ah, wait: she loaned me a record by a hardcore band which I know she hates and will never listen to again if I give it back. Should I do the ethical thing and return her LP, make a clean break, a show of good faith? Or should I be in salvage mode, thinking of the cost-benefit relational breakdown: "at least I got this LP out of it, and that cup of coffee which I never paid her back for." Fuck it, I think, deciding to run with her no-prisoners approach, as I stick the record in the back of the pile.

I look around the room. It's hard to argue the case for me as a boyfriend. No furniture, no stereo, a sleeping bag on a sheetless mattress (came with the room) for a bed- no one could accuse me of living in a love den. The first time that she stayed over here, she asked me whether there was any other lighting option beside the naked 100 watt bulb dangling overhead. "Sure," I said, and turned the light off. I've seen some people's rooms and they are full of lamps and none of their lamps even illuminate a desktop or night table, or really any horizontal surface. These people creep me out, because all their lights are mood lights, and they are the masters of shadow and contrast and variations in "soft" lighting. Theses people have a lot of lights and I guess that implies a lot of moods, and that is weird to me. I have two moods, naked light bulb and total darkness.

Out on the porch to await her arrival. Whose fault is it really? I muse. What are the real reasons our relationship has broken down? Could I have done anything to prevent this dark day?

It is such a ludicrous attempt at a train of thought that I actually look around, embarrassed, as if to make sure no one even caught me thinking it. Yes, obviously I could have done something to prevent this dark day. I might have attempted to, in any way, shape or form, be nice to her. I could have taken her out on a date which didn't revolve around food stamps or shoplifting. Man, I was even kind of stingy with the food stamps, I recall, a bit chagrinned.

Well, that's all over now. One more nail in the coffin. I bang my head gingerly against the bannister, attempting mournful regret. It won't come. I'm still strangely happy about the actual dumping itself- so clean, so surgical.

This break-up itself is being handled with the utmost of social tact: *she really is such a nice girl*, I smile to myself. I am snapped out of my reverie by the car door slamming. Volvo station wagon, of course. Sometimes I'd go over to her house and hang out with her, and then she'd let me borrow her car to go home. It was always a nice, rare luxury to drive in this day and age of public transit, scary vagrants on the bus with their succubus energy, corrupting me to be more like them every ride. Oh, man, no more car, I think, on some meta-level berating myself for the crassness of the thought even as I think it. I feel like it's the sort of thing I ought to say to her- "So, no more using your car, huh? Well, that *really* sucks for me-" let her in on my Id, how bad I really am, to help her along in case there is a glimmer of doubt anywhere in her soul as to the correctness of one half hour ago's decision. But, as she approaches the porch, I can see pretty clearly that she is not harboring any secret flames or second thoughts.

"Hey, what's up." she says.

"You know, dumped." I shrug.

"Totally," she sympathizes. "So, this is it?" Pointing at the small pile of possessions on a chair in front of me.

"Yeah, that's all I could find, but, you know, if anything else turns up, I'll definitely call you."

"Fuck that, just keep it," she dismisses me with an aggravated wave, as if there are bugs in front of her face. She scoops up her belongings and turns to make a hasty retreat.

"Oh, wait. " I say.

She turns and glares across the lawn at me, her demeanor indicating that I am a mentally deranged misanthrope and am wasting her valuable time. I jump out of my seat and rush inside.

"Here," I offer moments later. "I almost forgot. The record you loaned me."

She looks down at it. "I hate that record."

"Oh, well. Uh."

"Why don't you just keep it."

She is down the stairs and gone, slams the Volvo door, accelerates, out of my life, gone. Until the next time I go over to Andrew's house.

Jason straggles out on to the porch; the sun is setting over the pink and blue houses of Southeast Portland, bathing everything in a super-cinematic hue of oranges and long, contorted green shadows. Jason has just woken up.

"I've been dumped," I brag.

"Yeah," he nods, smiling broadly, a connoisseur. "By the sixteen year old?"

"She's not sixteen," I grumble, irritated. "she's a perfectly legal early twenties-year old."

"Man, I'm not criticizing you," Jason smiles, and then wanders into the house again.

"At least I got this," I cackle, patting the LP. I follow Jason in, put the record on in the living room. It's pretty good.

23.

Nine O'Clock.

A lot of pot smoking going on in this part of town, a lot of D&D playing and bad 70's movies being preened over. I'm at Nick Holzgum's (sic) house in Northeast Portland; Nick Holzgum, characterized by Wells as "Nick? Nick needs to get his shit together. Nick needs a plan." But what kind of plan do you prescribe for someone like Holzgum? He's eighteen years old, showed up in Portland on a train one day loaded down with suitcases full of recording gear and a cello which had been terminally mauled in transit; he has no particular interest in going to school or pursuing any sort of managerial aspiration at a Starbucks or Subway franchise. A broken cello and a bad attitude- what can a young man do?

Actually, I think the plan is pretty admirable. Nick moved to Portland carrying as his only form of ID a North Carolina drivers license whose lamination he has pried open, for purposes of modifying his age with a bic pen. Arriving in Oregon, he traded his doctored ID in for a perfectly legal Oregon driver's licence which says he is twenty-four years old. It's amazing- I moved to Portland when I was eighteen, but I went to college and had to actually come up with ways to fill up all those days, frittering away years until I arrived at twenty-four, broke, sketchy, and planless. Nick simply used a bic pen to arrive, in one transaction with the department of motor vehicles, at the exact same point. And now here he is, and here I am, and we're both twenty four.

You have to admit, he's efficient.

We sit on the porch of his house, bathed in the dim glow of the green porch lightbulb, which casts sickly shadows on our faces, and makes us look like grinning mischievous leprechauns when we crack jokes at each other. Nick has moved into the sketchy part of town, where there is nothing to do after dark because there are no yuppies around to fuel the café and chi-chi shopping emporium economy which has provided gold-plated lamp posts and water-fountains which spew evian in the downtown and Northwest areas. In Nick's neighborhood it's not uncommon to warily dismiss gun shots as probably just a car backfiring.

Northeast Portland reminds me a lot of my home town of Durham, North Carolina, another city where nightlife generally revolves around drive-by shootings, and wandering stoned and slightly terrified around the desolate landscape has an unlikely pacifying effect; it feels homey and secure to be reminded of my dour and mortifying teenage years, an eerie reminiscence made playful in the post-modern kitsch reclamation of acting like a teenager when you should really be working on your Plan.

Right now it seems like there are enough people orbiting in our general solar system of extended friendships that Nick and I can talk about it forever, lovingly psychoanalyzing and taking apart all our friends and acquaintances, even as we secretly nod and deconstruct each other, in the short silences in between subject switching to subject.

"People!" Nick exclaims, "That's really the most interesting thing. I can just sit and think about any person and they are so endlessly complicated and bizarre that I can be entertained forever."

"And just think," I say, "sometimes they'll even *interact with each other*. There's just no end to the analytical tangents then."

Analytical tangents induce hilarity, stress me out. A nice night makes me love Portland. It's strange to love a place, just the geographical area itself, separate from the people you know there. Portland is full of lame motherfuckers, junkies and hipsters, but the place itself is good. Sometimes it's enough just sit on a porch. You feel your hand on a railing, you look across at the row of porches facing you down, and it seems like something just to be around the architecture, the sidewalk, the sky.

24.

Over in Northeast Portland,

where rent is cheap and will remain so for a few more years, people eye me suspiciously when I walk down the street. The white kids are moving in to Portland's few predominantly Black and Hispanic neighborhoods, first in scattered outposts of rat-infested punk-houses and then in the form of bohemian college students and artists. "Good," says Andrew, "the more white kids move here, the less likely, statistically, that I'll be the one to get shot." This seems to me at first to be an extreme thing to say, maybe even borderline paranoid. I figure that, having grown up in the South, I've experienced the world of racial tension. But a few days in Andrew's neighborhood leave me with his same nerve-rattled paranoia, as I find less tension and more, well, just open hostility. Nowhere in North Carolina have I ever experienced people actually stopping me on the street to ask angrily why I'm here, in this part of town. "My friends' house is around the corner," I answer. "Yeah, but *why*? Why are you people here?" the accuser insists. I don't really have a good answer. Uh, because your neighborhood is being gentrified?

Walking home from the store with Andrew and Bill one night, we pass Andrew's neighbors and out of the darkness, from the unlit porch, we hear cackling and a woman's voice, loud and jeering. "Is that white boys I see? Are you white boys?"

Bill addresses the porch, nodding resignedly. "Yes," he sighs. "Yes, we are."

The porch explodes with merriment, and the woman's hoots. "Quick! Steal their wallets!" she yells, taunting in the hopes that we'll flee in comic terror, limbs flapping wildly in a hilarious inversion of some slapstick blackface routine of the bumbling negro. Confused, we just stand there, nodding and smiling.

"Was there a better answer I could have given?" Bill ponders aloud, back in Andrew's room. "I mean, it's a pretty open-and-shut question." I must admit, the anger expressed against us seems pretty justified to me. After all, these cycles are not new in urban areas; everyone who was living here before the white kids started moving in knows exactly what's going on. College-educated kids who, no matter what their current economic status, come from affluent backgrounds, are as much an assault on the indigenous population of America existing in a ghettoised third world as the "peacekeeping forces" amassing in Viet Nam before the Gulf of Tonkin incident were an encroachment of the First World's institutional grip. We act as the advance scouts of gentrification, preparing the area for eventual full-on takeover. People like me, slumming around on foodstamps, jobless, we just become the smallpox-infected blankets, we carry the disease in to new and exploitable neighborhoods. With no agenda above and beyond maximizing my own personal ennui, I've been transformed, molded inadvertently into one more foot-soldier in the march towards gentrification, personal-size Trojan Horse built around my head, thinking that the thrift store clothes make me invisible or invincible.

"You see that empty building across the street from my house?" Andrew points out. "That's going to be a fancy restaurant called the frying dutchman or something. It's going to be the kind of restaurant which no one who lives in this neighborhood can afford to eat at. I think that's fucked up, but, man, I'll probably end up eating there," he concedes.

25.

"I'm young, I'm free, I'm single, and I insist on exercising my rights as a young single person," says Bill, by way of explaining why he has placed an ad in the *Willamette Week* personals. The fact that he has a friend whose job it is to type in the personals is also a factor, of course. "I went to this singles party," he elaborates. "The paper throws them once a month. I went for the food, of course. There were certainly no eligible singles whom I'd be interested in at the party, but they did have computers set up and you could type an ad in right there. *And it was free*," he reminds me. His personal ad says:

If you love Clint Eastwood but are ashamed to admit it, call me for your own personal Escape from Alcatraz. Seeking woman, 18-40. Bill, ext. 3241187.

"Eighteen to forty?" I say. "That's quite an age range."
"Yes.... I kind of regret that. Perhaps that was a little, um, impulsive," Bill says, the first notes of anxiety creeping into his voice.

There is a message in Bill's voicemail box a day after the ad appears. The woman sounds nice, and she leaves her home phone number. She is thirty-five, eleven years older than Bill, but he is undaunted, and calls her.

"It was totally fucked up," he tells me later, "I'm on the phone with this woman and we're having this really heavy conversation, I mean, the innuendos were flying! It was completely sexually loaded. What have I gotten myself into here?" But he does not seem entirely displeased, and calls the woman back to arrange a meeting place. The second call is significantly more disastrous. In the course of conversation, as befits two people who have met through a personal ads, the topic of hobbies and interests is discussed, and Bill mentions that he plays the bass. "I'm trying to imagine what you look like," the woman coos, "do you look like a rock musician type?"

"Well, I don't look like Tad," Bill quips, invoking the porcine rocker from Seattle, and adding for good measure (later he will moan, "I don't know where that came from! It just slipped from my subconsciousness and right out of my mouth!"), "Uh, do you look like Tad?"

There is an awkward pause, and the woman mutters, "well, I probably look more like Tad than you do." Bill ignores the comment, cooly reiterates the time and place they are to meet for their date, and, after hanging up the phone, proceeds to have a fit. He is still having it hours later when I see him, and he relates the whole story to me. "What does that mean? *'I look more like Tad than you do.'* Oh, man, it can only mean one thing, can't it? She's probably really, really obesely fat!"

"Yeah, probably," I agree.

"Oh, God!" Bill yells. "I feel horrible for even articulating that! This experience is really bringing out the worst in me! I can't believe the values I'm espousing when my back is up against the wall. Do you think I'm acting wrong? Is it totally immoral for me to be freaked out as hell right now?"

"Oh, I'm the wrong person to ask," I say.

Bill consults his friend, the personals typist, presuming that she has a firmer grasp on personals etiquette than he or I. She informs him in no uncertain terms that it is completely immoral for him to be freaked out as hell. She then accuses him of crass misogyny and, within a few minutes, has Bill swearing various oaths that he will, in fact, go through with the date.

I run into Bill at a party a few nights later, slouched in a bean bag in the corner and somberly swilling down a forty ounce bottle of fine domestic malt liquor. "Hey," I recall, "wasn't tonight.... aren't you supposed to be on a date right now?"

"I got there and instantly panicked. I had a beer with her, and told her I just couldn't go through with it."

"Did she look....?" My voice trails off.

"She didn't look like Tad."

"Hmmm."

"But it was too late. It was already blown out of proportion in my mind. I just told her that the, uh, age difference freaked me out too much."

"What did she say to that?" I ask.

"Oh, she just... kept telling me, 'you don't know what you're missing with an older woman.' Oh, it was terrible."

This ends Bill's experiment with being a carefree swinger type, an inhabitant of the underworld filled with heartrending despair and strange acts of desperate lonely flailing. It takes a grim view of humanity to stare these shadowy alleys and back doors down, let your eyes adjust and take in what's going on. He's really not cut out for the lifestyle, it seems. And really, who can blame him.

26.

Being,

depending on your leniency and willingness to accept romantic reinterpretation, either fickle and foolish of heart or morbidly insane, Ramsey's complete disinterest in ever being in the same room with me again elicits in me, predictably, the cultivation of a pathological new hobby, which is trying to be in the same room with her as often as I possibly can. I gawk awkwardly and make everyone involved or even peripherally located feel the bad vibrations.

One afternoon I stop by Andrew's house to find Bill and Andrew in a state of animated excitement bordering on crisis.

"Manpower has a show at Satyricon," Bill explains, "and... it's...... with.... Hammerhead."

"Woah," I exclaim, "that's pretty heavy, huh?"

"Yes." Bill stares into the distance.

"Man," I exclaim, "I want in on that. Let me play with you guys."

They ponder the prospect.

"You do work for Manpower, so it's thematically consistent," Andrew concedes.

"Think about the implications," I reply, "It actually elaborates on the theme. I wouldn't necessarily be in your band. I could just be temping for that show."

"Hmm, yeah," the idea seems to sit well with Bill.

"But you have to pay me for four hours even if the job takes only an hour," I remind them.

It is settled; we practice twice. I learn the Public Enemy song, the Blake Schwartzenbach song; I'm also introduced to "Safeway Select: the Indulgence," an epic power-ballad/product endorsement with its titanic he-man chorus: "Safeway Select! It's in effect! Give it respect!" ("Why, Bill?" I ask. "Why write a song extolling the virtue of the Safeway generic brand?" "Look," he explains to me patiently. "I'm not going to fabricate some cause to get behind. Product endorsement is the only valid statement I can make. I sing about what I know.") We also have an instrumental entitled "2000 Flushes: a Space Odyssey." And with this set-list in place, we're on our way.

The big night arrives; I am, of course, amped because I know that housemate cordiality is going to dictate that all of Andrew's housemates show up and watch us play. Somehow, I can't escape the notion, juvenile as it is, that this performance is really going to win me back into Ramsey's good graces. Even as the notion plays itself out in my mind, I cringe at the utter foolishness of it. I must concede that it is a compelling American myth, and I am trapped in the spell of it. Boy wins girl by beating up sand-kicking bully/ scoring wining touch-down/ brilliant, emotionally moving rock music performance. (This archetype is nowhere better illustrated than in the film *Purple Rain*. Appolonia arrives at the club where the Kid [i.e, Prince] is performing, only to be flocked with admirers, not the least imposing of whom is Price's arch-nemesis, Morris Day. Prince, seeing these events unfurl beneath him, begins to squeal and writhe around on the stage, rubbing the microphone on his genital area in a fever of sexual spazzardry. Cut to a close-up of Appolonia, transfixed by what is occurring up on that stage: lip trembling, a single tear streaks her mascara'd cheek-bone and you know, in that moment, that she is all his.)

We arrive at the Satyricon, a rather odd little dive which floats incongruously on a refurbished strip of yuppie comedy clubs and upscale steak and/or sushi huts. The place pre-dates its more upscale new neighbors, and still clings half-heartedly to the veneer of grime and low-grade sketchiness which used to just be part and parcel of running a business in "old town." The city has pumped a lot of money into gold-plated street lamps and shiny new street signs to make this particular avenue more user-friendly, but one street over there are still shady drug dealers and muggings waiting to happen. It's an identity crisis in progress, one of those self-indulgent crises you can't really have too much sympathy for. Economics create social conditions, social conditions are deemed poetic, scenic or "cool" by the strange insect hipsters who abstract and aestheticize things; this adds value and the economic conditions shift, taking away the elements which made it so quaintly prole and risqué in the first place. The vultures move on; confused tourists remain, and the drug trade moves one street over.

The people who populate this particular establishment seem to fall into a very particular and hard to categorize little sub-sector of the sub-sector which comprises the chronic boozers and marginally employed consumers and producers of, uh, what do you call it? "Night life?" Most of these people seem to be bikers or hoods, the kind of people who snort lines of industrial-grade detergent in the stalls, but you listen in on their conversations and they're footnoting Foucault as they argue heatedly about brand loyalty to regional micro-brews. They probably all write for the *Willamette Week* on occasion, and probably all do heroin on occasion.

I'm nervous. We set up our dinky amps and the sound guy smirks maliciously, his jagged grin smeared across the jowly chin as if the taut pony-tail he sports is pulling his face tight against his skull. I want to tell him to fuck off, but it is generally not a good idea to voice such sentiments to the sound guy, especially if you have little amps.

In the cavernous bathroom, the trough-style river Euphrates of urine has been recently renovated into more first-world style urinals. It's disappointing; I always liked the sheer barbarism of the long, communal bucket, of sidling up to wasted junkie bikers, swaggering all macho, like characters in a western, catching their mostly self-referenced Nietzchian notations as you nod and pee down their leg and on to their shoes. Now it's a little more well-lit in here, and everything seems more civil. I spot the bass player of Hammerhead, the producer of the sonic mattress, peeing. He is a mean-looking motherfucker.

Out at the bar, I drink free drinks and make conversation. A couple of my friends have shown up- Dave has made it out of the house, Nick sports a recently sprouted mustache. It looks good on him, and I catch various household-cleanser-huffing low-lifes stroking patchy goatees as they eye him enviously.

"You're killing everyone in here," I note with admiration.

"Thanks," he replies, nonchalantly, turning his head in a slow arc, his mustache like a high-powered beam which sends the roaches scurrying for shelter.

Bill is over in the other corner, where he is attempting to strike up conversation with the mean-looking bass player of Hammerhead. "It is really an honor to play with you. It's always been a goal of mine," he confesses.

"Cool," the bass player says, robotically.

Their conversation continues for a moment, but the mean bass player's apparent religious conviction against polysyllabism whittles it down to an eventual, "uhhh...OK....well, nice talking to you," on Bill's part. He stands there, awkwardly, as a few seconds creep by.

"Cool," the mean bass player says, looking Bill straight in the eye, dead serious.

By the time someone taps me on the shoulder, indicating that I need to appear on the dilapidated stage at the far end of the room, I have had several free drinks, am filled with a newfound courage, and also feel heartened to note that a fair number of people have arrived to witness our cacophonous spectacle. All the housemates are in attendance, clustered together as if forming a force-field representative of their respective fortresses of solitude. They move in lumbering, dozen-legged packs about the room, sucking people into their midst for a moment, making small-talk, spitting them out. I don't talk to anyone, though, although I do see Ramsey and as usual she ignores me.

We get up in front of the people and a moment of dread sweeps over me in the second after I turn on my crappy amp and turn to face the people, but then we begin to lurch and screech along and everything seems in order. Only after I disembark the rickety stage do I notice that I have dislodged my knee-cap in the jumping around process. It's not too serious- I pop it back in place, but can already feel it, hot with pus, purring under the skin like a hot rod engine. I'll limp for a few days, that's all. It's not terribly serious.

When Hammerhead plays Bill, Andrew and I watch them intently, but, despite the wall of monstrous amps, there is something not quite there in their performance. It isn't overwhelming. Maybe it's my knee hurting, or Bill's earlier conversation with the bass player. "Hmmm, you know, I may have made a grave miscalculation in my musical tastes," Bill ponders. "What do you guys think? When it comes right down to it, do they really just sound like the retarded, painfully post-pubescent squawling of testosterone-overloaded tough guys?"

"Well.... I mean, you know...." says Andrew.

"Come on, what are you going to do, Bill?" I admonish him, "become an indie-rocker?"

"Fuck that," he agrees. Despite his doubts, there is an air of accomplishment about him at this moment, the feeling that, even if it is all nothing more than testosterone and suburban angst, at least he's flexed with the meanest, angstiest of the bunch.

And, for only having practiced twice, we seem to have been received fairly well. The housemate amoebas lumber over to offer their drunken encouragements. Nick tells me it sounded indecipherable and horrible, a pretty good review for him: "No, you know, in a good way, though." Ramsey pats Andrew on the back and congratulates him, then heads off to make it to a party across town. I stand speechless next to Andrew as she walks away, watching her leave. Then, a few steps away, she turns back and looks right at me. I try to smile nonconfrontationally. She acknowledges me, and it seems to be not in a spirit total loathing. She looks sort of, I don't know- amused.

After she exits, I exhale nervously. "It worked," I mutter. "I can't believe it worked."

27.

Bill, Andrew, Kevin and I
have all procured the same temp job.

It's sort of annoying, the condescending cheerfulness
with which Kelly greets us when any member of our squad shambles in
the door- "Well, well, if it isn't the crazy crew! What are you zany
guys up for this week?" On the other hand, the perk of the whole
arrangement is that, unlike in high school, where they'd make sure to
put you and your cut-up pals in different sections of Algebra, in the
actual (or at least virtual) employment world, they like it when you
volunteer a whole gaggle of dudes to work with you on a job. It makes
the slot-filling tasks that much easier for them, it makes it less
likely that you'll be loaning some fellow temp your lunch money for
amphetamines (or at least more likely that you'll get paid back),
and, unbeknownst to the Manpowers that be, it makes it all the easier
to arrange the sort of multiple-member inside jobs of slacking off
which only a Unionized wall of silence can really facilitate.

The job we get is, as usual, mind-bogglingly weird: we have to
affix UPC codes to clunky 1950's style computer "disks" (they are
actually archaic black boxes, each the approximate dimensions of a
good-sized sandwich), and then run these UPC-encoded files through
a laser to determine whether the codes will scan. I am told that this
in preparation for the instillation of a friendly robot who will roam

the vast warehouse space we are working in, using a laser-beam eyeball to pluck files from the shelves and do god knows what with them. Friendly robot? I am very incredulous, imaging the tin-can contraption from Lost in Space hunkering around, whistling a merry tune in a creepy digital voice. Have these people ever heard of a microchips? Do they realize they are being sold a technology which is a decade out of date in Bulgaria?

These are the questions which illustrate why I work for an agency called Manpower as opposed to Manbrain. No one asked for my opinion, so I content myself with the fact that peeling stickers is easy and fun, if I can only transcend my being and enter the consciousness of a thirteen year old girl, and imagine that these UPC codes all scan "My Little Pony." Non-stop hilarity is provided by the deadpan monologue of a Portland State student whose abnormal psychology class has recently opened him up to various alternative lifestyle options, his explorations of which he has no hang-ups about relating.

"So, when you wear the rubber suits, then what?" Kevin wants to know.

"Well, you lay on the bed and, you know," he pauses for effect. "Well, then your partner takes a shit on your chest."

"And then you rub rubber suits."

"Well, yeah."

"And then do you have sex?"

"Oh, there's no sex," he explains. "it's more about the defecation."

"You took a class on this in college?" I interrupt, from my station over at the laser.

"Well, that was one unit." he clarifies. He rates the practice highly, though he admits that in the long run it's "kind of too messy."

Andrew is oblivious to all of this, wearing a walkman and air-guitaring frantically in front of his laser. Occasionally, a managerial lady stops by to berate us harshly for talking and carrying on. I can't escape the feeling that we are in grade school, that triumphant feeling of a class out of control, a class which has seen the fear in the substitute teacher's eyes all too clearly. Bosses and teachers who treat their charges as some vaguely terrifying species of borderline-feral monkeys get what they deserve.

Of course, things go slightly over the edge around mid-afternoon when the hilarity becomes too much for me and, swinging my arms around wildly in the throes of some extended anecdote, I knock the laser I'm in front of off of it's precarious stand. It goes crashing to the ground, shattering into various pieces. There is a moment of tense quiet, and then the room explodes with even more vigorous laughter.

"Come on guys," I choke out between tears of mirth, "This is serious. Help me out here."

Andrew helps me to rig the laser back into looking sort of assembled, and then we prop it precariously back on to it's stand. It doesn't work, of course.

"All right, none of you people better sell me out," I threaten, pointing around the room. I resume my station in front of the defunct scanning device, pantomiming labor on already scanned black blocks. This is, of course, even easier than the actual work. "Man, if you need a break, you can get in on the leisure station," I tell Andrew.

A half an hour or so later, he is daydreaming in front of the leisure station when the high strung manger enters the room to berate us on our progress. Of course, she makes a B-line for Andrew. "How's it going with this thing?" she asks, giving the old laser a poke. At her gentlest touch, it falls into about five sections and clatters to the floor. Andrew stares down at his feet. The room tenses up.

"Woah, looks like you broke it," he says to the boss.

She seems to want to control her temper (those assault and battery lawsuits are costly, as she seems like the type to know from experience), and speaks in even tones, face growing a purplish-red hue in the effort of containment. "Er... was this unit giving you any problems?"

I'm squirming in my seat, my back to the manager. Will anyone try to save themselves? Will I be sacrificed for the collective just because, well, technically it *was* me who destroyed the laser? How much do those things cost anyway? How many years of polishing the friendly robot will I be sentenced to?

"Man, not until you showed up." Andrew says.

The woman stares hard into his face, trying to find a flinch in his expression which will indicate a lie. She can feel the hot sweaty wool being pulled over her eyes, and it is driving her mad, but she finds in Andrew's face only a cool look of bored annoyance, as if he's thinking, "great. Thanks a lot, Lady. Now, how am I going to provide my excellent standard of service?"

She scans the room. We all look down at the floor, or focus on our tasks, unpeeling stickers and other such attention-absorbing activities.

"It's that god damn night shift!" she explodes, finally. "Last night they poured coffee in one of these machines! Now this-*sabotage!*"

"Night shift people are slackers," I agree.

I escape this volatile situation without reprimand, but I am psychologically scarred. Things are going too far. I'm over the edge, and I never work at a job without obsessing on how to steal as much stuff as possible or hide in the back room the entire time. Bill and I work a job at a bar called the "Rockin' Rodeo" a week or so later, and when we arrive and find that the job is not as fun as a job with the word "rockin'" in the title would suggest, we essentially refuse to work and spend our whole shift plotting how to steal microphones from their powerful square-dance-related public address system.

My last job for Manpower involves working for the post office. I show up, stand in a room for an hour without doing anything, and am fired. When I insist that Manpower policy states that you have to pay a temp a minimum of four hours wages no matter what, the supervisor begins screaming at me. I walk back up to the office to turn in my time card. The postal manager has already called ahead to complain about me.

"What's this I hear about your poor performance today," Kelly asks in a voice which betrays the deep hurt of a trust bond trampled.

"You believed that guy?" I say, astounded. "An obvious psychotic delusional schizophrenic? Do you know how many postal killings occur every year? There are no standards involved in the hiring of those people except for meeting legal quotas of mentally deranged people in government positions. I'm shocked, frankly, that Manpower sent me in to such a dangerous situation."

Kelly frowns and doesn't seem to quite buy it, but she signs my time card and sends me home. Riding the bus home, over the bridge with the afternoon off, I realize that there's a reason they call it "temp." I should probably get more into the temporary aspect of temping. I probably shouldn't call anymore.

28.

The weather drives me crazy.

It rains for seven days in a row- which is not to say that there were seven consecutive days on which it rains; it rains for a solid one hundred and sixty eight hour period. I'm floating, aimless drowning. It's like the Bible come to life, my high school guidance counsellor liked to say about knots in trees which looked like the Virgin Mary and cried real sap tears.

Kevin is bailing on Portland. I'm not surprised. He's been working at an insurance agency translating documents into Spanish, but he hasn't found the experience especially fulfilling. His problem is the classic too close for comfort syndrome: he studied Spanish in college, but working for an insurance agent was probably not his ideal. A big dilemma people tend to face is when the conception of self begins to shift from the childish notion of who you are to the more adult what you do. Most people do not do exactly what they want to with their time. I try to spend my employed time doing the opposite of anything I'd ever actually want to do, in order to keep my free time more pure. My theory is, if you want to spend your free time painting, don't get a job painting houses. That's just way too much paint.

But Kevin flew where angels fear to tread, and tried to use his temp agency, of all places, to get a fulfilling job, one which might bear some relation to his actual interests or skills. Poor, wayward Kevin. What other result could ensue but that he'd find himself staring into the abyss? Which thought do you find more comforting? a) "My life and education have been spent in preparation for this job," b) "I have definitely never done anything in my life which indicates that I deserve to work at this god damn job."

The desertion seems to have materialized overnight. He has purchased a sad little station wagon, duct-tape intensive in it's non-essentials but apparently sound of motor, loaded up the back with his items, and prepares to depart. I can certainly relate to the sentiment.

There is a big going away party for him. Most people I know are there, at some sketchy house in southeast, dancing in the basement. A very drunk girl from Reed college is trying to back me into a corner and kiss me. Being the meanest person in the world, I tell her it will cost her a dollar. "I'll kiss anyone for a dollar," I explain. "Oh yeah?" Kevin interjects, grinning.

"You? I'll kiss you for free," I say, grabbing him. I'll probably never see him again, I figure, and he's a cute guy. I've never kissed a boy before and the experience leaves me acutely aware of how important it is to shave if you want to make out. His stubble crushes me. He has a solid face, like a brick wall, different from the mushy faces of girls. It's kind of appealing. "Ouch," I say, rubbing my chin, red from bristly friction. Kevin is laughing and dances away. The girl goes looking for a dollar.

29.

The tape player in the blue van (borrowed) broke, which has helped me out immensely in my pledge to listen exclusively to NRK radio rock and drive myself irrevocably over the edge.

Ain't that America, squawking out of tinny speakers, rattling my teeth loose with saccharine power chords and whittling away at my will to live. The radio keeps me in tune, so to speak. I know my enemy, I have seen the enemy and he is me. I have a tag which I stole from the Meier and Frank warehouse when last I worked there, and it says "visitor." I wear it all the time. It seems appropriate. I wish I had a tag which said "alien." I can't cope, I can't relate. I'm a dead man. I hope, sometimes, vaguely, that I don't offend people's sensibilities, but I can't really tell-- I've been wearing the same clothes for weeks on end, I believe. I have lost track.

You develop routines to keep yourself sane- I go to the same coffee shop every day, spending seventy-five cents on a cup of coffee which I milk for about three hours.

It's Halloween: I have no costume. I feel like a dork, walking down Hawthorne Street and everyone is dressed to the nines of garish excess. It's inevitable: either way I'll feel like a dork, costume or no costume. A no-win situation.

The rain is nowhere in sight, a sweet reprieve for fall in Portland. The streets are dry and it is bright out, a red sky overhead. The sky is huge. Everyone looks unnervingly attractive; girls waltz up and down Hawthorne in all manner of strange gear and for some reason I can't seem to pick out a face in the throng which isn't the most attractive face I've ever seen in my life. Everyone who appears in front of me has been the most beautiful person I've ever seen in my life, a cavalcade, for several hours now. Poor rattled brain- too little sleep, too many weird interactions, an absurdly weighted pendulum swings my moods erratically back and forth, seasick and crazed. I look straight ahead and try not to stare, thinking about Gregorian chants and shaving my head, and remembering the sound of Dave's voice in the solitary confines of a one room bachelor apartment I have recently helped him move into- "it's kind of lonely," and me trying to keep that same quiet desperation from creeping into my own thoughts. Everyone I know is gearing up to go to the big party at Andrew's house, and it's a week night! Doesn't anyone I know have a job? Doesn't anyone have anything to do in the morning?

I couldn't sleep all last night and spent the whole night searching for Nick Holzgum (sic). I went to every conceivable place I could imagine he'd be loitering around in, but he was nowhere to be found. Finally, defeated, I found myself walking down Powell, past the run down strip clubs around Thirty-ninth street. Impulsively, I decided to walk in. I couldn't really believe there were naked ladies inside. I entered the den of ill repute to find that, yes, there are. A couple of haggard and coked-up looking women gyrating on a pole. There was absolutely no one else in there, just me and the haggard ladies, spinning on the poles, stone-hard faces like they were at office jobs. It was a bad scene. I turned and fled.

At the coffee shop, I get a cup of coffee and sit down to collect my thoughts, and devise a plan of action for the night. The guy behind the counter is listening to some band which I recognize and I manage to make small talk with him for a while- a success, a social coup.

The air is abuzz with people scheming, making plans to go to parties, crap like that. I feel pretty weird. I drink four more cups of coffee.

A middle-aged woman enters the café, sits down, and begins peering intently at me. Eventually, she stands up and saunters over to my table. "Are you Peter?" she asks expectantly.

I'm momentarily confused, my dad's name being Peter. "I'm, uh...no.... my name.... Uh, no."

She sits back down, but keeps glancing over at me. She's almost glaring. It suddenly occurs to me that she is here to meet a *blind date*, someone named Peter whom she has never met, whose name she probably got out of the Willamette Week personals. She is convinced that I am actually Peter, but that I took one look at here and decided to pretend that I wasn't. I wonder if she is Bill's Tad, still in desperate pursuit of an escape from Alcatraz? Happy Halloween, lady! She glowers across the room- I become nervous, trying to avoid her gaze, intently watching the door, hyper-attuned to every guy who walks in, glances around and leaves again. God damn you, Peter, how could you sell me out like this?

It is almost too much to bear. Finally, she leaves, huffing in indignation and embarrassment. I wait for a few minutes, to give her a head start down the street, before leaving myself. Even then, I'm freaked out, expecting her to jump out of an alley, accost me, force me to attend a musical with her.

Outside, things aren't much more in line with my world view. All the trick-or-treaters seem to be twenty-something slackers wearing half-assed costumes. None of them have any respect for culture or tradition; they are all just in it for the candy. It's disgusting, really.

Tedra is having a Halloween party, so I walk over to her house. There is a small gathering of people there, Tedra and her housemates, of course, as well as a few strange familiar faces which I can't place until I realize one of them is a guy named Ben from North Carolina.

"What are you doing here?" I ask, surprised.

"Just got off the boat," he grins, "I'm moving here, dude!"

"Ohhhh..." I groan nonchalantly, my voice trailing off into a muted croak.

"Yeah, our whole band is moving here, man, it's going to be killer." he asserts.

"Great," I say. "Well, it's funny to run into you here."

"Man, everyone in this world is connected by a no more than two factors," he tells me, as if this explains it quite thoroughly.

"Those must be some sketchy factors," I muse. Holzgum has a jacket, the back of which simply reads "factors," printed up like it's the name of some team. I've always admired that jacket- it seems to be explaining it all away, excusing everything which might possibly happen, because, after all, you never can tell, you can never account for all the factors.

"No costume?" Tedra says, approaching me, simultaneously greeting and reproaching me.

"I just.... couldn't do it." I say. "If you could see what I've seen tonight, Tedra. The horrors. Grunge rock dudes wearing the most pitiful attempts at costumery I've ever seen. I can't be one of those people."

"Oh, come on...." she consoles. "I have an idea. Why don't you just wear my surgical scrubs from the clinic?"

"Oh, that's OK."

"Come on."

I ponder the proposition. "Can I tell people I'm dressed as an abortionist?"

"You can tell people whatever you want," she sighs, unamused.

"I'll try them on."

I close the door to Tedra's room and begin awkwardly trying to fit myself into the muted green gauzy garments which comprise her work gear. My limbs flail around spasmodically as I attempt to wriggle my way in. Too many cups of coffee keep my coordination in check, and I find myself performing a mutated ballet pirouette around her room, crashing clumsily into the wall and knocking over a shelf. "Woah," I mutter, and in trying to right myself fall over into a wall-mounted bookshelf, whose contents are also scattered to the floor. Son of a bitch, what is happening here? I feel like I'm possessed by the spirit of Buster Keaton and he's not used to the size of my lumbering limbs.

I do emerge fully scrubbed and the assembled guests oohh politely to make me feel good for participating in their little games. Tedra, presumably alarmed by the elephantine noises emanating from her now decimated room, peeks her head in and shudders. "Hmmm, the shelf fell over," she mutters to herself when she emerges, smiling in dazed politeness. Well, I'm in costume now- no time to waste on pleasantries. It is now imperative to get as loaded as possible, go over to Andrew's house, and make as many enemies as I can, or at least really cement the ones I already have.

Catch a ride, stopping at the Plaid Pantry along the way, guzzling nervously in the car- fall up the steps of his house and kick open the door. All hell is breaking loose inside, a thousand of my peers are dressed in all manner of absurd outfits, everything drowned out by the dull low-end hum of a band destroying their instruments in the basement, which seeps up through the floorboards, rattling your legs and reducing conversation to shrill screams , everyone crowding in on you, instantly screaming at you, and you just start shrieking back, belligerent nonsense, "bleeeeaaarghhhh!!!!" at the top of your lungs but they can't tell the difference, they make sense of your nonsense, or aren't listening, and nod as if to signal deep-felt connectedness and rapport, before gliding on to the next cretonious spectacle of mortality, bumping shoulders. There is Bill- he is dressed as a convict, in striped black and white with a funny little hat. And I see Andrew, whose face is painted ghastly white and who smiles broadly to expose his vampire fangs. He is wearing a leisure suit and later informs me that the concept for his costume was "Laid-backula." Nick Holzgum is here, startlingly convincing as a mustachioed twenty four year-old caveman. Everyone I know is here, except for Ramsey.

Well, no time to waste. I've got a town to be run out of. "I'm sorry about this!" I scream through the murk at Andrew. "What?" He screams back. I turn over a table, spilling bottles of half-swilled warm beer everywhere. I jump on a chair, and then tackle Holzgum's hapless housemate, wrestling her to the ground. Then up on a table and dance maniacally- people are enthused, no one gives a fuck. It is impossible to crack these people. You can set their houses on fire, disseminate genital herpes, kill their pets, nothing affects them. It all just makes you more the kind of person they want to know. It makes you great to have at parties. I'm struggling in quicksand. The more I try to alienate them, the more I try to engineer my own social downfall, the more parties they invite me to. Maybe they're one step ahead of me, reverse-psychologizing me. I have to admit, it's about the worst punishment I could receive.

Downstairs into the basement, where the atrocious rock band has segued into a drunken D.J. I'm waving my arms around like a poor, deluded dodo, a flightless bird still intent on keeping it real, struggling against inertia, straining for take-off. The party is dragging into the early AM hours, the dance floor growing creepy and disgusting as the gyrations of the ameba horde of palpitating arms and legs slowly undergoes multiple mitosis, splitting into paired off groups of two, grotesque in their costumes and lambada-like dances. Certain particularly far-fetched costumes circle aimlessly, like drunk bumble bees, trying vainly to make the chemical connection in a dance partner which will lead to embarrassing early morning sexual encounters.

About then Ramsey enters the room. She is dressed as a nurse, all in white, with a scarlet cross over her heart. She looks great. I pause, mid-gyration, stunned for a moment, and then realize that I am dressed in surgical scrubs. Hey, great! The costumes have thematic continuity. It must be more than a coincidence. I gyrate on over to her. Dance music overwhelms. Lights are pulsating and the lurid scene flashes yellow, blue, green, as Ramsey eyes me warily and I attempt to yell pleasantries in her direction. It is, of course, much too loud to talk in the thunderous cavern of this basement, and I am out of breath anyway, panting, trying to smile with my tongue lolling out of my mouth.

"HEY! HOW'S IT GOING!" I yell.

"WHAT?" she screams back.

"HOW ARE YOU DOING?!"

(momentary conversational pause. pounding bass drum beat. thump, thump, thump- electronic rave heartbeat, stuck in throat.)

"WHAT?"

Oh, well. Conversation seems out of the question here, so I kiss her instead. Astoundingly, she kisses back. I'm amazed. This is just way too killer to be actually working out. We are making out on the dance floor, and I am vaguely aware, from somewhere in the haze of my stupor, that people are gasping and laughing behind me. "I can't believe what I'm seeing!" I hear Bill exclaim with obvious social faux pas-induced bliss. He seems amused, at least, and in providing him this small service I feel a lot better about my life generally, for a moment.

30.

I'm sitting in the kitchen of Andrew's house the next day, surveying the wreckage. I caused most of it. It's embarrassing. I woke up at eight AM in Ramsey's room and immediately began having an intense anxiety attack. Five hours later it has really not subsided at all. I need to get out of this city. It's just too much. After months of trying to burn my bridges, force myself into a corner where I would be shunned by the populace, ostracized, tarred and feathered, run out of town- well, it just isn't working. My best attempts at wrecking my own life and the lives of those around me lead only to widespread recognition and acceptance, offers of places to live, employment opportunities, significant others. There is something horribly wrong with the psychological state of affairs here. These people are not humans.

31.

A week after Kevin's departure

from Portland, the rumors are circulating that he is back in town. I find them hard to believe. After the tremendous production he made about leaving, and with all his disdain and alienation in regards to the Northwest, how can he have chose to return? Besides, I say, he would have called me. No, the rumor-mongers insist. He's in hiding.

I finally see him at a party one night. "What the hell are you doing here?" I laugh.

He does seem embarrassed. But he swallows his pride and tells me the tale:

"Man, I only got about three hours outside of Portland in that damn station wagon before it completely broke down. I ended up checking into a motel and just sitting there for a few days, thinking it over. I guess I really had no choice. I came back. Gravity won. I feel OK about it, now.... guess I'm back in Portland, at least for a while."

I'm glad it wasn't me, hurtling out of the magnetic field of this godforsaken monsoon town, thinking that I was going to escape the yoke of my geographical oppression, probably listening to the new rock station one last time, drinking a Mountain Dew big slam and feeling pretty good about the world out ahead as the numbered streets on the overpasses changed from the familiar, Thirty-ninth, Forty-fifth, to the outlandish One-hundred and Sixtieth streets of Gresham and surrounding Portland suburbs; seeing the mighty Columbia river gorge stretch out and unwind along highway 84, idiotic skiers and windsurfers skittering about on the water like aquatic bugs, oblivious to the radio-active sulphurous sting of a river contaminated by the leaky nuclear power plants upstream in Washington- leaving all this behind, pushing hard on the accelerator, and then, BAM, the transmission drops out of the bottom of the car, careening off in the rear-view, the hood pops open and the carburetor shoots straight up, jetting steam in a swirling air-ballet of metal and wire, flames spew out of the radiator grill, and the whole journey comes to a screeching halt. I can imagine the jolt of that reality kicking in, the way everything becomes so concrete and static when the car stops, when the view out the window un-blurs and you face up to the fact that, yes, you are here. You're not going anywhere. Portland wins, it reels you back in. I'm glad it wasn't me who had to sit in that motel watching cable TV, contemplating the rest of my life. That sounds depressing.

32.

Down by the waterfront

in Portland, Oregon, walking through the remnants of the Saturday Market, as the first real moments of darkness set in, among tents filled with strange incense and nervously scuttling gipsy-turned-venture-capitalist nineties hippies- Andrew and Bill and me, squinting into the darkness at skateboarders with boards under arms scuttling into alleys to do who-knows-what. "Kids today," I mutter. I love to say crap like that; it makes me feel *mature,* which is at this juncture in my life still an occasional novelty, like the initial rush you get from huffing gas before years of the practice leave you with permanent migraines and brain damage. It's few days before election day- one guy I know has already voted by absentee ballot "on the toilet between acid trips;" most of my friends won't vote- it's easy to imagine that fascism is impending. The polls (correctly as it turns out) forecast new lows in voter turnout. Who cares? Not the droves of swarming teens in baggy below-the-butt pants and athletic gangster gear, or the pacifier-sucking rave kids bumming change as a fashion statement. When Charlton Heston is elected and institutes the new regime, it'll be guys like me being rounded up, the bad seeds.

"Man, look at us," Andrew says. " We're sketchy. We're the reason all these teenagers' parents are worried right now about their kids hanging out downtown. They might run into some dudes like us."

I pause to consider this. It always makes me feel creepy to have it brought into focus that I am, perhaps, a bad element. Bill, however, disagrees strongly with Andrew's thesis.

"There's NO WAY we're a parents' worst nightmare! We're all civil humans, from middle class backgrounds; we all have college degrees!WE COULD GO GET JOBS RIGHT NOW IF WE WANTED!"

We all have a good laugh about that one, and then imagine walking into the department store we're passing by and procuring employment. Man, I would be bummed out if I woke up tomorrow morning with a job at Meier and Frank. But, it is true, we could all probably get jobs right this moment if we tried. I've got the standard nineties hipster indie rock/punker short hair cut, i.e, the "hey, I'm still employable," look. Indie rockers are all bound by their common disdain for the *schlong* haircut (you know- the short on top, long in back hair cut) sported by various type and creed of redneck the world over, but the subtext to the vehement condemnation of this hair-do is a little disturbing when you think about it in employment terms-- I mean, at root, doesn't the hipster argument boil down to, "what kind of job can you get with that?" A few summers ago one of my housemates was the topic of much derisive commentary (behind his back, of course) from the other apartment-dwellers, and the main dis I remember is Dave saying, "I mean, he's got tattoos on his neck. You know what that means? It means he'll never work indoors." Me and Dave will always work indoors. I myself shave regularly, try to keep a modicum of employability at all times, even as I try to avoid actually being employed as much as I possibly can.

"Being unemployed in America is a disgrace," said a character in a movie I saw recently, "being unemployed in Paris is a noble act." The movie was set in the much mythologized Paris of the 1920's, a decade the youth of today, hungry for ideological constructs to support their sloth, turn to eagerly for re-affirmation. Portland seems sort of European, maybe self-consciously so, when you walk under bridges and find tents full of weird nicknacks being vended by strange men in garb which causes them to resemble wizards. Why not? What city wouldn't want to be Paris in the twenties?

Andrew supports the theory of Portland's self-conscious bohemianization, and he has the inside track, access to whole vistas of information which I am not privy to. Working on that NBC Movie-of-the-Week has brought him into contact with the alien and mystifying world of downtown commerce, the strange and amorphous entity he calls, "the new Portland." "The pressures always there," he says, "Are you part of the *new Portland*?" Within a revitalized and booming economy (Portland has ballooned from a population of 300,000 to 500,000 in the last few years, the local paper tells me) the new bourgeoisie flexes conspicuous muscles. The downtown is clean and modern, and often thriving; it's like being in some emerging nation-state, giddy with growth, reeling like a drunk.

A new restaurant is having a grand opening that night, packed to the rafters with well-dressed thirtysomethings, none of whom I've ever seen in my life, but who all know each other and knew that this was the place to come tonight, to see and be seen, to meet for drinks at the new spot previewed in this week's *Willamette Week* restaurant preview. Walking by, I stare in the window, make dumb faces, try to make the diners uncomfortable. Of course, just across the river I could be seeing and being seen by my own personal little cultural ghetto of dishevelled twentysomethings, in some place like the Montage.

It seems ironic that right in the geographical center of Portland you find the industrial wasteland of train tracks and homeless encampments, a chancre sore of desolation that just unabashedly sucks. From the Burnside bridge, which cuts right across this center, you can get a vantage on the various centers of gentrification and beautification which spread out from this center, attempting to make the city a *Money Magazine* winner for top ten places to live for the twenty-first century. The convention center, newly built, stands garishly illuminated at all hours, epitomizing this dream; the bizarre twin towers, garish and functionless, stand perpetually bathed in light, a self-conscious attempt at becoming a logo. The convention center would love to be the iconic representation of the "new" Portland, like the Empire State building for New York. It's a nice allusion- you look over to the other side of the river and see the old Steel Bridge, which sits dilapidated and dark at night, a silhouetted husk of a time when Portland was all about steel and industry, a blue collar town held together by rust and sweat. The two arches of the bridge are mimicked by the two towers of the convention center, which mimics the form of the bridge but is is always lit, all glass and plastic and shining twenty-first century newness. You look at the two sides of the river and it asks you the question: which side are you on? The downtown still smells like hops, but the old breweries are now micro-breweries churning out luxury items, and the most working class of beverages, the traditional crappy cup of coffee, has been reinvented as the most snooty of luxury items, that great Northwest export, insanely overpriced and fetishized espresso beverages. Over in Northeast, the insinuations have turned real: some friend of Andrew's has been hit-and-run by a speeding car while crossing Alberta, knocked off his feet and left there(alive, fortunately) for some angry motorists' dark amusement.

This is a strange city and a strange, strange time to be alive. I wonder what is going to become of all of us, bound together in this moment, arbitrarily, soon to be exploded and sent to the far corners of existence.

"I think it's important to have a concept of yourself ten years from now," Andrew says. "some people, it's like, 'I don't know where I'll be in three months, dude!' That's OK, but, really, it's the people who have a vision of themselves, no matter how improbable or far-fetched, who are the interesting people in the long run, the ones you really want to stick with."

Damn, dude, I think. I wonder where *I'll* be in three months. I wonder, in ten years, will any of us even recognize one another?

Navigating the boundaries of the possible, feeling our way along the sketchy shores of that dark continent which looms ahead, the future, we all choose our sides. We have that option; we're the lucky ones. I get depressed walking around downtown and thinking about how things have changed since I arrived here five years ago, took my first walk in the then-still-decaying downtown and thought, "wow, this city blows." That was the beginning of an abusive relationship, a horrible common-law shacking up which had both Portland and myself holding steaks over our black eyes, ice cubes over swelling skulls, swearing to the neighbors every morning that we just tripped on the stairs last night, that's all.

It's probably time to leave now. Renovations occur all the time and I recognize the place less and less. The constant shifting mass of disillusioned people marching in and out is one thing, but the actual physical transformation, the realization that in ten years I'll inhabit an alien landscape, is something I can't accept. Industry and commerce are powerful alienating forces. Or am I morbid, only feeling OK when a place is dying?

We walk into the downtown Safeway as I try to articulate this feeling to Andrew, who stops in front of a towering wall of Select brand grape soda and stares, awestruck. He gestures at it as if it's the answer to all my fears. "Man, there's all the commerce and infrastructure built to entertain us, to create these artificial needs to buy which force us into being consumers," he says, "but if you can just be entertained by being in a grocery store and checking out all the fucked up shit in here, you've beat the system. Because it's free to hang out in here, and you can do it as long as you want!"

So we stay in there a while, beating the system.

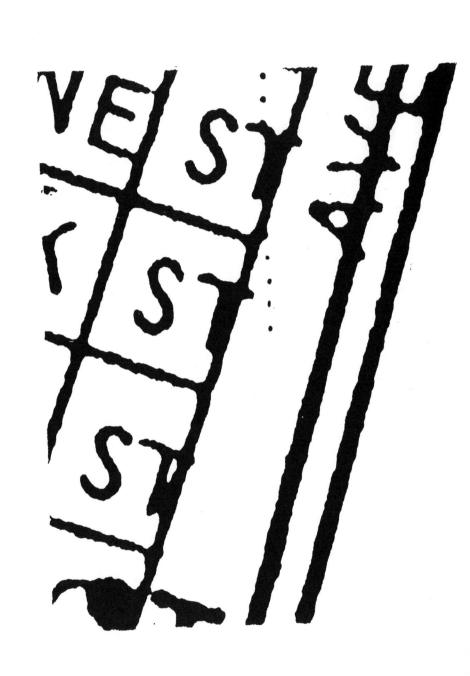

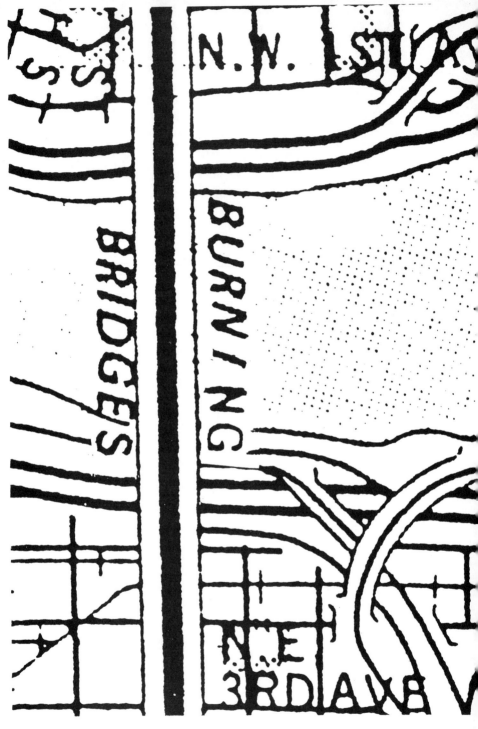

al burian• 307 Blueridge Road• Carrboro, NC 27510•US

9

BURN COLLECTOR

Hey there!

How's it going? Pretty good?

I wish I could say the same, but I'm committed to complete honesty and forthrightness in the realm of artistic expression, and so I'm going to have to come clean and give you the old "it's going pretty fucking sucky" response, even though when you said "how's it going?" you were just responding to my initial "how's it going." It was an act of social propriety on your part, not a legitimate expression of concern, kind of like when I say "what's up" and you respond by saying "what's up," even though that's not an answer to my question; now you're stuck staring at me uncomfortably, wishing I'd just said, "it's going pretty good." Oh, I'm sorry, did you just want me to say pretty good? This is just one of those conversational formalities? Whoops, the faux pas is all moi. Uh, it's pretty good. There. Better?

Really, though. Since you ask: things are bad. The reasons, at least, are simple: I'm cold. Winter has descended on North Carolina, a fact which registers only abstractly with my housemates, who have to grapple with the new challenges of color-coordinating all those extra articles of clothing, the jackets and hats and assorted Norwegian traditional beanies knit by senile Scandinavian grandparents. I am much more acutely and uncomfortably aware of the seasonal shift, being that I live on a glass sun-porch which is entirely uninsulated. I don't actually mind the cold per se- it's actually kind of nice, and I enjoy sleeping in sweatshirts, wrapped up in a sleeping bag under a comforter. My housemate Kate pointed out quite correctly that cold is a great stimulant- not only does it keep you alert, shivering and wide-eyed with that subtle primal panic you can only get from being exposed uncomfortably to the elements, but, according to Kate, the cold actually stimulates brain activity. This is, according to her, a scientifically verified fact. I believe it, only because the other scientifically proven brain-wave enhancer which she cited is classical music, and I know this to be a scientific fact because I remember the day my dad heard about it and came down from his study to gloat about it to me. "According to NPR," he said, "They timed mice going through a maze, and then played them Brahms for ten minutes at a certain decibel level, at which point they could run the maze three times as fast! Then, " he continued, "they played these same mice ten minutes of the rock group Anthrax at the same decibel level. The result: it took the mice five times as long to run the maze, and they kept running into walls."

I've been listening to rock music at high decibel levels on my sun porch and it's been very hot up until now. I've been relatively happy and stupid. But now, it's getting cold, and I've been getting smarter and smarter. Unfortunately, my sky-rocketing I.Q. is not leading to my running mazes faster and getting things done in a more efficient manner. Living on the porch makes me feel alienated and crazy, makes me loathe and resent my foppish housemates who loaf around inside in undershirts. My overstimulated brain comes up with a million long-winded reasons why they are worthless jerks. If I was in an alien land they'd think I was the shy, quiet foreigner, not the brooding menace, the mad-woman in the attic, clacking away all night on a typewriter, huddled in a sleeping bag, writing the great American assassination manifesto because its too cold to sleep.

I've always found the youth cultural practice of naming houses annoying

(and, after the classic crushing co-option of the practice in the Winona Ryder-Ethan Hawke cinematic character assassination of anyone born after 1965, "Reality Bites," with its cringer of a scene in which the Winona-Ryder's-dumpy-sidekick character welcomes the protagonists to her sordid little domicile by screeching, "welcome to the maxi-pad!"-- [ah, I'd just love to meet the scrotally-challenged screenwriter who came up with that gem, it's just so perfect; so close to actually mimicking the "reality" it is attempting to "bite," and yet so tragically just missing the mark that it inadvertently lays bare the sad, socially inept psyche of it's author, replete with junior high school beatings and torturous tauntings which I'd like to suggest we carry on as soon as we track this individual down] —after the "maxi pad," who could argue for house-naming as a valid expression of creative impulse or autonomous will?). But despite the fact that I do not endorse the practice, I do, as it happens, now reside in a house called the Spy House. This specific designation does make a lot of sense. The house is practically a mansion. It looks exactly like the sort of place James Bond might relax in, when not busy ridding the world of international terrorist menace.

The rental application for the Spy House was turned in almost facetiously. It really did not occur to me that we would possibly be approved to live here, in a suburban neighborhood overlooking a golf course and botanical gardens, where the average car driven is a BMW or Jaguar, and most people have small children and meticulously shaven lawns. Our neighbors are probably dentists, lawyers, long-tenured college professors. We do not belong here at all.

Surprisingly, the various half-baked lies on our rental application somehow worked. I am proud to say that not one of the four people who turned in applications were employed at the time, and yet somehow we rigged the numbers so that it looked like we were big-time movie producers. Ben Davis, I believe, actually told the realtors that he works for Steven Spielberg, and that he is paid in fist-fulls of wadded-up hundred dollar bills, which Steven Spielberg pulls periodically out of jumbo-sized trash bags labeled "Schindler's List." Despite these fantastic fabrications, here we are now, in charge of a mansion, which has quickly filled itself with habitators- every available space is now occupied, including all rooms, my porch, and the shed beside the house, to which electricity is run via a lengthy extension cord. Already one broken-down car litters the yard, and the motley collection of rust-buckets wheezing their way up and down the driveway must be a grim sight for the dentists across the street.

I *feel* like a spy- like a mole, a secret agent of sketchiness in the land of order and banality. There is something surreal and beautiful about the situation. Just a few months ago, I was living in a rotting shed of a house whose former tenants were illegally squatting, anonymous crack addicts who we'd accidentally displaced by our presence, and who registered their displeasure at this turn of events by defecating on our back door. "Don't worry about the drug dealers," a neighbor had told me one night, when I ran into him drunkenly wandering the streets, on a last bender before a month of house arrest began the next morning, " If they do their business on your lawn, just come out, politely tell them to leave, wave a shotgun around, and, after you do that a few times, they'll get the message." That was the house where I lived in the crawlspace, and where conditions with the utilities (or lack thereof) deteriorated to the point where we decided to go on rent strike (see Burn Collector #7). Unfortunately, the landlord was not familiar with the concept. He approached my housemate Seth one afternoon, and informed him that we should vacate the premises as soon as possible, for our own safety. "That old place could burn down any day," he said, smiling ominously. Seth noted the charred, empty lot across the street, also owned by this same landlord. We were out within forty eight hours.

The neighborhood by the old Columbia street house, where house shows and punk rockers somehow turned a run-down, working-class area into plastic Barbie-dream-home condominiums overnight ("We pretty much ruined this neighborhood," my friend Richard concedes, as we walk by the new development one night), or the slow climb towards coffee shops and knick knack boutiques of Alberta street, Northeast Portland, Oregon-- I've lived in enough run-down neighborhoods, and watched them gentrify because of my presence, and, having realized that I am disease-ridden, what is there to do but bring the germ back to its source? Let our presence here bring the property values crashing down, let our heaping garbage and dirt bring in plague-ridden rats to nibble at the dentists' children. The best soldiers are the ones with nothing to lose, and it's abundantly clear to me that we won't be getting our security deposit back.

September

September						
S	M	T	W	T	F	S
1	2	3	4	5	6	7
8	9	10	11	12	13	14
15	16	17	18	19	20	21
22	23	24	25	26	27	28
29	30					

Fall setting in as of today: you can feel it, the coming long pants and sweat shirts, the chill in the air around three or four am which will slowly spread, like a stain on a table-cloth, soaking the entire season, eventually, in its cold clamminess. I'm down with that; fall tends to be a good season for me. Summer is lethargic and depressing, one long let-down. Have I written this exact sentence before? I've thought it before; I'll think it again.

Around six in the morning, as it gets light out- fifteen minutes ago, standing in the driveway of the house with a date, watching as the sky turns grey and then red, awkwardly trying to say our good byes- she said the time of day reminded her of summer camp. Why, I wondered. What's the last time you were up at this hour, she asked, and I said I'm always up at this time of morning, I rarely miss it. This is my room, the private space which I inhabit and rarely hang out in with others, this time of day. It seems normal, a breath of relief to look out at the neighborhood, know that it mirrors in its slumbering state all the other neighborhoods, and know, *oh, good, all the bastards in the world are asleep- it's just me again.*

I'm starting to get minorly obsessed by the 80's and it's not because I've recently realized that the soundtrack to Purple Rain is one of the best records of all time. At least not completely for that reason. The passé cultural aspects aren't as interesting as the weird political phenomena that transpired then. Anyway, I've been listening to the last song on the Jello Biafra/DOA record, the fifteen minute one, and the last line really resonates with this neighborhood and the whole paranoid home security feeling of the world around me, especially half-hallucinating after staying up into another garishly lit florescent day. "If some one came for you in the middle of the night and dragged you from your home, do you really think your neighbors would even care?" The neighbors would definitely not care. That line really sums up my delusional paranoid state in relation to this house.

When you have a weird personal obsession for a while, you start to read into every conversation the conspiracy theories and innuendos of shared interest. Or is there actually some strange stream of cultural conversation, the big brawl of accumulated babbling which eventually produces things like urban legends or phone lists for booking punk rock shows? It's like learning a new word and then seeing it everywhere. It's not a conspiracy, you just couldn't see that word before.

I'm obsessing about the nineteen eighties, trying to decipher its history through garbled and esoteric references on punk rock records, and all of a sudden it seems like everyone is in on it. It's like people are waking up out of mass hypnosis, simultaneously, rubbing their eyes and muttering, "wha....? What happened? Oh wait..... hey, that SUCKED!" I pick up an issue of the Nation which I somehow read to have a story on the nineteen eighties, and when I get it home realize that I misread, that it actually has a cover story on the (current) threat of nuclear holocaust, and I realize that the nineteen eighties and nuclear holocaust are synonyms in my subconscious, they are inseparable, the same concept, the spell-checker of my brain interchanges the words automatically.

Then again, you've got the WXYC 80's dance. Oh, sure, I was there, dancing around and all, but I certainly wasn't having a good time. It wasn't because of the unfortunate confluence of every girl I've kissed in the last three months all being there at once, although all eyewitness can attest to the fact that that was a sort of awkward navigational situation; it wasn't because I lied about being XYC DJ Bo Williams in order to get in free only to discover that the door man was not only close personal friends of Bo Williams ("And you, sir, are no Bo Williams!") but that he, in fact, also knew exactly who I was, much to my chagrin. I could do little but stand there awkwardly, and shrug, muttering, "OK. Busted." A very acute social crusher indeed, although only because I happen not to be in "I'm actively trying to get run out of town" mode, at least not as of yet. But, no, let me just say that what really problematizes the whole event for me is the presence of, and dumb hooting for, the barbaric and soulless corporate retchings which passed for mainstream popular music in that unfortunate era. Is the undertow of nostalgia really so powerful that it can cause these people to reinterpret such hideous offenses to human decency as "Come on Eileen" and the collected oevre of Cindi Lauper as reminiscent of glorious times of innocent frolic? Were you all really having a good time back then, which you need fervently to be reminded of? A much darker and more suicidally maddening thought is that I am surrounded by people who are not reinterpreting, submitting to the false consciousness of memory-renovation- these people may have actually liked all these stuff at the time. If so, the 80's dance should be a Nuremburg trial of the aesthetic, where such people hang their heads in shame and claim to only have been following the dictates of the popular media. Because, come on, that shit blows.

Perhaps it has to do with an age bracket difference. I was old enough in the mid-to-late 80's to really loathe everything that was going on. How can I embrace the culture of the 1980's when I spent that decade defining myself as *counter-cultural*? Do I have to vote Republican now too, but just ironically? Of course, at this point, the needle scratches off of the well-worn grooves of Duran Duran's "Rio," (OK, I actually will defend the artistic merit of "Rio." Maybe this is just my own personal biases talking, but I just feel that--Oh, never mind), and the usually drab-garbed gas station jacket hipsters, decked out tonight in hairspray and parachute pants, stare at me with a dumbfounded horror tinged with pity, like I just said, "hey, this is cool and all, but after this let's all go back to my house, the MAXI PAD!" After a moment of this accusing silence, someone stammers, "You.... *vote?*" Well, yeah, I mean, not lately. I have done it, even non-ironically once or twice. Although, my straight Socialist ticket in the last presidential election was not even categorizable as "protest vote"- that was more "something funny to say I did at a party later that night" voting. We've hit the root of the problem- there is no such thing anymore as culture or counter-culture, or any mode, be it political, social, artistic, or even fashion-oriented, of expressing an allegiance to anything. Believing in something, as opposed to kind of checking it out and giggling about it, is an historically outdated mode of thinking. The barbaric and soulless corporate retching of the 1990's actually passed themselves off as being counter-cultural, at least on the most surface aesthetic level, so if culture is counter culture, than counter-counter culture would be-- uh, that's a double negative so-- uh, I guess that does makes Cindi Lauper subversive in some roundabout way, as much as anything else is. The record player resumes its rotation, people start breakdancing; some of these people are breakdancing majors, or urban anthropologists writing theses on the cultural impact of Huey Lewis, or deconstructing the cultural geography of fictional worlds inhabited by Donkey Kong and Super Mario. The machine drones on.

Montana

Montana in the middle of the night-

the dull rumble of the bus engine, the shivering sleep of the passengers, huddled against each other to escape the draconian air-conditioning vents hissing cold along the windows. No one ever does ask the driver to turn up the heat, despite his invitations at the outset, delivered almost like a dare. Roby Newton and I, dressed identically, in drab blue and black, sweatshirts and stained work pants, our hair bleached blonde and our eyes hollow orbs, planets orbiting the dim sun of the mind nourished for way too long on peanut butter jelly sandwiches, sit uncomfortably in the way back.

It's been a pretty good ride: somewhere along the route we stopped at a diner to eat lunch and I sat down next to a wall-eyed, buck-toothed man who was grinning and chortling as he surveyed the menu.

"Hi, my name's Al," I introduced myself.

The bucktoothed man nodded and extended his hand. His name, it turns out, is Andy and he is on his way home to a small town in Washington State, after a disastrous, abortive trip east to visit relatives in Green bay, Wisconsin. Andy arrived in Green Bay and telephoned his relatives, but they refused to come to the station and pick him up. Andy stayed in a Motel Six across from the bus station for three days, vainly leaving messages on their machine, but to no avail. "But I did walk a lot! Yes sir. One day I walked all the way down from the bus station to down where that big drug store is." Being unfamiliar with the landmark drug stores of Green Bay, Wisconsin, I nodded thoughtfully, stroking my chin. "Hmm, yes. Very good."

Andy never got to see his relatives, and running out of money, he climbed back aboard the unforgiving Hound, to be shuttled back home, completely unfazed by the experience. "I have lots of good friends at home," he cackles. Andy is not quite all there, I gather. Right now he has his overhead dome light on, several rows of seats up, and he is pawing a gigantic red bible, which he reads intently, muttering to himself and giggling.

Across the aisle, the lights are off and the young Bernard-Goetz-style aggro-nerd is shifting and squirming in his seat, feigning sleep so as to better put the grope on his seat-mate, a wide-eyed young girl who only a few hours earlier was reading her poetry aloud and regaling us all with the tale of her fiancé running off and leaving her in the lurch. Roby maintains that a young girl's only motivation for broadcasting that her fiancé just left her to a busload of strangers is as a green light for nearby aggro-nerds to put the grope on them. People are always looking for romance in the most unlikely places, and I have seen more than a few failed attempts to kick it to a fellow passenger on these long drives. Then again, you also see the phenomenal odds-defying success stories, and these are even more disconcerting, really.

Another passenger you just have to admire is the Cat-in-the-hat Hat wearing, Megadeth T-shirt sporting, braces-laden, Dutch hessian kickboxing champion, who tells me that he lives near Amsterdam on a pot farm. He says he is visiting relatives in Montana and will stay "as long as people get me high." This poor kid has been sucked into a particularly bizarre back-of-the-bus netherworld, where the lost souls always congregate, and the specific theme of this joy ride is the variety of lost soul known as the single mom. Squalling, bawling, crazed infants and their bovine, doped-out California moms, more than one of whom seems to have some Mansonesque cult leader to thank for their offspring, have created a gauntlet of terror back there, pushing the other passengers forward, setting nerves on edge. Our friend the pot farmer knows no fear, however, and he's become a surrogate dad for the duration of the trip, changing diapers, burping toddlers, listening to extended explanations of alimony settlements, and just generally hating it. Europeans, you'll notice, tend to do a lot more volunteer work, a lot more freelance child-rearing and house-cleaning. They make great houseguests, unlike Americans, but their nations rarely kick very much ass.

Staring out the window for hours into total darkness puts you in a kind of dream-like trance; like floating in a sensory deprivation tank, the removal of stimulus exacerbates your reactions to whatever information your senses can glean. You become hyper-aware of every little interaction and disturbance in the hypnotic web spun from brain to brain by the dull engine rumble- and you start to hallucinate narrative and emotional attachment.

Up front, two guys in mesh hats drink whisky out of thermoses and guffaw a lot. Behind them sit two nice, quiet college kids. I talk to them for a while. The boy, a clean-cut fraternity type, reveals his secret fetish for wearing leather bondage gear and going to homo-erotic goth dance clubs within three or four minutes. It's funny how the social vacuum of these situations sucks the truth out of people, turning them inside out in front of your eyes, skeletons clattering out of closets. Right behind me- an older lady from upstate New York is chattering away, at whom I do not know, crushing me with her world view, her "I'm going to retire to Mexico-- live like a king for two dollars a day; such nice people down there" fascist proclamations.

Outside, Montana rolls by. My whole life seems erased. You think of times in transit as the necessary filler between points A and B, but once you're in motion, whatever you were doing before fades into obscurity, like a dream of comfort and ease you awoke from to find yourself still here, on the eternal Greyhound ride. As for where I'm heading, I'm so far removed from Portland, Oregon, that it's like visiting Stonehenge because my ancestors were druids. Every place is the same. Some people have just been dumped by their boyfriend, some people are on heroin now, some people used to be into heroin and now they are even more into it. The bar that used to be the cool place to hang out is still pretty much the cool place to be. Context is a dangerous thing. The brain rebels against it, eradicates your memory of things so that you can't compare. I fuck up the whole system by writing things down and getting depressed about them.

The guys in the mesh hats have gotten out of hand. One of them is standing up, and I get a good look at him- puffy alcoholic nose, mustache, tattoos on his arms. He is sort of a decrepit Tom Selleck look-alike, and he is carrying on about being a Navy Seal and challenging the other passengers to engage in hand-to-hand combat. ("If he's a Navy Seal," the aggro-nerd mutters behind me, pausing in mid-grope, "I'm the President of the fuckin' United States of America.") The general populace of the bus shifts uncomfortably and shrinks down in their seats, trying to appear as inconspicuous as possible- not an easy task for a busload of people. "Shut the fuck up," the other mesh hat mutters. "What?" snarls the Seal, and they are staring each other down. I cross my fingers for a fight. I can tell that the mesh hat will cream the Navy Seal.

The situation is diffused at the next stop. The drunken passengers are ejected. Roby sits on a stoop in front of a nearby grocery store, eating peanut butter out of a jar, which induces a near-riot on the part of the populace of whatever microcosmic shithole of a town this is. "Jesus, are you OK?. What are you?" They demand. Cars circle the block for a better view, CB radios crackling as they broadcast the news to their fellow teen hoodlum compatriots, and you get the sense of local militia groups mobilizing to advance on us, so we retreat to the bus. Our morale is low.

In Billings, the bus stops for an hour, and we make a desperate trip around the corner to the Empire bar to guzzle a few of the advertised specials, dollar beers. "Dollar beers," we say in unison, looking probably pretty unusual for Billings: monochromatic blue with twin bleach-blonde heads, speaking in unison as we simultaneously slap dollar bills on the counter. I feel like I'm the protagonist in a Saturday Night Live "coneheads" skit. The bartender smirks; "Greyhound?"

"Yes," I mutter. We guzzle dejectedly. The bar is dark and dusty. Shafts of light cut across the floor from venetian blinds in a window, illuminating celestial configurations of dust and debris, galaxies of spores and sawdust, finely coated with the sweat and pheromonal excretions of whoever frequents this bar. You breathe it all in and wonder what the presence of this primordial substance will do to you. It's like sucking on an asthma inhaler filled with alien anxiety and inertia.

Our second beer is committing its Niagara Falls plunge down our gullets, when a haggard Native American man stumbles in to the Empire bar. He starts laughing when he sees us, but not in a hostile or discomforting way. It's more like, he's had a bad day and when he sees us he starts nodding emphatically as if to indicate, "Yeah! That's more like it! I'm about to get drunk and there's some coneheads in here. Things are looking up." He is not about to get drunk, though, because he doesn't get paid until Friday and the bartender is wary of extending him a line of credit. I watch the interaction passively. Finally, the bartender relents. The three of us sit and guzzle in silence.

Fortified, we walk back towards the bus stop. A little self-medicating really hits the spot sometimes. My outlook on things is improved tremendously since my experience at the Empire, I must admit. Back at the station, we have a few minutes to kill before they begin reboarding.

I am startled to see the Navy Seal, who we had left in the dust a couple of hundred miles down the road, sitting in the corner, still obviously obliterated by booze, scowling into his mustache and clutching his re-boarding pass in a white-knuckled, slightly quivering fist. He lights a cigarette, sucks on it, looks up, and catches me staring.

"Wuzzup," he slurs. I can't resist talking to him.

"How did you get here?" I want to know. "You got kicked off the bus a ways back."

"God damn it, I'm a Navy Seal," he barks. "You think I'm not trained to deal with a situation of that kind? Hell, this is nothing!"

"Well....?" I say. "OK, so how did you get here?"

"I rented a limousine!" he tells me. "It cost me three hundred dollars, but god damn it if I didn't catch up to this bus."

This strikes me as a highly implausible recounting of events. "A limousine?"

"A limo," he nods.

"And it cost you three hundred bucks?'

"Yup," he grunts, flatly.

"Why?" I ask. "Why not just take the next bus?"

"It's a matter of principle!" he states. "My ticket is for this bus! I need to be in Spokane, Washington at the time stated as the arrival on this ticket!" he thrusts forth his albino-knuckled claw, shaking the crumpled ticket at me.

His mysterious appearance, and ludicrous alibi, almost do convince me that he is a Navy Seal. I mean, how *did* he get here in time to reboard the bus? Even under the best of circumstances, it seems like he should just be coming out of his alcoholic stupor right about now, his brain catching up to the industry standard RPM, reconstructing events and determining that he has been ditched in a terrifying tiny redneck outpost in the middle of post-apocalyptic survivalist Montana, at which point he might begin to process the situation to enough of a degree that he could either choose to take up residence in this town or seek out a local limousine service willing to accept three hundred dollars in exchange for hauling him across the desert at top speed, big V-8 engine howling as the chauffeur turns to offer back a silver tray of caviar to our heroic mesh hat mastermind. More realistically (*realistically* being an already severely compromised term, since all the explanations for his mysterious re-appearance are beginning to accept as a fundamental premise that he really *is* a Navy Seal), he probably used some CIA-assassination-manual death-grip on one of the unfortunate heckling hooligans cruising the grocery store parking lot in a monster truck, disposed of the corpse with a pen-sized container of highly concentrated sulfuric acid, and then drove that monster truck two or three hundred miles an hour across the Tundra to arrive in time for boarding in Billings, Montana, so that, secret Navy Seal mission to Bosnia or the Ukraine or wherever completed, he can get on that bus and arrive tonight in Spokane, Washington, where his dentally-challenged wife and children can meet him at the gate, completely buying his story about having spent the week "out east with my buddy Earl from boot camp making six seventy five an hour picking blueberries for the Hostess fruit pie company." And, the craziest part is, despite all that CIA training, the elaborate alibis and cover-ups, the steps taken to insure national security and keep a lid on everything, he cannot finish this final leg of his top-secret mission because, basically, he's just too damn drunk. He gets on the bus and immediately starts picking another fight with some random passenger. The bus has not even started moving, and already he is being forcibly removed, again, swearing profusely and creatively as the second ejection is enacted. I watch him wander back over to his seat in the corner of the bus station, stewing sullenly, examining his new surroundings with the uneasy glare of a prisoner surveying the yard on his first day in the pen. There are still a few minutes before we leave, so I get off the bus for a moment to say my good-byes.

"What are you going to do now?" I ask, trying to be consoling but pragmatic.

"Oh, I'll be in Spokane when you get there," He assures me, teeth clenched in an action-hero grimace of determination, staring blearily straight ahead.

"I almost believe you," I say.

He snaps to attention, bloodshot eyes honing in on me. "You'll see," he says. "You'll see."

I am seized by a sudden inexplicable impulse. "I'll bet you a hundred dollars," I say.

"You be there," he says. "Have the cash on hand."

"OK," I say.

I reboard the bus, and tell Roby what happened. She reminds me that he has already flouted the laws of physics once, and that his second performance is likely going to cost me one hundred bucks. We'll see, I say. We do. He never shows up.

1980

I was nine in 1980 and had my first moment of political conviction

in front of a television, watching a befuddled and embattled Jimmy Carter debate the public-opinion-poll favorite, Ronald Reagan. I didn't understand metaphor and so I took it way too literally when Reagan, in reference to the lazy ingrate welfare cheats he was so sure were responsible for siphoning off the majority of hard-working Americans' tax-dollars, said, "sometimes you've got to cut off a kid's allowance." Instantaneously, I hated him. And, in a way, now, I love him for that. Ronald Reagan was directly responsible for more punk rockers and social deviants than any band or comparable public figure could ever be. He just had that charisma, the polarizing persona which made you take a side and believe in it. He was a zealot, and he spawned zealots.

I lived in Washington DC at that time. My parents took me to the inaugural parade. Carter had walked down the streets of DC four years prior, stepping out of the limo in a symbolic gesture to the pedestrian, the people here on earth, connected to the cement. Limos were back in 1980; Reagan ushered in the decade of hyper-consumption and excess with a fittingly grotesque spectacle of motorcades and ticker-tape. Vendors on the street sold cardboard periscopes, which people devoured ravenously, so that the crowd looked like a strange flock of robotic ostriches, necks craned and little cardboard heads distended, yearning for a glimpse of the Big Man. I sat on my dad's shoulders, craned my own neck, stared as the cavalcade rumbled by. Reagan, on a float, was a tiny speck of history, arms pumping the air, up and down, waving, easily, the crowd in his command.

At the same time, of course, the US hostages in Iran, one of the pivotal symbols of the election, were being released, coincidentally enough right on inauguration day, in a synchronicity of gloriously well-timed media spectacle. No one knew yet that Reagan's handlers had bought that piece of advertisement coup in exchange for promises of arms to the very "terrorists" holding these hostages-- and, amazingly, that was less than twenty years ago. It's hard to imagine that the public, as calloused to the most spectacular advertising gimmicks as it has become now, didn't see through that, didn't find it a little obvious. I guess people really wanted to believe, in the same way that you can't, apparently, hypnotize people without their consent.

The second time I had a run-in with Ronald Reagan

was a few years later. I was fifteen or so at the time, and Reagan's tenure in office was drawing to a close. By now those who chose to tune in to reality were pretty aware of how insanely corrupt and immoral a regime had been run in the past near-decade. Reagan was coming to speak in North Carolina, at Duke University. I can't recall why. My high school organized a field trip. Bob Fulks, the school's misanthropic Marxist principal, has a good story about Reagan, actually, which I remember him telling us on the way to the actual field we were visiting (one of the few times "field trip" has been literally descriptive of the activity in which I partook): apparently at some point during the eighties my high school won a federal award of some dubious sort for killer schooling, and as a result Bob and various other high school principals from around the nation representing these award-winning sinking ships were shuttled up to the white house to receive some congratulatory remarks in a private meeting with El Presidente. Fulks related that Reagan entered the room and launched into a classic Peggy Noonan-penned diatribe about the importance of Principals, principles, the imperativeness of leading America into the 21st century, educating our youth, and all that kind of crap. However, midway through, some kind of voltage irregularity in his hearing aid must have kicked in, sending a jolt to the neuro-transmitters of his brain, effectively derailing the speech and, even further, causing his train of thought to seamlessly jump rails on to the next track over, which happened to be a Peggy Noonan-penned inspirational speech for high school seniors. "Those SAT's are tough, and college admissions can be competitive," Reagan advised the room full of high school principals, who stared at each other, dumbfounded and too mortified to speak. "but you kids can do it. America is counting on you to carry the banner forward, no matter what field you choose to pursue!" It was at this moment, Fulks related, that he realized that the country, and by extension the ultimate fate of all life on the planet, was in the doddering hands of a senile, gibbering idiot. The experience seemed to have scarred Fulks, who I remember fondly as a bitter and sullen man, unusually so particularly in the context of the all-smiles Brave New World of the Carolina Friends School. He quit his post as school head soon after my graduation, and I've heard rumors to the effect of his making his living now either as a union organizer or state fair carny.

We gathered out on a field near the stadium where Reagan was scheduled to speak. A throng of fairly unsavory-looking onlookers had amassed, shifting around, wandering or staring expectantly out onto the empty lot. Finally, there was the whup-whup-whup of a distant helicopter, which grew louder until suddenly the contraption appeared in the sky, barreling downward, wringing hoots from the assemblage of assholes. The machine landed gracefully, and a door swung open, in perfect choreography, spilling out a beaming president, who, stumbling forward, found himself in front of a microphone. The crowd cheered; Reagan waved, looking much the same as on his inauguration day. He was senile and insane by this point. The crowd shouted at him, a mass of indecipherable gibberish; too many people trying to scream to many things at once. Reagan cupped a hand to his ear. "What's that?" he croaked, voice booming across the field, amplified through gigantic speakers. "Did someone say, JUST SAY NO?"

Ah, yes. JUST SAY NO, the "Where's the Beef?" of Reagan's personal fast food franchise of the mind, one of many popular advertising slogans delivered by delightfully Alzheimers-addled geriatrics in this time period, all to great public acclaim. Reagan was a washed up actor; Ernest (Of "Ernest goes to Camp" fame) began his career as geriatric spokesmodel around then, washing up as an already washed up actor before he ever had the chance to be legit, to head the NRA or run for President.

Then they whisked Reagan away to give a speech in the football stadium or something. I didn't get to go to that. Most of my classmates sauntered off to the Duke student center to play arcade games and buy soft drinks. A few of the more diligent ones found their way down to the stadium, to the back exit, where a throng had assembled, awaiting the presidential departure in a flurry of armored limousines. I pushed my way to the front, up against the yellow police line tape. I had a perfect vantage point. The gates opened, and the sleek black cars slithered forth, first a car full of grim-faced security, then another, then the presidential limo, and there he was, behind bullet-proof glass, grinning like an idiot and waving, his face perhaps two feet from mine. Our eyes met for an instant. Reagan looked at me, beaming and smiling, waving emphatically. Stone-faced, I lifted my hand, extending my middle finger. His smile did not waver. He seemed not to register what was in front of him at all, as if, perhaps, the window of the car was a one-way mirror, but turned so that we could see him, but he could only see himself; as if he was, in fact, smiling and waving idiotically at himself. In the next instant, a person in plain clothes was directly next to me with a camera. Click. And then, just as quickly, this person vanished into the crowd. I hadn't even had time to de-extend my bird.

November

November						
S	M	T	W	T	F	S
					1	2
3	4	5	6	7	8	9
10	11	12	13	14	15	16
17	18	19	20	21	22	23
24	25	26	27	28	29	30

I'm sitting in the waiting room of UNC hospital- serene and clean, very unlike so many other emergency room waiting areas, both experienced and imagined- last time I was in a hospital waiting room was in Providence, Rhode Island, waiting to be diagnosed with bronchitis, reading a pamphlet on tuberculosis symptoms, all of which I had, and realizing with creepy horror that probably the best possible place to pick up an airborne pox would be here, in a weakened and immune-deficient state, slouching in a cold plastic chair while all around me winter-scarred New Englanders hacked phlegmy, germ-cloud coughs into the atmosphere. Before that, an emergency room in Berkeley, California, where seven hundred bucks got me an X-ray verification that my leg was not broken and an extra fifty bucks got me (I received an itemized bill for all services rendered) something called "crutch training," which was, literally, a guy giving me a pair of crutches and going, "Do you know what these are? You put them under your arms."

But now I'm just waiting; I'm just the ride or the concerned housemate, or something. A little kid with a raccoon haircut runs spastically between weary people's legs, annoying them- having found a pair of latex gloves he terrorizes his little sister, brings her to tears, and the mom, immobilized and unable to assert control, mumbles inert, lifeless phrases like, "hush, now."

I remember, my brother called me up once, back when he was in college in upstate New York and I lived in Providence. He was having girl problems. Why anyone would call me for consolation or advice on that topic is something I cannot answer, as I have both the most dour view on the general subject of human pairing and a track record of dismal failures and inexcusable behavior in the area of romance to back up the abstractions. In any case, my brother seems to always have the exact opposite girl problems of myself- I'm always trying to extricate and untangle, he's always trying to involve and immerse. I suppose he called me because his immersion had gone wrong and now he needed extrication information. I do not like hearing myself articulate advice on the subject. I found myself giving the most ludicrous pronouncements, actually saying things like, "you should try a petty act of revenge," or "I find drinking helps a lot." I was coming across as callous and insensitive, I fear, but there comes a certain point, when you listen to a sibling mope and pine for too long, and then consider his enrollment at a college which boasts a 75% female student body, where you have to kind of come out and say, "wait, you're like twenty years old and single in college. How can you be having a problem which doesn't fall into the category of 'not enough time?'"

The girl problems were not to be cured. After carrying out my words of fraternal wisdom, my brother arrived at my doorstep in Providence, hung over and facing various lawsuits for destruction of property. His arrival was a quite killer turn of events. Winter in Rhode Island was in full swing, and a layer of icy mud covered the streets, wind biting into uncovered skin as we walked up Brook street. We talked about what we want to do with our lives, a common topic for college juniors and a strange and uncomfortable topic for me at times, because I am, actually, in the process of doing something with my life, and so all I can really talk about as I watch myself do it is whether it is completely lame and invalid, which, upon acute examination, I usually find reason to believe that it is.

My brother has it relatively easy in this department. He wants to be an ambulance driver. It's one of those youthful ambition leftovers, like when I was five and wanted to be an astronaut, except that my brother has stuck with it. It's not just an abstract idea, either, like my various conceptual employment schemes (the post office, the library) - he has actually taken the necessary steps to achieve this goal, he has undergone EMT certification, he's actually held down a job in the field, riding with a rescue squad in lovely East Orange, New Jersey (one of my prized possessions, actually, is a T-shirt his squad had printed up, which was found to be defective on the grounds that they accidentally spelled it like "bar-b-que": "RESQUE SQUAD."). He even has a tattoo of the snake twined around the staff, found on most ambulances, which somehow symbolizes good medicine.

I can really get behind my brother's vocational choice, in fact I envy it in a way. It is a straight-forward, simply deconstructed occupation. People get hurt, they need a ride to the hospital. There's very little in the way of hidden agenda there, very little political or ideological nuance to the occupation other than a general altruism, a rejection of the pure Darwinistic notion that people should be eaten by wolves unless they're healthy enough to outrun them. The world is complicated and it seems appealing to find a slot within that complexity which is straight-forward: a maintenance/technician position. You can be a surgeon or you can be a philosopher- one finds holes and sews them up, the other finds holes and tries to complexify and convolute them into even more and bigger holes.

Talking to my brother makes me feel profoundly useless at times. My vocation is a problem, comparatively. I am a bohemian artist type. Seriously, I write it on my tax returns under "current occupation." What this means, essentially, is that I have chosen to live extremely irresponsibly and self-indulgently, not only failing to give people the proverbial ride to the hospital, but what's more, when *my* ride to the hospital comes, I'll be unable to pay the bill. My entire life ambition and "occupation," if I can even be so brazen as to call it that, requires so much ideological padding and such a complex explication of world-view that it is nothing but a sordid mess. You can explain the use-value of the ambulance driver to the average American, but try explaining Andre Cerrano's *Piss Christ*, or why it's not immoral to steal from corporations, or that there is no God and everything is meaningless and void, and therefore the only response which makes sense is to cover yourself in blue paint and run down the street playing a tuba amplified through distortion pedals.

"See, you've got it made," I said to my brother, as we walked, "You want to get a girlfriend who treats you well and you want to perform altruistic acts for a living. I believe that all relationships are horrible lies which people construct out of the sublimated urge to destroy each other, and my sense of self-worth is premised entirely on my appearance in the readers' poll of various obscure and irrelevant hardcore magazines."

"Yeah, but then again, you get to perform in front of people, have them read things you write, and that must be pretty gratifying," my brother consoled.

"I think it really boils down to it just being more *fun* to be a bohemian artist type," I lamented sadly, "which is pretty immature. Pretty socially unconscionable."

"But people need artists," my brother insisted, perhaps just to derail another of my usual "oh, I'll just sleep out in the snow tonight" self-pity seminars.

"Hmmmm, that's true, I guess." I thought about it a bit, walking in silence. "I mean, abstractly I guess I'm glad someone's driving the ambulances. But I've never ridden in one. Hopefully I never will. If I do, it'll probably only be once or twice in my life. Crucial moments of transport, no doubt. Still, when you compare that to all the artists and writers and musicians who enrich your life on a daily basis, who, in fact, might be said to be the people who make life enjoyable and worth living, you find that, in terms of contributing to the social fabric, these people are actually monumentally important!"

"Sure," my brother agreed.

"Still," I said, "It's a strange thing to do, to decide that you are one of those people who enriches peoples' lives by your very existence. It's pretty damn audacious. You know, artists in America complain that society treats them so poorly, relegates them to poverty and marginalization. But, really, why shouldn't it? The amount of self-indulgence it takes to declare yourself an artist clearly indicates that you are a total egotistical asshole and should be marginalized as quickly as possible."

"Hmmm, yeah, that's probably true as well," my brother agreed.

An interesting predicament, the ambulance driver versus the artist. I remember that conversation in Providence often, though I don't think I was thinking about anything like that at all tonight, as I biked home from work, stopping at the traffic light at the bottom of the hill from whence Chapel Hill derives its name, warily assessing the intersection of Laurel Hill and Highway 15-501, a treacherous and potentially deadly crossing on a bicycle. Noticing the traffic blocked off and the flashing red and blue of police sirens, a car pulled over to the side of the road and a human figure sprawled out on the pavement, with police huddled over. An uneasy feeling creeps over, a physical nausea of anxiety, and the light just won't change, as I contemplate who the figure on the pavement might be, knowing somehow with a sickening psychic certainty that it is someone I know. The light changes and I bike across, to find my housemate Kate, who flags me down. "It's Roby," she says.

The ambulance shows up right then. I stand too close, and the paramedics seem to want to ask me to back away, but maybe they can just tell that I'm not going to, so they don't say anything. A police officer asks me who I am. "Housemate," I say.

She's lying on her back. Her jacket and sweatshirt have been jaggedly slashed open, so as to allow access to her arm, which lays stiffly at her side. A paramedic turns her wrist and elbow this way and that, asking her to indicate when it hurts and when it doesn't. They keep asking her to move her feet. She does. Roby seems as calm as a person can be under the circumstances- she answers questions lucidly, winces when they prod her in a way that hurts. She seems to be OK, but it's creepy, watching her, in shock, staring up at the sky without blinking, as they strap a neck brace on her ("just a precaution," they're saying- I'm torn between the horrific thought of Roby with a broken neck and the more likely scenario of Roby with a $75 *neck brace training* bill later on) and affix her to a stretcher, which they slide into the florescent-glowing womb of medical technicians and whirring machinery. She's OK, I assure myself, she's talking, telling the para-medics jokes, even as she seems about to start bawling hysterically. Roby always told me that if I ever see her about to be taken away in an ambulance to stop them from doing it. The classic bravado of the uninsured. I hope she won't be mad at me later.

Her bike lies mangled, both wheels bent out of shape, in the ditch nearby. The car which hit her is undamaged. The driver wrings his hands nervously. He seems nice enough; shocked and sorry. I'm glad: if it were some collegiate frat boy smirking moronically or an executive fretting about being held up on his way to some late-evening power dinner I feel sure the situation would be unnecessarily complexified by my arrest for assault. The ambulance staff seems professional and courteous, doing their best to make her seem comfortable. *That's my brother*, I'm thinking. *That's what he wants to do with his life.* They close the doors and she is off to the hospital. The artist in the ambulance. Matter and anti-matter.

Dave shows up- he walked down from the house because of the lights and commotion- and I tell him what's happened. We stand around for a while, dazed. A cop is questioning us and we give our address, give Roby's first and last name- all things we get the feeling we probably shouldn't be doing, but we don't have a plan prepared for this situation, no alibis, fake names or fraudulent Blue Cross/Blue Shield cards to present.

Which brings me back to the waiting room, hours later. The kid with the raccoon hair goes from person to person, bugging them each in some unique and brilliant way. He is oblivious to the vibe of anxiety which pervades the room, and his parent is too crushed under the weight of it to impress it upon him. People deal with the spazzy child with grim, mute smiles to each other. It focuses things away, at least, from whatever it is which brings them here, the unifying blanket of tragedy and disaster. Perhaps he will be a great artist one day. He shows all the signs.

I'm just waiting for them to discharge her at this point, slightly worse for the wear and carrying a prescription for fairly heavy pain killers. Roby will be OK, but her right arm is broken and will take a while to heal, and she'll be out of commission for a while. I could easily have come upon her dead, or much more severely maimed, and this scares me profoundly, it makes me realize that there is a certain basic level of life and death which is obscured by the complexification, by trying to make everything as multi-faceted and profoundly referential as you can. The surgeon exists because holes are bad and need sewing. At the end of the day he goes home and knows he has sewn up thirty cuts, splinted ten broken limbs, and the world is closer to life and further from death over all. The philosopher exists because holes are bad and proceeds to find new holes, or take existing holes and try to tear them open further. At the end of the day, the job is never done, there is never anything concrete to show for it except confused looks, cluttered offices, and a few corpses of people who lived their lives and never got it anyway. Band practice is off because I'm at the emergency room; further filming on the house movie is postponed. It seems fine; that all seems so pointless here, now.

The question of the artist versus the ambulance driver, I've come to realize, isn't a simple question of how to live. It's a question, too, of how to promote living, how to stave off dying. The ambulance driver does it by simply entering the fray, plucking the wounded off the pavement and trying to sew them up. This is a noble thing. It's this nobility which makes the artist look bad, because how do you pluck the wounded off the pavement abstractly? How do you pluck yourself off the pavement? In order to live, in order to justify living, we can't just fill the space of our lives with empty amusement, with pointless light and sound and words- we're going to have to try harder now.

Al Burian
Burn Collector
307 Blueridge Rd
Carrboro NC 27510

ABOUT PM PRESS

PM Press was founded at the end
of 2007 by a small collection of
folks with decades of publishing,
media, and organizing experience. PM Press co-conspirators
have published and distributed
hundreds of books, pamphlets,
CDs, and DVDs. Members of
PM have founded enduring book
fairs, spearheaded victorious tenant
organizing campaigns, and worked closely with bookstores,
academic conferences, and even rock bands to deliver
political and challenging ideas to all walks of life. We're old
enough to know what we're doing and young enough to
know what's at stake.

We seek to create radical and stimulating fiction and non-
fiction books, pamphlets, t-shirts, visual and audio materials
to entertain, educate, and inspire you. We aim to distribute
these through every available channel with every available
technology—whether that means you are seeing anarchist
classics at our bookfair stalls; reading our latest vegan
cookbook at the café; downloading geeky fiction e-books;
or digging new music and timely videos from our website.

PM Press is always on the lookout for talented and skilled
volunteers, artists, activists and writers to work with. If you
have a great idea for a project or can contribute in some
way, please get in touch.

PM Press
PO Box 23912
Oakland, CA 94623
www.pmpress.org

FRIENDS OF PM PRESS

These are indisputably momentous times—the financial system is melting down globally and the Empire is stumbling. Now more than ever there is a vital need for radical ideas.

In the three years since its founding—and on a mere shoestring—PM Press has risen to the formidable challenge of publishing and distributing knowledge and entertainment for the struggles ahead. With over 100 releases to date, we have published an impressive and stimulating array of literature, art, music, politics, and culture. Using every available medium, we've succeeded in connecting those hungry for ideas and information to those putting them into practice.

Friends of PM allows you to directly help impact, amplify, and revitalize the discourse and actions of radical writers, filmmakers, and artists. It provides us with a stable foundation from which we can build upon our early successes and provides a much-needed subsidy for the materials that can't necessarily pay their own way. You can help make that happen—and receive every new title automatically delivered to your door once a month—by joining as a Friend of PM Press. And, we'll throw in a free T-Shirt when you sign up.

Here are your options:

- **$25 a month:** Get all books and pamphlets plus 50% discount on all webstore purchases
- **$25 a month:** Get all CDs and DVDs plus 50% discount on all webstore purchases
- **$40 a month:** Get all PM Press releases plus 50% discount on all webstore purchases
- **$100 a month:** Superstar—Everything plus PM merchandise, free downloads, and 50% discount on all webstore purchases

For those who can't afford $25 or more a month, we're introducing **Sustainer Rates** at $15, $10 and $5. Sustainers get a free PM Press t-shirt and a 50% discount on all purchases from our website.

Your Visa or Mastercard will be billed once a month, until you tell us to stop. Or until our efforts succeed in bringing the revolution around. Or the financial meltdown of Capital makes plastic redundant. Whichever comes first.